Praise for the n[...]

"The cultural diversity represented [is historically accurate], beautifully integrated, sensitively explored, and incredibly refreshing. It's high time romance diversified its tales of dashing dukes; Herrera doesn't disappoint on that front."
—*Publishers Weekly*

"Adriana Herrera has created something extraordinary."
—Zoraida Córdova, award-winning author of *The Inheritance of Orquídea Divina*

"With fascinating historical detail, suspenseful drama, and scorching hot intimate moments, this story hits all the notes of a superb romance, while the setting and characters make it fresh and exciting. In a word, marvelous."
—*Kirkus Reviews*

"Adriana Herrera is a fun, frothy, feminist voice in historical romance."
—Sarah MacLean, *New York Times* bestselling author

"Adriana Herrera's stories of brilliant and mission-driven Afro-Latinx heroines are not to be missed."
—*Entertainment Weekly*

"This gorgeously penned book fuses together scorching chemistry, textured characters, and a searing examination of power and colonialism, all while scratching my favorite romance itches: witty, stubborn leads, intense (and sensual) swoons, and, of course, an ensemble that already has me dying for the next book in the series. Adriana Herrera is magnificent."
—Sierra Simone, *USA TODAY* bestselling author

"Historical romance at its very best—fresh, lush and full of steam!"
—Sophie Jordan, *New York Times* bestselling author of *The Duke Gets Ravished*

Also by Adriana Herrera

Las Leonas

A Caribbean Heiress in Paris
An Island Princess Starts a Scandal
A Tropical Rebel Gets the Duke

Dating in Dallas

Here to Stay
On the Hustle

Sambrano Studios

One Week to Claim It All
Just for the Holidays...

Dreamers

American Dreamer
American Fairytale
American Love Story
American Sweethearts
American Christmas

Also available from Adriana Herrera

Mangos and Mistletoe
Finding Joy
Caught Looking
Her Night with Santa
Monsieur X

For additional books by Adriana Herrera,
visit her website, adrianaherreraromance.com.

A Tropical Rebel Gets the Duke

ADRIANA HERRERA

CANARY STREET PRESS

CANARY
STREET
PRESS™

Recycling programs
for this product may
not exist in your area.

ISBN-13: 978-1-335-47696-8

A Tropical Rebel Gets the Duke

Copyright © 2025 by Adriana Herrera

For questions and comments about the quality of this book, please contact us
at CustomerService@Harlequin.com.

TM is a trademark of Harlequin Enterprises ULC.

Canary Street Press
22 Adelaide St. West, 41st Floor
Toronto, Ontario M5H 4E3, Canada
CanaryStPress.com

Printed in U.S.A.

To Kerri Buckley, a true Leona and a treasured steward of my vision and voice as an author.

This book discusses abortion and aftercare.
Please see the Author's Note at the end of the book for more information.

"Let grief convert to anger; blunt not the heart. Enrage it."

—William Shakespeare, *Macbeth*

"One day a woman is going to blow your life to smithereens, and I will be there to laugh in your face."

—James Evanston Sinclair to Apollo César Sinclair Robles,
A Caribbean Heiress in Paris

Prologue

July 1889
Paris, France

Aurora Montalban Wright was no rebel.

At least that was what most who knew her would say. It was not an unfair assessment of her character. After all, true rebels never bothered with consequences, not when a glorious mission lay in the balance. No one would label Aurora a carefree sort, and that was fine by her. Because what she'd learned early in life was that rebellions cost blood, sweat and tears, and she had none of those to spare. This, of course, did not mean she was above bending a rule—or five—if the situation called for it.

In fact, twice in her past, she'd broken every rule set before her in order to escape her circumstances. Once, humiliatingly, for a man—which came to a disastrous end. The other—equally catastrophic—for her freedom. Despite this, Aurora was not rebellious by nature. It was simply that she was galvanized by the word *no*. The more she was told she could not do something, the more creative she became at conquering it.

No, Aurora was no rebel, but tonight she felt like one. The worst possible news had come at the worst possible time and she desperately wanted a distraction. In fact, she wanted far more than that, she needed the kind of oblivion that only came from terrible decisions. Thankfully she was in a city where immoral diversions were easy enough to procure, if one knew which objectionable doors to darken.

Her destination, the clandestine apartment of Apollo César Sinclair Robles—a man who'd just claimed his place as the heir to a dukedom by destroying his own father—could be considered a particularly ill-advised one.

As her fiacre came to a stop on the Rue de Volney, she fleetingly considered if there weren't less potentially disastrous ways to deal with her current mood. Then she felt the weight of the key she'd kept in her pocket for weeks and concluded there definitely were, but she still wanted to do this.

The building looked exactly as she remembered from the night she'd spent here a month earlier. It was one of those modern, luxury apartment buildings near the Parc Monceau, kept by wealthy aristocrats and business titans to commit their more slanderous peccadillos in decadent discretion.

When she reached the door, she took a moment to examine herself in the sparkling glass window. The walking suit she'd donned that morning showed the strain of the day. Her face was framed with wisps of loose curls that had escaped the braid pinned to the nape of her neck. Her hat was a bit more askew than what was fashionable and there was a stain on her left cuff she could not quite identify and was reluctant to smell.

She ought to go home, clean herself up and come another day.

She wasn't presentable and she was certainly not in a state of mind to interact with someone who had a natural gift for trying her patience. Coming to Apollo for what she needed tonight was the furthest from sensible she'd been in a long time.

The thought sent a flash of alarm through her body. She decidedly ignored the cardiovascular admonition.

Undeterred, she pushed the door open and strode right up to the porter with the key dangling from her hand and her heart making another valiant effort at warning her off.

"Oui, madame." The porter greeted her with the detached politeness of someone too well trained to openly scowl at her clothes, but too French not to appear at least marginally aggrieved at their deplorable state.

"Lord Darnick." The two words did the trick, and with a nod, he stepped aside and directed her toward the lift operator, who was already pressing buttons.

Clearly, women coming to see his lordship at all hours of the night was a regular occurrence. Not exactly a surprise. From the moment she'd met the man at a soiree months earlier, he'd been an unapologetic reprobate. She'd never encountered anyone who cared less about other people's opinions than Apollo César Sinclair Robles.

The evidence of that lay in the way he'd arrived in Edinburgh like a dark avenging angel and exposed his father as a liar and a thief. Upending in a single night one of the oldest dukedoms in Britain while establishing himself as its rightful heir, leaving the peerage reeling, and his own father a social pariah.

He was arrogant, rude, and blatantly ridiculed the societal norms she'd so carefully ascribed to. From that first meeting, she'd found herself equally appalled and intrigued by him.

A smile tugged at her lips at the thought of what the new Earl of Darnick would do when she turned up at his apartment and told him she was there for sex, and the more depraved, the better.

He would probably think she was out of her mind.

Out of her mind or not, she had it made up, and whatever lapse this was, she would deal with it in the morning. Four steps forward and two firm knocks were all it took for her, a respected physician, to announce herself at a man's tryst apartment somewhere between one and two in the morning.

Her heartbeat marked hurried footsteps on the other side, while she took in slow, calming breaths. The moment the door finally opened, it was suddenly clear that she had not properly prepared herself. The rapid escalation of her pulse told the story.

He looked like the very last stop on the train to ruination. All languid grace, and the ease of a man who was well aware of the damage he could do on a woman's good sense with a mere wink and a smile.

Aurora, to her eternal shame, was not immune to either.

"Bella Doctora, I didn't know you made house calls." He spoke in that lazy drawl he always used with her, but there was an alertness to his gaze that betrayed his indifference.

"Don't call me that," she rebuked, then remembered she was here to ask for something and tempered her manner with what she hoped was a comely smile. "I came to return your key." She held it up as she endeavored, and failed, not to gape at the triangle of bronzed, muscled chest. She didn't dare look below his sternum lest she encountered bare forearms and swooned before she could tell the man what she was about.

"My key," he drawled, without reaching for it. "After more than a month, you've decided to deliver it at one in the morning, on a Tuesday." He'd given it to her on the night he'd brought her here, after her friend Manuela's wedding day devolved into a scandal that had all of Paris talking for weeks. She hadn't seen him since.

"I was looking in on a patient close by," she retorted, truthfully, dropping the key into the pocket of his dressing gown. The other truth she failed to disclose was that she'd kept the damned key in her pocket like some kind of talisman since he'd given it to her.

"Ah yes, Doctora Montalban and her causes." His voice dripped with cynicism, as if it amused him that she considered her profession anything serious.

"Why is it every time you call me that it feels like an insult?"

"That might have more to do with you than with me."

It irked her that his barbs always hit their targets. She'd made an art of letting men's opinions roll off her back, not a difficult task, since a significant number of men she encountered were imbeciles. But not this earl, not the man who'd ambushed the British aristocracy like Simón Bolívar did with the Spanish at Boyacá.

She wished that diabolical grin of his didn't start a sizzle under her skin. "Are you going to invite me in?"

He cocked a thick, dark eyebrow at whatever he heard in her tone, but instead of inviting her inside, he braced a large hand on the top corner of the doorjamb, until his very distracting mouth was close enough to kiss. She swallowed audibly when she caught a glimpse of the corded muscle of his forearm, thick veins and dusting of dark hair. Her salivary glands seemed to run out of fluid just then.

"First you have to tell me what you're really here for, Doctora." He was showing off his size for her and it was fruitless to pretend it had no effect. Everything about the man eroded every preservation instinct she had.

For over ten years, she'd avoided any scenario that could place her in a vulnerable position. She'd practically forgotten that under her walking suits lived a woman with very real urges and burning desires. Until this man had crossed her path. Since then, he'd been like a toothache. Making himself known, throbbing, gnawing at her, until she'd had to do something about it.

His closeness sent her blood from a canter to a gallop, and her breaths became shorter, more erratic. The undeniable biological evidence of arousal and desire. She might as well get on with it. She locked her own gaze with the Earl of Darnick's, took a breath and leaned in.

"I came here for sexual intercourse, my lord." It was gratifying to see his predatory gaze replaced by genuine shock. But as expected with a hunter, he recovered quickly.

"Well, in that case, do come in, Doctora Montalban," he told her with a wave of his hand before stepping aside.

She decided to ignore the sarcasm in his voice and walked into the apartment.

The moment she stepped inside, she was once again surprised by how different this place was to what she envisioned for Apollo's lair. Instead of a showroom full of ostentatious furniture and excessive gilt, what she found was a comfortable, unpretentious room. He had an impressive collection of books. One of which was sitting open on the armrest of a chair by the fire, next to a tumbler of amber liquid. He also collected art, which to her astonishment was tasteful and interesting.

He was rich, handsome, well-read and had an uncanny eye for art. Not that any of it mattered to her. She was not here for a marriage proposal and took a few steps toward her place by the bookshelf.

She was not here for a marriage proposal, she was here to return his key, and avail herself of his body. When she turned to look at him, she found him leaning against the door, his expression dark as he ran his eyes over her, then he pulled a watch out of his pocket.

"I've got an hour before my next rendezvous arrives," he informed her from his loose-limbed stance. He was obviously trying to irk her, but he would not get the best of her tonight.

"I'm surprised you didn't have them lined up outside the door." He grinned at her. The tip of his pink tongue caught between a line of straight, white teeth.

"Bosom size makes things go faster." He made that declaration while openly admiring her chest. His eyes perused her so lasciviously she almost covered them.

"You're a pig." A crack of his laughter resounded through the small space.

"I assume that's at least partly why you're here," he retorted with frustrating assertion, before pushing off from the door and taking a few steps toward her place by the bookshelf. "Let's reserve the endearments for later and see what we can do about all these clothes you're wearing."

"What?" She sounded like a dolt. This was what she'd told him she wanted. What did she expect after propositioning a scoundrel? Sweet nothings in her ear, passionate declarations?

"Your clothes, sweetheart." He wiggled two fingers somewhere in the vicinity of her chest. "The infernally unending layers of fabric you insist on wearing. They give a man a devil of a time surmising what you've got under all that wool and linen." He made a face, and her mouth twitched. Of all the things to fluster the wicked Earl of Darnick.

She took another look at him, those winged cheekbones, skin like the most perfect caramel, and the umber curls, which made her think of days in bed and rumpled, sweat-soaked sheets. It was a face a woman could ruin her life over. It was a good thing she'd already done that once and had no intention of ever doing it again.

"This is just for tonight." It needed to be said, but he remained unbothered.

"That you don't need to worry about, sweetheart." He lifted a shoulder, his gaze still suspended somewhere below her neck. "I've never had much craving for seconds."

She shrugged and looked away, what more was there to say to that?

"I'd appreciate it if this stayed between us."

"Keeping secrets from your pride, are you?" he asked in a mocking tone. He was referring to her two dearest friends. The friends with which she arrived here in Paris months earlier: Luz Alana and Manuela. The only two people in the world who knew every one of her secrets, *except for this one now*, she thought grimly.

"My dear sister-in-law will be scandalized to know you've come to me in your hour of need." Of all the unlikely twists of fate the last few months in Paris had yielded, Luz Alana finding a love match with a Scottish whisky distiller, who turned out to be an earl *and* Apollo's half brother, had been one of the most surprising.

"It is not as if you're the Marquis de Sade, you're just convenient." He laughed again and this time it reached his eyes. "Besides, Luz Alana and Manuela have their own lives."

"True love *is* miraculous." For her friends, it seemed to be. She'd seen enough people entrapped into those cageless prisons of duty and guilt to have any use for the sentiment.

But even she had to admit, Luz Alana and Manuela seemed to have found partners worthy of their devotion. She was glad for them, but that was not what she searched for.

Her friends believed in love worth any sacrifice. That soulmates and fairy tales were possible. Aurora did not. Not for herself, at least. She was too…marked. Too jaded to ever believe in the lies of the heart.

Love, for her, had only ever served to remind her of the ways she never quite measured up, how hard it was for her to inspire that sentiment in another, and she would never again risk her freedom for that chimera. She had a feeling Apollo César Sinclair Robles, in this at least, was a kindred spirit.

"Why are you really here, Doctora?" Apollo asked, taking another step in her direction. He was merely a couple of feet away now. From this distance she could see that his lips had a pink tint to them. She allowed herself the distraction of that perfect mouth for a moment as she considered his question.

She *could* confess that this very evening she'd received a letter from her brothers informing her they'd suspended her ability to withdraw funds from her trust. She *could* tell him she'd been using those funds to operate a clandestine clinic that helped women in a certain kind of trouble. She *could* even say that the friend who delivered the correspondence had seen the man who'd ruined Aurora at the of age fifteen aboard a steamer headed to France. She might even admit that the possibility of running into the villain of her past made her so sick with dread and shame she'd run here, to Apollo. To ruin herself again, by choice, this time. But none of those pitiful confessions would be conducive to what she'd come here for, not comfort or solace, but escape.

"Let's just say I'm in a fairly destructive mood," she declared, looking at him square in the eyes. "I would very much like to do something utterly ruinous and you were the first thing that came to mind."

That damned grin… The road to hell had to be paved with renderings of it. "*That* is one of the nicest things anyone has said to me."

In reality, all she wanted was to prove to herself that her body still belonged to her. She'd been a girl the last time she'd allowed a man to touch her like she wanted to be touched this night. She'd been so eager to please then, so grateful for any kind of affection. A sad, lonely child desperate for any sort of connection. That sad girl still lived in her, but along the way, she'd learned to be selfish too. She'd also learned to please herself when she could.

A man like Apollo was quite the self-indulgence.

"May I?" he asked, bringing a hand to the top button of her jacket. Her stomach gave an anxious swoop at the touch, but she made herself bow her head in assent. With practiced ease, he flicked the small black buttons with one hand while he kept his gaze locked with hers. That persistent regard should've unnerved her, but she found it oddly riveting. It was as if he was forcing her to stay with him. To not allow her mind to wander from what was happening in her body.

Once he was done, he lowered his head until his lips brushed the shell of her ear.

"You're quite skilled with buttons," she said a bit breathlessly, if only to keep from begging for him to tear the rest of her clothes off.

"Well, I'm not just a pretty face." He was using that teasing tone again, but this time, she thought he intended her to be in on the joke too. Aurora could not be bothered with humor in that moment. Not with him so close. She'd had no idea what his hands would feel like, or how she would react to it. It had been so long for her and those memories were not exactly pleasant. But she hadn't expected anything so…alarming. The friction of his mouth on her skin ran through her body like flashes of lightning along the sky. It made her knees weak.

"Are you certain this is what you want, Aurora?" he asked, and her name on his lips turned that lightning into thunder.

For once, his voice was devoid of any affectation, his eyes clear of any ridicule. He was giving her the chance to reconsider. Instead of gratitude, she was suddenly irritated. Wasn't this man a supposed scoundrel? What would it take for him to treat her like a trollop?

"Despite your assessment of my condition of hopeless spinster," she told him cattily, "I can assure you, this is no deflowering, I'm no maiden, Darnick." If he was surprised, she could see no evidence of it on his face.

"Is that so?" he asked, seemingly unimpressed by her confession to a shocking past. "I assure you there's nothing maidenly about what I want to do to you." He purred as he coasted perfect lips over the curve of her neck, up to her jaw. Her body swayed toward his, the urge to touch him winning out over her usual restraint. "And I'm beginning to grow fond of that sharp tongue of yours." She gasped as his fingers slid up her back to the nape of her neck and held her in place as his mouth continued its wicked exploration.

"You talk too much," she complained, then immediately felt the ghost of a smile brush against her skin. He palmed her neck possessively as he coaxed her lips with gentle, velvety slides of his tongue. She parted for him and he made a sound that set off fireworks in her belly. She remembered this part not being to her liking. Philip, she recoiled internally at the mere thought of his name, had been aggressive. His tongue drilling into her mouth. But Apollo's kisses were the most seductive invasion. Pushing in just enough to weaken her defenses, then quickly retracting until she was the one chasing after more nips and little kisses.

She needed more contact, hungered for it. Her body softened and he caught her by the waist, holding her up as he took her mouth with breathtaking skill. She never knew a man could make love to a woman's lips, but if there was one to do it, it would be this devil with the face of a god.

"Is this what you wanted?" he asked, before latching his mouth to hers again.

Oh yes, she thought, this was what she'd come for. This man's mouth would make her forget. When he pulled away, she gasped in protest, her hands scrambling to bring him back.

"Who are you rebelling against tonight, Fiera?" Her body reacted to that last word. A hot, languid sensation spread through her even as she narrowed her eyes at the irritating precision of his words. He'd called her a wild woman, a ferocious thing. It was exactly who she was tonight.

Then, be it, she told herself. *Se feroz.*

She closed the space between them again, and strong arms came around her. She shut her eyes and swayed her head. Playing the part of the swooning virgin to his ravishing rake.

"This is no rebellion, my lord," she told him, her lips grazing his collarbone. His breath hot against her face. "Let's call it a reclaiming."

He stiffened, as though her choice of words caught him off guard, but in the next second, he was lifting her off the ground.

"I will be gentle," he told her, and she made an offended noise, which pulled something out of him that in any other man would've been called a giggle. "Unless, of course, that's not to your liking, Fiera."

In fact, it was not to her liking.

Philip had demanded she lay perfectly still. Like an inanimate object while he rutted against her. And she, little fool that she'd been, had thought it all so romantic. The consummation of all her dreams. The thought of how stupid she'd been made bile crawl up her throat.

Pendeja.

"My previous experiences involved being treated like a doll," There was no hiding the bitterness in her tone. "I'd like something a bit more inventive." He cocked an eyebrow at that, his eyes penetrating. She made sure she gave away nothing. Apollo didn't need the details. Rogues never did.

"How far into the realm of depravity are we talking here?" His hand had traveled behind her head again and it seemed he was as good at taking out hairpins as he was at undoing buttons. "Know that the more depraved, the better," he whispered, but she was much too entranced by the brush of his fingers in her hair. He tugged and pulled until she felt the long braid coming loose at her back. "This is magnificent," he told her, as he finally undid the braid and her dark brown curls spread over her back and shoulders.

It was her one vanity that she kept it too long. Which meant it was almost always in a braid, to keep it from her face when she worked. Of all the places for him to focus on, she never thought this was where a rake like Apollo Sinclair would begin. But the man was only predictable in his unpredictability.

They were standing so close she could see the catch and release of his breaths. His scent of leather and cedar enveloped her. She was very tempted to reach out. She was wearing gloves and wished she were brave enough to take them off so she could run the back of her hands over his cheeks.

"I'm not afraid," she declared into the small space between them.

He looked at her curiously, as if he could tell that statement had been more for herself than for him.

"Can I ask a few questions?" His voice was so soft she wondered if she was not doing a very good job of hiding her nerves.

"Yes, but I reserve the right not to answer." He laughed, a low, rumbling sound that crept deep into her bones. Made her limbs heavy, made her aware of a pulsing ache between her thighs. It made the want grow into something more like need.

"All of my questions have to do with extracting every ounce of pleasure from you as I can."

He went to her right hand and pulled on the tip of one glove, and she stiffened, suddenly self-conscious.

"I must say, I didn't think this would be the part of your body I'd encounter resistance." He kept his voice light, but his eyes were intent on her face.

It was silly, but she didn't want him to see her hands. Hers were not the soft, delicate hands he was almost certainly used to. They were rough, angrily red in places where the carbolic acid she used to prevent infection in her clients irritated her skin.

"They're very dry and scaly," she said in a caustic tone, angry at herself for her embarrassment. "Working hands, which might be a foreign concept to you." She could see the calluses on his palms even as she said it. She'd been exceedingly rude, but there was no anger in his eyes at her words, just more of that puzzling inquisitiveness. When most men would recoil at her barbs, he seemed to take them as a challenge.

"I had to work in the coffee harvest for my uncle down in Antioquia every year until I left for school." He showed her nicks and cuts on those beautiful, big hands. "I know the work you do, Doctora."

"All right," she sighed, tugging the gloves off brusquely, then lifting her bare hands for his view. "Happy?" He took one of them in his, rubbed his thumb over her flaky knuckles, touched the angry red spots where the chemicals burned her sometimes.

"A healer's hands," he observed in a voice she'd never heard before.

He placed a butterfly-soft kiss on her palm. She sighed at the contact, self-conscious and moved by the gesture. When he took the other hand, he suckled the tip of each of her fingers, which had a different effect on her. From her hands, he moved on to the remaining garments on her person.

She was on fire by the time he had her just in her chemise.

"No corset," he remarked admiringly, before taking a step back without letting go of her hands.

"The things I've seen corsets do to women's bodies would give you nightmares for the rest of your days." She could not seem to be able to talk to him without lecturing. But if he caught her tone, he didn't seem bothered by it. He was much too busy cupping her breasts over the muslin of her undergarments.

"It's criminal to hide this under all that wool and linen." His eyes were hot. His big hands massaged the slope of her breasts, flicking a nipple with his nail, which incited a feline bowing of her spine. She'd never been touched like this, and she liked it.

It was carnal and yet so gentle. So devastatingly tender.

"Do you like having them kissed?" The question stumped her. She'd thought he'd begin with something simpler. Easier to answer without blushing. She could just not respond or she could lie, give him an impression of her experience which provided some armor for what was about to happen, but she had the feeling that being honest would not put her at a disadvantage with him.

"I hope to find out tonight," she remarked, honestly. He raised an eyebrow, obviously wanting to ask more. She braced herself for it, but instead he continued to caress her breasts. Each time he ran the pads of his fingers over one of them, the sensation shot a current of pleasure to her core.

"May I see them?" His fingers were poised on the top button of her chemise.

"Please," she breathed out, shivering from the effects of his light, sensual touch. She'd thought of Apollo as a hunter, one who would make quick work of his prey, but Lord Darnick would not be rushed.

His mouth was right on her clavicle, and she had to start mentally reciting the bones in her hand to keep from moaning.

"I find many things about you arousing, Doctora." She wished she could open her eyes. Watch him as he mouthed at her skin. Look at his fingers flexing into her flesh. She imagined her muscle and bone reacting to his hands. Molding to them. Had a silly thought of his heat searing past layers of flesh until he warmed up the coldest, darkest parts of her soul. "I'd love to lay you out in the sunlight," he told her as he suckled one of her nipples over the fabric, with such ardor that she found herself clutching handfuls of his shirt. "I'd love to learn if they flush with a hint of red like your cheeks do."

"I know you enjoy conversing, but if you could please do more of what you just did with your mouth," she urged. He let out a surprised laugh before applying himself to tracing her areolae with the tip of his tongue.

"I have a very detailed program for my tongue, involving every inch of you," he promised as he focused on undoing her skirts. He divested her of her boots and stockings with impressive alacrity, and in seconds, she was sitting on his sofa with Apollo kneeling at her feet. He traced his hands over her ankles, her calves, the underside of her knees. He'd removed his dressing gown, but he still had on his shirt and trousers. But even under the fabric, she could see powerful muscles contract and flex.

"Are you certain of this?" he asked her as he parted her knees.

"Please don't ask again, or I'll start to wonder if *you* are." At her words, he leaned in and caught her skin between his teeth and growled.

"I'll have to work to remedy that, then." He offered her a disarming smile that made her insides quiver. Then applied himself to her debauching with the same intensity. She groaned as he ran his fingers along the inside of her thighs.

"I have French letters." He shook his head.

"We won't need them tonight, mujer," he informed her, then kissed the spot where his fingers had been. What did that mean? Was he only…? The question fled her mind when his fingers parted her sex. That deep ache worsening with every touch. Her previous experience had allowed no time for anticipation, those few occasions had been awkward and painful, and left her feeling repulsed with herself. She knew now, of course, that it didn't have to be that way.

Tonight she'd hoped for an equally impersonal if more pleasurable experience. But Apollo refused to let her go into her
own head. He kept pressing his hands into her, lapping at her
skin.

Whispering things that didn't allow her any distance from
what she'd asked him to give her.

"You are a luxury," he muttered against her skin. "Every
inch of you is delicious."

She sighed as she watched him work, the way he discovered
more places to kiss. She shivered, her hand fisted at her side as
he left small, teasing bites along her thigh, up and up until his
lips were so close to where she needed him.

"Apollo," she panted, her fingernails digging into the cushions as he tortured her.

"This is lovely," he admired, as he played with her mound
of curls. With one finger, he pierced the seam of her. "Look
at me," he ordered as he continued to stroke his thumb up and
down her swollen labia. With great effort she opened her eyes
and found that bone-melting gaze fixed on her. "What?" she
asked, much too breathless to actually sound as peevish as she
intended.

He grinned, teeth flashing white. "It's only fair I receive a
medical lecture in exchange for my efforts."

"You want a lecture, now?" she practically sobbed.

He nodded, gripping her hips until her bottom was at the
edge of the sofa, his mouth just inches from her heat. "See, I
was absolutely terrible in anatomy class," he pretended to explain, as he applied burning flicks of his tongue to her skin.
"I could never remember the proper name for any of the important bits."

"Won't that be distracting?" she breathed out as he pushed
her chemise up to her waist.

"Take it off, Fiera." His voice was barely above a whisper,

but she found herself doing his bidding. Something wicked stirred in her, a need to have him see all of her.

As she pulled the muslin over her head, she heard him make a sound that was something between a growl and a grunt.

His big shoulders nudged her thighs apart as he focused on her sex. "Lie there and let me work."

She winced at his words, which were an unwelcome reminder of her previous experience. Apollo was nothing like the man she'd been stupid enough to almost throw her life away for, but the request for her to "lie there" brought back unwanted memories.

You're much too wanton, Aurora. If people knew how shameless you are…

"Are you still with me, Fiera?" He tugged on her curls, bringing her focus back to him, then buried his nose in that hot, aching place.

"Yes," she breathed out, as his mouth did something depraved to her sex.

"I'd like my lesson now," he demanded, petting her mound.

"That's the mons pubis," she gasped as he inhaled her. He left traces of fire all over her skin. She wanted to touch him, but she couldn't. She didn't want to seem too eager, to show him a need he could later throw in her face.

"I like your scent," he whispered, as he took her in again.

Even as her mind reeled, her body still reacted to his touch. A point of boiling-hot need grew into a chasm inside her as she watched him. "So wet, mi Fiera," he admired as he administered the filthiest of massages. The pads of his fingers slid over her wet flesh. He plucked her open and licked that secret place until she cried out.

"So pretty and pink." He scraped his teeth against her sensitive skin. Making her moan. "The prettiest brown," he whispered, then pierced her with two fingers. "You make me feel like a starving man, Aurora." He looked up at her then, and she almost looked away. His eyes were hot enough to set her on fire.

"That's the labia minora," she gasped when he slid the tip of his tongue along it. He lapped at her, so achingly slow. Once, twice, then faster until she was panting. She whimpered when his fingers tapped on the tight bud. Her mind began to swim, and her limbs felt liquid, and her existence seemed to whittle down to the place where his mouth met her skin.

"I think I know this one." He pulled the clitoral hood and blew on the nub until she was shaking all over, begging him to do something, anything to give her release. "Yes, sweetheart," he muttered, and she moaned in response. "You needed this," he crooned as she writhed into his ministrations.

"Apollo," her voice didn't sound like hers, hoarse and reedy. Like she'd been screaming for hours.

"How you move." His voice sounded almost admiring. He palmed her hip, cupping his hand around it as she rocked in a rhythm that sank his fingers deeper inside her. "You love this. What idiot made you think you should keep all this leashed?"

"Don't speak about that," she pleaded, not wanting any memories of Philip Carlyle tainting this.

"Shh," he soothed. "It's just you and me here, Fiera." Soon his mouth was back, right where she needed it. His tongue stroking her sensitive flesh until she thought her heart would explode.

"Oh." She could not keep quiet, her back arching as the orgasm tore through her. She moaned, cupping the back of his head as he ate at her. His fingers and tongue relentless.

After he'd managed to pull out another orgasm from her, she slumped against the sofa, eyes closed and her legs as limp as wet noodles.

"I will not ask for an assessment of my skills," he finally

said, while she struggled to regain her faculties. "Your tongue is much too sharp, but I'll take your near-comatose state as a stamp of approval." She merely shook her head and threw her other arm across the one already over her eyes.

Blindly she reached for her chemise and slid it over her head. When she opened her eyes, he was still kneeling in front of her. Impulsively she brushed an errant curl at the center of his forehead.

"I should reciprocate," she told him, her gaze fluttering down to his crotch. But before she could reach for him, he took her hand and kissed the roughened palm again.

"You should be more selfish, Fiera." She didn't like the way her heart pounded when he called her that. It tempted her to ask for things she never wanted to need. "I was desiring a distraction this evening and this was a most welcome one," he told her, lifting to his feet. The dismissal smarted, but she'd told herself a hundred times tonight this was precisely why he'd been the ideal man to do this with.

By the morning, he wouldn't even remember she'd been here.

"I should go," she told him, in as airy a tone as she could manage when she was still fairly out of breath. But his attention was no longer on her. He was serving himself a drink.

"Rum?" he asked, as he went to the decanter.

She shook her head. "I'm not much for spirits."

The last thing she needed was alcohol in the mix. Her body thrummed decadently, aches and sore spots that should've made that familiar shame erupt in her, but somehow did not. She thought this would quelch the disquiet in her, but now she was confronted with the fact that once did not feel like enough.

When he didn't answer, she decided she'd probably outworn her welcome and reached for her skirt. She slid her shirt on next, grateful for her sensible clothes that did not require a lady's maid's assistance.

"Are you one of those ladies who march for the temperance movement?" She sent him a cutting glance and focused on buttoning up.

She took no offense to the assumption. She knew women who advocated for the prohibition of spirits. Having worked in the care of women, she'd seen firsthand what happened when violent men vented their drunken frustrations on their wives.

"No," she told him, reaching for her boots. "I just don't drink on an empty stomach, and I assume you still don't have anything to eat in this den of iniquity." For some reason, her taunt seemed to deflate the tension from the air. When she turned to Apollo, he didn't seem quite as aloof.

"I'm afraid the only things on offer here are sin and vice." That sardonic smile was back in place. She was looking around for her jacket when he pulled open a drawer on the sideboard and lifted out a wooden box. "Chocolates count as vice, do they not?" He lifted the lid, and the aroma of cacao filled the room. "It's Ecuadorian cacao, made in Switzerland."

"If it were an éclair or a canelé, perhaps I'd be tempted," she prevaricated. In truth, she was more than tempted, mostly by him, but lingering here was not a good idea. "I should head home, I have surgeries tomorrow."

"I'll have the porter call you a carriage," he offered, but once again, she shook her head. This gentlemanly side of him distressed her. Did the man think she would launch herself at him, if he came too close?

"That's all right," she said, moving toward the door. For a long moment, he just stared at her, and once again, she got the feeling that he was attempting to extract her thoughts from her mind.

"As you wish," he finally said, reaching for her jacket, which he'd apparently settled on the back of the armchair. He held it up for her.

"Thank you." Awkwardly, she lifted her arms for him to slide it on. When he didn't back away from her, she almost leaned against him. Wondered if he'd wrap his arms around her if she did. But that was not what she wanted. She didn't need a man to rely on, she could stand on her own two feet.

She turned to face him and let herself admire him for a moment. He *was* beautiful, a man who turned heads in whichever room he entered. A peacock when she, even on her best day, was barely an above-average crow.

"This was an invigorating evening, my lord."

"It's 'Your Grace.'" She was so consumed by her own conflicting feelings it took her a moment to understand what he'd said.

"I'm sorry, what?" she asked, dumbly.

"The manner in which you addressed me is no longer appropriate." He said the words very quietly, but something about his expression made the hairs on her arms stand on end. "You were not the only one in a volatile mood this evening, Doctora." His mouth lifted into a self-mocking grin. "It appears that as of this morning, I am to be referred to as 'Your Grace.'"

"Tu padre—" she began, turning to Spanish for some reason.

"Is dead," he confirmed, then exhaled. "It seems I've finally gotten what I wanted."

In the darkness of the room, she could not see his face clearly, but the words descended like a heavy cloak. She couldn't imagine what he was feeling. She had a complicated relationship with her own father, but what his own had done was unforgivable. The man had abandoned him after his mother died in childbirth, then absconded with her fortune back to Scotland. And now he got to carry that man's legacy.

"How do you feel?" She didn't quite know what exactly she

referred to. The fact that his revenge was now final, the dark
legacy he was now stepping into, that he was now an orphan.

"The funny thing about revenge is that one never thinks
about what happens after." He didn't seem like the kind of man
who failed to think ten steps ahead, but she supposed even the
Apollos of the world might contemplate failure when the adversary was the British aristocracy. Then again, he probably
thought he'd have more time. "For now, I'm quite content
with the knowledge that my mere existence will forever be
cause for gnashing of teeth the empire over."

"I'm surprised their opinions would matter to you." It was
one of the things she admired about him. Not that she would
ever tell him.

"Their discomfort matters greatly to me."

That might be true. She could certainly see Apollo taking great pleasure in driving all the society snobs absolutely
mad. But she also knew what it was like to not be wanted in
a place you *should* belong. He wanted justice for his mother,
but perhaps he also wanted to be recognized by his peers, such
as they were.

"You could set an example," she heard herself say, and immediately regretted it. This man didn't need her advice and
he certainly hadn't asked for it, but she was who she was and
opened her mouth again. "You could be better, show them
that they're the problem, that the rot is in them."

"I'd have to be a better man for that, Doctora," he told her
with a shrug. "We can't all be martyrs for our cause." She'd
expected a cynical answer, but she'd been there that night
when Apollo confronted his father and exposed him for what
he was. She'd heard his voice shake with fury when he'd said
his mother's name in front of all those people and sworn to the
Duke of Annan he'd make him pay for what he'd done to her.

"Violeta." The name had an instant effect on him. That languid body, stiffening with alertness. "I remember you saying it on that night in Edinburgh." His face crumpled, and for a fleeting instant, he looked as lost as the child he must've been.

"Yes," he croaked, then took a long drink of rum. "That is my mother's name," he told her, in a voice which seemed to come from very far away.

"Her legacy's the one that matters," she told him. If she was expecting a reaction to this, she did not receive one. Apollo's mask of indifference was solidly back in place. He probably didn't want to hear her opinions, she certainly wouldn't have wanted to if she were in his shoes.

"Good evening, Doctora," he told her, clearly wanting her gone.

And what did she think she was doing here? Coming to an aristocrat for this? She thought she'd learned her lesson, but perhaps not as well as she would've liked to.

"Congratulations, Your Grace," she said, before opening the door and walking out of the apartment.

It was only after she was in a fiacre on her way home that she noticed the key was back in her jacket pocket.

One

September 1889
London, England

Apollo César Sinclair Robles, Duke of Annan, had prepared for many eventualities as he assumed his new title. He anticipated, for example, dealing with open hostility toward his person and the means by which he'd regained his title. He even expected to be a social pariah, rarely acknowledged by peers who held him in contempt for his undeniable—and unavoidable—existence. But as it turned out, the most formidable foe he'd encountered in the British Isles was the food.

"Basura." He gagged as he forced a bite of what he'd been told was very fine mutton by the butler of Travelers, the only gentlemen's club in London Apollo could stomach. "How do you eat this?" He pushed the plate away with disgust before turning to his brother, Evan, who seemed to delight in watching him suffer through British culinary experiences.

"My palate, like the rest of my countrymen's, is irreparably dead," Evan said with gusto, before handing Apollo a glass of amber liquid.

He mistakenly drank too deeply and almost spit *that* out. "What is this?"

"My competition," Evan informed him with a very satisfied laugh. "It's horrid, isn't it?"

This place, this unseasoned food, this insipid whisky was rubbish, and now, thanks to his damned obsession with revenge, his future was inextricably linked to all of it.

"I should've shot you when I had the chance," Apollo muttered, wincing as he put down the glass. Evan smiled, utterly unaffected by the threat. His brother, aside from being Apollo's right-hand man in managing the affairs of the duchy, was also a whisky distiller. He loved surprising Apollo with competing spirits. It was almost never a good experience.

"We could be eating well at your residence, if you weren't hiding from your aunt." This came from his oldest and supposed dearest friend, Gilberto Dossantos, who had come from Paris solely to aggravate Apollo. The mention of his dear Tia Jimena made Apollo groan. The woman was the only mother he'd ever known, but since she'd arrived in London after hearing of Apollo's father dying, she had been on a mission to find him a perfect duchess and orchestrating his entry into society.

He was to blame for voicing these desires to his aunt, but she'd taken to the task like Simón Bolívar on his quest to forge La Gran Colombia.

"I'm not hiding," he muttered, making Evan and Gilberto laugh at his expense.

He considered his brother, who had only learned of his existence a year earlier and yet had been his most loyal ally in a scheme that could've cost them both everything. Apollo had grown to care for him and had been surprised by Evan's desire to continue their friendship. His two sisters, Adalyn and Beatrice, who he'd expected to take their father's side, had surprised him too. In fact, they'd forced themselves into Apollo's life and affairs with the subtlety of a bull run.

He didn't quite know how to feel about any of it. He liked his siblings, he was glad to have his aunt and his cousin here with him too. But he loathed this world. It was all so damned silly.

These clubs were the prime example of the things he most detested of the aristocracy and the theater that was the life of a peer. The only reason he was here was because it was the only place to get a reprieve from the constant parade of debutantes his aunt seemed to find everywhere she went.

"How much longer do we have to be here?" he asked morosely, putting down the glass of terrible whisky.

"Until you receive all your new admirers," Evan said acerbically, which only served to incense Apollo that much more. In the last couple of weeks, he'd discovered that the wrath of the aristocracy only went so far when one arrived in the British Isles with coffers full of money. Not that all of them were happy to have a Black duke among their midst, but a surprising number of them were happy to overlook that attribute if it meant they got a chance to sell the new Duke of Annan on one of their demented schemes.

So far tonight, he'd been offered the opportunity to pay off the debts of a marquess in exchange for his daughter's hand. He'd been informed he could have the honor of attending a hunt hosted by a bankrupt duke for the right price…and covering the costs of the entire affair. But the winner of the evening had been a baronet's attempt to sell him a mine the scoundrel didn't own himself and had no clue where it was located. Blatant attempts to fleece him, apparently, were the ton's way of welcoming Apollo into the fold.

Unfortunately for them, Apollo thought less of the regard of the so-called ton than he did for what passed for food in this godforsaken damp rock they called England.

"Oh, here comes another welcoming party," Gilberto whispered, and all three men turned to watch the approaching twosome, one short and jowly, the other of an impressive stature and pale complexion.

"That's Barton, and one of Ackworth's acolytes," Evan informed Apollo, who sat up on his chair and sneered.

"Ackworth," Gilberto mused, shifting his large body. The spindly chair under him squeaked in protestation. "Why does that name sound familiar?" his Carioca friend asked no one in particular.

"Because that's the miscreant whose family ransacked the coast of Brazil from Recife to São Luis until they were forcibly removed." Then they'd gone down to Cartagena to do the same. But it seemed that was all in the past. "Now the man has dedicated himself to denouncing the arrival of foreigners and usurpers who he claims are destroying the fabric of his fair Britannia," Apollo relayed with a generous serving of sarcasm.

Ackworth, who'd spent the better part of two decades, when he was the third son of a destitute lord, declaring his love for the Americas and denouncing the prejudiced nature of his countrymen toward the "natives", had become a staunch nationalist after the death of a distant cousin made him Viscount Ackworth. Ackworth was now an advocate of maintaining the purity of the aristocracy, declaring which the very idea of a duke of mixed race was an abomination that could not be allowed to stand. The journey across the Atlantic seemed to have erased any memories the man had of his many years in Brazil.

Since the scandal of Apollo's claim on his father's title, the new viscount had a newfound zeal for the aristocracy as "the anointed, sacrosanct institution of the great and good of the empire" and had tasked himself with spreading all manners of rumors about Apollo's illegitimacy. How Apollo invented his father's marriage, that he forged the marriage certificate for his parents, that the photograph of the wedding was a forgery.

"Right." Gilberto's own father had been an admiral for the Royal Navy, who'd married a Brazilian heiress and remained in his adopted country for the rest of his life. Gilberto and his father had feelings about men like Ackworth—and the late Duke of Annan—who treated former colonies as their own personal playgrounds to reenact their berserker fantasies.

"I can't believe anyone's listening to that imbecile." Evan's expression was thunderous. Righteous in his affront that anyone would dare question Apollo's title. He, on the other hand, expected this to go on for the rest of his life.

"I'm quite amazed that this surprises you, brother," he said, laughing at Evan's pugnacious expression. "You really thought the great and good in the House of Lords would just allow a Black man to be made duke without so much as a complaint?"

A pair of the great and good within earshot emitted a few gasps of disbelief at Apollo's words.

"I expect them to abide by the bloody rules they created!" Evan glowered menacingly at them in return. This was one thing Apollo had not been able to disabuse his younger sibling from, this need to fight battles for him with the bigots they were forced to deal with.

How did Apollo explain to Evan that there was no rational thought, no logical path forward for men like Ackworth? A man whose family squandered everything they'd stolen, and when they did, went and stole some more from the very people they considered their inferiors.

"They can't refute what's there. The duke recognized me as his legitimate firstborn." The duke had not done it happily, but in the end, he'd complied.

Gilberto made a sound of agreement. "They might not like

it, and I'm sure they will do so vocally whenever he's there, but they can't refute it." Evan remained visibly displeased. Apollo had no comfort to offer.

"Unless they have me killed." Evan paled at the jest, turning his intense gaze toward Apollo.

"Don't say that." Despite his general annoyance, his brother's fierce reaction to possible harm coming to him moved Apollo. These past few months had been such a whirlwind of confusing emotions. He'd gained so much and lost just as much. A father he'd never known but whose death had brought life-altering consequences for Apollo. But the one thing that had not faltered was his brother's affection and loyalty.

When Evan's expression remained vexed, Apollo threw up his hands in defeat. "I won't say it again, but I was only joking. I doubt the complaints Ackworth put forward will go any further than that."

"I still don't like it," Evan finally said, grimacing at the whisky he'd ordered, likely regretting not ordering a dram of his own spirits.

"You'll like it even less in a second," Apollo murmured, tipping his chin toward a third man walking in their direction. "He's headed here."

As Ackworth neared, Gilberto glared openly at the blond, bunching his fists on the armrests in a less than friendly gesture. His friend was a master of the Brazilian capoeiragem, the martial art brought to the North Coast of the country by Angolan slaves. There was nothing Gilberto enjoyed more than intimidating a bigot.

"Annan." Ackworth's attempt at civility only managed to infuriate Apollo further. As if he didn't know what the man had been up to in the House of Lords. If they were back in Colombia, they'd work things out with a few obscenities, perhaps a blow or two, and be done with it. But this was not how wars were fought in the aristocracy.

Ackworth was in his finery today, a far cry from the shabby suits he'd worn during his Rio days. Still handsome with that lustrous blond hair, blue eyes and a trim form. But the man had come into money recently, no one knew quite how. His cousin the viscount had died in poverty.

"Ackworth," he almost spat out, making sure the man knew they were not friends. Men like this were reared with this sense that the world owed them everything they desired. When fortune smiled upon them, they were happy to boast it was all their own doing, and when they lost it—due to their own stupidity—they moved in an affronted rage looking for some-one to fix it or to blame for it.

"Say, you seem to be settling into your new role." The words were welcoming enough, but his expression was communicat-ing "don't become too comfortable" quite loudly.

But that was probably what Ackworth was after, prodding him into a fit of temper. Give the club an excuse to chuck him out. Remind Apollo again that he might have sneaked into their midst on a technicality, but they would let him know at every opportunity that he was an outsider.

"Ackworth, I doubt you can do much to help me," Apollo countered with a smile, standing up to his full height, which came to a good five inches taller than his rival. The man stepped back with a sneer. "Dressing smartly these days, I see." He tugged hard on the man's lapel, making Ackworth splutter. "Who did you swindle this time?" The viscount balked, then quieted when Gilberto stood up next to Apollo. "The last I heard, you were embroiled in a fraud scandal that involved at least three countries."

Ackworth choked on his own outrage, a blotchy red flush

covering his neck and face. Apollo moved an inch closer, hoping the bastard would give him an excuse to settle this like men.

"You are insolent, sir," Ackworth finally managed, his face growing redder by the second.

Apollo bared his teeth and considered how bad he might hurt himself politically if he wiped the floor with this cretin.

"I can afford to be, Ackworth," Apollo told him, and this time the smile on his face was not feigned. He leaned into the shorter, slender man. "Can I share a secret?" A nervous puff of sour breath escaped the viscount, turning Apollo's stomach. "I don't give two farthings about respectability or any of your lot's regard. I couldn't care less about you and your little band of zealots." By now, Ackworth's eyes were bulging out and his two associates were standing a good five feet away from him. "If you know what's good for you, worry about what I'll do once I get my hands on whatever you're hiding under the floorboards."

He was being loud now, and the heads of half the men in the room were turned in his direction. Good, let them look. He would be damned if he allowed any of these parasites, born and bred to leech off the work of others, to believe even for a second Apollo would be bowing and scraping for their acceptance. "It would be in your best interest to remember—" still fisting one of the man's lapels, he pressed a finger into Ackworth's chest, hard enough to bruise "—that unlike your bark, mine comes with a bite." Apollo let go of the viscount, who wobbled backward with his mouth hanging open.

"I think I've had enough of my peers for an evening," he told Evan and Gilberto in an amiable tone, which was a sharp contrast to the icy glare directed at Ackworth.

As they exited the Travelers Club, Evan let out a long sigh. "That won't help matters."

"I'd burn down the House of Lords myself before I gave Ackworth the satisfaction of saying I tried to curry his favor."

Evan lifted a hand, shaking his head. "I'm not telling you to refrain from directing your derision when and where it is merited, I'm just pointing out facts."

"That man is hiding something," he said to his brother, who was looking at the darkened street like it held the answers they needed. Ackworth had been practically indigent when he'd left Cartagena years earlier. "We need to find it, and when we do, I'll expose him for the hypocrite he is." Gilberto emitted a sound of approval while Evan stood silently, very likely devising a plan to do that very thing.

"This is not a war we win with public outbursts," Evan muttered, without looking at him.

Apollo clenched his jaw in frustration. He knew his brother was right. He was already tired of this. These men, this world, and yet he was loathe to let it go. He was determined to prove that he could be a better duke, a better kind of aristocrat than the lot of them ever could. The thought reminded him of a certain short-arsed physician who had fled his apartment like a thief in the night and had never returned.

He'd been a cad, dismissing her words, because she'd laid bare his greatest fear. That he would never be able to honor his mother's legacy. That perhaps he was not much better than those men he despised.

The theater of position, of good breeding, was a rotten, foul thing, but it was what he'd come here to claim. Any sane man would walk away from this putrefaction, this dying institution and the men who inhabited it. If he had any sense, he'd be on the first ship to Cartagena, but then he'd prove *them* right.

He'd confirm what they all were whispering behind his back, that because of who he was, because of his mother's African roots, because of who birthed him, he was not fit for purpose. And he would never give the Ackworths of the world the satisfaction. He would flaunt himself in their faces and remind them every day who the people who actually built this empire looked like.

Which only brought him right back to pondering Doctora Montalban. Despite her continued insistence among their shared acquaintances they were polar opposites, their struggles shared many similarities. Her womanhood kept her on the outside of her profession. Within the rooms she was allowed in, she was regarded as a novelty or as an abomination. Tolerated, never fully accepted. He wondered what havoc she'd been wreaking in Paris in the months since she'd come to him.

That hour she'd spent in his rooms still woke him up some nights, hard and wanting. Craving more of her. She'd surprised him, the prim and proper Doctora Montalban, with her secret desires and hungers. Heat surged in him at the memory of her soft thighs and wonderfully slick sex. He winced internally at his claim that he didn't crave seconds, when barely a day went by without him thinking of how sweet she'd tasted, how desperately he wanted to sink into her heat.

"Mon amis!" The shout from within an approaching conveyance snapped Apollo from his erotic musings. He was happily surprised to see their friend Sédar's pomaded head sticking out of the brougham.

"What are you doing here?" Apollo asked, as the proprietor of Le Bureau, the luxurious Paris brothel—and one of Apollo's favorite haunts—threw the door to the carriage open.

"Rescuing you from the doldrums that is the Travelers!" he offered jovially as they all climbed into the carriage, grateful to be taken away from the club.

"Are you a member?" Evan asked Sédar as he dropped onto the bench seat next to Apollo.

"I am," he said with one of his there-are-no-doors-closed-to-me expressions. "I assume they have not improved on their hospitality?"

"If you mean are they still offering gray food and allowing all manner of bores," Apollo said, "you assumed correctly. I'm going back to Paris," he declared with a flustered exhale. "I can't take this any longer."

Gilberto nodded in grim agreement as Sédar instructed the coachman on their destination.

"Isn't your aunt hosting a dinner for some dollar princess?" Evan demanded, while Apollo groaned. "Don't shoot the messenger!" His brother threw his hands up at Apollo. "That is the life of a man hunting for a bride." A little too pleased with himself, he smoothed his lapel and grinned. "I have no such difficulties. My bride is awaiting my arrival to our marriage bed, as we speak."

"You're absolutely insufferable since that Dominican hellion tamed you," Gilberto observed with humor. Evan beamed. The man was a besotted, absolutely hopeless case. Apollo could not begrudge him his marital bliss. Luz Alana, the rum heiress he'd entered into a marriage of convenience with only three months earlier, was formidable. Beautiful and tenacious. He liked her and, despite himself, felt a little envious of what his brother could have now that the duchy was not hanging over his head. That sword of Damocles now solely hovered above Apollo.

Once again, his mind drifted to another tenacious hellion hailing from the Caribbean. Perhaps he could call on her if he ever got back to Paris. Which would be idiotic because he had no time for any of that. He was in the midst of lifting the dukedom's affairs out of the dark ages. He was vying for more influence in the Lords. He had no time for chasing women who could not abide his presence.

"Paris has been quite lively as of late," Sédar quipped with an impish glint in his eyes, which he directed pointedly at Apollo.

"Oh? What juicy bits can you share?" Gilberto asked eagerly, the man loved a bit of gossip.

"My sister just employed Evan's wife's friend at Le Bureau." Apollo had only been half listening, but the mention of "Evan's wife's friend" was enough to bring his full attention back to the conversation. There were only two options when it came to his sister-in-law's friends, and one of them was of high interest to him.

Evan scoffed, shaking his head with amusement. "Is Manuela painting one of her orgiastic pieces for Seynabou?"

"Oh, it isn't the artist." A simmering heat began at the base of Apollo's spine at his friend's words. "We now have an in-house doctor for our staff," Sédar said amiably, happily ignorant of the fact that he'd just turned the duke sitting in his carriage into an active volcano.

"Aurora is working for you?" The three men swiveled their heads in his direction at the gruff question.

"She is," Sédar asserted, with a nod. "Seynabou's been trying to convince her to come to one of those masked parties she hosts for ladies." The man grinned, as if the idea of Aurora at such a thing was absurd. But Apollo knew the fire Doctora Montalban kept banked inside. Although, it was true that the Aurora he'd met earlier in the summer would've never agreed to be seen at a brothel. She also wouldn't have gone to a man's apartment to initiate a tryst either. But he now knew she'd done both those things. Something was occurring with the doctora and he was here on this damned island dealing with the likes of Ackworth.

"Are you quite all right, Apollo?" Sédar asked at the same time Gilberto informed him that he was "making growling noises."

"Tell your driver to take me to Charing Cross Station," Apollo demanded of the brothel owner, whose mouth dropped open.

"Where the devil are you going?" He only glared at Gilberto as he considered the benefits of simply launching himself from the cab and running to the train.

"To Paris," he replied, after Sédar spouted some nonsense about luggage and evening plans.

"Brother, might I ask why you're suddenly in such a rush to return to Paris?" Evan asked, amused.

"Because I damned well want to, and because if I see another bowl of smashed peas, I might do someone violence," he barked, which his brother apparently took as the height of humor.

"So, you mean to say it has nothing to do with Aurora frequenting a brothel alone?"

"Evan," Apollo warned, trying mightily to remove that picture from his mind. But his brother seemed much too amused to heed it. From the opposite bench, Gilberto reached out and clapped Apollo's knee playfully.

"It's about time a woman made you lose your head." He didn't know about that, but he was quite certain Doctora Montalban might try to remove it if he attempted to insinuate himself in her business. Which he planned to do the moment he arrived in Paris.

Two

One Week Later
Paris, France

As Aurora came face-to-face with yet another etching of what could only be considered an anatomically aspirational phallus, she concluded that in the future she ought to make more inquiries before she accepted invitations from her friends.

It was true that the phallus in question was part of a—as much as it could be—fairly tasteful and feminine-focused exhibit of erotic art. It was also true said exhibit was being displayed by one of her current employers, the famous Parisian brothel Le Bureau—where she'd been functioning as a physician for the past few weeks, thank you very much. But one would think Manuela could've at least warned her what she was walking into.

"There you are." The boisterous call was from her friend, who was serving as the hostess of the evening's event. A party to celebrate the birthday of her beloved, the dowager Duchess of Sundridge, at their private rooms in the upper floor of Le Bureau. It was still hard to comprehend that merely months earlier, Manuela was set to marry a man and live her life as a society wife in Caracas, Venezuela.

Now she was a working artist and teacher in Paris, a union organizer and living with her female lover, but most important, she was radiantly happy. For people who didn't know Manuela, it was perhaps not very dramatic, but to Aurora, it was a complete transformation. It wasn't that the old Manuela would've balked at the idea of hosting a birthday party for her lover at a brothel. Her friend had always had a penchant for scandal. But the old Manuela would've done it to shock, to horrify the hypocrites in their midst. This Manuela did things only because they made her and the woman she loved happy.

"I was going to go find you in the catacombs. Was the clinic all right?" Manuela exclaimed, all smiles in her lovely saffron gown.

"Everything was fine," Aurora said with a roll of her eyes. "I told you I'd be late." The "catacombs" were the small set of rooms the owners of Le Bureau had set up for Aurora to see staff who required or desired medical attention. Though they were in the cellar, Aurora did not have any complaints, Sédar and Seynabou Cise-Kelly were excellent employers, who compensated her exceedingly well and made sure she had everything she needed.

"You work too hard, Leona." Despite her annoyance at the comment—why was everyone perennially preoccupied with her work schedule?—she did warm at her friend's use of the nickname they'd been given in finishing school by the other students. To the heiresses from the Americas who ran together like their own pride of three.

"You work too, Mademoiselle Professeure," Aurora retorted, forcing levity into her voice.

"This is true," Manuela admitted, with a shrug. "But I take every opportunity available to engage in decadence and depravity." She knew Manuela said this to shock her, and while in the past the implication that Aurora was a boring stiff would've annoyed her, now she had her own decadent secret. The knowledge was surprisingly satisfying. But she also knew her friend's concerns were not merely about Aurora's working habits, but about her brothers cutting her access to her trust.

This was something she did not want to discuss again. Every time the topic of her recent liquidity woes came up, it resulted in one more, embarrassing, offer of help from her friends. Aurora didn't want help. She could support herself just fine with the money she made from her work here at Le Bureau. It was true that she could no longer afford an address at the Place des Vosges or shopping at the Rue de la Paix, but she never cared for those things anyway. It also felt hypocritical to accept money that could go to other causes, like Manuela's artists union.

The truth was that Aurora could have as much money as she wanted or could ever need from her family. As long as she submitted to her father's and brothers' many requisites in how to live her life.

Though the events that led to her departure from the family home thirteen years earlier effectively severed her relationship with them, she'd never been denied access to her trust. But like most women, the independence she thought she'd fought for when she left home was in many ways an illusion.

She could be a doctor as long as she never attempted to have any power or contradicted any of the rules the men had set. She could have her own life as long as her brothers controlled her purse strings. She could be her own woman as long as *men* got to draw all the lines she was not to cross. When, as she always did, she pushed back on their efforts to control her, they extended threats and ultimatums.

A heaviness filled her chest when she remembered her oldest brother's last letter. *Why must you always be so angry?*

That had always been the seed of all her troubles. Her insistence in exhibiting her displeasure had been a constant source of bewilderment for the men in her family since she was a child. In adulthood, that bewilderment had turned into scorn.

Angry girls were unlikable, but angry women were detestable.

If she could only learn that lesson.

"This is quite the display," she commented, if only to take her mind off her brothers, though she was not quite certain what she was looking at. As she'd been lost in thought, Manuela had moved them along the art displayed and they were now in front of what appeared to be a Japanese illustration of a sea creature performing impassioned cunnilingus on a woman.

"Is that a squid?" she asked as she took it in. The woman's face twisted in pleasure brought back memories she simply did not want comingling with this amorous mollusk. The memory of Apollo's shoulders surging between her thighs, bloomed like a rose of fiery petals in her belly.

"It is indeed," Manuela confirmed, happily unaware of Aurora's thoughts. "It's called Shunga, it's quite old Japanese erotic art." It was intriguing, and the illustration so detailed. But the skill of the artist was not responsible for Aurora's flustered state. "We're quite fortunate there are so many artists from all over the world here for the Exposition Universelle." Aurora nodded, but did not risk speaking. It was as if she could still feel that hot tongue sliding over her flesh.

"Is it too hot for you, Léona?" Manuela asked, with a concerned frown. "Cora likes to keep the room warm, I asked her to open a window." Aurora waved a hand in dismissal, and hurried to the next piece, before she began to perspire in earnest.

The painting was of an orchid which looked much too anatomically correct to be a mere flower.

"Is this yours?" Aurora asked, unable to suppress a grin.

"It is indeed." Her friend's artwork had always been a bit risqué, but lately, Manuela had lost any remnants of constraint when it came to announcing to the world who she was. "It's one of Cora's birthday presents."

Aurora didn't choke at the implications of that, but it was a close thing. "I did not need to know that."

"You look at vaginas all day! How is it that you still get flustered by them?" Manuela protested with a laugh, making Aurora's face heat.

"Where is your keeper, Manuela Caceres?" She spoke loud enough to be heard by Cora, who was coming toward them. Her friend only waggled her eyebrows in answer, then thrust herself into her lover's arms.

"Mi amor, are you torturing your friend again?" Cora asked with a fond smile on her lips as she embraced Manuela. In her hunter green trousers and suit jacket, Cora cut quite the figure. Corazón Kemp-Bristol, the Chilean born Dowager Duchess of Sundridge, was a tall, slender woman, with a sternness to her that verged on intimidating, but there was no denying her adoration of Manuela. "Doctor," she said with a nod. "There are a few guests who are interested in hearing about your work."

Aurora knew this was likely a good opportunity. She and Virginia Morelos, her partner in the clinics, had been trying to find more sources of funding for the operation in Paris as well as the plans they had for them in the Americas. She needed money, but she hated this part. She didn't like feeling like anyone's cause, which she knew made her a hypocrite. Besides, Luz Alana and her husband were already planning to host a garden party for this very purpose and that was already going to be enough torture.

"I have one more patient to go see tonight, for the clinic," she said with a wince, knowing her friend would have something to say about her extracurricular activities.

"But you just got here!" Manuela threw her hands up and turned to the duchess with an expression that said "talk some sense into her."

"I don't like the thought of you out on your own seeing patients." Manuela paused, looking around as if to make sure the coast was clear. "I worry about your safety."

"You were the one who told me to be more adventurous," she retorted, proud of herself for getting her friend back for once.

"Erotic, sinful adventures! Not for you to run around Paris doing who knows what in the middle of the night," Manuela balked, then turned serious. "We just worry about you getting hurt."

This had been an ongoing issue since Aurora began working with a few other physicians to provide women confidential and free services and procedures that were not exactly within the purview of the law. The idea was born at a meeting months earlier when she'd mentioned that the Exposition Universelle brought to Paris thousands of women from countries where contraception was forbidden.

Virginia, one of the doctors in her group, had created a small flyer that they distributed to women at the fairgrounds, offering free consultations with doctors specialized in "female ailments." Within a week, they'd received dozens of requests for appointments. It was a logistical nightmare finding secure places to perform those riskier procedures, and for the safety of the patient and the doctors, they usually did them at night when there were less chances of being caught.

"I will not be totally alone, the patient will be there." Manuela did not like that answer, if the scowl on her face was any indication. "Abelardo will be there as well, he's meeting me here soon." This seemed to somewhat mollify her friend. Abelardo, a Dominican medical student who assisted them for the more complicated cases, was also an artist and had become a close friend of Manuela's.

"Fine." Manuela dropped her shoulders and Cora instantly wrapped an arm around them. "But you must stay a little longer, Luz Alana should be here any minute," Manuela cajoled. "She had to attend a party at some diplomat's house, but she and Evan will come here after."

It would be lovely to see Luz Alana. She hadn't since her return from London. She was mulling that thought when Cora spoke up.

"I wonder if they'll have Annan with them." Aurora didn't blink, she didn't breathe at hearing the name said out loud. She simply admired the orchid vulva and pretended this wasn't a question that had been buzzing around her head like a mosquito since she'd heard Luz Alana and her husband were returning to Paris from London for the closing ceremonies of the Exposition Universelle. "Apparently he's come back with the intention of razing through every ballroom in Paris until he finds an eighteen-year-old foolish enough to marry him." The information caught her like a slap in the face. Shocking and more humiliating than painful. Of course, he'd be looking for some infant with a fat dowry and a conscience like driven snow to make his duchess.

It was what dukes did and the doings of dukes were not of her concern.

"Perhaps I should go look for Abelardo before it gets too late," she said, pointing to the clock, with every intention of getting out of the building before the Duke of Annan entered it. She had not prepared herself to see the man tonight. She didn't think she could abide his smirks and suggestive quips without committing some violence. Which would only lead to questions from her friends she had no intention of answering.

Her downfall came, as it was prone to do, served to her on a silver tray. She was close to making an escape when a procession of servers in Le Bureau's gold-and-burgundy livery entered the room holding trays laden with all manner of confections.

"What is this?" Manuela exclaimed as they watched the small platoon heading in their direction. "Did you do this, mi amor?" Cora shook her head, and from the frown on her face, she seemed to have no idea who did.

"Are those canelés?" Aurora asked, her mouth watering at the sight of a pyramid of the French pastry. Behind the bearer of canelés, a tall young man was carrying what had to be a tower of a hundred profiteroles.

"Aurorita, you must stay now, these are your favorites!" Manuela sent her a pleading look and Aurora felt her reservations drain out of her.

She did love her food. It was one of the few indulgences she allowed herself. She was not one for fashions, rarely took in theater or musical entertainments. She couldn't give two figs about dances or balls, and roaming the halls of museums utterly bored her. But she loved a delicious bite of food. She fantasized about her favorite meals like other women did their weddings days.

She let out a tiny gasp as one of the servers stopped in front of her with a tray of éclairs. They were lined up like little soldiers. The golden tops covered in a shell of milk chocolate, a tiny dollop of custard peeking out of the ends. Just the aroma made her mouth water.

"I guess I could stay a few minutes." They *were* quite small. She would eat one in a few bites and take a few others for later.

"Mademoiselle, s'il vous plaît," a liveried server said encouragingly, passing her a small plate. The éclairs came first, then when the tray with the profiteroles appeared, she plucked a couple from the very top of the tower. She also took some canelé—for after she saw her patient—and only when her little plate was heaping did the servers move on from where she stood.

By the time she bit into a flaky, buttery éclair and felt that decadent custard on her tongue, she'd forgotten entirely about the reason why she'd been trying to leave Le Bureau. She was on her second profiterole when a very tall, very large reminder made his entrance.

Three

"She's practically making love to that damned cream puff," Apollo muttered to no one in particular as he observed Aurora Montalban devour a mountain of pastries with a single-minded passion that was nothing short of pornographic.

The muscles in his neck spasmed as she delicately picked off some of the cream from the pastry with the tip of her tongue. In hindsight, knowing what he did about the doctor's appetites and the effect their display had on him, he should've thought the gesture through. "She's a bloody public menace with an éclair in her hands."

He was quite transfixed by Aurora Montalban's appetites. The way she ate, drank, worked...the way she demanded pleasure, all of it with such vigor. He wondered how no one else noticed that the forbidding Doctora Montalban was a secret hedonist.

"Are you drooling, brother?" His sibling's irritating laugh forced him to tear his gaze off her for a second.

"Why are you bothering me?" he growled, prompting another amused laugh from Evan. "Aren't you supposed to be chasing after your wife's skirts?"

As expected, his brother did not take his bait. On the contrary, Evan seemed to relish any references to his utter infatuation with his wife. While other men might bristle at the implication that their woman had them wrapped around their fingers, Evan relished it.

"My wife." His brother loved saying those words, *my wife.* Like there was no higher cause a man could hope to achieve than that of being someone's husband. "She stopped in to see Seynabou, she'll be here shortly." Evan's beloved had inherited a stake in her family's rum distillery in the Dominican Republic and, in the months since she'd arrived in Europe, had made impressive inroads to offer her spirits in quite a few markets. Now she was looking to fill every pleasure palace in the continent with it. "I came looking for you, Sédar is waiting for us." Watching Aurora tongue the cream off a bit of pastry blasted any thoughts of business dealings right out of his mind.

"Sédar is here all night. He can wait for ten damned minutes." Evan raised both eyebrows at his tone, which only made Apollo more cross. This woman made him volatile.

"I thought you'd be happy she's enjoying what you sent her."

"Who said it was for her? Maybe I wanted to do something nice for Cora." Evan scoffed at the blatant lie, while Apollo practically choked on his tongue at the sight of Aurora using hers liberally over a bit of frosting. "Besides, she'd come and throw it all in my face if she knew it was from me."

"She probably would," his brother agreed with a knowing grin. Aurora Montalban's disdain of Apollo was no secret. Which made the one they shared even more delicious. Because she might despise him, but she wanted him.

"I still can't believe she's working here," he mused as he watched her. Aurora's first time at Le Bureau was the stuff of legends, when she'd accidentally entered a live fellatio demonstration and practically fainted from horror. He knew that was not the only side to Aurora Montalban. There was also the woman who'd come to his apartment in the dead of night asking assistance in her sexual rebellion. But she'd always been cautious about not doing anything that could impact her professional reputation. Working as a brothel physician was not exactly the most respectable of occupations. "She used to be more careful."

Evan was quiet for a long time, which told Apollo there was something he was reluctant to say about his wife's friend.

"From what Luz tells me these days, she can't afford being too careful." How could the heiress to one of the biggest fortunes in Mexico not afford to stay out of Parisian brothels?

Was that the reason she'd come to him that night? Had she been disowned? Cut off?

Aurora didn't seem the type to be reckless with money. He gave her clothes a look and frowned. They were as shabby as always and seemed to hang off her, even more ill-fitting than usual. There were also dark circles under her eyes. She looked tired, like she hadn't been sleeping. Was she in trouble? He turned to his brother again, tempted to push him for more information. He could probably get it out of Evan if he prodded, but he'd had enough of cowering behind columns.

"Excuse me, brother." He didn't wait for Evan to answer, his feet carrying him to where she sat. She was so distracted with her pastries, she didn't notice him until he was right in front of her.

"Annan." She spoke around a bite of éclair, with a gloved hand over her mouth. But he could still see a tiny spot of cream on her bottom lip he desperately wanted to lick off. He was transfixed by her damned gloves, and he was not ashamed to admit he'd lain awake imagining himself sliding them off with his teeth while she whispered utterly depraved things in his ears. He was so caught up in the fantasy, he almost missed her insult. "Did you knock out some poor unsuspecting woman with your excessive use of cologne and need me to revive her?"

If he'd had a drink, he would've spit it out. She was so deliciously vicious. She fixed him with one of those icy looks she favored in his presence and turned that button nose up at him. He didn't know where to look first. The chocolate bonbon eyes that burned like embers. The sweetly curved cheeks, the pugnaciously pointed chin.

"I've come to offer my aid in finding you a less depressing wardrobe." He made a point of looking at the cuff of her shirt, which was missing a button.

"How generous of you," she sneered in between bites of food. "If I ever decide to dress like an out-of-work court jester, you'll be the first person I call on." Her undisguised vitriol felt like a fresh breeze after weeks of dreadfully boring conversations about fossils and English rainfall. The way his pulse raced, it might as well be foreplay.

"You say such sweet things," he told her in response, before pulling up a chair and sitting down. He noticed that despite her claim about his appearance, her eyes seemed to be taking stock of his person in minute detail.

"I did not invite you to sit down." She shot him another one of those dirty looks which stirred him up to a frenzy and gave a dismissive wave of her fingers. "I'm waiting for someone." *That* he did not like.

"Very naughty, Doctora. If you needed a tumble, you merely had to say."

"I've already partaken," she said, with a yawn, then flashed those white teeth in his direction. "The profiteroles are *much* more satisfying." If she only knew what her insults did to him, she'd truly be furious.

"I can see that from the way you were lapping up the cream from that éclair." He made a point of lingering a moment too long on that spot on her lip. "Incidentally it brings to mind another kind of cre—"

She let out a horrified little cry that ran right through his bloodstream. "You're disgusting. Is sex the only thing you think about?" She was livid, but not quite enough to keep from staring at his mouth.

"We *are* in a brothel." She growled, baring a row of white teeth at him and brought her plate closer, as if concerned it would become contaminated with all the sexual innuendo.

"You're quite fetching when you growl, you know," he whispered, pulling his chair close enough to hers that the tips of their boots kissed. "Now that I think about it, when was the last time I heard you growl?" He tapped the table with two fingers while she glared at him. "Oh, that's right, it was when I— Ow! Dammit, Aurora," he cried out, rubbing the spot on his arm where she'd pinched him.

"We agreed not to speak about that night, you cretin." She bit out the words, pointing at him with a gloved finger. He hadn't intended to, but she was so damned prickly. One of the things no one told him about this new title was that even the people who hated him would never contradict him anymore. His brother did, his aunt, but there were days when he felt like Apollo didn't exist anymore, just the Duke of Annan. Aurora's utter disregard for his feelings—never mind his title—transfixed him.

"My apologies," he finally conceded, reaching for a frosted pastry, but she caught his wrist.

"I will pinch you again," she warned him, before finishing the bun in her other hand in two ferocious bites. "Now, go away, I'm busy."

"Busy with what exactly? You can't be working at one in the morning." He didn't expect her to take his prying well, and she did not disappoint.

"I don't know how to say this without offending, but there is nothing that is less your business than mine, Your Grace."

"I just thought an heiress so mindful of her social standing would be more careful, that's all." She sent him a scathing look while she licked sugar off her leather gloves. If she kept at that, there was a high probability he'd disgrace himself in this room full of people.

"I thought all new dukes were supposed to be getting indoctrinated in exploiting the poor and stealing with impunity, but here you are." She made a sweeping motion with her hand.

"That's uncalled for." He pretended to be offended, but she was utterly unmoved.

"What's uncalled for is your attempt to question my presence here when you're doing the exact same thing." He opened his mouth to say that, unlike her, he was not an employee, but she held up a finger and pointed it right at his face, in warning. "If you utter the words *I'm a man*, I will commit violence on your person."

"I would not dream of it," he said in as conciliatory a tone as he could manage, putting a hand to his chest. Which she regarded mutinously. "I rather enjoy thinking of you engaging in unladylike activities."

"I'm warning you, Annan." She threatened him with a very small fork.

"Is that the way you thank me for sending you trays of your favorite treats?" Immediately she narrowed her eyes, then lowered them to her plate with a regretful expression that had him very close to laughing out loud.

"Mentiroso," she finally bit out. "Besides, how would you know what I like?"

"I'm not lying." He ought to scrub the smugness out of his voice, if he didn't want to lose an eye to that tiny fork, but he could not control himself with her. "Besides, you told me yourself." He was violating the promise of not bringing up their night together, but how else would he know.

If it were an éclair or a canelé, perhaps I'd be tempted.

That was what she'd told him that night when he offered her chocolates. The profiteroles had been pure indulgence on his part, as well as a secret hope that she'd lick some chocolate off her lips.

For a few moments of taut silence, she glared at the remaining treats before finally looking up at him.

"If it's true—" she clearly didn't quite believe him "—thank you." She expelled the words from her mouth with the sweetness of a viper. Heat stirred in him at the absolute noxious glare she sent him.

"You're welcome, Fiera." As expected, the color rose in her cheeks, a flush of pink making those delicious freckles scattered over her nose and cheeks stand out.

"I don't like that nickname." She ground out each word like she was attempting to curse him and his progeny for generations to come.

"You've forbidden me from calling you Bella Doctora too."

"Then, call me Doctora Montalban." She waved away whatever she saw on his face, then surprised him with her next question. "So, what is it that you intend to do with your duchy, besides find some dollar princess with a fat dowry? Get richer? Hoard more resources?" He had come to poke at her, and turnabout was fair play.

"Don't go easy on me because I brought you treats," he said acidly, which earned him the first real smile from her that evening. She had not been kind in her questions, but they weren't unfair either. "And did I detect a hint of jealousy regarding my hunt for a bride?" She actually snorted, as if the notion itself were beyond ridiculous. He retaliated by stealing a canelé from her plate, which he popped into his mouth.

"Get your own!" she protested, sliding the plate far from his reach. "And don't avoid my question."

"I don't quite have an answer," he heard himself confess. "I'm still figuring that out. I never thought I'd actually be in a position to consider what manner of duke I'd be." Seeking revenge on his father had always seemed like a mission one didn't return from. And even if he'd considered that success was actually attainable, he'd never expected to become duke so fast.

Once he saw for himself the state his father had left things in, he wondered if the bastard was laughing at him in hell. He'd spent weeks visiting tenants who were living in deplorable conditions. Hundreds of people under their care who had been left to their own devices while the duke kept his second wife in diamonds and Worth gowns. Evan had tried, but he didn't have the means to fix every problem. Apollo wasn't quite sure how he would.

"To be fair to you, I don't imagine any of the dukes in your line ever gave it much thought either," she said, not unkindly.

"I'd like to think I can do better than that." He tried not to get his hackles up when she made a skeptical sound.

"So what's the problem?"

"I need alliances. I need leverage."

"I assume the House of Lords is of no use," she said with unsurprising perspicuity.

"You assume correctly," he sighed. His peers were quite useless in fact. The ones who were not actively trying to boot him, like Ackworth, were either lukewarm about his presence or so financially desperate their support scarcely mattered. He had some friends, but they were not enough to grant him the leverage he needed to actually have influence in the Lords. "And the white burghers who do have influence and solvency are not exactly rushing to form alliances with a Black duke."

"So boring and predictable." He liked her sharp tongue,

and despite her disapproval of his position, it was a relief to speak frankly on this without being bombarded with a barrage of platitudes. Aurora Montalban had no interest in putting him at ease.

"Then you need to look for other powerful friends to ally yourself with." He raised an eyebrow at this, because it was exactly what he'd been thinking since he arrived in Paris. "You can't allow these pilferers to rob you of your senses, Apollo." Every time she said his name, even in obvious rebuke, his entire body seemed to catch fire from within.

"I'm pretty certain my senses are still in place," he told her, trying very hard not to smile at her zesty expression. She turned in her seat, so that they were facing each other, her lovely heart-shaped face glowing like bronze in the gaslight.

"Are you not a Black man who owns a respectable amount of the coffee in Colombia?"

"I am." Or he had been. He'd dissolved a lot of those holdings now.

"My father is one too, a direct descendant from Mexico's first president, also a Black man." It was the first time he'd heard her speak of her father and she did so almost with reluctant pride. As if she was not certain if she liked the man yet could not help but feel pride for his accomplishments. "The Brits may have sold us the story that the sun never sets on their empire of thievery and rape, but we don't have to believe it."

"I don't," he protested, but she had more to say.

"This isn't our world, you and I know there is a lot of power out there that doesn't belong to the couple of hundred men in that house you now belong to. A lot of those who wield it are in Paris right now."

He knew that, in fact half of them were already invited to his villa in Nice as part of his aunt's scheme to find him a wife. Apollo thought of the businessmen, heads of state, scientists, inventors he'd met at the exposition. Many of them from the Americas, South Pacific, Asia, Africa, the Middle East. Hell, a significant number of the most powerful men in the Americas would be in Paris until the end of the fall. She was right, he could use those connections for business.

"That's good advice," he admitted, bowing his head.

She rolled her eyes at the compliment, primly dabbed the corners of her mouth with a linen napkin, then turned to face him. "How hard is it to throw a party? Isn't that most of your job as a duke?"

He wanted to lean down and bite that sneering lip. "Among other things," he acquisesced with a shake of his head.

"Excellent." She flecked the crumbs off her skirt and pushed her plate aside with a flourish. "Now that I've given you a task, I'd like for you to leave." She made a shooing motion in his direction. "My friend will be here any minute, and I don't want him thinking we know each other." That he did not like at all, but he knew he had to proceed with caution.

"Who is this suitor you're waiting for? I won't divulge your secret, I promise."

"I'm not here for an assignation." She didn't look at him, focusing her attention on gulping down a glass of lemonade. Her throat moved as she drank thirstily, and Apollo could not tear his eyes off her.

"But we were having such a lovely conversation."

"Fine," she huffed, standing up when he didn't immediately move, and, with an air of dignified outrage, plucked up the remaining pastries on the table, placed them delicately on a linen napkin, which she promptly shoved into that horrendous Gladstone bag she took everywhere. "I'll go, then. He's here anyway." She pointed a gloved hand at a slender man with dark brown skin and a Byronic air that instantly annoyed Apollo.

This man could not handle his Fiera. She'd gobble him up like she had those buns.

"I'd like to meet your associate." He also stood and for a second, he wondered if she was going to try and shove him away. Despite her being a good foot shorter than him, he had to admit he liked her chances. She was that fierce.

"Abelardo is very shy, and your gigantic size will scare him," she whispered, as she sent the man a smile and beckoned him over.

"I promise to be polite. Besides, we're practically related. It's my duty to make sure you're not mixing with the wrong sort of man." He grinned shamelessly when she sent him another of those icy looks.

She took a step toward him. "For the last time, he's not a suitor. He's a colleague." She stomped her minuscule kid leather boot on the floor. Which only brought to mind the shapely legs she kept so well hidden. "I have a patient waiting and Abelardo's escorting me to the appointment."

The outrage came upon him like a wave. Had she really said she was going to see a patient? It was past one in the morning.

"You can't be serious, it's the middle of the night." He tried to keep his voice level, but the cool indifference he'd relied on his entire life seemed particularly fleeting when it came to Aurora Montalban.

She hefted that ugly leather bag and skirted around him. "I don't have to explain myself to you, sir." He had the most overwhelming urge to put her over his shoulders and drag her to a dark corner where they could really unleash whatever was brewing between them.

"Aurora, there you are." Abelardo sounded like a happy enough fellow and didn't seem particularly lecherous, but Apollo did not like the sight of the man's hands on the doctor's shoulder.

"Abe, thank you for coming." She was all smiles now as she offered her cheek for a kiss. What was this familiarity? He'd been seen by doctors all his life, and he'd never known them to smile or cluck around, patting people on the arm.

"Won't you introduce us, Doctora?" There was no helping the menace in his voice. He was tired and he did not feel like exercising restraint. Abelardo at least had a good sense for danger, because the moment he saw Apollo, he took a full step away from Aurora.

Excellent. "Abe" might get to his bed with all his fingers still attached.

"I'm sorry." Apollo reconsidered his assessment of the man's instincts when he extended a hand. "I'm Abelardo Bona."

"A pleasure," Apollo said, applying enough force to the handshake to get his message across. "Duke of Annan." The man paled upon hearing the title. Aurora made a face of disgust, then pulled Apollo's hand away.

"Stop that, you're hurting him." Instead of continuing to yell at him, she turned to Abelardo with an apologetic expression.

"Abe, could you wait for me by the entrance downstairs? I left something in the women's surgery I must retrieve before we leave." To Apollo, she sent a very hostile look. "You, behave."

With that, she took her leave. Abelardo, the poor sod, actually attempted to engage him in conversation instead of heeding her warning.

"Is this your first time here, Your Grace?"

"Abelardo, are you a gambling man?" he asked, to which the other man reacted with a nonplussed expression.

"Not particularly," he answered, pushing a pair of spectacles up his nose. "I do play dominoes occasionally, but mostly with my—"

"What do you think are the odds of you getting lost between here and your meeting place with Doctora Montalban?"

"Lost?" Abelardo looked around wildly, and Apollo should've felt bad for the man. He didn't.

"This is a big building, and one could get turned around easily," he said pointedly at a confused Abelardo.

"I don't understand."

"I'll escort her to where she's going."

His view on Abelardo improved when the smaller man shook his head. "With all due respect, Your Grace, Aurora's my friend, and I don't know what your intentions are with her."

"Are you implying a duke could be capable of hurting a woman in his care?"

The doctor squared his shoulders and pursed his mouth mutinously. "I'm implying that the fact you are a duke makes me think you almost certainly will." Apollo thought he might even come to like the man.

"Annan, take your hands off the poor man." Abelardo slumped in relief under Apollo's clutches as Manuela and Cora sauntered up to them.

"I was just explaining to my new friend here that I would be glad to assume the responsibility of escorting Doctora Montalban to see her patient." Manuela nodded slowly, while Cora perked up in a very worrisome manner.

"That's an interesting offer, Annan." Cora spoke in her usual bored manner, but her eyes were the very opposite of apathetic.

"It's the least I could do. The doctora and I are family, after all."

Abelardo frowned again, likely remembering the barrage of nonfamilial threats Aurora had tossed at him before leaving.

"Family?" Manuela asked dubiously.

"She's grown quite attached to me." He had a hard time keeping a straight face for that last one.

"He's a jackass," Cora said, turning to a now fully befuddled Abelardo. "But he," she continued, then seemed to reconsider, "or more likely, his man Jean-Louis, will make sure she gets there safely."

"If you're sure," Abelardo said dubiously.

Cora shook her head, as if this was all beyond what her patience could handle this late in the evening. "She'll be if not in 'good' hands, at least in hands capable of decimating any villain she encounters on the way."

That and the arrival of Cora's stepson, who Abelardo was quite giddy to see, seemed to settle matters, and mere minutes later, Apollo arrived at the meeting point right outside the brothel. Aurora was already there, holding that blasted Gladstone in one hand and some kind of metal canister in the other.

The moment she saw him, she let out a curse in Spanish that had him biting his lip.

"Language, Doctora, this is a respectable establishment."

She snapped her teeth and hiked up that metal canister menacingly. "What did you do with my friend?"

"Doctor Bona sends his regrets," he informed her, sliding both hands into his trouser pockets.

"You bastard," she spit out, as she waved that big metal can in the air. "Do *not* follow me." She turned on her heels and loped down the sidewalk like a very furious, and adorably mussed, medical fairy.

"Wait for me, Fiera," he called out, but she only walked faster.

"Don't call me that," she shouted over her shoulder, lifting the canister over her head for emphasis. Even with his significant height advantage, he had to pick up his pace to keep up with her. The little diabla was quick, and before he knew it, she had a few hundred yards on him.

"Demonios, mujer!" he called out to her in Spanish, but she ignored that too. He had to break into a run to catch her, and almost lost an eye for his trouble.

Four

As she held up her glove with sharp blades on the fingertips at the Duke of Annan, it occurred to Aurora that some
might consider her actions a mite dramatic, but the man had
a gift for driving her into a rage.

"I will stab you, sir," she warned, thrusting her claws in a
small forward movement.

"Que feroz." The smile he offered her then was the one
he'd used that night when it had been just the two of them.
The one that made that nauseating chasm in her stomach open.
The one that reminded her of things she ought to not want as
badly as she did.

They were standing about a foot apart on the illuminated
pedestrian walk of the Boulevard de Clichy.

"Might I ask what the hell you have on your hands?" he
asked, staring at her hands with a baffled expression. She looked
down at her gloves, then back up at him.

"They're special gloves I had made." She always felt silly
wearing them, but they were very effective in deterring the
wrong kind of attention. "For protection," she added self-
consciously. She'd gotten them when she began seeing patients
in secret locations. Some nights, she only learned where she'd

be going a few hours beforehand, and some locations were riskier than others.

He looked at the gloves for a very long time, his expression mutinous, which was unexpected. She assumed he'd mock her for walking around with such a ridiculous contraption, but the furthest thing from his face was humor.

"Aurora." She didn't think she'd ever heard him sound so serious. Not even earlier when they'd discussed his duties in the duchy. "Why are you taking such risks?" The tightness in his voice was so foreign, she wondered if this was the first time she was actually hearing the real Apollo. She didn't know what to do with any of this. Why couldn't he just do what everyone else did and wash his hands of her?

"What is it with you, Annan?" She tried for callousness, hoping that would finally do the trick. It did not. "Is it that you can't abide the idea of a woman not falling all over herself for you?" She expected him to return her rudeness in kind, but he seemed offended by her accusation. Like her opinion of him was the furthest thing from his mind. He looked almost confused.

"I'm merely making sure you arrive in one piece wherever you're headed, on foot, at one in the morning." He was so damned reasonable, in that impeccable blue suit, just the color of midnight, cut to mold perfectly to his imposing frame.

She'd made jokes about his clothing, implying he didn't look the part of a duke, but she'd been untruthful. He was the physical manifestation of what all that power and birth *should* look like. Shoulders that could carry any load, but hers would not be one of them. She was no one's cross to bear.

She could stay here and argue all night, but she did have a patient to see and tried for a more conciliatory approach. She put away the gloves, deciding they might not be communicating the right message.

"I can see myself home. I'll be fine." She attempted to sound reassuring, but the man was not budging.

"But you're not going home." No, she was not. She was going to see a patient about a fistulotomy. A patient who in her letter requesting the consultation advised Aurora that since her husband disapproved of her receiving medical care for her ailment, she could only come to the appointment while he was away on business in Loire. From Aurora's experience, this likely meant her patient was taking great personal risk to seek treatment, so she could not arrive late with a very large, very noticeable, stranger to their meeting place.

Abelardo was different, he knew how to put patients at ease. Apollo was a damned giant, and with all the scowling he was doing tonight, he'd probably frighten the poor woman to death.

She had to get rid of him. With great effort, she managed to tip up her lips into some kind of a smile.

"Your Grace—" she could be civil "—truly, I'm not too far from my destination and don't require an escort this evening." She exerted herself further and managed to reveal a few teeth. He frowned, as if the glimpse of her teeth was the most puzzling part of the evening so far.

"I noticed you never said *what* your destination was."

Demonios, did the man miss anything?

"I did not," she conceded, waving a hand at the few stragglers making their way up and down the avenue. "As you can see, I will have company in my journey."

He gave her another one of those looks that aggravated her.

"I'm not sure I'm making myself clear. I mean to accompany you where you're going." What did he want with her? Was this about showing her she couldn't look after herself?

"Is this some kind of game for you?" she asked, and the question seemed to catch him off guard. "Is that it? You want to prove you can take better care of my person than I can?"

For some reason, that made him angry. "Carajo, Aurora," he exclaimed with a frustrated laugh. Running a hand through his hair with clear barely constrained irritation. "Is that the only reason I might be out here with you?" It was clearly not a question that required an answer, so she didn't provide one. "The only interest I might have to escort you where you're going is only to humble you, then?"

He sounded sincere, his tone almost pleading. Had she read this all wrong? Was he actually concerned for her? She considered this for a moment, then decided he was probably just bored.

"I don't need your assistance. I walk the streets of Paris alone at night regularly. No harm has ever come to me." He stared at her for what felt like hours, his eyes softening into something that made her feel like she had no skin. She did not care for it.

"I didn't know you did this." He said it as if it was of significance. The man had clearly gotten in his head that he was somehow responsible for her safety, which was exceedingly tiresome. But it was true, she was perfectly capable of taking care of herself.

If he only knew he was standing in front of a criminal. Just in the last months she'd committed offenses that could send her to prison for years. She wondered what he'd think of her then? It was true her work put her in the path of the occasional rough sort. But beggars could not be choosers, and when one was operating an underground clinic for women, locations had to be in out-of-the-way places.

And she was going to be late. The last thing she wanted was a patient waiting for her in front of a building at this late hour when they were attempting to go unnoticed.

"You don't have to do this, you know?" She stopped in the middle of the street, turning to him.

"Do what?" He'd bent his head toward her, and she had an

almost irresistible urge to tug on his errant curls. It was only then she noticed that he looked tired, as if he'd had more than one sleepless night since she'd seen him. She almost wished it was in her nature to put her guard down. That she hadn't been so abrasive when he'd been honest with her back at Le Bureau. That she hadn't picked a fight the moment she saw him.

"This. Being my custodian." She waved her hand between the foot of space that separated them. "Feeling obliged to me in any way because we were intimate once."

A myriad of emotions crossed his face, and how she wished seeing them didn't affect her. "You should know by now that I don't do anything I don't want to," he told her, without a semblance of his usual diffidence.

Then why was he here? Was he entertaining himself by making her believe he cared about her well-being? No, this was his damned sense of chivalry.

She should let him walk her. Just get to the meeting point and make him turn back. What was the harm?

The *harm* was that she was beginning to feel warm and soft about his insistence to make sure she was safe, and that way lay danger. The *harm* was that she didn't want to rely on this man, or any man, ever.

"I didn't want to say this, to preserve your pride," she told him, in the most contrite voice she could manage. She looked down at the cobblestones for additional effect. "But Abelardo, in truth, was not escorting me to see a patient, he was accompanying me to meet a…" She stumbled then, her mouth going a little dry.

"A…?" He arched one of those thick eyebrows, his face otherwise the picture of imperviousness.

"A new lover." Her face was so hot, she wished she'd moved farther into the shadows before she began her deception. "He's waiting for me."

"Is that so?" His eyes crinkled in the corners, which didn't seem to her like the reaction she wanted. "Then I should love to meet him."

Argh.

"Meet him?" she asked dumbly, and he nodded soberly.

"I'd love to get his advice on what kind of trap to set to keep you from fleeing my apartment the next occasion you come calling." This pendejo, the man made her want to scream.

"That is absolutely uncalled for." He laughed at her, the bastard.

"You're not getting rid of me, Aurora, so you might as well start walking, if you don't want to miss this rendezvous." The humor had completely drained from his voice now, and something about the obstinate glint in his eyes told her she didn't want to test him further.

"Oh hell, suit yourself," she exclaimed, throwing her arms in the air. Absolutely at the end of her patience. "Come with me to the damned meeting place, but you cannot be seen by the patient. These meetings are supposed to be anonymous."

She could see the questions forming in his head.

"What exactly are you doing for these patients?" he asked calmly as he kept pace with her. She opened her mouth to yell at him again, then decided to not further waste her energy. Her displays of temper seemed to have no effect on him.

"I can't tell you what I'm doing and I can't tell you who I'm meeting." She held up a hand before he even had a chance to speak. "This is my private business, and though I cannot prevent you from walking me there, I *will* ask you to respect my work."

He did not answer as they turned off from the main boulevard and into a poorly lit street.

"That's fair," he conceded, surprising her. "Is there so much demand for your services that you have to see patients at these hours?"

She noticed the absence of his typical sarcasm. Maybe she was just so tired she was hallucinating, but she thought she could almost hear genuine curiosity.

"We have so much demand we could see patients every day, for twenty-four hours of the day, and we still would not fulfill the requests we receive." He whistled in surprise, which she found irritatingly charming. This was the disorienting thing about Apollo. He looked exactly like a duke should, but he behaved like a man she would like, if liking men was something she did.

"If business is so good, then why are my brother and his wife hosting a charity event for you?" he asked, astutely.

"We only charge those who can pay, and we assure clients anonymity." She felt great pride in that. Their clinic turned no one away, ever. What they couldn't do, they found someone who would. "We also work under strict hygienic protocols. Word spreads fast when the need is great."

He slowed his pace and reached out for her bag. Her instinct was to resist. She found it very difficult to put down her guard, especially with someone who tested her patience like he did. But so far, his questions about her work had at least been respectful, and her hand *was* aching.

She let go and he caught the bag with a sound of satisfaction that tugged at something in a reckless part of her that still believed in chivalry.

"Are you the only one doing these clandestine visits?" These kinds of questions she didn't like. They were the ones people usually asked before making judgments.

"I'm not," she answered truthfully. He remained contemplative for a while, before speaking again.

"This life is not the typical one for an heiress," he told her, then raised an eyebrow when she scoffed.

"I'm not the typical heiress, Your Grace." If he only knew just how atypical she was. "Nor am I interested in living like one." In fact, her little life with a modest room at a boarding-house in Montmartre run by Manuela's friend and an occupation that allowed her to fulfill the promise she'd made herself at fifteen suited her just fine. It was a distant existence from the comforts she'd grown up with, but she preferred the freedom which came from cutting the controlling strings those comforts came with.

"Does your family ever worry about you doing this work?"

"They never have." That was more than she'd wanted to say. She was not one to indulge in self-pity and that answer reeked of melodrama. But it was the truth.

She'd always felt like a burden to her parents. Her mother was never warm to her, and on the rare occasion her father remembered she existed, he was always distant.

As a small child, she thought if she was very good, then maybe they would allow her to accompany them on the family drives into town. But no matter how quiet, how obedient she was, it was never enough. As she got older, she became angrier, rebellious. She doggedly protested every rule she found unjust, flew into rages when she was punished for it, and that made everything worse. She didn't want to think about any of that.

"How about your family?" she asked, needing very badly to veer off the topic of her familial catastrophe. "Are they helping you with your obligations?" They were only five minutes away from the turn to the clinic in Le Marais. If she kept him talking about himself until then, she might get out of this without too many of her secrets uncovered.

"Evan is of great help, and my sisters." Though she'd never had any kind of bond with her brothers, she recognized the affection in Apollo's voice. He'd only met his siblings recently and it already seemed like there was genuine care between them. She was glad for him.

"You must be pleased to finally have some close family."

"I always had my aunt Jimena and my cousins," he told her, before plucking the ether canister from her hand, with a stubborn expression. She let it go, too curious about this aunt. It was the first time she'd heard of any other family.

"Is it your mother Violeta's sister?" He turned to her then and the smile on his lips made her heart stumble for a moment.

"Yes." He smiled wider then, and she thought what a gift it must be to think of family with such fondness. "She raised me after my mother died and is the architect of this so-called hunt for a duchess." She pressed a fist to her chest at the sudden tightness there. Likely indigestion from all those sweets. "Since she arrived from Colombia last month, she's taken a very invested interest in my taking the right wife." He didn't sound too excited about the prospect and that didn't affect her or her mood in the slightest fashion.

"Shouldn't *you* also be invested in who you take as a wife?" She'd long given up on the notion of marriage for herself. Like any girl, she'd had her fantasies. But there weren't many men out there who delighted in a wife with no interest in domestic pursuits and endless opinions.

"I'm invested in rebuilding what my father destroyed," he said with gravity, once again displaying a side she'd never seen. "I'm quite set on finding uses for all the land we've hoarded for generations that would benefit more than just those in our scant bloodline." He lifted his shoulder, as if what he'd just suggested wasn't breaking with hundreds of years of aristocratic greed. "I'd also like to use the vote I have in the Lords to help advance the rights of the more disadvantaged. Like I told you earlier tonight, for that I need the right alliances." He looked down at her, then back to the street.

"And the right wife could help with that." He grunted in agreement, but she could not surmise much from his face.

"So do you have any prospects, Your Grace? Or are the aristos refusing you their innocent maidens?" Why did she insist on bringing this up at every opportunity? From the look he sent her, he was likely wondering the same thing.

"You would think so." He sounded amused, but there was an edge to it that made a shiver run through her spine. "But for the right amount of money, even the most hardened bigots are perfectly willing to bring their daughters to the beast."

"I find it hard to believe there aren't some ladies in the ton willing to marry you." From the looks he received from the women present in every room she'd seen him in, she hazarded to guess some were throwing themselves at him.

"Are you saying you consider me a good catch, Doctora?" She was the one laughing then. She had talked herself into this corner. But what about it? He was clearly a desirable match for any ladies of genteel breeding looking for a husband. He was rich, charming, beautiful.

"I'm not your audience, Your Grace." Or anything close to a suitable prospect. He needed a wife with a pristine past. The right breeding and not a hint of scandal. She had a past murkier than the Seine. Not that it mattered. She had no interest in marriage. "This is where we part ways," she said, relieved to finally have reached the destination.

"Absolutely not," he said, pulling his hand back when she reached for her bag.

"What do you mean, no?" she asked in a furious whisper.

"I'm not leaving you in a dark alley, Aurora." She was being punished. Some deity had decided she needed to learn a lesson about stubbornness and Apollo Sinclair was who they'd sent to torture her.

"No, you're not." She was done with amusing him. She

tugged on the bag, then stomped her boot hoping to catch his foot, and almost tripped and fell in the process.

"You're being reckless, Aurora." So what if she was? She didn't answer to this man, she answered to no man, and she liked it that way.

"Le Marais is perfectly safe." It had a few dodgy corners, but she had her gloves. Hell, in the mood she was, she might invite a fight with some ruffians.

"There are no safe places for women on their own at one in the morning," he retorted, mirroring her amiable tone while not being amiable at all.

"The house is merely one block in that direction." It was not so much a house as Virginia's brother's print shop, which they'd converted into a temporary clinic.

But it seemed the proximity to the place was not enough to make Apollo let go of the damned bag. He stood there, his mouth pursed, not budging an inch. It was like talking to a damned statue.

"If you scare my client, I'll take my blade gloves to your face," she warned him, and turned toward the lookout point on the north corner that allowed her to see if the coast was clear before going to find her client. "Stay on this side of the street," she whispered testily over her shoulder. She was so mad she could spit. "You better not talk to my patient, and must you stomp so loudly—" The anger bled out of her when she spotted three shadowed figures standing by the clinic's entrance. She froze in place, when she spotted the batons and uniforms.

"Oof, watch it, Fiera," he groaned as she stopped, causing him to collide right into her. She turned around to clamp a hand on his mouth, then pointed at the other side of the street where three members of the Parisian police seemed to be waiting right in front of the print shop's door, with her patient nowhere to be seen.

Five

It took Apollo a moment to realize what was happen-
ing. One second, he was on the receiving end of another one
of those bizarrely arousing tongue-lashings from Aurora, and
the next, she was staring at the street, frozen in shock. Then
he saw them, a cluster of coppers standing in front of what
looked like a closed print shop.

"Mierda," Aurora cursed under her breath, before taking off
like the hounds of hell were on her heels. For someone with
such short legs, the little wench was fast.

"What in the bloody hell?" Apollo spun around, chasing
after her, then winced, remembering the coppers were only
a few yards away. He gritted his teeth and sped up with the
damned Gladstone slamming his leg and the canister tucked
under one arm.

"Arrête!" someone shouted behind him, but he didn't stop
to look, chasing after Aurora, who was now at least ten meters
ahead of him. But he didn't lose sight of the dervish in front
of him as earsplitting whistles rang in the air.

"Aurora, que diablos—" She was racing up the street in
those damned split skirts she always wore. That was probably
why she had them, so she could evade the law.

"A la izquierda," she called out breathlessly, running into what looked like a wall but was instead a pitch-black alley. Despite his reputation as a scoundrel, in all of his thirty-five years, Apollo had never been chased by police. And yet, Aurora Montalban, the buttoned-up doctor, who had once been scandalized by even the mention of a brothel, was apparently so accustomed to it, she had escape routes.

And he'd actually felt guilty for pushing himself into her evening. Even now when he had half a mind to throttle her, he could not help but admire the cojones of Doctora Montalban. If he managed not to kill her for this, he might tell her so.

After a couple of turns and a treacherous encounter with a hedge of extremely prickly bushes, they managed to lose the coppers. She finally came to a stop on a poorly lit street, where she practically collapsed against a wrought iron fence, gasping for breath. By the time he came to a stop next to her, he could only stare in amazement as he struggled to get his own breathing in order.

"Que diablos fue eso?" he demanded between gulps of air. She sent him a sideways glance, with absolutely no contrition on her flushed face.

"I told you to go home," she managed to wheeze out.

I told you to go? That was her answer?

Apollo tried to never let his temper slip from his control, but on this occasion, he managed to govern himself with sheer force of will. Very slowly he placed the bag and canister on the ground between them while he listened to her labored breaths. He reminded himself that back there, as they walked, he'd seen the exhaustion in her face. That he'd watched her straighten her spine as if the whole weight of the world was meant for her shoulders. All important things to keep in mind, so he wasn't tempted to ring her neck.

When he was back in control, he crouched so that he was eye level with her. As expected, she instantly bristled.

"This is not your problem," she wheezed, still holding on to her knees like she was afraid she'd topple over if she let go. She was right. He'd inserted himself into her evening, bullied his way into her plans, but now there was no prying him away until he made sure she never did anything this damned foolish again.

"I've just made you my problem," he said in a low, nasty tone. Instead of looking intimidated—like any reasonable woman would—she narrowed her eyes and pursed her mouth, as if she was considering the virtues of spitting on a duke's face. "So help me," he bit out. Feeling every muscle in his neck tighten. "Do not test me, Aurora." He stood up and began to pace, furious beyond belief. "You really think running around with those ridiculous gloves is enough to keep you from harm?"

"I am not answering—"

"No more lectures, Aurora." He picked her up by the waist and forcibly carried her deeper into the park, where he could get some bloody answers.

"What do you think you're doing, sir?" He almost laughed at the haughty tone she took with him. She thrashed in his grip, testing his already perilously low patience.

"Do you want to attract attention from lawmen who are probably now looking for you, Doctora Montalban?" he asked right against her ear as she writhed in his hands. Even now, as furious as he was, he could not help but notice her curves were not as lush as they'd been the last time he'd touched her, and that only made him angrier. "What are you involved in, Aurora?" he asked, as he set her unceremoniously back down.

"It's none of your business," she seethed, looking up at him with that ever-present pugnacious expression.

"Since I was just chased down the streets of Paris by police, I would say that it's somewhat my business," he told her, with just as much animosity. Her clothes were so big her skirt had been practically down to her knees from when he'd picked her up. She wasn't eating, she wasn't taking proper care of herself and she was putting herself in danger. She was running herself ragged and no one was paying any attention. He would be damned if that went on for another second. He was so preoccupied with his thoughts he barely heard her.

"Who said they were looking for me?" She sounded so genuinely affronted that had he not seen her face when she caught sight of the police, he would've bought the lie.

"Listen to me very clearly, Aurora."

She opened her mouth to object, but after looking up at his face, she seemed to think better of it and closed it.

"If you don't want me to drag you back to my brother's flat, wake up Luz Alana and let her know what you're up to, you will tell me the truth." That seemed to mollify her somewhat, which meant she'd also been lying to her friends about what she was getting up to in these clinics. "What exactly does this appointment entail?" The prevarication began instantly.

"Why do you care?" She beat her fisted hands against her sides in obvious frustration, and he could not deny she had him there. She was a grown woman and what she did or didn't do was well beyond his jurisdiction. But the truth was that he did care. Maybe this was his own self-destructive attempt at avoiding his own problems, or maybe he was just bored, but he could not walk away from this.

"Why don't your friends know what you're out here doing?" The mention of her two friends took some of the wind out of her sails, so he tried his luck and pushed a bit more. "You're supposed to be the sensible one."

"They know the important parts." Which meant they had no idea what she was truly up to. "Besides, this is my affair."

"An affair that had you running from police, which I suspect is a common occurrence for you." She set her mouth, stubbornly turning her face from him. He lowered his hand and clasped that proud chin between his fingers.

He could see the battle inside her in the way her eyes flew back and forth. This was a woman who didn't trust anyone, not even her closest friends, with her secrets. Because she didn't want to be dissuaded from her mission.

"There are others involved and I will not reveal anything that could hurt them." Her eyes, which had been flashing with anger, now simmered with repressed frustration and obvious defiance. He could feel the tremors in her body, but she was not standing down. "In our night clinics," she began, her eyes defiantly locked with his, "we provide some services for women that are not regarded positively under the guise of the law."

He didn't need her to tell him what that was.

"Diablos, Aurora." She was not cowed by his censure. On the contrary, it seemed to puff her up. It was like sparring with a damned windstorm. He was constantly being knocked on his ass.

"We don't only do *that*," she explained with an air that said she thought him much too simple to be privy to this. He crossed his arms over his chest and listened. "We provide women with information, we instruct midwives in sanitary measures, we educate young women of marrying age, we help women prevent pregnancies, and provide assistance if they come to us in need of other services." She was careful with her language, but he could read between the lines. The long and short of it was that the fastidious, forbidding, scrupulous Aurora Montalban was spending her nights committing crimes under everyone's nose. "If that gets a bee in the bonnet of the law every so often, then I deal with it." She was practically daring him to judge her.

This was how she did it, he thought. She hid behind all that vitriol so no one noticed they were in the presence of a woman with a spine of steel. Anyone could take risks for their own gain. He had, and he thought himself bold and tenacious for it. But to risk it all, her fortune, her standing with society, even her family, for the well-being of others, that was what warriors did.

How had he not seen this? Even when she'd come to him that night and brazenly asked him to help her in her *reclaiming*, he had not appreciated the strength in her. That did not mean he wasn't on the verge of putting her over his knee.

"You 'deal with it,'" he echoed, eliciting a disgusted sneer.

"Yes, *I deal with it*. On my own." She bared those perfectly straight teeth at him again—it had to be the fifth time that evening—and despite everything, he could not help but wonder how they'd feel on his skin. He just knew she bit and scratched. Fiera. "Now, are you finally done entertaining yourself with me? Because I still have a patient to find."

"You cannot be serious," he growled, at the very edge of his control.

"This was where we told the patient to come in case there was trouble, and since she's not here—" she used a very nasty tone while making sweeping gestures with her hand "—I have to go and see if she's lost."

Go and see? She was going back there?

Once again, he was struck speechless. And by the time he reacted, she was already walking away.

"Oh no, you don't," he said, reaching for her.

"Oh yes, *I do*." Her sable curls, had come loose from her very sensible coiffure and framed the sides of her face. She looked disreputable, so wild. He'd been bored to tears for the past month meeting perfectly lovely and nice girls who left him cold, but one night with this hellion reminded him the world he came from was nothing like the frigid, vapid world of the ton.

She flew in the teeth of all common sense and did so unapologetically. Willful and impetuous when she believed in her cause. A woman who guarded her secrets fiercely and made no excuses for the length she went to guard them. A woman very akin to him.

"Are you finally done amusing yourself, Your Grace?"

"You are not—" he began, then stopped. "I don't find you amusing." She raised an eyebrow and huffed with obvious disbelief. "I find you endlessly…" *Beguiling, provocative.* "Confounding…"

"I don't find you charming, is that it?" she asked in that impatient, caustic tone of hers, and the numbness that had dogged him since he'd gotten that letter notifying him of his father's death seemed to lift like the fog at sunrise. Life, energy, hot blood pushing through his veins once again.

"No, that is not why, Fiera," he said softly into the small space between them. Tired of arguing, needing her closer. "It's because ever since that night I told you I never craved seconds, you've made a liar out of me." She balked at his words, just as he reached for her face. He cupped her cheek and risked running his thumb over her plump bottom lip.

She had her face tipped up to him, eyes flashing with menace, even as she placed both palms on his chest. She was like a caged wolf, distrusting, but craving touch. He wondered if she even noticed the way her fingers dug into him. How tightly she'd pressed herself to him. Aurora Montalban Wright was a firestorm. They could burn each other down to ash. Too much spirit, as his Tia Jimena would say, in them both.

"Apollo, this is not the time," she protested weakly, even

as she ran her hands over him. "The patient might still be out there."

"And I'm coming to get her with you."

She made a noise between a sigh and scoff, but the curve of her mouth softened, and then she let go. Her plump form falling into his. "You don't give up, do you?" she asked, but the bite was gone from her words, replaced by something that sounded almost like bafflement.

"I'm a duke, aren't I?" This time she did scoff, and circled her arms around his neck in apparent defeat.

"Then why don't you kiss me," she challenged. He could've reminded her that she'd just told him to leave. He could've done all manner of things, but instead he did the only thing he was driven to do.

Her lips parted for him with ease as he lifted her by the waist against the wall. Her tongue slid against his with astounding eagerness. This was no delicate pretense, it was the kiss he'd wanted to give her that night before he let her walk out of his apartment. It was a rough caress, that coaxed eager little moans out of her. He kissed her hard enough to bruise, but she did not pull back. He was so lost in her scent, in her heat, he didn't hear the small voice calling for Aurora until the woman was standing right in front of them.

"Doctora?"

He let her go before she had the chance to push him away. Without looking at him, she went to the cloaked figure standing at the mouth of the alley.

"Doña Maria," she said quietly, sending a warning look to Apollo over her shoulder. He remained where he was, attempting to calm himself down while he observed the situation. He could barely make out the woman, but she was very small, smaller than Aurora. She seemed to be wearing a veil and spoke in hushed Spanish. He did manage to hear that she'd seen the police and retreated here to the meeting place like Aurora had instructed.

She had a damned contingency plan. He had to smile to himself, at the gall of Aurora Montalban.

Even in the dark and from a few yards away, Apollo could see that the manner in which Aurora spoke to her patient was very different from how she dealt with everyone else. She was gentle, respectful, her demeanor approachable and nurturing. Her movements careful and gentle.

He'd begun to think she'd forgotten him when she left the woman just inside the alley and walked back to him. All traces of the flushed, lusty woman from a few minutes before replaced now by a self-possessed, controlled doctor on a mission.

"I have a favor to ask." She sounded so affronted he almost laughed.

He crossed his arms over his chest, enjoying the first advantage he'd had since he'd set off on this demented caper. He leaned forward, cupping his right ear as though he had not quite heard her.

"My apologies, I thought the words *favor* and *ask* were just directed at me, but I'm certain I must be mistaken."

"I don't have time for jesting, Annan."

"Apollo," he said without thinking. "Call me Apollo." He rarely heard his given name these days. The only thing his mother left him with. That and a San Gregorio medal he wore on a gold chain around his neck. He liked hearing his name on Aurora's lips.

She seemed confused for a moment, but after sending a worried look to her patient, she only nodded in agreement. "Fine, *Apollo*." He knew she was trying, but she still sounded like it cost her to grind out each letter of his name. "I need to use your den of immorality," she informed him impatiently, and it had to be the late hour and the running from the law, but he almost laughed. She looked so damned put out.

"My den of immorality, which you now want to use to break the law," he said, too genuinely stunned at her shamelessness to manage any kind of cynical intonation.

She shushed him, then canted her head in the patient's direction as if *his* pointing out the nature of her request was beneath both of them.

"This procedure would be perfectly aboveboard." To hear the affront in her voice, a man would not guess she ran from the law so often she had escape routes. And damn if that didn't make her that much more beddable.

Given what he'd found out tonight, he wasn't about to take her word at face value. She sighed when he sent her a dubious look.

"It's true, she—" She cut herself off, looked over at the waiting patient and beckoned him closer. When he did and she still was not satisfied, she tugged his lapels down until he was at her preferred height. "You're too damned tall," she groused.

"Maybe you're too short," he retorted, and she narrowed those chocolate bonbon eyes at him.

"I am not arguing with you," she informed him, with a little huff that was much too petulant to be sending a line of heat down his spine. "I swear the treatment she requires is perfectly legal."

"Then why can't she go to a hospital?"

For once, she didn't send him a dirty look, and merely sighed. "What she has, most doctors won't treat." He pulled back at that, and she shook her head again. "It isn't a venereal disease." She blew out a frustrated breath, like his questions were an unnecessary nuisance. "Her situation is delicate, that's all," she offered vaguely.

"Meaning?"

"Meaning her brute of a husband, who is responsible for her condition in the first place, won't allow her to seek medical treatment." It was astounding how vicious she managed to sound in such a low tone. "We've been trying to get her to the clinic, but she can't get away and—"

"The illegal clinics," he added, which she did not like.

"The *women's* clinic," she corrected. "We've been waiting for her husband to leave town for long enough to do it."

"You're treating women against their husbands' wishes?" He didn't have the energy to sound outraged, and by now, he was past being surprised by Aurora's antics.

"Yes, *I am*." It was not like he expected her to sound contrite and it was much too late to pretend that anything would deter him at this point. So instead of doing the sensible thing and leaving Aurora Montalban to her illegal activities, he asked the question that had been plaguing his mind. "Do you still have your key, or will you need mine, Doctora?" She inhaled a quick breath, and the sound strummed every nerve in his body like a well-tuned violin.

She sent him one of those murderous looks, then dipped her head. "Yes, I have my key." The answer was raspy and low, and he wanted to ravish her again.

"Good." He took a step toward her and tucked an errant strand of hair behind her ear. "I like the idea of you carrying it all these months, Fiera." A shudder moved through her, even as she glared at him through narrowed eyes.

"I was waiting until I saw you again to throw it in your face." He swallowed down a laugh and wished more than anything he could pull her into that dark alley she'd brought him to and take her hard.

"I have conditions." She rolled her eyes and sighed. "I will take you to my apartment only if you agree to have a conversation about how you're protecting yourself in these harebrained outings." Her head snapped up at that, but he placed a hand over her mouth when she opened it to protest. "Don't fight me on this." He used the voice that usually sent men scampering to follow his orders, and it seemed, for once, Doctora Montalban agreed.

That didn't mean she was gracious about it, as she proceeded to let out an aggrieved breath while she looked between Apollo and the huddled woman waiting for them.

He could be enjoying a cigar and some of that fine rum his brother's wife produced, but instead he was being bullied *by choice* by a five-foot-tall tyrant. Maybe Evan was right and he needed some time away from this marriage-mart scheme, perhaps society altogether, if this was the kind of evening he was volunteering for.

"Are we going?" he asked, sending a look to the patient. But he could tell Aurora was still mulling over something. Given the revelations of the night so far, he braced himself.

"Please be kind about the odor." He frowned, certain he'd misheard.

"Pardon?"

With another one of those world-weary exhalations, she went up on the tips of her toes and clasped a hand on his neck and spoke hotly right in his ear.

"*I said* be kind about the odor." Her lips brushed the side of his face. It was a whisper of a touch, but he jolted backward as if he'd been shocked.

"That's all right," he told her. "I barely notice it these days." She frowned at his words, and he used the moment of distraction to pat her on the rump. "One gets used to the sulfur fumes after a while," he teased, which as expected, she did not find humorous.

"Not me, cabrón," she whispered hotly. "My patient." If she only knew how arousing he found her insults. "She has a condition which makes it hard to keep her hygiene, and people's reactions can be very unkind." For a moment he thought she'd cry, but when she stepped under the lamplight, her eyes were dry. "Stay there," she ordered, with the duress of a drill sergeant. "I'll inform her you are to come with us. This was not part of the plan she was given."

"What's her name?" Once again, she hesitated, then slumped her shoulders in surrender.

"You can call her Doña Maria." He was satisfied with that, but after a moment she came closer. "It's the name we give patients who don't give us theirs." He must have looked confused, because she leaned again. "Sometimes it's safer for them if we don't know." The more he learned about Aurora's dealings, the more he wondered if he needed to get her out of France altogether.

He dipped his head in silence, and she went off with that single-mindedness she seemed to do everything with.

"Monsieur," she called for him after a few moments, and he took his marching orders without argument. As soon as he got within a few feet of the women, he was indeed assaulted by a pungent odor. He had to school his features not to react. What kind of monster would force someone to live like this? Aurora, for her part, seemed completely unbothered by it. With a hand over the other woman's shoulder for reassurance, she turned to him.

"Shall we?"

Six

Later, Aurora would marvel at her ability to maintain her composure that night. As they dismounted a fiacre in front of Apollo's building, she could barely keep herself from losing the contents of her stomach.

This had been much too close. They had to find more secure locations. They could not be risking having clients' identities exposed or being arrested themselves. But the funds were running low and renting multiple locations was costly. Tomorrow she'd have to meet with Virginia and discuss a way forward. Despite her complaints, the truth was that Apollo's presence had at least allowed for the night not to be a total waste.

Not that she wasn't concerned about the tall Colombian-Scottish headache she'd acquired during the course of the evening. The situation with the Parisian police had been unpleasant, but she knew that could be solved—at least temporarily—with crossing the right palms with a few well-placed coins and being more discreet until the authorities lost interest. Keeping Apollo from sticking his incredibly large foot in her affairs would be far more challenging. She had not liked the look of him when he'd told her they'd have a conversation about her "safety."

Heavy-handed, overbearing pendejo. But he had been kind to her patient.

She'd assumed he'd be cross and surly when she'd asked to use his apartment, but instead he'd taken pains to put the woman at ease. The Duke of Annan had taken the entire thing in stride, as if he regularly rode around with strange women in the middle of the night. Then again, the cabrón probably did. That damned charm at least could be good for something, she thought ruefully as he made conversation with Doña Maria. Despite herself, a flare of gratitude ignited in her chest at Apollo's efforts.

"Here we are, mesdames." Apollo pointed to the sofa as soon as they walked into the small apartment. "The best seat in the house." The gesture was clearly for the patient, but Aurora's own face heated when a memory came to her of what he'd done to her on that very piece of furniture. It was unsettling to be back here for the first time after that night. She'd told herself she'd never set foot in the place again, and she likely wouldn't have. But here she was, maybe one day she'd walk in at a decent hour.

"Make yourself comfortable while I get things ready," she told Maria, who seemed to be hesitating by the door.

"It's better if I don't, I don't want to ruin it," she whispered, breaking Aurora's heart. She extended her hand to the slight woman and nudged her to the sofa.

"Our host won't mind," she told her.

"I'm honored to have you in my apartment," he confirmed amiably as he reached the bedchamber's door. "I'll make sure everything is in order there." He was probably making sure there weren't any ladies' garments tossed everywhere. Not that she cared about his libertine inclinations. "It's been a few months since I've been here." She would not muse or speculate what that meant, because as she'd told him various times that evening, they were not each other's business.

While he was in the bedchamber, she focused on putting her patient at ease. The poor woman was sitting on the very edge of the sofa, as if she was attempting to touch as little as possible of the furnishings as she could. Aurora was quietly asking after symptoms when the Duke of Annan reappeared in the room.

"It's ready," he informed them with a radiant smile. Even now, with a patient in the room, she felt the pull toward him. The faster this was done, the faster she could get away from the promise in Apollo's dark eyes. "Doctora, is there anything you need before you begin?" He was being so damned kind, it was driving her mad. She'd intended to hold on to her irritation for the way he'd commandeered her evening, but how could she when he was taking pains to make this easier for her and her client?

"I need to boil my instruments," she finally said, once she'd gotten herself in hand. "I also need some hot water for a tincture to relax her." They both looked at the small, veiled figure sitting on the sofa. She was yet to see the woman's face but knew she was only eighteen and already the mother of two girls. Which was probably the reason her husband insisted on getting her with child a third time despite her condition. This poor girl was suffering in silence from a completely preventable and highly treatable injury. She knew Apollo could not understand why she took the risks she did, but perhaps this would make things clearer. Not that she cared one way or the other about the Duke of Annan's approval.

"I can help boil the instruments and with the water for the tincture," he offered, bringing her out of her thoughts. She gave him the instructions, which he listened to closely without a single acidic remark or acerbic smile. While she worked, she could hear him talking quietly to the patient. When she came out of the bedroom a quarter of an hour later, she found him right outside the threshold with her instruments in hand.

"Thank you," she said, confused by the sudden and over-whelming urge to kiss him on the mouth.

"She's drinking the tea," he told her soberly, and she almost smiled at his ardor. She'd prepared the laudanum-laced con-coction to help the patient relax for the examination, but he'd insisted on mixing it with some tea and sugar to make it more palatable. He was a competent attendant, quick and thorough.

"Pass me that canister, please," she instructed, a little more sharply than she intended. But it was late, and it had been an exceedingly trying evening.

"What is this?" he asked, and once again she had to wonder if he was putting her on. Why did he care about any of this?

She smothered a sigh as she took it from his hand and care-fully placed it on the table.

"It's an anesthetic," she explained. "It's Dr. Bengue's ethyl chloride dispenser." She pointed to the place on the device where the inventor's name was engraved.

"Not coca, then?" he asked, and she shook her head. "I know of it because it's been used in Colombia for centuries," he explained.

"Cocaine is a popular anesthetic, but it can be addictive." He didn't seem surprised by her answer.

"So many of our practices become profane in the hands of the West," he said with a somber tone that brought her up short. "Us included." It was a sobering thought, and an as-tute one. One she would have been astonished to hear out of Apollo's mouth, but this evening was forcing her to see the man in a different light.

"I won't bore you with a long explanation, but this works much more safely and—" He was so close now, the heat of his large body eliciting very unwelcome reactions in hers. It damned near robbed her of speech.

"I find you a great many things, Fiera," he said in a husky whisper. "But boring is not one of them." That was not anything that she could take on. She was lucky not to drop the thing on the ground.

"Yes, well." She cleared her throat. "I need to go see my patient," she said, before she escaped the bedchamber. She didn't think she imagined the whispered "Fiera" that trailed behind her.

Aurora found Doña Maria slowly sipping her tea and wondered what the woman would say if she knew the man serving her all night was a lavishly wealthy duke. She'd think it was utterly ridiculous, just as Aurora did. But she could not deny the man made for a very handsome attendant and a dashing duke. She thought of their conversation about his duties, how he was still finding his way. It had surprised her to hear his genuine concerns for those he was responsible for.

But tonight she'd seen a man who was willing to lend a helping hand, even when the circumstances were risky. A man who was kind to a woman in need, and a much better partner in crime than she'd ever imagined.

"If you would remove your overskirt," she instructed her patient a few minutes later, once they were behind closed doors in Apollo's bedchamber. When she hesitated, Aurora attempted one of her reassuring smiles and tried again. "It'll make it easier for me to see the fissure." Her patient flinched at the word, and once again she felt that mix of rage and helplessness for the way women were forced to live. "I can leave the room and give you some privacy if you prefer," she offered.

"It's all right," Maria said from behind her veil, and moved to unbutton her skirt. "I'm just a bit nervous. Tonight has been much more adventurous than I'm used to." She sounded like perhaps the excitement was not altogether unwelcome. Her husband probably kept her locked in the house. So many women with her injury lived in confinement.

Maria was suffering from a fistula caused by frequent and difficult births starting when she was fifteen years old. Aurora strived to distance her own past from her patients' stories. It did her no good to conflate her own emotions with the troubles of the women she cared for. Some days this was easier than others.

"Nothing about your visit will leave this apartment," she promised, and to her amazement, she really trusted that Apollo would respect this woman's privacy. "You can leave your veil on if it's more comfortable for you," Aurora told her. She received a quick nod in answer. While the woman undid the fastenings of her skirt, Aurora took in her appearance.

Despite the odor, she was wearing a fine dress of lovely pale blue silk. The embroidery on the bodice was done with expensive silver thread. This was a woman of means, and yet in her letter to the clinic she'd indicated her inability to pay for her visit because she could not spend any money that could not be explained to her husband.

"How is the pain, Doña Maria?" she asked as the woman lifted her veil to reveal a face that was heartbreakingly young. Her brown complexion was lovely and smooth, but her eyes betrayed a life filled with pain.

"It's bearable." She sat down on the edge of the bed, her back very straight and her small hands clutched on her lap. Her gaze focused on something behind Aurora. "It's the smell I can't stand." Living with a fistula was a miserable existence.

"Is this from your most recent pregnancy?" Maria nodded. Aurora could see her throat moving as if she was holding back a sob.

"Yes." A small whimper escaped her anyway. Aurora fished out one of the many starched handkerchiefs she stuffed her pockets with and passed it to her. Perched on the edge of the bed, she was so small, her feet barely touched the floor. At eighteen, she was just out of childhood and yet this woman had endured labor two times in the last three years.

Minutes passed with the patient holding the cloth over her nose and mouth and sobbing quietly. Aurora was not patient by nature, and she had very little grace when it came to tears. But in these moments, she considered it her duty and her honor to be the one to at the very least bore witness to her patient's pain and resilience. If she was capable, then she healed the wounds, if not to their spirit, certainly to their bodies.

"It was a stillbirth," Maria finally said.

"It's been a year?" Another slight nod.

"He says I've had enough time to recover." She lifted her haunted gaze to Aurora finally, and what she saw there was stark resignation. "We have twin girls," she explained with a lift of her shoulder. "But he wants an heir."

And likely at whatever physical cost it came to for her.

"Surely the doctor that attended you informed your husband that a pregnancy is not advisable without addressing the fistula," Aurora stated with as much restraint as she could. She knew better than to assume the same male doctor who continued to deliver children for a man who clearly did not care about his wife's welfare would take any kind of stand against this inhumanity.

"My husband does not think it's necessary," she whispered, clearly embarrassed for her situation. "The doctor did not disagree."

There were many things she could've said in that moment, but she held her tongue. The so-called doctor was likely a pupil of Antonie van Leeuwenhoek, who espoused the brilliant theory that men's seed carried forth a fully formed human and women were nothing but an interchangeable vessel.

Aurora's blood boiled for her, but she knew that venting her frustration would possibly mortify her patient further.

"Let's take a look, then, and we'll discuss some options."

The patient backed up on the bed, distress and shame flushing her lovely bronze skin with an angry red. "The smell's worse the closer you get." Her breath caught as she struggled for composure.

"Don't worry about me," Aurora told her softly as she assisted her in lying down. "I promise it does not bother me."

A single tear slid down the woman's rounded cheek as she laid her head on Apollo's pillow.

This would've been me, Aurora thought. Had she not done what she'd done, she would have been another Maria. Bearing children for an indolent man until her body gave out. It had come at a high price, but she'd gained a life only she determined and that she could never regret.

Aurora forced air into her lungs and made her mind clear of any thoughts that were not the woman who she was tasked with caring for. There was no room here for anything other than the work at hand.

"You have taken good care of the wound," she said, smiling up at the patient.

"I saw a midwife," she said, her cheeks flushing again, but she looked at Aurora with something almost like defiance in her eyes, and she thought maybe there was a little ember of rebellion left in Maria. "She's the aunt of one of my maids. She came on one of the nights my husband was..." She trailed off, then shrugged. "Given my situation, he has to see to his masculine requirements from someone who is not so repulsive." The way she uttered the last word told Aurora that the young woman was merely echoing what had been said to her. "She gave me some salve and taught me how to keep it clean. She was who advised I come to you."

Their clinic worked closely with a network of midwives. She was always grateful for the women who, despite the constant disrespect from the medical establishment, continued to provide vital care for those who needed it.

"It was good of you to come," she reassured as she cleaned the wound. "Your fistula can be repaired with a minor procedure."

"Truly?" The relief on her face made tonight's ordeal and whatever fallout Apollo would dole out worth it.

"We'd need at least three hours," Aurora told her. "Can you do it now?"

Maria shook her head, regretfully. "I must be home before dawn, but my husband will have a trip to London soon." Already Maria seemed a bit more self-assured. It was incredible what the ability to decide for herself what happened to her own body did for a woman.

Aurora nodded, already running through the catalogue of locations available that could work for the procedure. "Send me a note and we will do it then." She made quick work of discussing the details of the surgery, then offered the patient some options in pregnancy prevention until then.

"I can't pay." The shame in her voice almost broke Aurora's determination not to go on a rampage. "He keeps a very close eye on my expenses."

Aurora waved Maria's concern away even as she thought of the funds her brothers had suspended, of the police and the bribes it would take to make them stop snooping, of the desperate need for secure locations. Those concerns were hers, not her patient's.

"Don't worry about that," she told Maria lowering the woman's skirt after she finished the examination. "Now, can you go to an apothecary to procure what you need, or do you prefer I give it to you?"

Maria wrung her hands again.

"If you have it here, that would be best." The woman was practically a prisoner in her home. Aurora almost asked her if she'd thought of leaving. But even the mention of divorce would probably send her running and she needed that procedure.

One thing she'd learned from her work was that sometimes all one could do was fix the most immediate problem and hope the person, restored, could do the rest. So she patted her patient's knee, forced herself to smile and pointed to her trusty Gladstone.

"Let me get it ready while you get yourself sorted," Aurora told her with a smile, before reaching for the remedies she kept on hand.

She might not ever be enough anywhere else in her life. She didn't quite measure up as a daughter, could be a distant and aloof sister, was even an impatient, and at times harsh, friend, but she was a good healer. With her tools in hand, she knew exactly where she belonged and that was more than enough to build a life on.

Seven

"Could you hail her a fiacre?" Aurora's faint request could've been a bomb going off in the silent room. He was on his feet in a flash, coming toward her. "She's doing well," she told him, and he wondered if it was because she thought he cared, or if it was just habit to reassure whoever one encountered after treating a patient.

"I've had one waiting for her," he said, resisting the urge to take her in his arms.

"You did?" Aurora looked up at him with a surprised, and perhaps marginally impressed, expression. "Thank you." Something fiercely protective ensnared him in that moment. Urges that he simply could not entertain. Not if he was to stay on course.

"You need to rest," he said, but she shook her head.

"I'm fine."

She looked a far cry from fine. In fact, she looked done in. Utterly wrung out. There were grooves on the sides of her mouth and her face was pinched and pale. He also knew that pointing out these details was not in the best interest of peace and harmony.

It was funny how he'd started the night furious with her,

and now he'd probably open his own vein and let her feast on his blood if it would ease the sheer exhaustion practically radiating from her.

By now he knew Doña Maria would be her priority. So he focused on getting the patient, who he'd become strangely invested in, to her conveyance. There was something about the woman that reminded him of his own cousin. She was much too young for such despondence, such abject hopelessness. His fifteen-year-old cousin Juliana's life full of dreams of pretty dresses and ballrooms could not be more different from Maria's. If he had anything to do with it, that would never change.

"Thank you both for your help," she said from behind her veil, which was still firmly over her face. Once she was seated in the fiacre, she reached out to kiss Aurora's hand.

"Make sure you change the dressing as I showed you," Aurora told the woman in answer, her face flushed with embarrassment at the praise. She was so prideful about her work, but she shrank at any kind compliment. "And this is for you to give to someone who might need help from the clinics." She pinned a little gold charm, which he couldn't make out the details of in the dark, to the woman's lapel. "I'll see you soon," Aurora finally said, before telling the driver to go.

For that hour he'd paced in the parlor, he'd thought of what he'd say to her about what she was getting up to. Imagined himself delivering a righteous monologue about the risks she was taking. Was she intentionally trying to get herself killed by some stranger in the streets? Did she realize those demented gloves would not protect her against the criminals roaming the streets at this time of night?

But when she turned to him, and he got a good look at her under the warm light of the streetlamp. The fury drained out of him and all he was left with was a staggering need to carry her upstairs.

"You saved me tonight." She was visibly shaking, her teeth chattering with such intensity he could hear them from where he stood. "I will just get my things and get out of your way." He tried to reach for her, since she looked ready to collapse, but she sidestepped him, stumbling back into the foyer of the building, toward the elevator. The entire ride up, she stood rigid, her arms wrapped around herself, while he helplessly watched the tremors rack her frame.

He opened the door of the small apartment in complete silence and only when they were back inside did he speak.

"Aurora—"

"I'll be gone in a minute," she told him, before picking up the teacup Maria had used and placing it on the tray he'd brought in from the small kitchen. "You probably want me out of here after all the trouble I've caused you." She was attempting to sound breezy and unaffected, but he could see the cracks all over her.

"Stop it," he said tersely, and she froze at the threshold of the bedchamber. "Stop this, Aurora," he repeated when he saw her shoulders slump. "Come here." He reached for her hand and pulled her to him.

"Let me go, Apollo." She resisted weakly at first, but after a moment, she let him cradle her to his chest. He tried to lift her face up, but she kept it pressed against him. Her fast, hot breaths seared his skin as he held her. He sensed the war waging in her, to resist his caretaking, to insist she needed no one.

It was a battle he'd waged for much of his life. Denying in every way he could how lost and alone he'd been. How badly he'd yearned for a mother and father who loved him, and instead was burdened with the knowledge that his existence had taken his mother's life. That his father was a monster who abandoned him. He'd turned that ache, that hole inside him, into his obsession with revenge. He'd plotted and schemed until he destroyed the man who'd taken his mother from him. Meanwhile, Aurora healed. At a cost he was only now beginning to comprehend.

At one point tonight, he'd wondered if she simply wasn't scared of the consequences. That perhaps she was somehow unaffected by the dangers she incurred to treat these women. That had made him angry.

It was worse to realize that she did all of it this afraid. That she knew exactly how absolutely mad it all was, and did it anyway. He wanted to make her stop. Wondered why no one had. But instead of badgering her with recriminations and questions, he held her. He ran his palm up and down her back while she quietly gathered herself. He suspected she'd never forgive him for seeing her like this, especially when he informed her he had no intention of walking away from that. He already had a plan. The challenge would be to apprise her of it without getting his eyes clawed out with those blasted gloves.

They stayed like that for a long time, him leaning against the doorjamb to the bedchamber and her hanging on him, her arms limp at her sides, like a battered vessel that had finally crashed against the wrong rocky cliff. He was working up to speaking when she pushed off him as though she'd been scalded.

He had to fight himself not to cage her in his arms.

"I'm grateful for your hospitality." The little devil actually extended a hand to him. He could only stare, all the while considering options to keep her there that didn't involve tying her to one of the chairs by the hearth until she saw some sense.

Even with an indentation on her cheek from the button of his vest, she was once again warrior Aurora, with steel in her spine and daggers in her eyes. But he wouldn't be steamrolled. Right or wrong, Aurora Montalban Wright was very much his problem, starting tonight.

"I'm not shaking your hand, Aurora," he told her, and for once, she seemed genuinely chagrined.

It only lasted long enough for her to summon that foul temper of hers.

"Fine." She retracted her hand. "I was attempting to be cordial," she retorted, before spinning on her heels and heading to the bedchamber.

"You had the police running after me tonight," he reminded her, as he followed her in there.

"It would not have been an issue if you weren't such a slow runner."

He had to be losing his mind, because he actually laughed, which only served to further infuriate her.

"What?" she asked through tightly gritted teeth.

It would never be easy with this woman. Not talking to her, certainly not bedding her, dammit, not even a meal with her could occur without some manner of hostility. Everything was a battle, but he'd never walked away from one before and he would not do it now.

"Am I supposed to become enraged at your insults, Fiera?" he asked, propping himself on a dresser to watch her carefully arrange her instruments. "Are the men you usually deal with so fragile they can't take a few barbs?" He had no idea why he was bringing other men into the conversation, but he was well past attempting to make sense of this evening or his reactions to Aurora Montalban.

"Very few men can keep up with me, Your Grace." Even dead on her feet, she was defiant. This rebellious bluestocking with more passion than sense was not an obsession he could afford to indulge in.

An ill-timed distraction if there ever was one. He had to find a way to neutralize Ackworth, he had a million things to think of regarding his tenants. Then there was the promise he'd made his aunt to find a suitable wife. He had obligations after all, not to his father, like Aurora told him that night, but to his mother. The last thing he needed was to be embroiled in another scandal, and one thing was certain, what Aurora was doing would almost certainly end in one.

And yet, as he looked at her, undaunted in her mission, clearly intending to carry on—despite the many setbacks of the evening—he knew Queen Victoria herself could not make him change course now.

"You should eat something," he finally said. Her head whipped in his direction, the challenge in her eyes replaced with genuine confusion.

It seemed like years had passed since they'd sparred over cream puffs at Le Bureau. He expected to be told to go to hell, but in the end, she sighed and turned back to cleaning her instruments.

"I thought you only kept chocolate and rum here." She didn't look at him as she wiped down a wicked-looking scalpel with a cloth soaked in something abrasive enough to make his eyes water. He still had to work hard not to laugh again, especially when he spied a small twitch of her lips.

"O ye of little faith," he proclaimed, but she didn't turn around. "I ordered a tray from the restaurant downstairs while you were with your patient."

This time she did turn. Her expression dubious. "Are they open so late?"

"It's Paris," he retorted. She still did not look convinced.

If she only knew that the morning after she'd come to him, he'd gone down to the building administration office and asked them to find a night cook for him. Tonight, he'd finally ordered one of the midnight meals the man had been hired to make.

"When you're done, come to the parlor." Without waiting

for her to turn him down, again, he went to the kitchen to fetch the plate of bread, fruit, cold meats and cheese. He was just opening a bottle of claret when she walked out of the bedchamber with that enormous bag in one hand.

"How can you run with that thing?" he asked, pointing with a wineglass at the Gladstone. "I thought my arm was going to be ripped from the socket, lugging it while those coppers chased us."

"I'm used to it." She shrugged after carefully placing it on the floor by the door. A clear signal she had no intention of staying very long. "I appreciate this," she mumbled as he handed her a glass of wine and slid a plate in her direction. After pouring himself a dram of rum, he sat down across from her.

"It's the least I could do after such an invigorating evening." If she heard the sarcasm in his voice, she didn't say it.

He had no intention of letting her walk out of his apartment until they'd had a serious conversation, but for now, he'd let the wine, food and exhaustion soften her up for him.

"You've fed me twice tonight," she told him, before taking a sip of the claret. When she licked an errant drop off her bottom lip, he had to shift in his seat.

"You need a keeper, Doctora." He expected an earthquake, but what he got instead was a grin which was much more effective at knocking him off his feet.

"*That* is the one thing I don't need, Your Grace," she quipped, before she popped a fig into her mouth, chewed and focused doggedly on the walls, the fire, her own feet. Anything but him.

"That's debatable," he countered, and decided he'd exercised enough restraint. "You've dropped at least one stone since I last saw you."

She put down the piece of bread and regarded him curiously, as though she was attempting a diagnosis of his tone. He was certain she was preparing for the best way to succinctly inform him the quickest route to hell, but instead she broached the last topic he expected her to.

"Besides balls, what does a duchess hunt entail exactly?" Her tone was casual enough as she pressed her finger on errant crumbs of bread scattered around the table. But this was not the first time this evening she'd brought up his impending betrothal. Perhaps it was merely to taunt him, but perhaps not.

"According to what my aunt tells me, my presence at an ungodly number of recitals and receiving a surprisingly large amount of embroidered cushions," he told her, if not for her benefit, then for his own.

"Is someone making these cushions?" she inquired with genuine bafflement.

"From the sheer number that arrive at my home, I would surmise all of Britain and certain parts of Europe are engaged in nothing else." She laughed this time, clearly amused by his flustered state. "I don't suppose you're interested in entering the aristocracy."

The amusement instantly vanished from her face. "I'm afraid I'm not suited for the life of an aristocrat."

He was beginning to wonder if *he* would ever be. But he didn't want to think about his own malaise then, he wanted to talk about her.

"What was the matter with Doña Maria?" She'd warned him that she wouldn't share any information about the patient. When she didn't answer, he figured she wouldn't tell him, but after sending him a long considering look, she did.

"It's called a fistula."

He knew about them. "My uncle owned cattle. I've heard of cows getting them after particularly difficult calvings."

She grimaced and sipped more wine. "It can happen when women give birth too young, before their body is ready for it."

He didn't have to ask for Doña Maria's, just from her voice he knew she was still painfully young. "It's a fairly simple injury to repair, but she's been denied access to medical care by her husband." He could hear the frustration in her words.

Men had so much to answer for. His own father had left his mother to die in her childbed. That thought suddenly put the entire evening in a different light. Aurora was saving mothers, daughters, sisters. Women who were at the mercy of callous men and an indolent society. He wondered if his mother's fate would've been different if she'd had an Aurora at her bedside.

"Have you seen many cases like this?" he asked, hoarsely, suddenly awash in emotions.

"Some." She nodded. "You want to hear something horrific?"

"I thought I already had," he muttered, unable to produce even a trace of humor. But she let out a tired laugh.

"I learned the procedure when I was working in Philadelphia. My mentor Sarah Loguen Fraser taught me how to perform it." He didn't know she'd been in Philadelphia. He thought she'd been living in Mexico.

"Your mentor was a woman?"

She narrowed her eyes at his question, but after a moment she must've have seen his curiosity was not malicious. "She was, she was only the fourth Black woman to become a doctor in the United States." He would not have expected any less from Aurora Montalban. "She's actually living in the city I was born in Hispaniola at the moment."

"Aren't you from Veracruz?" He'd asked questions about her to Evan here and there. Not too many, in case his brother became fanciful as he was prone to do now that he'd found true love. Apollo knew she'd studied medicine here in Paris, but he'd assumed that like a good little girl, she'd returned to the family nest the moment she was done. One more assumption he'd made about this woman he'd gotten wrong.

"I haven't lived there since I was fifteen." And from the way she held herself as she said it, he imagined the departure had not been a warm one. "I was born on the northern coast of Hispaniola in Puerto Plata, my mother's family is from there." Did he imagine that flinch at the mention of her mother? "My father was doing diplomatic work for Mexico in the Caribbean and asked to be posted near her home."

"Is that how you met Luz Alana?"

"Why do you want to know about any of this?" she asked warily, while she occupied herself with rearranging what was left on her plate without looking up at him.

"I'm curious of where a well-bred woman like you would've learned such evasive tactics when running from police." This time, the flinch was quite obvious. Something about this conversation was bothering her. He didn't think it was the mention of the police chase. If anything, she seemed to have taken it in stride.

"You are quite preoccupied with breeding, and no, I met Luz Alana in finishing school in Switzerland." She didn't say it waspishly. She sounded disappointed in him, which in turn made him defensive.

"I suppose all the thinly, and sometimes not-so-thinly, veiled implications that I'm a bastard and an impostor might have something to do with that."

She stared blankly at him for a long moment, then made a sound that should've been a laugh, but something about it sliced Apollo like a knife. "Well, there is no bigger slight than being called a bastard, is there?"

He'd hurt her, he realized. He didn't know how, but suddenly he felt like an utter ass. "Am I being a snobbish comemierda?"

he asked sincerely, and to his relief, this time her laugh reached her eyes.

"Not any more than usual."

"Fair enough." He dipped his head in acquiescence. "You don't want to talk about this, do you?"

She gazed up at him and shook her head. "No, I don't."

"Then, tell me about the fistulas." Just to make her laugh, he took one of the white linen napkins on the tray and waved it.

"Your humor is lacking," she told him without heat, and because he was a man prone to taking calculated risks, he veered into more perilous territory.

"I have other skills, as you very well know, Doctora." She coughed loudly, pounding her own chest as she swallowed the wine she'd been sipping. He grinned when she sent him a dirty look. But the tenacious Aurora Montalban did not take his bait.

"As I was saying, regarding fistulas." She emphasized every word, eyes very wide as she spoke.

"Chicken," he teased, provoking an adorable harrumph from her.

"The doctor who perfected the fistulotomy is American." She took another fig from the plate, but she didn't eat it. Just fiddled with it. "J. Marion Sims was his name." She said it with such distaste, that he braced himself for yet another emotional blow. "He used slave women to test the procedure, without anesthetic." That turned his stomach.

"Hijo de puta," he swore, and reached for his dram of rum, which had so far gone untouched. He took a long, burning gulp before he looked at her again.

"I don't do this work because I like to put myself in a position of danger," she told him, as if she knew where he'd been waiting to take the conversation all along. "I do it because women are suffering." She waved the hand with the fig in the air between them. "Especially women who look like you and me. And I'm in a position to help. So, I do." As simple as that.

"How are you funding the clinics?"

The moment he asked the question, any trace of humor vanished from her face. He could almost see the tension seeping back into her bones.

"That's a complicated question. I was the primary benefactor, but my trust fund is not available to me at the moment," she confessed without any prevarication. This was not a woman who ran from her problems, on the contrary, he guessed her trouble was more the tendency to ram headfirst into them. "Cora has been generous, and Luz Alana. I have a small bequest I'm in the process of liquidating that will allow us to continue to run until we find more permanent solutions." He didn't think he imagined the suggestiveness in her tone. "Would you like to help, Your Grace? You'd be the first man we ask."

"I didn't know you could say 'Your Grace' without spitting." Oh, but he liked that grin. It made her nose wrinkle at the top and it exposed one incisor, so that he didn't know if he was looking at an imp or a very cheeky doctor.

He'd get into a hell of a lot of trouble for one more glimpse of that grin.

One could not accuse Aurora Montalban of lacking brazenness. To dare ask a duke to help her fund a clinic where she performed what certainly had to be illegal procedures made her the bravest or foolhardiest woman in the world. Then again, maybe she was just desperate.

"I'll be one of your benefactors, Doctora." The offer seemed to only make her more suspicious. "I have two conditions," he began, but she interjected, holding up one finger.

"If it involves offering your unsolicited manly opinions on women's matters, I must politely decline." She said it so sweetly, she even fluttered her eyelashes, the incisor made another appearance. He wondered how it would feel on his skin.

"What if I told you I have a building here in the eleventh arrondissement, near Le Marais, I can gift to the clinic, as well an endowment for its maintenance." That made her sit up straight. Those curls fluttering around her head like antennae.

"I'm listening," conceded Doctora Montalban with a cautious expression.

"One," he continued, pointedly holding up a finger, and for once, she kept her mouth closed. "That you promise to stop using your personal funds to support the clinics."

"You can't tell me—" Whatever she saw on his face made her clamp her lips shut. He knew it was not cowering, but Aurora would be the kind of woman to set her pride aside for her cause.

"Whatever is happening with your trust, it's clear your family is using it to discipline you. If you allow me to help you, then you can hold on to this bequest."

"I don't enjoy having people in my personal affairs."

"I'm only stating facts." He knew he was on very thin ice, but he was not above extortion when trying to get his way. After what he'd seen tonight, he'd be damned if he left her unprotected. And damn it, she should not be left with nothing, no matter how worthy her cause. "You like your independence, and that only comes with money." Her jaw tightened and he could see she was barely containing the urge to fight him. But she managed to resist it. "You might be willing to sacrifice everything you have for your cause, but you don't know what it is to be destitute. If your family cuts you off for good, what will you do then?"

"I can make money as a physician," she protested, all bluster and pride.

"From whom? The Doña Marias who can't afford to pay

even for their fiacre?" Her shoulders were by her ears now, and she was practically bristling.

"You are transgressing, Your Grace." He was dangerously close to being slapped across the face, but she was still sitting there, which told him he was not completely off the mark.

"But I am not wrong, am I?" She lifted that pert nose in the air, refusing him an answer. "I'm not offering to give you money, only to help you keep the funds you do have," he reasoned with her. "You can't live on your convictions, Aurora."

She didn't like what he said, but the truth of it seemed to sink in, because she finally looked at him. "All right."

"That's only one of the conditions," he reminded her, and she was back on the defensive in the next instant.

"When will you sign over the building? I won't agree to anything without seeing the deed." She crossed her arms over that generous chest, and he could feel the blood rushing to every limb in his body like lava.

"I will have my solicitor send it over as soon as it's ready." Or more like once he found a building to buy, since he'd made the entire thing up. But she never had to know. "If you accept both my conditions."

Another woman would attempt meekness, diminish herself to make him feel big. Aurora Montalban leaned forward, took his glass from the table, crossed her legs at the knees and took one big gulp.

"Get on with it, Annan," she croaked after the rum sent her into a coughing fit. God, but he wanted to put her over his knee and redden those luscious nalgas.

"I'd like to teach you how to defend yourself in case you find you're in a situation like you were tonight." If he had to think of her trying to put off criminals with nothing but those gloves, he would go out of his mind. The mere thought that she'd been doing this for months had him clutching his chest.

"You'll teach me how to fight the police?" For the first time all night, she appeared genuinely energized.

"Not exactly, Fiera," he said, biting back a laugh. "But I am certain the police are not the only trouble you run into." The fact that she didn't argue told him everything he needed to know about his suspicion.

"What exactly will this entail?" she asked suspiciously, taking another gulp from his rum. Every time she sealed her lips to the glass, his cock pulsed.

"Let's just say you'll learn some basics of hand-to-hand combat from an excellent instructor." She sent him a look that said "what are you up to?" but she didn't refuse. He extended a hand to her, which she eyed with naked contempt.

"And what would you be getting out of this deal? Forgive me for doubting your selflessness." He knew she'd argue, but if there was something Apollo could do with great effectiveness, it was use an advantage in his favor. She needed what he was offering, and they both knew it.

"To be honest, I could use your expertise." She scoffed, but he was being truthful. "The way you were with Maria was—" he paused, finding the right word "—humane."

"That's a low standard you have for physicians, if basic kindness impressed you." Her caustic tone could not hide the flush in her cheeks. His compliment pleased her even if she didn't like the fact.

"I'd like your advice on how to operate a clinic of sorts in the dukedom's land." He and Evan were working to improve conditions on the housing, but he wanted to do more than be a landlord. He wanted to give those people the means to thrive. "I noticed that in addition to the need for a school, there are also many women and children who require care. I'd like to provide that for them."

As he expected, this seemed to soften her somewhat.

"You could hire a doctor in Scotland," she countered.

"I could," he admitted. "But my family is now here too, my aunt, my cousin. I have half a dozen trusted staff from our estate in Colombia making their way here as we speak, with their families. I'd like your expertise on how to set up medical care for them too. From people who they can trust." That got him another dubious look, but eventually she relented.

"Fine. We have a deal," she told him grudgingly, extending a hand. "But I'll bring my blade gloves and will use them liberally if necessary." Then, because she truly was the Fiera he'd called her, she lifted his glass. "More rum, please, it's been a long night."

"You drive a hard bargain, Doctora Montalban," he told her, rising to his feet to fetch her rum.

"I still don't like you, Annan," she volleyed back, as she leaned her head on the sofa.

"You can bring clients here, when you need to, while we sort out a more permanent option." He didn't want her in the streets, and he knew better than to tell her to stop until the fictional building he'd now have to find and buy to give to her was ready.

"Tuesdays," she whispered, her voice drowsy like she was only half-awake. "I'll come here on Tuesdays, thank you."

By the time he'd poured her the drink she'd demanded and came back to the sofa, she was fast asleep. He stood there with the glasses in his hand, watching her. Her pouty lips, which had been flattened by irritation just minutes earlier, were soft and parted just enough to blow little puffs of air.

His heart ached looking at her. Even in her sleep, she was restless. Her fingers twitching, her eyes moving fast under bruised lids. She reminded him of a young colt, unbridled and loose in the wild. Frighteningly unaware of the dangers in its path. But that wasn't true, was it? She knew exactly what she was doing, she just did it anyway because she was brave and noble.

He put the glass down and went to the bedchamber, which reeked of that carbolic she used to disinfect everything, and grabbed one of the blankets from the trunk by the foot of the bed. She'd slid down on the sofa and was now half lying on her side.

"What am I going to do with you, Fiera?" he muttered under his breath as he reached for her. Gently, he nudged her down onto the cushions, careful not to wake her. She mumbled something unintelligible as he pulled her boots off. They were the only beautiful thing she had on. Soft, supple burgundy leather, with lovely embroidery work. He smiled at this bit of vanity as he placed them on the rug, so she'd find them when she woke up.

He smothered a yawn as he walked into his bedchamber. The clock on the mantelpiece read half past four. The night had ended a lot differently than he'd imagined, but for the first time since his father died, he was looking forward to what the next day had in store, he'd make sure to tell her in the morning. But when he came out of his bedchamber three hours later as the sun was rising, he found the blanket folded neatly on the sofa and no trace of Doctora Montalban left in the apartment.

Eight

Somewhere between his insistence in helping with her patient and his extremely heavy-handed effort to help her protect herself, Aurora came to terms with the fact that Apollo César Sinclair Robles might not be the bastard she'd convinced herself he was.

This didn't mean she wasn't irritated with him. Last night had been shambolic, largely thanks to his meddling. Had she not woken up on Apollo's sofa at six in the morning, she would've tried to convince herself it had all been a bad dream.

Although she had to admit his willingness to let her use his apartment to see Maria had gone a long way to redeem him. And he had been kind to her patient. He'd been kind to her, other than the blackmail. She didn't know what to think about his offer to give her a building. But she could only deal with one crisis at a time, and her priority was letting Virginia know about her run-in with the police.

Only three months earlier, being involved in a fiasco like this would've had her fretting about her reputation, what the men in her profession would think if they found out. But the clinics, helping patients like Doña Maria had shifted something in her.

She reached the small green door of the print shop which now served as their temporary clinic and walked in with a sense of dread. She hadn't seen any suspicious people milling outside, but for all she knew, they'd raided the place this morning. She began to panic when she found the small waiting room empty, but a moment later Virginia stepped out from the consultation room, appearing as if everything was perfectly normal.

"I'm so sorry I brought the police to your building," Aurora apologized, but the Argentine doctor waved her off as she gestured to the chair across from her. As usual, Virginia had her raven hair in a bun at the nape of her neck. Her hair had gone silver at the temples, which made for a striking contrast. She was an angular woman, very tall and thin, with a pointed chin and aquiline nose that gave her the air of a very friendly crane.

"Sit here. I was just about to have some coffee," Virginia told her warmly, pointing at the carafe and saucers sitting on the small table in the corner.

"I should've canceled the appointment last night," Aurora said tearfully, feeling truly terrible now that she was confronting what she'd put at risk in the light of day.

"Todo está bien, querida." Virginia clucked her tongue, like Aurora was the one in need of comforting. "My brother Giovanni was upstairs last night and he said they've been circling the neighborhood like this for weeks," she assured Aurora, handing her a cup of black coffee. It was not exactly a relief to know they were being watched, but it was some comfort to learn it hadn't all been her doing. "I was here late myself."

"An emergency?"

Virginia's face fell for a second, and she noticed her friend looked a bit pale today. "It was a midwife case, one of Renata's," she said, grimly. A referral from a midwife was nothing unusual. All the physicians from the clinic viewed midwives as an essential part of the medical profession and considered the establishment's dismissal of their skills a grave injury to the well-being of women.

For centuries, midwives were the primary source women had for information and means to prevent pregnancy and receive humane care. But once men took over the medical field and "professionalized" it, they realized births were a profitable venture and proceeded to push midwives out. Their clinic embraced them as partners in women's health and was the better for it. Renata was one of the more experienced midwives they worked with, if she could not deal with the patient on her own, it must have been fairly bad.

"Was it a birth?"

Virginia shook her head, her expression dark at whatever she was recalling. "She brought in a young lady in fairly bad shape. The daughter of a wealthy banker." That brought Aurora up short. They served well-to-do women, of course, but it was unusual to have them as emergency cases.

"Is she all right?"

"She will be. It was a close thing." Virginia sighed. "The patient's older sister goes to Renata for our Dutch caps." Despite the horrible situation, Aurora felt a surge of pride at the valuable services they provided. The mention of the expensive contraceptives brought to mind Apollo's offer to become a benefactor. The Dutch caps were distributed for free to anyone who asked. At the moment, they could not keep up with the demand, much less their goal of supplying them in the Americas. With the Duke of Annan's funds in their coffers, that could change.

"Did she purchase one of those unsanitary pessaries?" It was a common occurrence for less scrupulous vendors to take advantage of women desperate to prevent pregnancies by selling them useless junk that only made them sick.

"No," she answered after a long pause. She was clearly preoccupied, which in turn worried Aurora. "I'm sorry, querida, my head is in the clouds today," she apologized.

Whatever it was, had to be serious. Aurora had never seen her this vexed. She was usually utterly unflappable. At thirty-six, Virginia Morelos was one of the most notorious fighters for women's rights in all of the Americas. She'd been ousted from Argentina for her radical views, for goodness' sake. Seeing her so affected shook Aurora.

"What happened?" she asked a little impatiently, eliciting another worried sigh from her colleague.

"The girl went to someone to bring down her menses and whatever they did to her brought upon a terrible infection." This was what happened when women had to seek medical care in secret. They ended up in the hands of butchers.

"Was it done by someone we know?" It was hard to track all the charlatans in Paris, but they tried to keep a record, if only to warn the midwives and apothecaries they did business with.

"They didn't have a name," Virginia said, with a shake of her head. "Just that he had a well-appointed office in the third arrondissement." That was probably how he got away with leaving women at death's door. A good address and promise of anonymity. They knew none of those society ladies would report him to the authorities, for fear of their own identities being divulged. "We'll make sure to put a word out. We'll find him."

"I just wish we could do more than warn women off when we do." Because there would be no punishment. If Virginia alerted the police to a bad actor, it would only turn the attention on their clinic, even if they spent half their time cleaning up others' crimes. Sometimes she thought her body would simply go up in flames purely from raging at society. "And after all that, I brought more trouble to the clinic."

"It is not your fault." Virginia insisted.

"I wonder who could've tipped them off," Aurora mused, deciding to set aside her guilt for the moment. It was unnerving to think someone had betrayed them. They were all so careful.

"Who can say?" Virginia threw up her hands. "It could be one of the hacks who sees us as competition. It could be one of the pious ladies who likes to burn our pamphlets and shout about eternal damnation in front of the clinic. It could be the husband of a woman who came to us against his wishes because her body could not bear another birth."

At that, her friend stood up with a sigh and retrieved a metal box from the sideboard and opened it, before offering it to Aurora.

"Unfortunately, this kind of thing is as much part of the work as the patients are." Virginia's words stole Aurora's appetite, and she shook her head at the cookies. "Eat, having one won't hurt, and who can resist my alfajores?" she said with a wink. "I know you have a sweet tooth." Which only reminded her of the éclairs and canelés she'd put in her bag last night.

When Virginia shoved the box in her direction, she relented with a laugh and reached for the shortbread cookie sandwich filled with delicious dulce de leche. Aurora had become addicted to the Argentinian treat that Virginia always seemed to have on hand. The butter cookie and the nutty and sweet taste distracted Aurora from her worrying for a moment.

"Were you able to see to the patient?" Virginia asked, catching Aurora off guard. She'd been so preoccupied with what she might find at the clinic that she didn't consider how she'd explain where she'd gone after the encounter with the police.

She had no idea what Virginia—an avowed anarchist—would think of her taking a patient to a duke's apartment, but she could not lie.

"I did." She focused very carefully on the cookie, until she could no longer use it as an excuse to delay her answer. "I knew of a place that was quiet and out of the way." Her colleague gave her a curious look, before sipping her coffee.

"That's what we need," Virginia told her. "Something permanent and out of the way, so we no longer need to do all this running around."

Her stomach fluttered as she thought of the deal she'd made with the Duke of Annan to secure that very thing. She was well aware she'd consented to doing business with the human equivalent of a semidomesticated tiger, but how could she turn an offer like that down?

Besides she didn't think Virginia, despite her views, would be totally opposed to taking a building from an aristocrat, she was much too practical for that. But for now, she'd stick to the funding streams that didn't have over six feet of trouble attached to it.

"My friend Luz Alana and her husband have offered to host a garden party to help us meet potential benefactors."

"That's good news." Virginia seemed genuinely excited and that was a relief.

"I am so happy you think so!" Aurora exclaimed, finally feeling more at ease. "We'd need to talk about some of the work we do," she explained. Luz Alana had insisted that in order to get benefactors to open their purses Aurora would have to convince them that what they did was important. "A redacted version, of course," she told Virginia with a wink, who let out one of her boisterous laughs.

It would indeed have to be a very curated account of what they did. All manner of things that ranged from moral offenses to serious crimes occurred in this small space, and in the last three months, Aurora had been at the center of most of them. She was a full-fledged outlaw and had every intention of continuing on being one for as long as she could.

It had been transformative to function not for the approval

of the men in the medical establishment but for the benefit of those who needed her skills. These past months were the best thing Aurora had ever been a part of and she'd do anything to keep it going, even if it meant dealing with a few society snobs.

"You will have to be our voice, Aurorita." That she didn't expect. Virginia was so passionate about what they did, Aurora assumed she'd jump at the chance, but she was shaking her head.

"But it's your clinic."

"It's *our* clinic!" Virginia countered, her brow lowered as if Aurora's words had vexed. "Look at the night you just had, seeing a patient against all odds, even after being chased by the police." She shook her fist in the air, as if Aurora had accomplished a great feat. "And here you are this morning, facing the music." Aurora found herself quite suddenly on the brink of tears at Virginia's words. She'd always had to fight to be seen. Only the Leonas had ever accepted her with open arms. But this was another Leona in front of her.

Aurora looked around the cramped space neatly stacked with freshly laundered sheets clients were offered for modesty. There were crates with carbolic soap and Abelardo's special antiseptic mix. The other room was outfitted with a brand-new examination table, desk and privacy partition Aurora purchased during her first week as part of the clinic.

Today they were closed, for inventory, to devise a schedule of shifts here at the day clinic and to consult on the more delicate cases. This small space ran like a battalion that deployed its efforts to help the women of Paris, the least she could do was stand in front of strangers to convince them to support a more than worthy cause.

"And you're certain you are amenable to receiving help from aristocrats and capitalists?" It had to be asked, and it wouldn't hurt to know where she stood if Apollo was telling the truth about the building.

Virginia raised an eyebrow, seemingly amused by the question.

"Will I use the money acquired on the backs of women like the ones we serve in order to help them?" She crossed her legs with gusto and flashed Aurora a very saucy smile. "Absolutely, my dear, take *all* their money. I have my morals, but I am a pragmatist."

Aurora thought that Virginia and Apollo would probably get on very well. And why was she constantly thinking about the man?

"Now that's all sorted, tell me about the party at Le Bureau, since my emergency kept me from attending."

"Well, I didn't stay very long," Aurora said evasively while smoothing her skirts. "I had my patient." Her face heated when she thought of her jaunt through Paris with Apollo on her heels. She could not believe she'd pulled the blades gloves on him.

"Did you not enjoy yourself?" Virginia asked, pulling her out of her musings.

"I am not much for parties," she admitted. She never had been, and now that she had her work, she preferred focusing on that. "There is so much to do here."

"You deserve to enjoy yourself too, you know," Virginia said, to Aurora's surprise. "I've learned that running myself ragged to prove I can work 'as much as any man' is not good for my heart or my head."

It took a moment for the words to sink in. She didn't think she'd ever thought about what was good for her heart or her head.

"But so many people need us," Aurora retorted, unable to suppress the urgency that constantly dogged her.

"The work is endless," Virginia agreed, kindly. "But our energy is not. We must protect it."

Aurora was at a loss.

"But the work, the struggle." She knew she sounded like a child, repeating herself. But how could Virginia be so cavalier when she knew they were always short on able hands, on funds, on hours of the day?

"I see my words trouble you," Virginia said with a smile, reaching to pat Aurora's knee. "It's not that I don't I love my work, or that I wouldn't do what I must to continue it." The Argentine looked around her little clinic with such affection and pride. Aurora aspired to one day build something as worthy as what Virginia had. It was quite a feat to go from exile to being at the center of such an operation as this. "With the years, I've become quite vigilant in not letting the work become a burden." Aurora frowned, which made Virginia shake her head at her affectionately. "The need is great." She said so with a clap and a smile, as though to snap them both into action. "But I can't forget my own needs and I require divertments. God forbid, I require leisure!"

"Leisure?" It was beyond Aurora to hide the scandalized tone in her voice. Virginia only threw her head back and laughed.

"The horror on your face," she said, amused. "Yes, *leisure*. Something that brings *you* pleasure," she pressed, then lifted a shoulder with a very suggestive smile on her lips. "Or *someone* who does."

Aurora, to her eternal mortification, spluttered like a damned maiden. "Oh no, I don't—" Even as she said it, Apollo's wicked smiles appeared in her mind. The kiss they'd shared last night in that alley, the way his hands could rouse her body with a mere touch. Despite the folly of it, she could not deny the man was pleasure in the flesh. To look at him was decadence, to kiss him...a delight.

"I've tortured you enough," Virginia said with a laugh, breaking Aurora out of her reverie. "Tell me about the fistulotomy patient from yesterday." From there, the conversation went to safer topics, but her friend's words lingered.

She was still mulling them over hours later as she made her way to meet the Leonas for lunch.

"There you are," Manuela exclaimed. Aurora had no time to react, because she was soon engulfed in a hug from Luz Alana.

"Leona! I missed you," her friend said in her ear, and Aurora let herself sink into her embrace.

There was much to worry about. The clinics, the pile of unopened letters from her brothers and this Faustian deal she'd struck with Apollo, but at least she didn't have to do it alone.

"I missed you too."

"Now it's time to get to the real business," Luz Alana declared, as she hooked her elbow with Aurora's.

"Indeed," crowed Manuela, leading Aurora to believe that the business they were interested in was not the garden party. "Please, do regale us with every detail of what you and the Duke of Annan got up to after you left Le Bureau together."

She should've known.

"I thought we were here to discuss this charity event for the clinics." Her attempt at a diversion was received as well as expected.

"You see the avoidance?" Manuela asked Luz Alana.

"Nothing happened!" she insisted, but neither of her friends were buying her story. "He accompanied me for a portion of the journey, and then he must've gone home."

"That is interesting," Luz Alana mused as they walked down the crowded pedestrian path. "Because this morning we received a note from my brother-in-law with an offer to host your garden party at his home." Aurora was very proud of herself for not stumbling, falling on her face or running away screaming. Instead—as she'd been trained to do—she stared at the crisis straight on and then pretended to have it all under control.

"Would we call it *my* garden party?" she asked, without making any kind of eye contact.

"We would, yes," Manuela offered. Aurora countered with a dirty look.

Luz Alana nodded in agreement before continuing her probing. "And now this sudden desire by the Duke of Annan—"

"The man you claim to hate," interjected Manuela.

"I never claimed that!" Aurora protested.

"I recall you calling him an oversized buffoon with an inflated sense of his own importance and a serious misapprehension of his effect on women."

"That was in jest," she protested, veering off into the first café that looked open for lunch. With a huff, she dropped onto one of the chairs. "Maybe he's after some philanthropic endeavors to champion."

"He is," Luz agreed, primly taking the chair next to Aurora's. "What is curious is the timing and intensity of his interest."

"I think it's wonderful," Manuela declared, waving over a harried server. "And who knows? Perhaps the doctor and the duke can find some common ground."

"Exactly," Luz Alana concurred, and Aurora got the feeling the conversation was headed in a direction she would not like.

"And then," Manuela sang happily, "once that common ground is firmly in place, maybe they can lie down on it and forni—"

"Manuela Caceres Galvan!" Aurora cried, clapping her hand over Manuela's mouth while both her friends dissolved into laughter. She had to bite the inside of her cheeks to keep from joining in. "I will leave," she threatened. "Be serious. Besides, isn't he looking for a wife?"

"He is," Luz Alana concurred, and that lurch in Aurora's

stomach at the confirmation, had to be a reminder she'd only had an alfajor for breakfast. "Although I'd say that effort is being spearheaded by his aunt." So, he'd been telling the truth last night. It was not a good sign this information seemed to ease her somehow.

Aurora didn't respond. She didn't want to say more than was prudent. Not about what happened the night before, and not about her changing feelings regarding the duke.

"I'm not the doctor here, but I think a torrid affair with a wicked and very large man would do you good, and as far as I know, he's not married yet."

"I never said I was opposed to torrid affairs?" Manuela practically fell off her chair at that, which was satisfying. Luz Alana, on the other hand, narrowed her eyes as if attempting to decipher what Aurora wasn't saying.

"You've changed in the past few months, Léona," her friend observed. "You're…" She paused, searching for the word.

"Less tightly wound?" she asked, in jest, surprising her friends yet again. Goodness, did she take herself so seriously, her two dearest friends were perplexed to see her cracking a joke?

"More spirited, lighter," Luz Alana said, kindly.

"It's her work," Manuela explained. "She loves those clinics." She did love them, that was true. But she'd also seen the change in her friends, how their lives were richer, because they'd taken risks. Though she didn't want exactly what they had, she wanted her life to be a little bigger than it had been. To live less like she was in eternal penance. Philip Carlyle had taken too much from her already.

"I like my work, but Virginia just reminded me I need to enjoy myself sometimes too."

"I like that Virginia," Manuela said, approvingly, and once again Aurora had the urge to shock her friends.

"Maybe I will take a lover," she mused, and the face of a certain duke ambushed her mind. Perhaps some "leisure" might be exactly what she required. Apollo would be willing. She had no doubt of that.

There was a certain comfort in knowing she'd embark on this possible tryst with a man who she could never have a future with. She was, after all, the furthest one could be from a suitable wife for a duke. Apollo was on the hunt for a wife, so perhaps Aurora would go after her own game.

"That is the face of a woman contemplating a sinful deed or two," Luz Alana declared with a grin.

Aurora's own lips inevitably tipped up as she focused her attention on their newly arrived server, but not before turning to her friends and saying, "You two would know."

Nine

"*What is this I hear about a tertulia I have not been* invited to?" A querulous voice snatched Apollo from his so-far failed attempt to recover some of the sleep he'd lost the previous night.

"It was too much to hope for a quiet morning," he muttered as the Duchess of Sundridge strode into his study unannounced—the staff were too terrified of her to challenge her penchant for turning up at Apollo's house whenever she wanted. "And how the hell did you hear about the tertulia? I sent the note to my loose-lipped brother only this morning."

Cora waggled her eyebrows with mischief as she sat down in his favorite chair. "My beloved and I were at Evan's for breakfast."

He should've known not to send notes to his brother after barely having three hours of sleep. But he'd woken up with the thought of Aurora trampling around town unprotected dogging his mind. She'd taken off on him before they could talk, so he did the only thing he could, offer to host the blasted garden party.

Half of Paris had been waiting for him to host some kind of event as the new duke. He did not have the patience for a soiree where he'd be expected to dance and make conversation, so a charity event, to benefit a worthy cause, was the perfect alternative. This didn't mean he was in the mood to explain himself to his nearest and dearest.

"Ah, Your Grace," Evan exclaimed from the doorway of the study, before turning to Apollo. "Not you." Then he smiled at Cora. "I'm speaking to the duchess!" his useless brother cried out as he walked in with a grin Apollo would've loved to punch off his lips.

"Why are you two here? It's barely been two hours since I sent the damned note, carajo!" he bellowed, coming to a stand so he could properly kick them out of his house. "I thought your little artist had conscripted you to a life among the proletariat," he said to Cora, who, as expected, laughed in his face and then went to the sideboard to drink his coffee. "And you—" he pointed an accusing finger in his younger brother's direction "—I know you're busy trying to pull a dukedom from the sinkhole our father chucked it into, so why are you in my house discussing garden parties for doctors?" He applied his most ire-filled voice into this last part of his rant. Not that it had any effect on his unwanted guests.

"We've come to inquire about this new philanthropic effort of yours." Cora slid a hand over her bespoke vest and tie, with a smug expression on her face. She had the look of a woman who had recently won a bet she'd fully anticipated winning but was still delighted to have trounced her opponents spectacularly. "It seems a bit impulsive, doesn't it?"

Evan, that wily bastard, nodded with an expression of utter consternation. "I find it to be quite a conundrum."

"A baffling one indeed, Lord Evan." Cora made a show of looking between Apollo and his brother a few times, as if the conversation was so confusing she needed to get her bearings. "And given His Grace's aversion to the person the party has been organized for, it seems—" She paused then, at an apparent loss of what word to employ for such a vexing happenstance.

"Perplexing?" Evan offered, while Apollo glared at them.

Cora applauded. Apollo didn't think he'd ever seen the woman's palms make contact with each other in such a manner in the months he'd known her, but here she was enraptured.

"Perplexing!" She hoisted a finger into the air with glee. "*Utterly* perplexing, to see our duke so invested in assisting someone who he's called infuriatingly abrasive—"

"And a diminutive demon," Evan added cheerfully.

This was a gauntlet that Apollo had to very carefully make his way through. They clearly suspected something was happening between himself and Aurora. If they got even a whiff of any actual confirmation, they would run back to their respective spouses, who would make their own fuss and he'd never see the pocket-sized escape artist again.

"Are you two finished?" He made sure to appear very bored at their games.

"He's so cross today." Cora didn't know the half of it. It had taken his man Jean-Louis half the morning to track down the boardinghouse Aurora was living in now. If the directions were any indication the establishment was a far cry from the town house in the Place des Vosges she'd been previously staying in.

He knew Evan and Cora had to know what happened with her family. But asking for details would only lead to more of this buffoonery. From the beginning, he'd found Aurora intriguing, then she'd come to him that night, demanding and hungry, and he'd barely been able to keep her out of his mind since. But after last night, his curiosity for Aurora Montalban had transformed into something akin to reverence. The truth of who she was, of her strength, had cracked something wide open inside him, he didn't think could be closed again. But those reflections would be for when he didn't have an audience, and right now, he had a building to buy.

"Duchess, I need the name of the man who helped you procure that building you very impulsively gave your lady." He made sure to harp upon the impulsivity, in the hopes of distracting her. But Cora was like a damned hound.

"I didn't know you were in the market for a building." He had not been, until he'd offered one that he didn't own to a certain doctor.

"Since when do you know all the comings and goings in my life?" he volleyed back, but Cora was much too focused on figuring out what Apollo was truly after to care about the barb.

"What kind of building exactly?" she inquired, crossing her legs. "This, too, is quite impulsive, is it not? First the charity event, now this new building."

These two had some gall pointing a finger at him about impulsiveness, after they'd both turned their lives upside down in recent months for the sake of love.

"I'm not being impulsive," he denied. "Besides, I'm only hosting the salon as a favor to Evan."

As expected, his brother instantly protested.

"A favor to me?"

"Yes, to you," Apollo declared, then pointed at each of them. "Now that both of you have fallen in love and decided to live like commoners, I'm the only one with a decent place to host the kind of people one asks money from." He made a show of resting a hip on his desk and crossing his arms over his chest. "Which is why, as a favor, I'm offering you one of the most enviable gardens in Paris." He waved an arm toward the windows, which displayed the north side of his very elegant grounds.

He was on the cusp of winning the argument when his aunt barreled into the room. For a second, he was tempted to jump through the window and run off to parts unknown. As expected, Cora and Evan were ecstatic to have another conspirator join them. He loves his aunt, but she was the last person he wanted nosing around any of his business with Aurora.

"Sobrino, what is this I hear about a party?"

"You've been saying we need to have some kind of social event," he reminded her, which only made her scowl deepen.

"An event for you to meet a suitable bride, not to have our house overrun with scientists." The way she said it, it made him wonder if she actually meant *satanists*.

His aunt, who was still standing by the door of the study, sighed heavily and shook her head like the very idea was chipping away at her soul.

She was in one of her Worth gowns, this one in pale green and silver. She looked elegant and lovely. Even at her fifty-three years a beautiful woman by any standard. The most important woman in his life. The only mother he'd known, but his aunt's obsession with this so-called conquest of the aristocracy was beginning to wear on him.

"We are hosting the charity event, Tia," he said with finality, and sent a warning look to his brother, who was one of his aunt's favorites. He was grateful to his aunt. He owed her his life, but this was his house and hosting Aurora's event was his wish. That was the end of it.

What was he supposed to do, now that he knew Aurora Montalban was putting herself in harm's way? He knew he could not solve everything with money, because her damned pride survived on notions of merit and sacrifice.

Aurora wanted people to see the value of her work and support it. She didn't want a handout, she wanted compatriots, and she needed a victory, more than anyone he'd ever met. And because it was his damned prerogative, he was determined to be the one to give her both.

That explanation was not one he could offer his aunt.

"He's a bit distracted today, isn't he?" Cora said unhelpfully.

"Because he was in the streets all night," Tia Jimena lamented, with her eyes to the sky. "You're supposed to be behaving respectfully, instead you are gallivanting like a sin verguenza all over Paris."

He was starting to hate the words *hunt* and *bride*.

"Tia, as you well know, this bride hunt is not exactly a quest for a love match, and I assure you none of the gently bred ladies you keep shoving in front of me are expecting fidelity." He thought of the hellion who had kept him from his bed most of the night and sneaked out on him before dawn and wondered what life would be like with the unpredictable Doctora Montalban.

She'd demand loyalty, of that he was certain, and, though she'd likely lash out at him for saying so, she'd expect to be satisfied. A woman of appetites and passions, and with secrets and crimes, but not ever dull, never uninteresting, not to him. Despite her efforts to appear so.

"Pero Apollo," his aunt protested, "Lord Forsyth advised us to not host any large social events here in Paris."

The last person he wanted in his affairs was his aunt's new beau. The man had latched on to her in Colombia a year earlier and was now in Paris "guiding her into all the right spheres of the bon ton."

He was insufferable and much too slick for Apollo's comfort, but his aunt was fond of him, and he wanted to see her happy. But he was not going to allow Philip Carlyle, some two-bit baronet, into his affairs.

"This event is my business, Tia," he said, short on patience. "We already have everyone with a fortune and marriageable offspring coming to Nice, don't we?" he asked with a raised eyebrow. "Vamos Vieja," he said, vying for a more cajoling tone, and went over to put an arm around her.

"Don't try to soften me up," she groused, even as she patted his cheek. "I just want everything to go perfectly, mijo." He knew it was true. This was what she'd wanted for him all his life, for him to claim his rightful place. But he had to do it on his terms and not those of the ton.

Which reminded him of what Aurora said to him about remembering there was power beyond the British Isles. It had been some of the best advice he'd received since he'd become duke.

"Besides, inviting some of the leading businessmen of the continent and the Americas who are here for the closing of the exposition to join a worthy cause will not hurt me in any way." He knew that would do the trick, instantly her eyes lit up.

"Well, that is different, isn't it?" She lifted her face and Apollo dutifully lowered his cheek. "We want you to appear generous."

"And with half of the daughters of these new business magnates marrying aristocrats, we might have a house full of ladies and lords, Tia," Evan chimed in, *in Spanish*, because the man had become an unrepentant adulator of any women hailing from the tropics he encountered. Of course, his aunt ate it all up, sending the cabrón a besotted smile.

"Your Spanish is improving so quickly, Lord Evan."

"Stop encouraging him, Tia," Apollo teased.

But it was true that his Scottish brother had taken to his wife's—and Apollo's—Caribbean culture a little too well. The man was so obsessed with his woman that he was on a mission to absorb every part of her. He was learning Spanish, practicing the dances, demanding their cook learn her favorite dishes, everything he could to make her new home familiar.

It was as if he wanted to immerse himself in her. It was as

if Evan's life had been devoid of a North Star until Luz Alana assumed that place. Which was all well and good, but what if she was suddenly gone? What if she stopped loving him? What then?

That kind of love, that level of devotion was terrifying to Apollo. Like walking along a very steep, very high cliff with no protection. He enjoyed a risky business proposition, had reaped the benefits of many ventures of that nature. With people, he liked safer bets, like potential entanglements with women who had less use for marriage than he did. Once he managed to track her down, that was.

Aurora walked briskly along the pedestrian walk, lost in her thoughts, as she made her way to her rooms. Next to her, Abelardo seemed to be equally vexed.

"What are we to do?" Aurora asked as they rounded the corner leading to her boardinghouse. They'd just spent two discouraging hours visiting apothecaries. Their intention had been to ask some questions about any new doctors providing services for women. Not only had they learned nothing in that regard, but their most reliable supplier for the materials they needed to make their contraceptive tinctures and pessaries informed them they could no longer do so.

"I don't know," Abelardo answered, with a weary sigh. "This is the second apothecary we've lost in the last three months." One more problem to add to the mountain of them they seemed to be constantly managing. They had a very small reserve that could keep them afloat for a couple of weeks. After that, they'd have to send their patients to take their chances on unknown vendors.

"We have to find our own supplier of the herbs," she mused. Abelardo didn't speak, which Aurora took as tacit agreement.

"It's too risky to continue to rely on apothecaries that can refuse to supply us at any time."

"It would make things easier," he admitted.

"The apothecaries are under as much scrutiny as we are, they're no longer dependable," Aurora added, her stomach in knots as she considered their situation. It was true the establishments were taking risks by working with them. It only took one complaint to the authorities to make trouble for a business.

"There must be someone at one of the markets that can help us," Abelardo mused, as they trudged up one of the steep hills of their neighborhood.

She didn't answer, thinking that however it was one went about finding a supplier, it would likely require funds.

"We have the charity event, which will help," Abelardo reminded her, with a pointed look she ignored. Then instantly recalled the invitation in her Gladstone she'd received from Luz Alana that morning.

The Honorable Earl and Lady Darnick with His Grace, the Duke of Annan, cordially invite you for an evening to honor physicians and scientists from the Americas at his residence...

She'd not heard from him since the morning she'd left his apartment. Who could blame him, after she'd run out on him like she had?

She'd felt bold enough after her talk with the Leonas. She'd been determined to brazenly make him a proposition the next time they met. But after two days without a single word, she was beginning to wonder if all she was to him was a charity case.

Apollo César Sinclair Robles kept her in a constant state of turmoil. She craved his attention but didn't want to crave it too much. She wanted him but didn't want to have to tell him she did. Mostly she was irritated by how much she longed to see him again. But it seemed she was the only one who felt that way and she refused to throw herself at him again.

A whistle and sound of surprise from Abelardo rescued her from further agonizing thoughts about the Duke of Annan.

"Someone's got a fancy suitor," her colleague commented, lifting his chin to the carriage sitting in front of her boarding-house. It was probably for her landlady, a famed former cour-tesan.

"Claudine has many friends among the higher echelons," she told Abelardo, as she inspected the crest on the side. There was a chance it could be Manuela, but she didn't recognize the seal, or the impressively large man standing by the conveyance. She also noticed the stranger was not merely standing there, he was on the lookout. Watching every person who entered Claudine's like a hawk. For some reason, the realization made her slow her steps.

For a moment she considered the possibility this could be Philip coming to harass her, but how would he know she was in Paris? And it wasn't as if he'd ever attempted to contact her before. No, she was certain whatever her brothers had done to send the man away thirteen years ago would keep him away for good. It *could* be her brothers, but they would be the ones standing guard at the door, not that they would ever make the trip across the Atlantic to see her.

"Do you know him?" Abelardo inquired, then took a cau-tionary step back when the man waved at her in greeting.

"I do not." He *was* quite focused on them. He'd pushed off the carriage and was now standing between them and the en-trance to her house.

"Doctora Montalban?" Relief coursed through her when he addressed her by her title, then felt a little silly for suspecting the man. This had to be about a patient. She almost laughed with embarrassment at her fretting. It was true that she didn't have any patients with such fancy modes of transportation, but it could be a referral.

"I'm Doctora Montalban," she offered, deciding in this instance to be honest. "This must be about a patient," she said, turning to Abelardo.

The big man frowned at that. "No, ma'am. The Duke of Annan has sent his brougham for you." The mention of the man sent a jolt through her system, she could feel her pulse racing. While Abelardo made a sound of distress, then took a much bigger step away. So large, in fact, he was now on the street.

"And where exactly am I to go, unchaperoned, in the duke's brougham?" She could practically hear Apollo laughing at her for that.

Undaunted by her corrosive tone, the duke's messenger pulled out a small envelope from his coat jacket and handed it to her. She took it, but only after making her discontent known to the man as she opened the missive. There were only four sentences.

Fiera,
You are an exceedingly troublesome woman to pin down.
   Your first lesson awaits.
   Make sure to bring that devilish temper and tongue of yours.
I've missed them.
AC

He'd signed his initials, as if he was a regular person. She only wished her body would react in a proper manner to the man's high-handedness. Rage and fury were the only suitable responses to this. Instead, her belly swooped with frustrating anticipation, and she was quite certain a humiliating flush was even now rushing to her cheeks.

"Thank you for this," she said, sliding the note into her pocket and turning toward the door of her boardinghouse. "I will respond to His Grace at my convenience." When she tried to take a step in the direction of the building, the man blocked her path. "Get out of my way, sir."

"I'm afraid that won't be possible, madame," the man informed her. "You see, I've been tasked with bringing your good self to the duque." His tone was not exactly menacing, but she had the sense that she would find herself in that carriage whether she went peacefully or not. It would not be peacefully.

Who did the Duke of Annan think he was?

"I think you should go see what it's about," Abelardo advised from his place on the street.

She rounded on her so-called friend. "Truly, Abelardo? You're fine with an aristocrat having me abducted?" she asked incredulously and obtained a shrug and a smile for her trouble.

"He seemed quite taken with you that night at Le Bureau."

This was what she got for letting one act of kindness blind her to Apollo's manipulation and high-handedness. Just because she'd made an agreement with the man didn't mean she was at his beck and call.

"Tell the duke I'm indisposed at the moment," she told the large man, very cordially, given her mood. "I will send a note when I'm available." Aurora was sidestepping him with the intention of going home when she was lifted off the ground.

"What are you doing?" she demanded as she was hauled up to the carriage and unceremoniously dumped on a bench seat.

"Delivering you to the duque?" the brute said, with a grin, as she bounced on the seat like a rag doll.

This was absolutely unacceptable. She would not be carted

around like a damned parcel whenever Apollo deigned to summon her.

"I would like to get out of this conveyance," she told Apollo's lummox, who closed the door in her face.

"I'm afraid I can't do that," the giant responded. He had very white teeth and he seemed to be enjoying his task a little too much. Aurora was close to combusting from pure fury.

"Abelardo, do something!" she pleaded, as the conveyance pulled away. But her colleague was waving at her as if she was about to depart on a pleasure cruise.

"This is the leisure Virginia was referring to!" Abelardo called out as the conveyance moved forward. "I'll let Claudine know you won't be in for supper."

"Tell her I'm being kidnapped!" Aurora shouted, hanging from the window, but Abelardo was already skipping up the steps to the boardinghouse and the carriage halfway down the street.

Ten

"*This is outrageous,*" *Aurora protested as the carriage* came to a stop barely ten minutes later. She was going to scratch Apollo's eyes out the moment she saw him. The nerve of the man.

"Mademoiselle can direct her grievances to the duque," Apollo's manservant—Jean-Louis, she'd been informed—advised as he pointed to the entrance of the building.

"I intend to," she assured him with an aggrieved huff as she headed up the couple of steps to the door. "And I could've walked here," she protested. Unlike his den of iniquity, this place was in Aurora's neighborhood. Their meeting place, it seemed, was right in the heart of Montmartre.

She rapped twice with the door knocker and looked nervously over her shoulder while Jean-Louis stood like a sentinel a few feet away, clearly intending to personally deliver her to his overlord if she attempted to flee.

After the fourth knock, the door finally opened and a very slender, very pretty gentleman appeared in the doorway. He observed her curiously, but he didn't seem surprised to find her at the door. This was likely another of the "duque's" minions.

"Bonsoir, Docteur Montalban." He bowed when he greeted her and stepped to the side to allow her in.

He was certainly not dressed as Apollo did in his bespoke suits. Loose trousers and a simple shirt and vest. His hair was very long and black, hanging down below his shoulders, and he had kind eyes that crinkled at the corners. Despite her general displeasure at her situation, she liked him instantly.

"I've been summoned by the duke, but I suppose you already know that."

The man's mouth twitched. "Indeed, we were expecting you." He turned to the side, and she stepped through the door. "I'm Mihn."

"Are you my instructor?"

"No." He shook his head, still smiling as he pointed at a long hallway. "But I will take you to him." With that they began their brisk walk through a long corridor. Mihn moved very fast, but his footsteps were light. Meanwhile she was stomping down the corridor like a bull.

The place was bigger than it seemed from the outside. She tried to take a peek as they passed empty open rooms, but they were walking too fast to take a good look.

"What is this place?" she asked, a bit breathless as they passed a room with a boxing ring.

"This is a club," he told her, with another of those warm smiles.

"What kind of club?"

"A club to learn and practice pugilistic arts." Of course, this would be the kind of club Apollo Sinclair visited.

"Do women belong to this club?" she asked, certain what the answer would be. To her amazement, he nodded. "There are women who practice, yes," Mihn told her with a grin that said "you didn't expect that did you?" She did like the man. There was something very easy about him and it was a rare man who appreciated a woman with questions. "One of the owners of the club is married to the daughter of Charles Lecour and she has a class only for ladies." She had absolutely no idea who Lecour was, which clearly showed in her face, given Mihn's consequent explanation. "He was one of the masters of Savate, the art of French boxing." She *had* heard of Savate. She knew it came from the streets of Paris and involved punching and kicking. Not exactly her areas of interest, but she could not deny the idea of learning how to throw a proper punch intrigued her.

"Is that what I'm to learn? Savate?" she asked, as they rounded a corner.

"Not quite," Mihn answered with an air of mystery that piqued her interest despite the situation.

As they reached the door at the end of the corridor, she thought she heard the sound of drums coming from the other side. "Are those drums?"

Mihn nodded. "There's a sparring session in progress," he answered vaguely, then put a finger over his lips.

She sent him a dubious look, but kept her mouth shut. She'd never heard of drums in a sparring session. "The drums are part of the background to them, but any other sudden noise could result in an accidental blow or kick."

"Oh." She nodded, solemnly waiting for him to open the door. When he did, she understood why he'd warned her.

She put a hand over her mouth to keep from crying out as she crossed the threshold. The sparring session, as it turned out, was not taking place in a room like the ones they'd passed. This was some kind of outdoor arena. It was a rectangular lawn lined with torchlights on all sides. Beyond it, she could see shadows of larger trees, and possibly a garden. They were standing on a concrete landing, which led down to a sunken green lawn, where two shadowed figures were circling each other in quick, graceful movements.

Both men were well-built and powerful. They were stripped to the waist, and the light of the torches turned their brown skin into a brushed gold. Her attention kept returning to one of the fighters. Her gaze hungrily roaming over his form. He wore only loose white trousers, and the sight of his broad shoulders, leading to a lean, tapered waist, stole her breath.

This display should've caused discomfort. Apollo bringing her here to watch him spar half-naked should've offended her. Offense was not what swirled and coiled hotly inside as she watched him move. Something possessive and hungry pounded through her as she took in that lithe body, his powerful form. She could not look away from the sinew and brawn on display. Brown curls bouncing as he swayed to some inner rhythm and circled his opponent. Even from a distance, she could see their skin slick with sweat. The two men crouched, bent at the waist with their feet moving almost in unison, forward and back, back and forward, as they rocked on the balls of their feet, tracking each other like a pair of fighting cocks.

"What is this?" she asked Mihn, a little breathless. She'd almost forgotten the man was there, she'd been so entranced with the view.

"It's called capoeiragem or brincar de Angola," Mihn explained in a hushed tone as they both watched the fighters. "It's Brazilian. I'm told it was brought there by the men bought as slaves from Angola."

"I've never seen anything like it." As if he could sense he was being watched, Apollo's movements intensified. He became quicker, and to her delight, the drums matched his rhythm. "It's like a dance." She was not certain if she was saying this to Mihn or to herself.

"It is," her companion said appreciatively as his gaze followed the two fighters.

"I've heard the practice is so popular and has been used so

effectively by slaves to defend themselves that the Brazilian government is in the process of outlawing it." That did not surprise her. She could only imagine the horror of the wealthy landowners watching the men they had in bondage displaying this kind of power, this prowess, to the sound of these drums.

As she watched Apollo move and sway, she was quite suddenly overwhelmed with emotion for what she'd been invited to witness. He could be learning to fence or box or whatever his peers did in their clubs, but instead, here he was uncompromisingly himself. Apollo César Sinclair Robles might have claimed his place in the British aristocracy, but he was not theirs, he was his own. He could live in their world, but he knew what blood ran through his veins. She'd asked him to bear in mind that there was power in the world the two of them came from, in him, and tonight he was showing her he'd never forgotten.

The Duke of Annan might have his father's blood, but he was his mother's son.

His very existence was a rebellion.

A six-foot-tall, brown-skinned ambush on the ton. And he moved like he knew it. Limber and dangerous, prowling as he harnessed and unleashed power in equal measure. How would it be to be the one to unravel him?

Her rebellion could be this man, taking him into her body, into her bed, not out of duty, or penance, but because it pleased her to do so.

Oh yes, the two of them could be quite a revolution.

It was enough to make her forget she was supposed to be very mad at him. Just then, as if her thoughts had drifted from her head to his, he turned. His body rocking in that ancient cadence. He faced her, and she thought her heart might have actually stopped then. Collapsed against her sternum as she took in the glory of him.

I want this man, she thought, as she watched him crouch on the ground and sweep his impossibly long legs under his opponent, felling him swiftly. Apollo did not boast or crow. He simply offered his opponent a hand, helped him up, and they both went back to that constant back and forth. She'd never been particularly attached to things or money, but in that moment, she understood greed more than she had any emotion before that.

Soon he will be some gentle lady's husband, said a shrewish voice in her head. *Soon someone will be able to call that body her own.* The thought made bile rise in her throat. Her body almost physically rejecting the idea. But it was the reality, she could never own this man. But she could have him for a time.

He'd brought her here, after all. A man who dragged a lioness into his lair had to know he might walk away with a few teeth marks on his person. That thought agitated her so, that her Gladstone slid out of her hand and crashed to the ground. The contact of the leather with the flagstones finally seemed to snap Apollo's concentration. He whipped his head toward her and stood stock-still. His dark eyes boring into her. She thought she could sense the places he looked at.

After a moment, his sparring partner turned his gaze in her direction and grinned widely. Then he leaned to whisper something in Apollo's ear that the duke seemed to not find nearly as humorous. His eyebrows dipped and he shook his head. The other man laughed then, loud and deep. Aurora noticed that he was even bigger than Apollo, and handsome. Both men turned to the drummer and bowed to him.

Apollo's partner stayed in the pit, but the duke began walking toward her.

Apollo's long strides covered the distance in a half dozen steps, and all the while, his eyes were locked with hers. He came to a stop a few feet from her, and she had to work hard to hold on to her earlier anger, when all she wanted to do was touch.

He was so magnificent. She raked her gaze over him freely, his broad mouth was now parted as he sucked oxygen into his lungs. There was stubble on his cheeks, which she'd never seen before. His cheekbones stood out on his face like birds' wings. She noticed a medallion nestled in the divot between his pectoral muscles, which glistened with sweat in the dusky light of the torches. There was not much hair on him, just a trail traveling from his lower abdomen to a place she intended to see before the night was over.

She held herself very still as she watched him. Locking every muscle in her body she could. There was no way to fully conceal the effect his semi-nakedness had on her, but she was fairly certain she could keep herself from leaping at him like a trollop.

"Fiera," he drawled huskily. "You were not easy to find."

"You had me kidnapped, Your Grace." To her frustration, her complaint was much too breathless to be considered a satisfactory reprimand. She might as well have complimented the man.

"I *sent* for you," he told her, coming closer. Close enough to smell his sweat and the hints of vetiver on his skin. Close enough to see a drop of perspiration gathered at the base of his throat.

"I'm not yours to send for," she countered, resorting to the safe waters of outrage.

"We had an agreement." He was merely inches away. His body so near, in fact, that if she were to lean in, barely a centimeter, she'd be able to lap up that drop with the tip of her tongue. Demonios, but she wanted a taste. She squeezed her eyes shut and forcefully reminded herself that the man had her manhandled into a carriage.

"This is highly inappro—" she began to protest, but he put a finger over her lips and shook his head.

"Hush, Fiera." That command, as unwelcome as it should've been, melted her bones. Tiny, agitated puffs of air escaped her nose as she attempted to rein herself in from the sudden contact. She should not like this manhandling. Shouldn't feel a flutter in her chest at the thought that he'd wanted to see her. She knew Apollo hadn't been pining. He was asserting himself. Reminding her he was a man who got what he wanted.

He was torturing her, flaunting that toned chest and flat stomach. He wanted to agitate her with his nakedness. To humble her with his carriage and his manservant. But he had no idea how reckless she could be. It seemed he'd forgotten how far she'd go to satiate her hungers.

So, she reminded him.

Eleven

She bit him. The little diabla bit him.

"Ow," Apollo cried, tearing the finger from its trap while she bared shiny white teeth at him. "That hurt," he protested, looking down at the injured digit.

"I didn't bite you that hard." She was nothing but sweetness now that she'd almost maimed him, not that his wayward cock noted the difference. "Besides, I thought I'd show you some of *my* self-defense tactics."

She did look radiant after she took the skin off a man, positively bloodthirsty.

"Ah, my new pupil has arrived," Gilberto, his old friend and sparring partner, called as he made his way to them. Apollo had a feeling he'd regret bringing her here. His house would've been a much better choice, but he'd wanted her to see this.

"Gilberto Dossantos, Doctora." Apollo noticed his friend's fingers didn't get bitten off. "You're already displaying excellent instincts," he complimented her by pointing at the injured finger. The wench tittered at the joke at his expense, and that only made him more obsessed.

"Should I go with him?" Aurora asked innocently, which he knew by now was when he could absolutely not trust her.

"I think I can handle things from here," he grumbled, shoving Gilberto aside. "Biting is not allowed," he grumbled, which earned him a surprised look from Aurora and a snort from Gilberto.

"Is he always this sensitive?" Aurora asked her new best friend.

"I'm not—" They were baiting him, and Apollo was allowing it. How had he lost control of the situation so damned fast? The answer to that was standing next to him, in one of her woolen monstrosities. "Let's get on with the lesson, shall we?" he finally said. Aurora instantly stood at attention, like a very short and well-endowed cadet.

"I'm ready." Demonios, but he wanted to kiss her.

Gilberto considered her a moment, likely assessing what to start her with.

"Should we have her change into something less—" Apollo waved a hand toward her attire at a loss of what to even call it "—constraining?"

She stared down at herself, then glared up at him, looking quite offended.

"I'm not changing." Then she turned to Gilberto and pinned him with a flirtatious little flutter of the eyelashes. Was she trying to get the man killed? "If this is self-defense, shouldn't I do it in the clothes I'd be typically wearing in the event I'm attacked?"

Dammit, she was right. It was a conclusion he'd surely have reached if his brains weren't scrambled from lusting after the pint-size hellion.

Gilberto nodded with a grin, clearly already smitten with her too. "Precisely," he told her, sending an amused look at Apollo. "I will make sure to teach you—"

"*I*," Apollo corrected, pointing at himself, then pulling on Gilberto's arm to wrench him away from Aurora. "*I* will be teaching her."

Gilberto guffawed, allowing himself to be dragged away. "Oh, it's like that, is it?" his old friend asked, and Apollo only grunted. Then turned to Aurora, who was watching them with interest.

"Ignore him," he ordered, with a sideways look to Gilberto, who was still snickering. "Tonight we'll go over a few simple moves to help you get away from an assailant."

"But you told me that I'd be learning from a master."

"I'm perfectly capable of teaching you some defensive tactics," he assured her, while behind him Gilberto laughed so hard Apollo hoped he burst something.

"*Capoeiragem* defensive tactics?" she asked, with narrowed eyes, and that was the precise moment when he knew this woman could quite easily take possession of his entire existence.

"Not exactly," he hedged, knowing that was not a good enough answer for Aurora Montalban.

"What you did there." She pointed a gloved finger toward the torchlit pit. "That's what I'd like to learn," she informed him, with that authoritarian way of hers. He thought he would very much like to hear it right in his ear while she instructed where and how to put his mouth on her next.

"What we were doing took us years to learn," he explained in what he thought was a very sensible manner, but his Fiera would not have it.

"Then why did you bring me here to watch you do it when you were not planning to teach me anything useful? Or am I getting the girl lessons while the men actually learn how to defend themselves?"

"No, that is not..." he growled, then pinched the bridge

of his nose, took a breath and recalibrated his tone when she pinned him with a nasty look. "I brought you here because I watched you put yourself in danger more than once and I didn't like it."

"You weren't so worried, to send word in the last two days."

From any other woman it wouldn't have been much of declaration, but for Aurora, to actually admit she'd noted his silence made it very hard to keep himself in check. "You were waiting to hear from me, Fiera?" he asked, cupping her face.

"No," she denied, but she didn't reject his touch. "I was irritated at not knowing how your little lessons would impact my schedule." He had to bite his lip to keep from grinning. She was so damned ornery.

"Why didn't you send me a note?"

She shrugged and looked away. "I figured my safety was not as important as you'd claimed."

He could tell her his first instinct was to force a carriage and bodyguard on her. That he'd been tempted to send Jean-Louis to shadow her every movement. But he knew how that would go over. But whatever she saw in his face seemed to finally soften her.

"We should get on with this," she told him, but not before sending him a rueful smile. He made some kind of gruff noise in place of a yes. "And I do want to learn the ginga," she said, walking past him down to the pit, where she assumed the ginga stance, with that heart-shaped bottom swaying. The only thing keeping him from groaning in agony was Gilberto's presence.

"Who knew a short-assed fireball like that would be the one to knock down the great Apollo César a few pegs."

"Vete a la mierda, Dossantos," he told the man as he followed Aurora into the pit.

"Is this right?" she asked, face serious as anything while she whirled her arms in front of her and swung her bum.

"You know that will be absolutely useless in an encounter in an alley with some lowlife," he told her. Not to mention the fact that she'd likely attract every male in a two-mile radius.

"Come on," she urged him, dancing around him on the balls of her feet. The little jaunty hat she usually sported was lopsided and her shirt was half out of her too-big skirts. She was, in one word, *chaos*, and he would have ravished her right on the wet grass in an instant if she'd let him.

"Your movements should be stealthier," he instructed and got himself in position to demonstrate. "Give yourself time to locate a weak spot." She followed his lead, a little wrinkle of concentration forming between her brows as she did.

"Use your arms, Doctora," Gilberto called from the sidelines, lifting his to show her how. She nodded at him, very seriously, then turned her attention back to Apollo.

"Like this?" she asked, with her elbows exactly where they needed to be. She liked to do things right the first time, his Fiera. He could only nod as a frantic heat sputtered inside his chest from looking at her. "How do I topple you?" She had the same glint in her eye he'd seen when she was admiring a particularly indulgent pastry.

"To start, I thought we'd focus on how to get you away from a hostile situation, not necessarily *engaging* with it," he said in an attempt to redirect her.

"Fine, I'll ask Gilberto," she threatened, turning to his friend, who grinned back. Gilberto did not fancy women. In fact, he'd been devoted to Mihn for the better part of the last decade. Still, the thought of his hands on her made Apollo want to dismember things.

He exhaled, attempting to expel the cocktail of frustration and lust flooding him, and focused on the source of it.

"All right, I'll teach you." The moment he said it, the little vixen stopped to do a victory dance. She was being a brat and damned if seeing this side of her, didn't make him want her more. "Come here." He crooked a finger at her, which provoked a very unfriendly look. But she unbent from her crouch and made her way to him.

"How do you want me?" she asked with a hint of uncertainty as she looked him over. His pulse was racing, so much so, he thought he could hear the blood rushing in his ears. The top of her head barely reached his chin, but she looked formidable with her wild hair and her fists on her hips.

"Turn around." She eyed him with suspicion, but when he twirled his finger in the air, she did as he asked.

"Do not take liberties, Your Grace," she tossed over her shoulder.

"I've only ever taken the liberties you've given me, Fiera," he whispered as he slid his arms around her waist. "But we can discuss what other ones I'd like to take on your delectably short body, after your lesson." He had his lips right above her ear, and he could hear her quick breaths. A sweet little growl escaped her lips. He slid his hands to those wide, lush hips. "Now, be a good girl and lift your trasero." She looked up at him with fire in those dark brown eyes.

"I will not," she protested, and he decided it was time for her first lesson. Without warning, he slid his legs under her. "Que diablos?" She landed on the grass with a thump.

"An opponent is going to provoke you, Fiera." He tried for a conciliatory tone, which she did not find amusing. The moment she stood up, she was back on guard. Her body taut as she awaited her instructions.

"Now, attack me," he encouraged, thinking she'd waver, but she came at him without hesitation. Her smaller body rushing his much larger one. Her breathing was hard as she did her best to take him down. She wrapped her arms around his waist and tugged with surprising strength in an attempt to topple him.

"You barely budged," she cried, sending a pleading look to Gilberto. "How do I take him down?" She was mightily pissed off, and he wanted to kiss her so badly, his teeth ached.

Gilberto took a step toward them but looked at Apollo first. He needed to get himself under control. He couldn't expect her to learn if he didn't allow anyone else to touch her.

She was not very good, bless her, but she had brio. It was the only word he could think of. Spirit, valor, resolve. Gilberto did not go easy on her, but she did not complain. Every time she fell, she got back up and into position.

Una Léona, esta mujer.

He thought he might never tire of her, if she was his.

"Come, do the leg sweep," he told her, and she came at him again. She was relentless, crashing her body into his, until he was certain she'd have bruises from head to toe.

"Again," she demanded, from where she'd landed on her side. After an hour, he was slick with sweat and she'd taken off her jacket. Her shirt was ripped at the collar. She barely seemed to notice. "I'm not very good at this, am I?" She didn't seem particularly distressed by the fact.

"As long as you have one move that can neutralize an attacker," he told her.

"You only need one good defensive move," Gilberto concurred.

"I think I have one that might work," she told them, between harsh breaths. She looked exhausted, but he knew better than to underestimate her. He could only imagine what it would be.

"Show me, then."

She held up a finger, still breathing hard, and put her hands on her knees.

"Is she going to swoon?" Gilberto asked, while Apollo wondered the same thing.

"She's reaching for her ankle," Apollo observed, as he tried to figure out she was doing to her foot. He thought he saw a glint of silver, right before she popped back up with a tiny pistol in her hand.

"Would this do for a defensive maneuver?" she asked, still a little breathless. Gilberto started laughing, while the little imp grinned at him with a look of utter satisfaction on her face. "Maybe distract my opponent with my terrible ginga before I pull out Juana Inés?"

Of course she'd named her damned pistol after a radical, sapphist nun.

"Why didn't you say you have a pistol?" he asked, struggling not to laugh, especially when Gilberto began rolling around in the grass.

She lifted a shoulder, then slid the weapon back into her boot. "Because I don't plan on ever using it, unless I absolutely must."

"Can you shoot it?" It was not an absurd question, as she had no coordination that he could see from her sparring.

She scoffed, all offended pride. "Who do you think taught Luz Alana to use hers?" His sister-in-law infamously carried around a flask and pistol under her dress. He'd mocked Evan for his obsession with that fact, now he understood, only too well.

"Then, why agree to the class?" he asked, quietly, not that anyone could hear.

Gilberto was apparently in such a state that he'd crawled out of the pit, likely gone to find Mihn. Which left the two of them alone with only Juana Inés for a chaperone.

Aurora looked up at the sky, then sighed, before returning her gaze to him.

"For one, it was part of our deal," she reminded him with a surprising lack of acid. "And I liked the idea of becoming stronger."

"I can understand that." He truly meant it. Apollo thought of his aunt and the lessons she taught his cousins about being "ladylike," to not display too much knowledge of a topic in order to allow their suitors their "pride." Women made themselves fragile creatures so men could feel strong. Aurora Montalban did not care about men's fragilities.

"Can I ask you a question?" There was a hesitation in her voice that seemed utterly wrong coming from her.

"Of course." He dipped his head and braced for something potentially scathing.

"Where did Gilberto go?" she asked, looking to the closed doors of the patio.

"Probably off to find Mihn," Apollo said, and she nodded. He knew that could not be the question. "They'll be a while." The confirmation seemed to scare and bolster her at once.

"Would you be interested—" she began, then stopped herself. She fidgeted and slid her hands into the pockets of her skirts.

"Would I be interested...?" he urged, when she seemed to become engrossed by the flickering light of the torches.

"I..." She bit her bottom lip in unusual diffidence. For a second, he thought she might not continue. But then he saw the Fiera return. She straightened her shoulders and tipped that pert chin up at him. "I would be interested in another kind of lesson, in addition to the self-defense instruction, which I would like for Gilberto to do. You fluster me." He opened his mouth to ask something appropriately inflammatory, but she paid him back by covering his mouth with her hand.

"I refuse to go into details about your effect on my person." Even in the torchlight, he could see the flush on her cheeks. Control was beyond him in that moment. He risked pressing the very tip of his tongue to her hand. She made a hissing sound, her eyes going wide, and languid. He licked again, and she made a needy little sound before removing her hand.

"What kind of lessons?" He knew the answer, but it seemed tonight he, too, wanted to test his fortitude. She played with that bottom lip again, until he considered pinching himself to keep from pawing at her like a rabid animal.

"Sexual lessons," she stated with finality, never breaking eye contact, while Apollo did a mental assessment of which horizontal surface he could conscript into service in the next sixty seconds.

"Like the night you came to me?" he asked, needing to set the expectations. He was perilously close to begging, and he wanted to delay that humiliating display as long as possible.

But she shook her head, denying his question.

"No, I want..." She looked to the heavens again, then back at him. "I want more." She shook her head after that, then emitted a sound of frustration. "*Physically* more. That night, it made me realize I don't know my body very well," she admitted, bravely. "I'd like to explore what brings me pleasure."

"I will give you anything you want, Fiera."

She exhaled, a shaky sound, then pinned him with one of those fierce stares. He could almost see a barrier forming around her. "Anything but emotions, and we stop when you select your bride."

He should rejoice that this woman was offering him exactly what he should want, in exactly the manner that would be most convenient to him. But for some reason the entire thing made him furious.

"What is so unsavory about emotions?"

She seemed almost confused by his question. "Neither of us have any use for them." She wasn't wrong, and still he felt slighted. "I won't marry anyone, and you must marry well. This could be a diversion."

All of it so perfectly fucking sensible.

He'd have her for a few weeks. He'd enjoy her as long as he could and then he'd do his duty. It was ideal. Truly he couldn't have asked for a more favorable arrangement, but for the first time in his life, Apollo didn't want to stay the course. He didn't want to do what would serve him in the long run, he wanted all of her, even if he could never keep her.

This would not end well. He was walking into some kind of trap. He didn't know which of them was setting it, but it would have them both dangling by their ankles over an alligator pit soon enough.

He'd always liked his trophies. Things he could flaunt in front of others to assert his prowess, the many ways in which he was better, faster, stronger, smarter. An abandoned, motherless boy showing the world he was not merely their equal, but their better. But those trophies had never been for himself, they were for the benefit of those he sought to humble.

Aurora would be his secret. The prickly, censorious doctor who behind closed doors became his Fiera. The one thing he wanted, not for duty or retribution, but purely because he could not help himself.

Oh, to hell with it.

He lunged at her, lifted her off the ground and pressed her against the nearest wall in seconds.

"I didn't mean now," she protested, even as she wrapped her short legs around his waist. "Someone will come."

"Gilberto and Mihn are probably engaged in the very thing

I hope to be doing in the next minute, if you cooperate," he said with his teeth scraping along her neck.

Her hands stopped gripping his shoulders for a second, and she looked up at him. "Mihn and Gilberto are a couple?" He didn't expect any disapproval from her given her support of Manuela and Cora's relationship, and he was not disappointed. There was only curiosity, and maybe a little wistfulness, in her eyes.

"Yes," he said, before biting her bottom lip.

"That's wonderful." She sighed as he licked the seam of her mouth, and his hands squeezed her still gloriously voluminous rump.

"I'm glad you think so, Fiera," he told her, as he pressed kisses to her neck.

"Not you," she protested breathlessly as she ran her hands over his bare back and shoulders. "I meant them, although your muscles are quite impressive." She followed this by latching her mouth to his. He groaned into the kiss, sliding his tongue along hers.

"I look forward to showing you my other impressive parts." She huffed a laugh and reached for him again. Just as he started to devise a plan to have her right on the ledge of the pit, the door slammed open.

"Gilberto, if you value your life—" he growled, beyond frustration. There was shuffling of feet behind him, preceded by a very loud slam to the patio doors.

Like him, Aurora's breaths were coming fast, he could feel the heat against his bare chest. He thought she'd be upset at being found out, but after a moment what sounded like laughter drifted up to him. She didn't laugh very much, this very serious woman. It seemed to him like a great accomplishment to be the cause of it.

That emotion was suddenly interrupted by a much more

pressing one when a hot little tongue began lapping at his chest.

"What are you doing, sweetheart?" He could barely make the words from how tightly he was grinding his teeth.

"You're salty," she told him between laps of her tongue while his cock jumped in his trousers. She lifted her eyes to him while she left wet trails on his skin.

"You like to taste, don't you?" he asked, huskily, and she nodded. "I have more things for that mouth of yours to try." Something hot flashed in her eyes, and she bit down again. This time it was more pleasure than pain. He needed a bed, he needed walls, he needed a door with a lock.

"Let me take you to my rooms," he told her, as his hands kneaded her rump.

"I didn't mean we'd start tonight," she told him distractedly, before tracing a wet line between his pectorals. Was he supposed to go merrily on his way after having his chest bitten and licked? "If I'd had you as a model, I would've had the best marks in anatomy class."

"What?" he asked, panting as she followed her observation with a love bite on his collarbone.

"I like your body," she told him, in a tone that implied he was being obtuse and irritating.

He was trembling from her touch, lost in her already. He was supposed to be the one seducing her. But with a few flicks of her tongue, he was practically on his knees.

"Aurora," he whispered, as her hands began drifting down his chest. "Aurora," he insisted when one of the hands breached inside his trousers.

"Yes?" she asked, innocently.

"I need you to understand something," he explained, taking her errant hands in his. "I intend to take you out of this studio, put you in my carriage, take you to my den of iniquity." He used her own words to hopefully drive the message across more succinctly. "There I plan to have you on every surface." She inhaled sharply at that, her eyes glowing with intrigue at the prospect.

His voracious girl.

"That sounds very tiring," she mused, wiggling her nose.

"I intend to thoroughly exhaust you," he confirmed. "I'll take you right against the door," he told her. "Lift your skirts and sink inside." The sounds she made. Like he was reciting the sweetest poetry. "Then I'm going to strip all your clothes off, lay you on the table and lick your concha until you cry out my name." She pressed into him, her hot breath searing his chest.

"What else?" she asked so quietly he could barely hear her.

"Then I'll take you to my bed and fuck you until the sun comes up." He was practically vibrating with need.

"I look forward to it," she said amiably, then pulled away, quickly moving out of the way when he reached for her. "I'll come to you this evening." This woman was so damned slippery. He was never on steady ground with Aurora. One minute she was fire in his arms. Hot enough to scorch and the next she was primly dusting her skirts as if they'd been discussing the weather. It was enough to drive a man mad.

"It is evening," he told her. It was barely seven, but that was good enough.

She shook her head as if that simply would not do, then plucked a timepiece out of her pocket.

"I will see you in your rooms then."

"Aurora," he warned, contemplating simply putting her over his shoulders and running off with her.

"I must bathe," she said, gesturing to her stained and wet clothes.

"*I'll* bathe you," he offered, almost shivering at the idea of running a sponge all over her as she writhed in pleasure.

"That sounds lovely," she said in a strangled voice. "But I much prefer doing so myself. I promise I will come to you."

She would disappear, never to be seen again, and he would combust from lust. At this point, he didn't think he could even become aroused by a woman unless she was wearing frumpy wool and reeked of carbolic.

"You will take my carriage." He used his most authoritative tone, well aware of the fact that it had absolutely no effect on her. Miraculously, she relented.

"I will need an hour," she retorted with her hands on her hips. "You've agitated me, and I must clear my head."

"You were the one licking and biting my chest merely a minute earlier," he drawled, which was received with a nasty look.

"I was hungry," she huffed, but her lips were tipped up. Then she turned around and began to walk toward the door.

She was luminescent after sweating and sparring with him, and just then, he finally saw her for what she was. A diamond hiding in plain sight. A treasure no one had been smart enough to claim.

"One hour, Doctora," he called out as he chased her down the corridor. It seemed this would be the way things went with them. Aurora setting on a path and Apollo loping behind her in an attempt to keep up.

"One hour, Your Grace," she echoed over her shoulder, smoldering him with those brown eyes. Brown like melting chocolate, like a good café de mañana. Dark and strong, waking up his blood, making it roar.

"One hour," he echoed as he shut the door to his carriage. She nodded, squeezing his hand for a moment, before letting go.

No one could've told Apollo as he watched his conveyance drive into the wayward Parisian sunset with Aurora Montalban in tow, that by morning, the tightly held reins of his life would be irrevocably in her hands.

Twelve

Aurora did not intend to insinuate herself into Apollo's bed. It was true that she'd considered it since her talk with Virginia, but she had not arrived at his fighting club with the intention to do so. Once she had, it seemed undeniable, as though the two of them had been on a collision course from the first moment they'd set eyes on each other.

In truth, it did not need to be a complicated affair. It was simply a liminality, a threshold on their way to their next destinations. His to a bride and life among the aristocracy, hers… ensuring that as many women as possible had access to the medical care they needed.

But these were things to ponder at another time, tonight was for… Well, tonight was for herself.

Her face warmed as she remembered the way she'd been with Apollo earlier. The wanton manner in which she'd lapped at his skin, bitten him. She stared at the mirror in disbelief as she attempted to button up the bodice of the dress she'd decided to wear. It was one Manuela had forced her to buy on a shopping afternoon in Manhattan before they boarded the streamer to France. It was not nearly as scandalous as the pieces her friend had purchased, but it was certainly a departure from her work suits.

The material was some kind of opal-colored silk, it could be sage or light blue depending on the light. It was soft to the touch, and it complemented her figure. She had wide hips and a plump bottom, and she was not very tall. One of the cooks at her family's house used to call her periquita. Because she said she resembled the small birds with ample posteriors and short legs. She looked like a parakeet tonight in all this green.

"I should take this off," she muttered to herself, turning this way and that, her eyes on the little bit of lace that concealed the swell of her breasts. She might as well have *ravish me* scribbled on her forehead. She sighed at the clock when she saw the hour she'd asked for was almost over. Apollo would probably laugh at her when she arrived at his apartment in these clothes. What had possessed her to put this on?

She wished she had Luz and Manuela there, but if she did, they'd be driving her mad. Manuela would likely suggest she wear something even more provocative and Luz would tell her to wear whatever she liked, as long as she was honest with herself about the reasons.

"I'm wearing it because I want him to look at me with fire in his eyes." The person in the mirror looked terrified at that confession, but it was at least the truth. She'd enjoyed herself tonight. Loved seeing him spar. The thought of the way his body moved under the torchlight made her stomach flutter. He was such a fine man and for tonight he'd be hers.

She pinned up a curl and arranged her collar one more time. She'd even donned her white lace-up boots. An indulgence she'd been too self-conscious to wear, but this evening seemed the perfect occasion to finally put them on. It was the most time she'd spent on her appearance in years, but it felt good to do so. She found that the anticipation brought her a thrill.

As she reached for the doorknob to her rooms, she glanced at her Gladstone, the urge to grab for it was great, but she reached for her reticule instead. She didn't want to make excuses or pretend this was something other than what it was. She was a free woman, an independent one, and she was on her way to take a lover.

The idea put a smile on her face as she descended the stairs to the ground floor. Apollo's henchman was probably there already, she thought. She allowed herself to enjoy that too. Perhaps Virginia was right and this leisure idea had some merit to it.

"Aurora." She was so lost in her thoughts she almost tripped down the final step at the sound of her landlady's voice.

"Claudine." She smiled, trying to shrink into herself as the woman took in her very unusual attire.

"You look lovely." Claudine beamed as if she was witnessing a miracle. That only made Aurora more self-conscious about her clothes. "And very popular this evening." Claudine's eyes shone from excitement as she looked at the closed door to her small parlor. Had Apollo come to fetch her himself? Her heart hammered in her chest hard enough to put a dent in her sternum. "Three callers, Doctora," she exclaimed. "And handsome ones at that." Three callers? Had the man sent an entire retinue to make sure she got into the carriage?

She didn't like how much the prospect of his unchecked possessiveness appealed to her, and still a small part of her wished it was him waiting for her. That even if it set the tongues wagging, he'd come himself. But the Duke of Annan had a reputation to protect.

"Gentlemen callers?" The landlady nodded, then gestured toward the small private room next to Claudine's own rooms.

"I put them there," she said amiably, then winked. "I'm glad you're being more social."

Was her personal life truly so pitiful that even her landlady noticed she did nothing but work?

"Thank you," Aurora said, then decided she needed to know exactly what she was walking into.

"Is the Duke of Annan among the gentlemen?"

The question took Claudine aback, but her shock soon gave way to delighted approval. "You have been quite busy indeed." Her own excitement at the prospect of Apollo personally coming for her surprised Aurora. "They did not identify themselves, but all three are quite virile."

Three Jean-Louises was excessive, but Apollo didn't seem to do anything in moderation, at least when it came to her. And who was she kidding with this, the man's high-handedness pleased her to no end.

"Go," she nudged Aurora. "They've been waiting awhile." She thanked her and briskly made her way to the small room. An eruption of something giddy and unfamiliar spilling inside her as she did.

She couldn't quite remember a time when she'd felt like this. Excited without the fear that someone would snatch it away.

"I must be quite intimidating if it truly requires three of you to get me into a carriage," she said boisterously as she entered the room, those bubbles of giddiness turning to ice when she saw who was there waiting for her.

Her brothers.

The moment she saw them, she was assaulted with the dread that accompanied any interaction with her family since she could remember. The happy jitters from seconds earlier replaced with nauseating unease.

She'd never been close to her brothers. There was the difference in age. Octavio, the youngest, was almost fourteen years older than her. Sebastian and Ramón had been married and out of the house before she could walk.

Out of habit, she scanned their faces, looking for traces of herself. It was a game she'd played obsessively as a child. They were tall and lean, while she was shorter and considerably plumper. Their complexions fair, while hers was a deep brown. Her hair was a mass of tight brown curls, while theirs had delicately soft waves.

There was very little that gave them away as siblings, other than their father's nose. The flat bridge and slightly flared nostrils that revealed the Olmec and African blood running through Fernando Ramón Montalban's veins. As a child, she'd told herself it was simply that she didn't take after their mother. Later she'd learn that she'd been wrong about that, as she had been about so many other things.

"What are you doing here?" She directed the question at her oldest brother, Ramón James, who was always the leader among her three siblings. Her tone was bellicose, and as expected, he instantly bristled. The four of them had not been in a room together since that awful night thirteen years ago. The weight of those memories settled over her like a shroud, smothering the excitement from a minute ago.

She should've known this would happen. It occurred anytime she was foolish enough to think she was free.

"You look well, Aurorita." That came from the youngest of her brothers, Octavio Peter. He'd been the only one who'd ever shown any interest in her. He smiled at her warmly and took a step toward her, but Ramón stopped him.

"We're here because you've ignored all our letters for the past three months." Those were the first words out of Ramón's mouth. She pretended not to hear him and turned to Sebastian and Octavio, who stood on either side of him like sentinels. "And we find you here, in this—" he gestured at Claudine's lovingly decorated parlor as if it were a hovel "—this pauper's house. Will you ever tire of embarrassing us?"

That enraged her, but she knew showing her temper to Ramón would only spur him on.

"I like this 'pauper's house,'" she told him icily. "And might I point out this is what I can afford now that I no longer have access to my trust." None of them responded, but she could feel the disapproval as if it were a presence in the room. "I thought the three of you and the other Montalbans would be delighted to not see or hear from me." Her brothers flinched when she refused to call their parents Mama and Papa. But why would she call them that, when from the time she could remember they'd both pretended she didn't exist. "Is this the chair for the accused?" she asked, scowling at the lone chair directly across from theirs as they each took a seat. As expected, it seemed she was going to be on trial. "I'd rather stand."

"No one asked you to vanish yourself." Ramón always spoke to her in an exasperated tone, like her very existence was more than he could bear. It was how her mother spoke to her too, and Ramón was the apple of Catalina Wright de Montalban's eye. "Why must you always make everything so difficult?"

He'd always been like this, haughty and cold. It was only later, after she'd ruined any possibility for any kind of peace with her brothers or her parents, that she realized the reasons why.

"In which way have I been difficult?" she asked, becoming enraged despite herself. "I have stayed away like she wanted." Her voice broke slightly at the mention of the woman she'd believed to be her mother for the first fifteen years of her life. At that, her brothers all began to fidget with discomfort, even Ramón. "I have given up my trust. I have virtually disappeared from your life. Surely that must be good enough, even for them and for you?" She held her back straight, her head high. She would not cower or beg like she'd done that night. She would never do that for anyone, ever again.

"You were spending recklessly." She knew it was moot to explain it was for a worthy cause, because her brothers likely saw it all as a waste. "And we never asked you to disappear," Ramón claimed, but she held her hand up to stop him. She didn't want to hear this, what's more she didn't have to. When her fate had still been tangled with the purse strings he managed, Aurora had to stand for her brother's sermons, but she'd cut those months ago.

"You sent me away," she reminded him. "When I needed my family most, I was ripped from the home I knew and *you*—" she thrust an accusing finger at her brothers as she shook with fury "—*you* vanquished me and punished the only person who cared about me enough to help me." Octavio paled at her words, but if they'd made their way from Veracruz to Paris to bring her to heel, they had another think coming. "And now that I've stayed away, that I've given up what rightly belongs to me, in order to have control over my own life, you come here to scold me?" Thirteen years of swallowing her family's disdain was long enough. She was utterly fed up with Ramón's sanctimoniousness, with Octavio's and Sebastian's complicity.

"We tried to protect you," Ramón claimed, and for the first time, she heard something other than recrimination in his voice. But what they'd done hadn't felt like protection, it felt like a shunning.

She'd been fifteen and terrified. So scared of what she'd done. She'd gone to the only person who had ever been kind to her for help. Her aunt Gloria, her mother's sister. She'd told Gloria that she'd been a stupid, gullible fool by falling for Philip Carlyle's lies—the handsome Royal Navy officer who'd promised to marry her and allow her to attend university in Europe.

She'd been so easy to ensnare. A lonely, neglected wallflower, desperate for anyone to see her, she'd practically thrown herself at him. He'd found her watching one of her parents' parties from her pathetic little hiding spot on the patio, and he'd been so handsome in his uniform and so gentle. He hadn't laughed at her or pointed out how she looked nothing like her brothers. Instead, he'd been curious about the book she'd had in her hands. He'd even seemed interested in her answers.

For the first time in her life, she didn't have to long or yearn. She'd wanted someone's attention and had received it without having to beg or plead. Without having to kick or scream. For once, she wasn't invisible.

Philip returned the next week to see her. With her parents and her brothers gone to see friends in New York for a few months—and as usual leaving Aurora behind—that first visit turned into more. Then there were walks in the park with Gloria as chaperone and carriage rides that had all of Veracruz talking. Philip didn't seem to care she was half his age, a child really, and Aurora was smitten. Hopelessly infatuated with his blue eyes and blond curls.

Then the secret meetings began. The once-charming Philip became aggressive, demanding she demonstrate her affection for him in ways that made her scared and uncomfortable. But she wanted to please him so badly. She was so scared of becoming invisible to him too. So, she succumbed to his bullying and pleading that she prove her love for him. That if she did so then they could be together, always. She did and then there were more tests of her feelings for him, and secrets, so many secrets. Until the secrets could no longer be kept.

It was not long before the dashing and understanding Philip transformed into a sadistic, greedy monster. Those cerulean eyes she'd found so kind were suddenly hard and cruel. His claims of affection were replaced by insults and reminders that no one would ever want her after what she'd done. That she was tainted, damaged goods and should be grateful he was still willing to marry her. The promises to assist Aurora with her dream of becoming a physician were replaced with lectures on the place of women in the home and boastful diatribes about what he'd do with her dowry.

Aurora, determined to escape the awful fate that surely awaited her, asked for Gloria's help. It was her aunt, after all, who she'd always confided in, and Gloria helped her. She arranged a short trip to Jalisco two weeks before her parents were scheduled to return from New York to see someone who could help bring back Aurora's menses. Aurora and Gloria returned only to find her parents and brothers home a week early, and Philip with them. What happened in the hour that followed was something she still could barely ponder on, much less discuss.

Philip's threats to turn her into the authorities for violating the law. The woman she thought was her mother calling her a whore. The heartless indifference of her father, whose only concern was how to keep all of it quiet, how to get rid of Philip, of her, of anything that could taint his reputation. Her on her knees begging for forgiveness, pleading with her father not to send her away.

It all went ignored, and in a matter of days, they had her shipped off to a finishing school in Switzerland and Gloria vanished back to Puerto Plata. She remembered how terrified she'd been for the entire voyage. The staff when she arrived was unfriendly, the food strange, and it was so cold. She didn't think she would've survived if she hadn't met her Leonas.

"Are you going to refuse to speak with us, Aurora?" Ramón's demanding voice pulled her out of those terrible memories.

"What do you want from me?" she asked wearily.

"We want you to respond to our letters," Sebastian told her, speaking up for the first time. "We want you to be residing in a safe area of town."

She scowled at that, irritated once again. "You have no

right to opinions on my life, brother," she reminded him, not bothering to keep the anger from her voice. "None of you do, and besides, why do you care so much? Why not wash your hands of me like your mother did?" Ramón flinched like she'd slapped him.

"You're still our sister." She could hear the sentiment in Octavio's voice, but it was too little, too late.

"I'm your *half sister,*" she said pointedly, eliciting uncomfortable groans and evasive looks. "I'm the child our father never wanted and only tolerated so his mistress would remain under his roof." She used the same words their mother had used that night thirteen years earlier when Catalina demanded that Aurora and Gloria leave her house forever, while her own father watched in silence.

"That doesn't mean we don't care about your safety, your well-being," Sebastian insisted.

"What is this sudden concern with my safety you speak of, brother?" she asked in a louder voice than was appropriate. "I've been on my own since I was fifteen years old and not once have you ever concerned yourselves with my well-being."

"Carlyle is in Paris," Ramón finally said matter-of-factly, and now she was the one flinching in surprise. Not at the information, she'd learned months ago that the man had been seen on a steamer headed to France. What shocked her was her brothers were apparently concerned.

"I heard he's here." That seemed to infuriate the three of them.

"And you're walking around without a care in the world?" Octavio's outraged tone took her aback. Were they here because they feared she'd take up with that desgraciado again?

"Why wouldn't I? Philip Carlyle is free to do what he likes," she said with a feigned indifference she certainly did not feel. Her heart was beating so loudly, she could almost hear it. "Besides, I thought I was at fault for what happened. Wasn't that what you told me that night, brother?" She didn't like the bitterness in her voice. Didn't like that she still harbored so much anger. "That I was a disgrace, a puta?"

"No seas vulgar." Ramón had the nerve to sound offended. Octavio sent their oldest brother a hateful look.

"We've come to realize that we were wrong. Haven't we, brother?" Octavio demanded harshly, but Ramón only looked away.

"How did you hear that Philip Carlyle was in Paris?" she asked Ramón, certain that he would be the one to know. He was the Montalban who was always willing to get his hands dirty. Her brother's defiant expression was answer enough, but he loved expounding on his machinations.

"We've had someone keeping an eye on him periodically," he explained, which was not surprising. The man posed a real threat to the Montalban name. "He's kept to the northern coast of Venezuela and Colombia for most of the last ten years, but it seems he's acquired a minor title and has now relocated to Europe."

"The man is likely up to no good," Sebastian voiced, venomously. He'd probably use the title to swindle some poor woman. Philip had been a conniving comemierda as a low-ranked officer, she could only imagine the pomposity a title, even a low one, would entail. Which only made her think of Apollo, whose own position put him only below the Queen of England, and just this evening had been sparring in a Montmartre club. She was so angry at her brothers for stealing this night from her.

"We'll find out what he's up to and remind him to stay away," Octavio declared.

Ramón, who didn't like being interrupted, sent a nasty look, but for once the quieter brother had something to say.

"We didn't do enough back then, too worried with gossips and not how that bastard got his hands on you." Ramón, to his credit, blushed. "No matter what, you're our sister."

Now she was their sister.

"Don't lose sleep on my behalf, I've long made peace with the truth about my birth." They all paled then, probably recalling the way Aurora had been informed about her real mother, but she was certain none of them wanted a reminder of that. "Can one of you finish this long-winded tale?" she asked impatiently. "I'm late for an assignation, and the gentleman does not like to wait." She could've used another excuse, but it was much too satisfying to see her three holier than thou brothers splutter about her scandalous declaration.

"You have always been insolent," Ramón seethed, back to form. It seemed Aurora already had him at his limit.

"I'm the insolent one, am I?" she demanded, with as much derision as he'd used on her. "Why, because I won't beg you to allow me back into the bosom of the family I was always a second-class citizen in? Because I won't beg and plead with your mother to forgive me after she called my mother, her own sister, and me trash?"

"There's no reasoning with you sometimes, Aurora." Sebastian had the gall to sound exasperated, when they'd come to her home to make demands.

"She's always blamed us for what happened that night," Ramón added morosely, as if he was the injured party. "And all this pretending to want a profession only to end up as someone's mistress." His mouth twisted in an ugly sneer as he moved closer. "Just like her mother."

She didn't realize she'd raised her hand to slap him until the contact with this face made her palm ache. She'd never hit anyone, but the words were so vicious, so ugly. She stood there stunned, her hand throbbing and fighting back tears, not of pain, but shame and frustration.

"Shut your mouth, cabrón," Octavio seethed, but Ramón didn't say anything, just held a hand to his cheek, as she turned to leave.

"Please don't go, Aurorita," Octavio pleaded and despite herself, she stopped, because no matter how much vitriol she spewed at them, all she'd ever wanted was for her brothers to see her as more than an embarrassment. "We said we wouldn't do this," Octavio told the other two. "We agreed that, for once, we would behave like her brothers, not her enemies." Aurora frowned at her brother's words, at the way the other two flushed at his recriminations. "We were almost grown when she was born, and we allowed Mama to punish her for Father's sins." Octavio had always been most docile of her brothers, but his eyes blazed with fury as he spoke. And though it might be too little, too late, the words still healed something inside her.

It wouldn't have made a difference. She knew that. Her brothers all depended on the family's fortune. Worked for their father, lived on his land. They would not have risked their security for her. And their mother had to vent the anger of having to put up with her sister's and husband's betrayal on someone.

"What were we supposed to do?" Sebastian balked.

"We could've gone to that little table in the kitchen they made her take her meals at and sat with her." She'd forgotten about that, or at least forced herself not to remember. She never could understand why she never sat at her parents' table as a child. Just one of the many things she only understood when it was too late. "We could've made her feel like our true sister. We could've confronted our father, but we were all cowards."

"Who are you calling a coward, cabrón?" Ramón shouted, lunging for Octavio, who instantly threw a punch, then Sebastian entered the fray, and before she knew it, a chair was knocked over.

"Stop this." None of them heard her, focused on tearing each other apart as they were. When a flying fist almost knocked her over, she cried out, and that was when the door to the parlor burst open and a mightily pissed-off Duke of Annan prowled into the room with violence written all over his face.

Thirteen

"There better not be a scratch on her, or heads will roll."

Apollo did not make a habit of making bodily threats to strangers. But like every other rule he'd observed without issue for most of his life, it went out the window with merely one word from Aurora Montalban.

To his relief, she seemed unharmed, though she was attempting to get between two men who seemed determined to beat the tar out of each other.

"Step to the side, Fiera," he said as gently as he could, before he bodily lifted her away from two pairs of flying fists. There was a third man, but he was simply watching placidly from the corner he'd wedged himself into, while Aurora tried to help end the confrontation.

She'd dressed up for him, swapped the wool for lovely green silk and lace, and he couldn't even properly appreciate it or inform her of all the ways in which he'd be peeling it off her as soon as he got her alone, because he'd likely have to turn these three imbeciles into pulp.

"Ramón, Octavio, stop it," she cried out as Apollo struggled to pull the burlier one away. Her pleas seemed to work on the shorter of the two, and he threw his hands up, backing away.

"Sueltame cabrón," the one with his head in Apollo's grip demanded. He was not planning on letting go of anything until he found out what the hell he'd just walked into.

"I think not, pendejo," he growled as he lifted the larger fighter off the ground and smashed him against the wall of the parlor.

"Be careful," Aurora cried, while she checked the other one's bloody lip.

"Thank the lady for the fact that your nose isn't being smashed against this wall," he whispered in the man's ear. But he wasn't listening, his sole focus was to get out of Apollo's hold so he could go beat on his adversary. "Hold still or I'll make good on that promise to break your nose," he grunted at the imbecile, who continued to fight him. Apollo kept his attention pinned on Aurora, who looked back at him with pained brown eyes. When she'd left him merely an hour earlier, she'd been effervescent, and now she looked haunted. Someone would have to answer for that.

"Are you all right?" he asked, then sent a cursory look at the other two men, who were now in a heated conversation in the corner, their heads bent toward each other.

"I'm fine," she told him, with a trembling voice.

"Of course she's fine. We're her brothers," the bellicose one in his grip protested in a muffled voice.

So, these were the brothers who cut her off and had her living in a boardinghouse.

"You better watch your mouth when you speak to her," he threatened quietly as the man fidgeted. "I'm quite talented at breaking bones and I'd love an excuse to smash you against this wall a few times." The man's breaths were harsh, as Apollo squeezed him tighter.

"Let him go."

With one last shove, he cut the man lose.

"Is this your supposed assignation?" Ramón asked Aurora in a nasty tone after he'd hobbled to the farthest point from Apollo he could get to without actually leaving the room. But at that moment Apollo was much more interested in the question the man asked, and the pleading looks Doctora Montalban was sending him.

What exactly was happening here? A question that became even more pertinent a second later when Aurora walked over to Apollo, hooked her arm into his and defiantly kissed him on the cheek.

"This is Doctor Abelardo Bona," she said without once looking at Apollo. "He's..." The pause could only mean that Aurora was about to proffer one of her lies. But to his alarm, she chose to tell the truth. "He's my lover." As expected, the declaration sent Ramón into a rage, which Apollo interrupted by reminding him that his nose and arms were still very much at risk of suffering a fracture or two.

"Is this why you cut off all contact with the family?" the one who'd fought Ramón asked, but he noticed, not with the same vitriol.

"No, Octavio," she admitted, pushing herself against Apollo so closely that he could feel the tremors running through her. He wondered how she could speak without her teeth chattering. "I did that because it's what you all wanted." She said the words with such resignation, his heart broke for her.

"We never said that." Ramón's self-righteousness was beginning to grate.

"In the last thirteen years, I've only ever seen you or heard from you to receive reprimands. My financial dependence on our family was the only tie I had left, so now you never need to be bothered by me or my choices again." She spoke like she was hollow inside, and he wondered how much it took for her to do that. Apollo might have been discarded by his father, but he had his mother's family.

He wanted to take each of these men out back and make them feel the pain they'd inflicted on this woman who spent her life doing for others. He knew that she'd resent his desire to defend her honor. But he could not stand by and watch her bare her soul for these useless sinvergüenzas.

"Would you like to leave?" he whispered, and received a short nod and a shaky breath in answer. But he would not go until he spoke his piece.

"I'm taking her away from here now," he told the three men, who reacted as expected with bluster and protests. "But I'd like you to know that your sister lied to you," he told them, and Aurora instantly froze next to him.

Ramón—who Apollo truly would love to trounce—emitted a triumphant "I knew it."

"I'm not only her lover but hope she also considers me her friend—a title I would value greatly."

"You don't have to do this," Aurora whispered, but he slid his hand over hers and held it tight.

"And I'm not a doctor," he informed the men. "I would never have the discipline or the intelligence that requires." He turned to grin at Aurora, who was staring at him with a shocked expression. "I'm merely a duke, after all."

"What?" The one she'd called Octavio spluttered, but Apollo was not done yet.

"I have seen your sister work," he said to them, incensed at their disrespect of this woman. None of them—Apollo included—was fit to kiss her feet. "I have seen the lengths she'll go to in order to make sure her patients receive what they need. That's where all the money you cut her from went." They looked embarrassed, and it only made his desire to throttle them that much more intense. "*You* should all be praising and supporting her, but instead you shame and punish her."

"You have no idea what she's done," Ramón declared, in an aggrieved tone, which made Aurora flinch.

"I know enough," Apollo told the man, infusing his voice with a hint of violence he hoped the Montalban brothers heeded. "But what I do know, and I'd like for you all to bear in mind, is that I'm not a very nice man." Sebastian paled at the unvarnished threat while the other brothers whipped their heads in unison toward their sister.

"You should know who you are threatening, sir." Ramón was in dire need of a fist in the mouth and Apollo was very close to obliging.

"Your Grace," Apollo corrected him, with an arrogance he rarely exercised when discussing his title. But the reminder did its work, all three men backed off instantly. Aurora seemed too stunned to react, and he decided he could flex this particular muscle a bit more. "And in case I was not clear enough earlier, I'd caution you in how you approach Doctora Montalban in the future." He bared his teeth then, and Octavio was now pressed so tightly to the wall he could've been a portrait. "Know that nothing would bring me more pleasure than to abuse a considerable amount of my power in thoroughly humbling the three of you." Only then did he turn to Aurora, who, as expected, seemed quite unhappy with his speech. "¿Nos vamos, Fiera?" he whispered.

"Yes." He'd never heard her voice sound so small. It made him fucking furious. He escorted her out without sparing another look at the three Montalban brothers. When they stepped out into the foyer, they found her landlady, clearly concerned about the shouting.

"The gentlemen will need a fiacre," he told the older

woman, pulling a few francs from his pocket. "I'm escorting Doctora Montalban to dinner."

The woman sent a forbidding look to the door of her parlor. "You take care of her," the woman said, kindly. "I will deal with them, Your Grace," she assured him, before walking in the direction of the Montalban brothers. Aurora didn't utter a word as they left the building, or as they took the steps down to the sidewalk. But the moment they reached the carriage, she turned to him with that peevish expression he was now quite familiar with.

"You don't need to be my champion, Your Grace," she told him with a petulant little sniff. "I have no desire for a protector." A month ago, a week ago, he'd have taken offense to this. He'd have turned on his heel, gotten in his carriage and fumed all the way home about Aurora Montalban's rudeness. But he knew what this was—this was Aurora wounded. Desperate to be alone so she could tend to her emotional injuries. Like she'd probably been left to do all her life, if those miserable excuses for men were anything to go by.

"I'm not leaving you here to be scolded by those pendejos, and if I have to physically put you in my carriage, I will do so." He had every intention of carrying it out, and she must have either been too tired to fight him or having a spurt of acquiescence, because she only sighed and emitted a mildly cantankerous "Fine."

"As if they'd dare to even look at me after all those threats." With a huff, she stepped up to the carriage, glaring at the footman by the door, who wisely moved aside as if telling Apollo "you deal with her."

"I can climb the damned steps, Annan," she protested, as he attempted in vain to assist her up. He bit back a laugh, because she was truly the most contrary human being on earth.

"Your legs are very short," he teased her, which resulted in him being favored with the same glare the footman had received.

"And you're an oversized cabrón, but you don't hear me pointing that out," she retorted, settling herself in the settee while offering a look that would've made a lesser man shrivel. But Apollo was becoming more and more adept in defending himself against Aurora Montalban's arsenal.

"It is truly astounding how sweet natured you are," he said insincerely, which earned him a rueful smile. Once he was settled next to her, the carriage began moving onto the street.

He frowned, watching her profile as she looked out the window at her current residence with a rueful expression.

Once the ride began, she continued to look out the window. She was deep in her thoughts, while he was close to bursting with questions. He could only imagine what it did to someone as proud as her to have a witness for her family's treatment of her. Aurora Montalban had never given him the indication she would share any details about her life she didn't want him to know. But surely by now she had to at least have some degree of confidence that he would not violate her trust.

"Are the three of them always such unrepentant comemierdas?" he asked and was glad to see a hint of a smile tip up her mouth. He'd only become someone's brother in the past year. But even with his cousins, who were much younger and quite spoiled, he'd never behaved like those three pendejos.

She pressed the back of her head to the plush headrest and turned those tired brown eyes in his direction.

"Ramón is the one who usually acts like an ass." She pursed her mouth, then closed her eyes as if the mere thought of her brothers robbed her of every ounce of energy. "Octavio's kinder and Sebastian does whatever keeps his allowance coming on a monthly basis and our father covering his gambling debts."

He made a sound of disgust and had to force himself to keep quiet.

"Did they force you to move here?" It was not so dark inside the conveyance he couldn't see the defiant look she was sending him.

"Why are you so interested in my life, Apollo? Is being a duke so boring?" She twisted her body so that she was facing him. This was bluster, she was embarrassed and hurt—with reason—and he was the only one here. She probably wanted him to respond in kind, get angry at her. He knew those tricks. He'd used them quite effectively for most of his life. You made everyone around you furious and they never noticed you were hollow inside. You pretended to sneer at everyone, and they missed the howl of that discarded creature inside you.

"I thought friends shared details about their lives with each other."

"Friends," she huffed, like the word itself was absurd. "Men have only ever wanted to know about my life so they could control it."

"Well, even if you don't consider me a friend, I think of you as one of mine." It was true that he'd never concerned himself with what his friends chose to do with their evenings or when they ate. He'd certainly never threatened any of his friends' relatives with bodily harm, but that was neither here nor there.

"I don't want to talk about my brothers." She was fuming, her nose turned up at him, and he wanted to take her mouth until she melted into his arms. He wanted to breathe in all that righteous fury until he was on fire from the inside too. Incandescent with conviction like the woman sitting in the carriage with him.

"What would you like to talk about?"

"Let's not talk about anything at all," she retorted with enough vitriol to strip the paint off the carriage. "I'm tired of talking to men, Apollo. Tired of telling them what I want, what I think, what I believe, and being ignored."

"I'm not like them, Aurora," he said, and the words sounded useless, even to him. "I respect you." The pitying look she gave him was far worse than anger. This woman's eyes seemed to hold an entire lifetime of dismissals and slights, and for all his power, his title, there was nothing he could do to make it better. Even for dukes, sometimes all there was to do was say, "I'm sorry." "I wish I could make it better," he whispered into the space between them. They were so close he could see the flutter in her jaw at his words.

She was still not looking at him, but he heard a long shuddering breath escape her.

"How much did you hear?"

She held herself tightly as she asked the question, which told him he hadn't heard nearly as much as she thought he had. "By the time I got to the door, your brothers were shouting at each other."

"Hmm." He couldn't tell if it was acknowledgment, relief or surprise in that sound. But it was all he obtained from her for a long stretch, then finally she turned back to look at him. "They're only my half brothers." She seemed much younger than her brothers and physically there was not much resemblance. But that wasn't uncommon in the part of the world he was from. In the Caribbean, five siblings could have five different skin tones, and she'd said her mother was from Hispaniola.

"Did your father remarry?" he asked cautiously. A fortune like the one her family had could generate a lot of animosity between the children of the first wife and those of the second.

"No," she said with a shake of her head. He thought that would be the end of it, but then she spoke again. Her spine was like a ramrod as she stared straight ahead, still avoiding his gaze. "I'm the by-blow, you see." She informed him of this with such grace, such dignity, in that moment he could almost see himself entering a ballroom with her as his duchess. If the mere suggestion of such a thing wouldn't send her running, he would've said it. "I'm the dirty secret my father forced his wife to endure."

The man had fathered a child and had her living under his roof. His wife, in turn, punished the innocent child for the man's betrayal. Aurora's father needed horsewhipping.

"I assume it was not your father who paid for that transgression," he said, helpless to conceal the anger in his voice.

She seemed surprised at his comment and once again closed her eyes. They were expressive, those chocolate brown eyes, and said too much. No wonder she hid them from him when she needed to gather herself.

There was an emotional isolation that came from being unwanted. The desolation of knowing the person who gave you life simply did not care much about your existence. Apollo's anger at his father's abandonment, at his treachery, had fueled his thirst for revenge. Only to discover, after he'd gotten it, that the hole inside him was not made any smaller. Not his position, the power, the title. The family he'd gained in Scotland. His sisters and nieces and nephews, a brother who had stood by him, even when it meant losing a dukedom. None of it quite made up for the fact that his father's greatest wish had been for Apollo never to survive infancy.

Learning that Aurora had lived with a similar wound was like a physical blow. Perhaps that was what drew them to each other.

"My mother, Gloria, was his wife's younger sister." When she opened her eyes, her gaze was distant. As if she'd retreated into a place where she could say these things and not ache from them. "She lived with us, and I never knew." Apollo cursed under his breath and reached for her hand, which to his astonishment, she let him take.

"Was she good to you, your real mother?" he asked, suddenly very much in need of knowing if at least one person in her childhood had made her feel wanted.

She was quiet for so long he didn't think she'd answer, and then she let out a shaky breath. "My mother loved me in her own way, but I think she loved the idea of being the one my father couldn't give up even more. He tolerated me if he got to keep her."

"What happened to her?"

She inhaled sharply at the question and once again looked away. "She went back to Hispaniola, she passed away while I was here studying medicine. I wasn't told until much later." He didn't think he could get angrier tonight, but the rage surged in him like a cresting wave.

"We both deserved better fathers," he bit out into the quiet of the carriage.

"And our mothers deserved better too."

"They did." He was debating how likely she was to attack if he attempted to bring her closer, when the universe conspired in his favor and jolted the carriage, sending her right into his arms.

He pulled her to him and sat her across his lap. She made a little gurgling sound of surprise, which spurred another one of those waves of tenderness and lust in him.

"What are you doing?" she grumbled as he adjusted her lush bottom on his hardening cock. Not even the emotional distress of the past fifteen minutes was enough to douse his hunger for her.

"I'm holding you, Fiera." He wrapped his arms around her and pressed a kiss to her cheek. "Let me." He expected her to fight him, but instead, the most astonishing thing happened.

She stayed and laid her head on his shoulder. Apollo knew this was likely more exhaustion and weariness than any kind of interest in being comforted by him, but he was not going to question it. All he wanted was to get back the playful, lusty Aurora from that afternoon.

"I don't want to talk about this anymore," she told him, pressing her nose to his neck. He made a sound of agreement and ghosted his lips over her temple. "I thought you'd be trying to ravish me by now." He wanted to. There was nothing he'd love more than to slide both hands up her thighs and tear through whatever linen impediments she'd donned under her pretty skirt.

He'd have her just like that with that luscious rump bouncing on his cock while they drove through the streets of Paris.

He needed to stop. This was not the time.

"I don't want anyone else with us in the room when I finally have you."

When she looked at him with furrowed brows, he decided to risk another confession. "That night you came to me was to prove something to yourself, or to someone, and I'd like our next time to be different, to be only ours." When she fidgeted, he held her tight and made the soothing sounds he remembered his tia making when his cousins were babies.

"Why does that matter?" She didn't deny it and he wondered if perhaps he was breaking through some of those carefully constructed walls of hers.

"Because you walked out of that encounter with your brothers with a wound, and I wanted to tend to that first." He didn't want her to let him touch her out of need for a distraction or spite. He wanted her lusty and wanton, he wanted the promise he'd seen in her eyes at the club.

"If you don't want me anymore," she began, attempting to

slide off his lap, but he held her there. She protested, but in the end she stayed.

"I assure you, my dear, a thorough ravishment is very much in the cards the moment I have you behind closed doors." He wrapped his fingers at the base of her neck and slid them down the lovely pearl buttons on her bodice. "Was this for me?" he asked, grazing his teeth on that spot on her neck that made her breathe faster. She scoffed, then seared him with those blazing chocolate eyes, and just like that, the ember that always seemed to glow when he was with her sparked into a flame.

"I dress for myself," she informed him. "And I do not find your arrogance charming." She said it with such a mischievous glint in her eye he could not resist testing that theory. He pressed up just enough for her to feel the effect she had on him. He was rewarded with the most delectable little moan.

"My charm is not exactly one of the attributes I'm interested in putting forward at the moment."

That provoked a lusty sound and wiggle of that decadent derriere, which had him gasping in seconds. Just when he was reconsidering his stance on carriage ravishments, the damned thing came to a stop.

"We're here," he groaned, keeping his hands firmly on her hips for one more second before she bolted off his lap.

"Will I receive my other lesson this evening, or have I worn you out, Your Grace?" The question seemed to come from a place he had not been allowed to witness before. Her eyes crinkled and she shook her head like she scarcely believed her own nerve, and he sunk an inch deeper into the murky waters of Aurora Montalban.

"Not only am I still up to the task, Fiera," he told her, right before the footman opened the carriage door. "But I intend to put that deliciously compact body of yours through its paces until neither of us can stand."

Fourteen

When she was a child, Aurora's mother—or the woman she thought was her mother—kept chocolates wrapped in pretty-colored paper in a glass bowl in the parlor, right next to her silver tea set. They looked like round jewels, so dainty and colorful. She was only allowed to have one when she was very good, which did not occur very often. On the rare days when she was allowed to play inside the house, she'd take them all out of the bowl and count them. She'd make shapes with them, a circle, a square.

She'd stand there, her mouth flooded with saliva and her hands full of the candy she could not eat. She could see it, smell it, touch it even, but she could not have it. Once, when she was about ten, her mother found her and furiously swept all the candy back into the bowl, then took it outside to the porch and left it there to melt in the Veracruz sun. Aurora watched in horrified disbelief for hours, tears streaming down her face at the waste, until her Tia Gloria coaxed her back inside with the promise of a dulcito de coco she'd made.

So much of her life was like those chocolates. A family she could see, hear, touch, but never quite belong to. Even her stint at finishing school felt like the final act in a farce. The bastard daughter who'd ruined herself sent to be trained as the lady she could never become. Never quite enough to reach for the things she yearned for.

Apollo was the latest of those things that she wanted but could never really have. But as she walked into his rooms, which still held a hint of the carbolic she'd used here days ago, she thought at least this time the punishment might be worth it.

She was probably not in the right state of mind for sexual lessons with the aristocratic equivalent of a werewolf. Her brothers' presence in Paris would surely be the source of future headaches. Then there was Philip Carlyle. For the past few months, she'd managed to put his existence out of her mind. She'd been busy with the clinic and told herself he could be anywhere in Europe. Now she was faced with the unavoidable reality of his presence in the city she'd begun to think of as a sanctuary and she did not like it.

"You are very deep in your thoughts, Doctora." Apollo's deep, raspy voice brought her out of her unpleasant musings and forced her to focus instead on her ever-growing obsession with the Duke of Annan's mouth.

She pressed her back to the wall, soothed by its solidness, lying to herself that it might be enough to keep her bearings. That somehow she might not fall.

"I was—" she began, then swallowed the sound that almost erupted out of her when he caged her in with his arms and body, making her achingly aware of her own.

She never gave much thought to her own body, not in any intimate manner. She appreciated it, of course. She marveled every day at the miraculously complicated system that was the human body. But who paused to think about the way their left arm felt right after the pads of a finger brushed it, or how their right ear could throb for hours after a mere graze of teeth?

She did, every time Apollo César Sinclair Robles touched

her. Every inch of her became a potential blaring siren of her hunger.

"I love seeing your hair down." When he spoke to her like this, low and hot, something like a tourniquet tightened inside her. Every word mounting the pressure, making her desperate for release.

"It's quite unmanageable when it's loose," she told him nervously as his finger traced her hairline from her temple, up to her forehead and to the other side. How could that simple touch have such an incendiary effect?

He raised a sardonic eyebrow, then tugged gently on a hairpin.

"You must know by now I enjoy you most when you're unmanageable." Her breath hitched and something like a squeak escaped her lips as he unraveled her hair pin by pin. "But you are a luxury, Fiera," he told her with an appreciative grunt as he ran his fingers through the mass of her hair. *Luxurious* was not anything that had ever been uttered when it came to her mass of curls. It was too thick, her coils could be temperamental in humid climates and was utterly uncontrollable in the summer. But one would not know it from the way Apollo was handling it right then.

"Coconut?" he asked, after pressing his nose to it.

"Yes, I brush it with the oil." It was the only way to get it to behave long enough to get it into some kind of plait. Once he'd arranged it over her shoulders, he stepped back and looked at her for so long her eye began to twitch.

"Are you taking me to bed or doing my hair, Your Grace?" she asked, with a bit more bite than warranted. But unlike every other man in her life, Apollo liked her bouts of insolence.

"Are you becoming impatient for my bed, Fiera?" he asked, with a slightly predatory growl as he slid a hand over her chest.

Her nipples tightened at the sensation, and her belly swooped with want.

"*Bored* would be the word I would use," she retorted, or at least tried to, but her voice cracked slightly when his thumb began circling one of her nipples.

"Boring you, am I?" he asked with an evil grin, as he took her wrists and pinned them over her head. "Would you like to hear what my plans are for you?" He sucked on the skin below her ear, which had a loosening effect on her joints. "Or would that be too tiresome?" It was hard to keep track of what he said, while he used his teeth on her. The sting of them sent a flash of heat through her that had her squeezing her thighs together if only to ease the ache inside.

"Perhaps a brief summary," she croaked as he dropped one of his hands to reach for the buttons of her bodice. The other, still wrapped tightly around her wrists, kept her in place. She was certain that if she asked, he'd let go, but she liked this game, she liked it very much.

"I've been dreaming about your breasts for months now, Fiera," he told her, before he plucked the first button. "May I?"

She nodded and he made quick work of it. Within seconds, the bodice was pushed down to her waist.

"No stays," he said with appreciation as he cupped a breast with each hand, before leaning down to kiss them over the sheer linen of her undergarments.

"You know I don't use corsets," she told him, lowering her gaze to watch what he was doing. His lips pressed up against a dark brown nipple, a lazy touch she felt to her very core. "I joined the Rational Dress Society when I was in Philadelphia," she mumbled, if only to try to keep her wits about her. "The society objects to the use of devices that could permanently damage women's organs." His errant curls were covering one eye, but she could still see a pink tongue laving each areola, while his thumbs played and flicked. It was quite an ordeal to maintain a conversation this way.

"I approve, such quick access," he complimented while he availed himself of more of her flesh with hands and mouth.

"It's not for men's convenience," she rebuked, though it might have gotten lost in her moans of pleasure. He did the wickedest things with his tongue. "I am not..." She lost the thread of the conversation when he pinched the underside of her breast.

"You are lush," he said, opening his mouth wide and sucking in a breast.

"Oh Dios," she sighed as fire licked inside her. He made love to her breasts, one then the other he worked with his mouth. As he whispered how lovely her skin was, the perfect brown, like milk and chocolate. That she tasted just as sweet.

"Do you like when I use my tongue on you?" he asked, as his lips drifted upward, leaving a wet trail along her collarbone, and up to her neck. "Hmm?" She shook her head and moaned as he pulled on her skin. "I can't wait to have my tongue in your sweet heat again."

"Apollo," she cried out, as he raked his teeth along her jaw.

"It's so hot and tight." Her limbs were heavy, and her body pulsed, throbbed with need. "Will you let me in, Fiera? Make room for me inside you?"

She nodded, unable to deny, even for a second, what they both knew she wanted.

"Stop teasing me," she groaned as he pecked at her, when she needed to be devoured.

"Tell me what you want, Fiera," he said in that gravelly, bone-melting voice of his.

What did she want?

She wanted everything, to be debauched, unraveled, taken roughly. She wanted to feel to her bones how badly he wanted her. She wanted her body to ache for days after. She didn't know if she could ask for any of it. But she was feeling bold enough to try.

She dropped one of the hands he'd placed above her head and slid it between them until she found what she'd been looking for. The Duke of Annan sucked in his breath as she tightened her grip and then she began a slow stroke, which rewarded her with a low, dangerous growl. And, oh yes, she liked this.

"Fiera," he whispered with just a hint of warning in his voice.

"Your Grace," she responded innocently, tightening her hold on him, while he looked at her through hooded eyes. "You asked me to tell you what I wanted. I've always been more of a tactile learner." She bit her lip and let her hand drift to his testicles.

"You think you can take me, Doctora?" His hips rocked into her touch, and his voice, raspy, deep, like he was already inside her, flooded her with heat. His mouth hovered over hers as he spoke, his lips grazing hers. It made her teeth ache with want. "Will you part your thighs for me and let me slide deep inside you?" She was humming, her throat making a sound she'd never heard, as he nipped at her. Her lips, her jaw. Sharp, rough kisses that made her tremble.

"Mmm," she moaned, instantly lost, but she never let go of him. Her hands exploring that part of him. So hard, so big she could scarcely believe it would all fit inside her. "This is intimidating, Your Grace." She circled her fingers around the head, and he growled again. Without warning, he scooped up her bottom and lifted her off the ground.

"What are you doing?" she squealed, letting her arms circle his neck as he carried her across the small space.

"I'm taking you to my bed, where I will fuck all this picardía out of you." He didn't sound too upset about her so-called naughtiness.

"Will you behave now?" he demanded when he walked into the bedroom.

"What would be the fun in that?" she asked, tightening her legs around his waist and leaning in to bite his earlobe.

His sensual laugh moved like a line of fire inside her.

She felt weightless in his arms. It was a rare indulgence to cling to such power like this. She could not make herself let go.

"Fiera," he whispered as he settled her on the bed. She was bare from the waist up, but he was yet to fully remove her skirts or her boots. "Finally, you're wearing something convenient for a quick tryst," he told her, before tugging the thing the rest of the way off.

"I don't make a habit of trysting," she retorted, lifting her feet for him.

"No," he told her, kissing a spot on her calf. "These are sinful. I want to leave them on." He gripped her calves and sank his teeth into her skin. "Como me gustas, mujer," he whispered, before reaching for her sex. He cupped her with one hand, tugged on her curls. "May I have this tonight?" he asked, as he tickled the seam of her with a finger. She lifted her knees and spread herself shamelessly for him.

"I will let you take it," she countered, parting her legs even further. She closed her eyes and pushed up her breasts for him. Imagined herself as a seductress, luring this man with her attributes.

She didn't believe in doing things by halves. If she was going to do this with him, she would do it without any reservations. Her encounter with her brothers had been crushing and now Apollo knew all about her. Knew just how inadequate she was for him, but that didn't mean she could not have him. That she would not take what she could and deal with the consequences later.

He ran his hands over her legs, from her ankles all the way up to the juncture that held her neediest place. She was so wet for him, she wished she were brave enough to tell him. "I'm going to lick every inch of you until you're screaming for my cock." If he knew how close she was to that already.

"I'm keeping a tally of all your promises, Your Grace," she teased. "I expect you to deliver."

He was still fully dressed, and she naked and wanton but for her boots.

"Spread your hair on the pillow," he said as he reached for that hot, aching place. She did as he asked and heard his breath catch as her curls tumbled on his sheets.

"Que delicia eres tu, Aurora." Her stomach tightened and her breath caught in her throat at the way he looked at her. Like he'd finally found his Daphne. His gaze on her was ardent, searing his desire onto her skin. His eyes didn't drift from her as he touched her. As if he wanted to see every reaction on her face. It was intoxicating.

"Abre tus piernas, Bella." It was not a request, and she parted even farther for him, her arms thrown over her head as his fingers traced her outer labia. "Resbaloza, mi leona." She moaned in her throat and pushed her bottom into the mattress as his fingers mingled with her wetness. She *was* slippery, ripe, weeping for him, for his touch.

"Apollo," she gasped when he slid the tip of his index between her folds and flicked it. "Don't," she cried as he snatched his hand away, then almost swooned when he stuck the finger he'd had inside her in his mouth and licked it.

The sound he made. She had to look away.

"Going to make many meals out of you." The promise ran up her spine like an electric current. She might not survive this. "Come here," he ordered. She clenched her teeth to keep from demanding he bring his hands back.

"Why should I?" she asked, peevish, while he licked his lips like the devil himself. "You don't do what I ask."

"Because I'd like very much for you to bring that sweet cunt—" he pointed at the edge of the bed "—here. So I can taste it." The things he said, they made her burn. How would she leave this apartment again, and behave normally after this?

She sat up, then crawled on her hands and knees to him, their eyes locked. He took her chin in his hand and lowered his head for a kiss. His tongue swept into her mouth and she whimpered as she tasted herself. He touched her as they kissed, his hand skating down her spine, to her nalgas. He kneaded, tapped, pinched until she was vibrating on the bed. Then he pulled away, leaving her gasping for breath.

"Undress me." His voice was stern, his eyes hard, but this game was thrilling.

"And if I don't?" she challenged, her hands behind her back. He bent his head and bit down on a nipple.

"Then I'll just add that to the tally you racked up when you pointed a pistol at me earlier this evening, Fiera." He made his point by reaching down again and swatting her behind with his open palm. He soothed away the sting, rubbing circles where his hand had made contact.

"That was in self-defense," she protested, even as she arched her nalgas for another pet.

"My shirt, Fiera," he reminded her, and with a huff, she began unbuttoning. All the while, he played with her body. He flicked her earlobe with his hot tongue while he entered her with two fingers. Pushing them in and out while she made those animal, keening sounds he could so expertly coax out of her. "I've been dying to know how it feels inside you," he told her with a low growl that made her hands slip from his shirt. "Going to take you slow, sheathe my cock to the hilt, stay inside, fill you up." That was when she ripped his shirt.

"Sorry," she whimpered, looking at the small tear in the sleeve, but he seemed oblivious to the damage to his clothing.

"Keep going, sweetheart, I'm getting impatient." He made his point by digging his fingers into the flesh of her bottom, where one of his hands was still plastered. "I'll slide right in," he told her. "Pin your hands over your head, spread you open and take you hard."

"Ah," she gasped, before she dug her own teeth into the pectoral muscle she'd just bared. He stiffened for a moment, then cupped the back of her head in encouragement. She sucked on his skin, grazing the nipple with her teeth. Licking the trench between the muscles of his stomach while he told her all the ways he'd have her that night.

"Asi me gusta, Fiera," he whispered in her ear as she used her teeth on him. Her nails leaving red tracks down his chest.

There was no precedent in her life for this. Hell, the few times she'd lain with Philip, he'd scold her simply for trying to kiss him. Nothing could be more distant from her previous experience than this carnal, heady sexual encounter where there were no rules but the ones they made together.

"Eager for me, Your Grace?" she asked, looking at him from lidded eyes, giving him her best impression of a lusty vixen, except that with Apollo, it didn't feel like an impression. He gazed at her with a fire that made her feel like the object of his every desire. The lustiest, most desirable woman in all of Paris.

She stroked him over his trousers, and he was hard as steel under her fingers. For her.

"You know what I thought that night at Le Bureau?" he asked, as he touched her in dark, needy places. She shook her head and arched into his touch. "I wanted to bend you over that table and have you right on that tray of cream puffs," he

said, before he took her mouth. "You were so damned contrary," he told her between kisses in that mixture of exasperation and delight he used sometimes when he spoke about her.
Like she was the most enchanting riddle.

"You annoyed me," she shot back cheekily, gripping the hair
at the nape of his neck, to make his kiss go deeper. He slithered
his tongue along her as his hands roamed her body. Blindly
she undid the placket of his pants, pushing them down with
his undergarments until he was, finally, as naked as she was.

She pulled back to admire him in the low light of his room.
And he was magnificent.

Nothing she could've imagined compared to this man in
the nude. The breadth and width of that chest, the sculpted
muscle of his stomach. It was like one of those Roman statues
at the Louvre, except this was no cold, pale marble, this body
was golden brown and pulsed with life.

There was no self-consciousness to Apollo's nudity. He
seemed as comfortable in his clothes as out of them, and she
could see why. While other men used their smart suits as armor,
Apollo's body *was* a weapon of war.

"On the bed," he ordered with another swat to her rump.
"On your back, hands over your head." For once, she took her
orders obediently. Her sex throbbed as she lay there supinely
while he stood over her. "Eyes on me, Doctora," he instructed.
And how could she look away? The man was beauty in motion.

She was still wearing her boots and he seemed particularly
drawn to them. He slid a hand over the laces, then up her legs,
stroking up, up, up until he was at her groin, which pulsed
for him. But to her disappointment, he didn't linger there for
long and glided his warm palms up to her belly, her breasts,
her shoulders and her arms to her wrists. He gripped them in
one hand again and sank his head to one breast and played with
the nipple. Tortured it with his teeth, suckling, nipping until

she was wild with need. Bucking into the sting mingled with pleasure. Every inch of her skin felt alive, buzzing as if she'd run through lightning.

"I want to slide my cock right here." He placed a palm between her breasts, making her gasp. Her hard nipples tingled with anticipation at the thought, imagining herself holding them together as his shaft slid in and out.

She couldn't believe she was aroused by such an act. But after the night she'd had, she didn't think there could be a better way to wipe the slate clean than letting Apollo take control and make her body feel as good as he had the last time.

"I have a hard time deciding where to start," he said, raking his burning gaze over her body. "Do you want my mouth, Fiera?" he asked her, kneeling between her legs. "Or do you want my cock?"

She wanted both. "Why don't you decide?"

"Because I want you to tell me what you want from me." So later she couldn't pretend this had all been a fluke. If she demanded, if she participated, she couldn't deny what she'd wanted.

"I want you to make me climax." It was not a specific request, but it was all she could manage with him hovering over her like a lusty god and her body close to going up in flames.

"But how, is the question, Fiera," he said, dropping his hands on either side of her head and pressing his mouth to her neck. "Do you want me to kiss your breasts?" he asked, before doing that very thing. "Or do you want me to lick your sex? Make it weep on my tongue?" He followed up the question by fluttering his tongue on her nipple, just like he'd done to her sex before.

"Yes," she gasped when he licked a path between her breasts to her navel.

"Yes, you want my mouth on your cunt?" he insisted. She

closed her eyes and moaned as his lips brushed the top of her mons. "Because that's what I want. I want to spread you open." His hands disappeared from where they bracketed her head and then they were on the back of her thighs, doing what he'd just said. He pushed her knees up, then parted her with a firm tug.

She thought she could feel her heartbeat between her legs. She wondered if he could too. "How does this feel?" he asked as his fingers flicked her clitoris.

She swallowed a desperate cry before mumbling something close enough to "Good."

He slid a finger inside her and her muscles spasmed around it. His chest rumbled with appreciation, and the praise made her smile. She never knew what to say or do when people complimented her work, her skills, her resolve, but Apollo's appreciation of her body, somehow felt right.

"I like it when you clench on my fingers," he told her, his gaze fixed on whatever he was doing between her legs. "You're so slippery and hot, and then you lock around me so tight," he groaned, like it was happening right then.

"Don't tease me," she moaned, desperate for him. So close to begging.

"Does this feel like teasing?" he asked, right before he lowered his head and licked along her seam. "You're so sweet," he grunted, lapping her labia with quick, rough strokes.

Something detonated inside her at the caress, his hands keeping her in place as his mouth ate at her. He pressed soft kisses right to the core of her one second, and the next, his teeth were on her, making her scream. Her back arched and she held to the bedpost. She imagined herself as a bow pulled tight before release. Pleasure radiated inside her, like tiny explosions all over her body.

"Apollo," she moaned, as he kept her open for his mouth.

She could hear her harsh breaths in the quiet of the room, her increasingly desperate sounds.

His shoulders moved up and down, only the back of his head and his messy dark curls visible between her legs. She felt when he flattened his tongue on her clitoris and began moving it up and down, then side to side, the pressure building and building as she pulled hard on the metal bars. He breathed as he worked on her so exquisitely, his mouth latched to her sex. She was so close her legs tingled, the tightness in her groin churned, ready to burst, and then he pulled away.

"No, por favor," she sobbed with frustration, tugging hard on his mess of curls.

"I'm not ready to make you come yet," he told her and moved up to kiss her. She could taste herself on him. His hands were in her hair, his body pressed to her. "You're the most delicious thing I've ever tasted." She knew it wasn't true. A man like this had any woman he wanted, but she appreciated his effort to make her feel this desirable. He pulled away to look at her, and what she saw in his eyes made her heart thump almost painfully.

"I need you," she demanded, even though she hardly knew what she meant by that. But *he* seemed to and this time she let herself trust that he would take care of her.

Fifteen

Apollo had already been half out of his head by the time they reached the bedroom, but seeing her like this, so free and lost in his touch, was making it too easy to forget this was a woman he could not keep. Not after what he'd learned about her past. He knew he could not be another man to hide her, to make her feel like she didn't fit in his life. But he didn't want to think of any of that tonight. Her pleasure was all that mattered in this moment.

He lifted her legs until those white boots were up on his chest and held them up with one hand, then pushed back so her pink, slick sex was on full display for him.

"Beautiful," he told her, running a thumb over her slippery folds. It was a secret pleasure to know that this was only his. That when she needed to be touched, to be fucked, it was his hands she wanted. "So ready for my cock, Fiera." She nodded in agreement, and he rewarded her with a pinch. She bucked wildly into his hand and licked her lips.

"You're torturing me," she croaked, and he soothed her with a kiss to a shapely calf. She was a roaring fire on his white sheets. Her brown skin glowed in the gaslight. He could devour every luscious inch and still want more.

"What's that?" she asked, with a little shudder, as he slid those gloves she loved so much over her pubis. He didn't answer, going lower. She let out a little gasp when his thumb pushed in. His cock bobbed every time she made one of those sounds, and he was aching to be inside her, but she was so delicious to watch.

"How does that feel?" he asked her, flicking the supple leather against her core.

"Good?" she moaned, her hips rocking back and forth. He did it and she cried out for him, her eyes screwed shut. "Do it again," she ordered, her voice eager.

"I'll ruin your gloves, darling," he told her, and she popped one eye open, an outraged look on her face.

"Those are very expensive," she protested, then gasped when he rubbed them again to her clitoris.

"I'll buy you new ones," he promised, swatting her again.

"Harder," she ordered, widening for him, giving him a better look of all that sweetness. He could live with his face buried there, inhaling her, with her arousal down his throat.

He did as she asked, striking her again and again until her legs began to tremble. Then tossed the gloves aside and lowered his mouth to her one more time, latching his lips to her sex, and nursing that sensitive pearl until he heard her cries of pleasure echoing around the room.

"So sweet, so damned good for me, Fiera," he soothed, delivering soft kisses to her thighs, her mons.

"You better replace my gloves," she huffed, making him laugh. But he was moving briskly now, his blood churning as the last threads of his control came very close to snapping.

"I have to be inside you." He loomed over her, examining that expanse of brown-sugar skin that made him lose his head. With a hand, he positioned himself at her entrance, kissing that delicious wet heat with the head of his cock. "Are you certain you don't want me to use French letters?"

She shook her head. "Dutch cap," she told him. "I put it on earlier this evening," she admitted cockily, and he finally understood then her insistence in going home. "I take other precautions too." He knew what the opinion of most men would be for her kind of brazenness, but this only made her more appealing to him. This was not a woman who left anything to chance.

He leaned down to kiss her, tasted long and deep until he could not wait another second. With one hand, he guided himself to her entrance and pressed inside just an inch, just enough to make them both cry out.

He pressed his forehead to hers and breathed, willing himself into control. "I can barely hold myself back, Fiera," he told her, his voice tight.

"Go easy on me, Duke," she returned, and he almost asked her to do the same. He was frantic, his body eager to take her, his need overwhelming well-practiced restraint. It took everything in him to only go in another inch, panting at the tightness enveloping him.

"You're perfect," he moaned truthfully, as he pressed inside. Slow, short strokes until he was seated to the hilt.

"Is this all right?" he asked, running a shaky hand over her flank, as he forced air in and out of his lungs while he waited for her answer. He needed to know this was good for her.

"Yes, it's just—" she gasped, slithering under him, until he began seeing black spots from holding his breath. "You're very large." He was not certain it was a compliment, but something primal still howled inside him at the way she held on to him while she said it.

"Does it hurt?"

She shook her head, which was a relief, then buried her face in his shoulder. "No." A sweet little puff of air escaped her, and he risked another thrust, this one longer, deeper. "I'm so full of you."

Bloody hell, the way she said it, with a touch of awe. Like taking his cock was a marvel. He never lost control with women. He could always deliver an elegant seduction where everyone got what they wanted. But tonight he was unraveled. Inside this woman, nothing he'd known before quite worked.

"I'm so deep inside you," he told her, starting to move his hips in earnest now. Braced on his hand so he could see her face. She met him stroke for stroke, her nails digging into him as he pushed inside her. He pulled almost all the way out and sank in again, and she sighed as though it was the exact thing she'd needed.

He put his arms around her and lifted her until they were both sitting with her impaled on his cock.

"Move these nalgas, Doctora." He added a swat to his command and bit her bottom lip for good measure. She met his challenge like the Fiera she was. Without shame or reservation, she grabbed on to his shoulders and hoisted herself up.

"Like this?" she asked, as she ground herself on him. "I've never…"

"Just like that," he encouraged, moaning as he felt her muscles flutter then tighten around his cock. He grabbed her hips and worked her up and down his length, the sounds of slapping flesh and harsh breaths reverberating throughout the room.

"I like this," she beamed at him, while he leaned in to lick a bead of perspiration from the hollow of her throat. He slid his hand between them and pressed on that tight nub of nerves while she took him inside her again and again. She threw her head back, eyes closed as she rode to her pleasure. He felt the contractions as her orgasm took her, and soon he was following her down. He roared as his climax tore through him, his arms like a vise around her.

He felt her drop to the mattress, her breath still fast and harsh while he attempted to regain control of his limbs. It took him a moment. He should've known bringing a cyclone like this to his bed would leave some kind of permanent alterations to his life.

The trouble was he was starting to think the kind of chaos Aurora brought was exactly what he needed. He'd intended to be gentler with her, but he wanted her so badly he hadn't been able to hold back. Her appetites matched his own to a degree that was almost frightening. He wanted her again already, but he couldn't even be sure she wouldn't be running out of his bed in the next minute.

How the mighty fall, he thought. He was usually the one escaping the bed of a lover. A small hand shoved at his shoulder and then her delectable body began to wiggle under his own.

"If this is your way of telling me you'd like a repeat performance, you just have to ask, Fiera," he teased, pressing a kiss to the round curve of her breast. She scoffed and shoved again, harder, then directed that bellicose gaze at him.

"If this is *your* way of obtaining praise, you're out of luck," she told him haughtily, while tossing that mass of mahogany curls over the pillow. "And you ruined my gloves." She was so damned prickly, despite her very slow, very thorough assessment of his upper body.

He was vain enough to show off a bit for her. He worked hard at his muscles, riding and sparring with Gilberto, and it was most satisfying to catch her admiring him.

"You're too attractive," she told him, glaring at his chest.

"Is there such a thing?" he asked, tucking an errant curl behind her ear.

"Yes," she assured him, then flopped back against the mattress, still wearing those fancy boots. "And incredibly pushy. And don't tell me I'm beautiful. I know I'm not." The defenses were already going up, but she was still touching him. Her hand possessively wrapped around his arm.

"I will be the judge of that, and I don't appreciate you making judgments on the women I bed." He swatted her behind in answer, which made her yelp.

"Hey," she protested, pulling away, but he convinced her to stay with a pat and a squeeze on her rump. She retaliated with a nip to his chest, which sent a spark of electricity right to his cock. He covered her with his body, eager to be inside her again.

"Don't manhandle me," she protested but let him nestle her between his thighs. "You are too sodding big." She accompanied the huff with a vicious glare, but when he tightened his arms around her, she didn't bolt.

"Gilberto and Mihn are hopelessly smitten with you," he told her, coaxing a sweet little smile out of her while she attempted to gather her hair in a gravity-defying coil with two pins that simply did not look up to the task.

"I liked them." And he liked her in his bed, a little too much perhaps.

"From what I gather, you like everyone on sight, except me," he told her, only half joking while she shook her head.

"Fishing for compliments is not becoming, Your Grace." Receiving her barbs was becoming his new obsession.

"I don't need compliments," he rasped against her ear. "The way your tight pussy clenches around me when I make you come is all the accolade I require." She sucked in a breath at his words while a little shiver ran through her.

"Usted tiene un boca muy sucia," she reproached, turning her head to sink her straight teeth into his bicep.

"Pero te gusta mi boca, Fiera."

"I might like your mouth some of the time," she admitted with a saucy grin. "Besides, it's not true that I like everyone," she argued, her tone very serious despite the smile tipping up her lips. "I despised the Hymen Brothers on sight."

"Did you just say the Hymen Brothers?" he asked, and now it was he who repressed a laugh.

"That's not their name," she tossed back, with an aggrieved exhalation. "They're disciples of Ambroise Tardieu in the forensic medicine field, who essentially made a science out of inventing 'detection methods' to ferret out women they believe had interrupted a pregnancy." She gave him a probing look as she said this, clearly expecting a certain kind of reaction.

"They ought to remember inquisitions never end well for anyone." This seemed to be somewhere in the vicinity of the correct answer, and he was rewarded with something akin to a smile. It only figured that Aurora's idea of post-coitus conversation would be a lecture on hymens. He was well on his way to a full-fledged obsession with this woman.

"I just call them the Hymen Brothers to annoy them, given their status as the foremost experts on the integrity of the maidenhead." She was particularly gifted in delivering the most shocking things impassively, so for a moment, he honestly thought she was joking.

"You're jesting."

"I truly wish I was." She shook her head, which made the loose bun on her head bob precariously. Her voluminous sable locks, as usual, were in a fight to the death with the pins, and the pins were losing. "They wrote an entire book on it, *The Hymen in the Americas.*"

For this next part, she turned around and knelt on the bed with her hands clasped over that enticing chest of hers. He had to force himself to focus on what she was saying as they bounced every time she moved. It was not easy to resist pinching one. "'Virginity is one of the most precious jewels for which man searches,'" she recited drolly. But he knew now to look for the spark of mischief in those cacao eyes. "'All civilized nations must prioritize its maintenance, establishing rigorous punishments against all acts committed against it.'"

"That is," he said, then closed his mouth again in honest astonishment, which seemed to amuse her immensely, "highly objectionable, though I am impressed with your memorization skills." She wrinkled her nose in distaste, but he didn't think the sentiment was directed at him this time.

"Wouldn't you memorize words used to whittle your worth down to the existence or absence of a membrane?" Apollo was not unaware of men's infamy, but there was something very humbling about the way this woman spoke of the hypocrisies they all held up as civilized behavior.

"I can't say I've ever had to think about it," he confessed, half expecting to have his head torn off.

"I wouldn't expect any man to," she said with an air of defeat he disliked with violent intensity. Anything that made Aurora Montalban despondent was now his personal dragon to slay.

"So, how do we fix it?" he asked, reaching for her again. "Do we put all the maidenhead marauders to death?" he inquired while he set her astride his lap.

"Maybe," she retorted, with an absolutely devilish glint in her eye, and Apollo startled himself with the sound of his own laughter.

"I thought doctors were invested in keeping people alive," he teased.

"I suppose." She made a face, then circled her arms around his neck, with a tipsy grin on her face.

"You know you can catch more flies with honey." It was an approach that had served *him* well. One could hide all kinds of wrath and nefarious intentions behind a smile. "'Kill them with kindness' need not be merely a figure of speech," he told her, to which she responded with an aggrieved harrumph, before sending him another one of those censorious pouts. He wanted to kiss it right off her mouth.

"Kindness might be an efficient method," she agreed, before pressing her lips to his. "But they die just the same if I use fire." She whispered the words right against his mouth, and he wondered how people saw and talked to this woman every day without ever realizing she was the single most glorious thing in Paris.

"But *you* might get burned in the process, Bella Doctora."

"It would not be the first time." The words could've been a punch, the way they knocked the air out of him. He had questions about her family. Wanted to know more about what had gone on with her brothers tonight, but he didn't want to ruin the fragile joy of this moment. He didn't want to see that hunted look in her eyes. "Tell me about Mihn and Gilberto. Are they really a couple?" She changed the subject, before he fully recovered from her previous statement, but Aurora Montalban did not dwell. She pushed on, focused on the things she could fix. It didn't surprise him that his friends had caught her attention.

"They are."

"Is Mihn a teacher too?"

"No." He shook his head, and with her arms still around his neck, he reached for the small jar he'd procured not long after that first time she'd come to him. "In fact, I had him make something for you."

He took her hand so that it was palm up between them and he put the round metal on it.

"What is it?" She kept her narrowed eyes on him as she opened it, then sniffed it suspiciously. The scent of lavender and lemongrass filled the space.

"It's a salve. Mihn's mother makes it," he told her and watched her take a deeper inhalation of the fragrance. "He said this will help you with the dryness in your hands."

She popped her head up and he saw she'd gotten a bit of cream on the tip of her nose. Just a tiny white dot, which made his heart ache. It was then that he came to a realization that had eluded him since he'd met her. The unflappable Doctora Montalban was a sweetheart. A sweetheart who secretly loved to be pampered, and that was information he planned to use in the future.

"Lemongrass and lavender are a rare combination," she told him matter-of-factly, then batted his hand when he attempted to swipe the bit of cream on her nose.

"You're so sweet," he joked, and she bared him her teeth.

"What I am is the owner of a large collection of scalpels," she huffed out, and by some miracle he managed to keep his grin on the inside. "Where does she make this? Does she have an apothecary?" Her brown eyes were alert now, the languidness from their lovemaking, replaced by clear interest. He could only assume she was asking questions out of more than curiosity.

"Phuong is her name, and she's from Vietnam, which the French call Indochine," he explained.

"I know what Vietnam is," she said with a roll of her eyes.

"She has a farm in Aix-en-Provence, where she grows lavender, among other things." She was definitely more than just curious. Her eyes were wide as saucers now and she was examining that jar like it held the secrets of the universe.

"She does?" She appeared to be filing away the detail for later use. "But how did you end up with a jar of salve in your bedroom?" she asked, then sent him another one of those withering looks he was starting to think were the closest Aurora Montalban got to outright flirting.

He refused to feel awkward about it. She'd confessed that insecurity about her hands and he'd asked Mihn for something that could help.

"You said you wanted soft hands," he told her.

"Oh." There was a hint of surprise in that short answer, and maybe even a little pleasure. Very carefully she scooped a bit of the salve and then rubbed it onto the top of her hand. She made a little sound of appreciation, which made something pulse white hot in his chest.

"Thank you," she finally said in that affronted tone of hers, a sharp contrast to the smile on her lips.

"You're welcome," he whispered, leaning closer and pressing their lips together. She sighed into the kiss, opening for him. She moaned eagerly when he sucked her tongue. But when he slid his hand up her inner thigh, she pulled back.

"We are conversing, Your Grace," she admonished, then softened it by laying her head on his shoulder. He tried not to show his shock at this overture. But she'd had to deal with that terrible scene with her brothers and then he'd brought her here and fucked her like an animal.

His Fiera needed comfort and this was the closest she'd come to asking.

"What would you like to know?" he asked, his voice a bit raspy with sudden emotion.

"How did you end up with this den of iniquity?" She looked around the place with a glint of ownership, and as far as he was concerned, it already belonged to her.

"It's where I lived during my time at the Sorbonne." She turned to him in surprise at that, making him grin.

"I didn't know you were also at the Sorbonne." He could see the pride in her when she talked about her education, and she should be proud, knowing what he did about her upbringing.

"It's not *that* alarming," he laughed, running a hand down

the curve of her rump. He could not stop touching. "There are many students from the Americas in Paris."

"That is true," she conceded, still sending him those suspicious looks.

"If you can believe it, I managed to scratch out an education in mechanical engineering."

"Engineering." He laughed at her astonishment. "That *is* remarkable."

"I finished with honors too," he added, grinning at how her mouth dropped open. "Have I finally impressed you, Doctora?" It figured that it would not be his title or his wealth that had, but his mathematical abilities.

"Well, it is notable." He imagined that would be as close as Aurora Montalban would come to admitting any kind of admiration.

"So, this place has not always been a den of iniquity?" she asked, and he suspected that was only part of the question.

"Not quite," he admitted, then corrected, in an effort to be honest, "Well, not entirely."

"I'm sure that's what you tell all the poor souls you bring here," she teased again, her amused expression hinting at a smile.

"For your information, Fiera—" she harrumphed at the pet name he'd given her, but he had noticed her demands that he stop using it had ceased "—you're the first woman I've ever brought here other than my aunt, and Manuela that night after she jilted that dolt she almost married, I suppose." Her eyes practically crossed in disbelief. But it was true, this had always been his sanctuary. Now whenever he walked in and she wasn't here, it felt like the walls or the roof were missing.

"Your aunt lived here in Paris?" He nodded and could not resist planting a kiss on her lips.

"No." He shook his head, smiling at the idea of Doña Jimena

in this small space, with no room for a retinue of servants. "She visited every year I was here in the hopes I'd leave Paris with an education and a lovely French wife." Even then his aunt was thinking entry into the aristocracy, vying for a wife who'd help him gain access to his father's circles. He'd refused, promising to settle down once he claimed his revenge.

"But her wish was not granted?" his bedmate inquired cannily.

"There's no wife hidden under the floorboards, Fiera," he teased, grimly pondering what his aunt would think of his infatuation with Aurora Montalban.

"I take it this new hunt for a bride is her way to remedy her past failures?" Another question that had a second question lying right under it. More and more, he found the topic of his future to be particularly repugnant.

"I suppose." He was tempted to tell her about the real reason his aunt's plans for him had failed in the past. But she'd probably get the wrong idea.

"I would've imagined a supple, virginal girl with a big bosom and no opinions would've tempted you out of bachelorhood long ago." This he recognized too. This was Doctora Aurora Montalban being provocative. He was more than happy to take the bait and do a little provoking of his own.

She gasped when he cupped the back of her head and brought his head down, so their faces were only inches apart.

"If I wanted that, I'd have it." She made a surprised little sound when he clasped her waist, pressing them together.

"You always get what you want, do you, Your Grace?"

"I usually do," he told her, carding his fingers through her curls. She was so lush. So warm against him. At times, he feared he'd spent so long scheming he'd forgotten how to do things for the pure pleasure of it. But Aurora in his arms disproved that theory in ways which seemed quite dangerous to him.

"Can I ask you something?" She looked very serious.

"Yes," he said, reluctantly, wondering if he'd misjudged what she'd wanted from him. Just because she hadn't run yet didn't mean she wouldn't.

"Do you have anything to eat?" He didn't think that was her real question, but he didn't want to push and end the night with her walking out on him.

"Is that what you came here for, to be well fucked and fed?" he asked with a grin, then nuzzled her neck. She stretched like a cat seeking his attention. Making happy little sounds as he worked to finally remove her boots. It took great doing to force himself from the bedchamber once he had her fully naked and resting on a bed of pillows, like an empress.

He found her snoring when he returned to the room. A soft purr that reminded him of a slumbering lioness. She'd been bedded and now wanted sleep. If he wasn't already half-smitten, this would've done it.

"I thought you were hungry," he said, when she perked up, likely from the aroma of the bread he'd brought her.

"I am," she told him, all mussed with sleep. She had a love bite on her neck and her hair was utter chaos. The sight of her robbed him of air and filled his lungs all at once. He watched her make quick work of a few slices of cheese and bread, then drink deeply from the goblet of water he handed her. By the time she was done, her eyes were half-closed.

"I will want to do that again," she told him, and rested her proud chin on his chest.

"That is a promise, Fiera," he said, with a grunt, when she pressed a chaste kiss to his cheek. By the time he eased her under the covers and used a damp, warm cloth he'd brought from the kitchen to clean her up, she was fast asleep.

He kissed the top of her head, at a loss of how he'd gone and fallen for the only woman on earth who considered marrying a duke tantamount to a life sentence. As he slid under the sheets and pulled her to him, he remembered what he'd told Evan months ago.

Caribbean women will turn your life upside down.

Sixteen

Aurora risked opening one eye first and then very slowly opened the other. She held in a breath then quietly exhaled as the evening before returned to her consciousness. Sparring with Apollo, then propositioning for sex lessons, her brothers, coming back to the den of iniquity, what they'd done after that...

She suppressed a groan and squeezed her eyes as the rest of the events of the evening flooded in. Her face heated as she noticed the aches of Apollo's lovemaking, which in turn kicked up a bothersome swarm of butterflies in her belly. She could scarcely believe the things he'd done to her, the things she'd asked him for.

How much she'd loved all of it. How badly she wanted to do it again.

But it was the way he'd been with her after that was the bigger problem. He'd held her, caressed her like she was something precious in his hands. The way he'd stood up for her with her brothers. He continued to surprise her in ways that only confused her feelings more.

She knew that if she stayed this morning, he would attempt to insert himself further into her affairs. The trouble was that she was not certain how much she could resist him. Because despite her insistence that she wanted independence, she could not deny his protectiveness made her feel cared for in ways she never had before. He'd barely batted an eye at her confession that she was not her father's legitimate child. Then again, it was not like that fact would impact him in any way. It was not like he'd marry her.

She needed to get some perspective. Find her footing after another night with Apollo which further eroded the assumptions she'd made about the man and revealed a picture that made everything confusing. An engineer. She suppressed a sigh and decided an escape was her best plan. He probably didn't want her there either. He had a dukedom to run after all and she had her patients. What did one do after a lesson was over? Leave. Besides, it was a week to the garden party, and she'd see him then.

She would write him a thank-you note for what he'd done with her brothers...and for after, then she would put some much-needed space between them.

He would understand. *He* didn't want entanglements either.

And she had much to attend to. There was the issue with the apothecaries, and her brothers. She didn't think for a second Apollo would scare them off for very long. For all she knew, they stood guard outside Claudine's all night.

But none of that could be dealt with until she actually extricated herself from this bedroom without waking up the very large duke currently slumbering with half of his substantial body on top of her.

With uttermost caution, she raised her head and confirmed that indeed his entire arm was currently over her chest. Holding her breath—which was not easy with a limb the size of a tree trunk on her—and wriggling her body like a worm, she managed to free herself from the arm.

Was the man made of concrete?

She could feel the beads of perspiration on her forehead while her heart hammered in her chest. She clenched every muscle in her body as she gripped the edge of the mattress, hoping to simply launch herself to freedom. Just as she was about to slide off the side, Apollo flopped onto his stomach and threw his leg out, effectively pinning her back under him.

She swallowed down a sob and thought these were the things people ought to warn wanton girls about. No one would risk this nightmare for a roll in the hay. Oh, who was she kidding? After what Apollo had done to her body the night before, she'd do exactly that.

After what felt like hours, but according to his clock was only two minutes, she pried herself from under the Greek column that was the man's leg. She let herself drop to the rug, praying the thump her bottom made when it hit the ground didn't wake him up.

She almost wept in relief when she saw her things neatly folded and sitting on a chair. She might have felt a tiny pang of guilt for leaving like this after he'd been so wonderful to her, but this was for the best.

As quietly as she could, she crawled to the chair and grabbed her clothes, then tucked her boots under her arm. She saw one of her gloves lying by the floor on Apollo's side, thought of what Apollo had used them for and decided she'd let him keep those. Finally, she reached for the doorknob and almost jumped out of her skin when she heard a rustling of sheets. She pressed her forehead to the cool surface of the door and held her breath, but the movement behind her continued. Reluctantly she turned her head only to find Apollo now sleeping on his back. The relief made her legs weak.

The man slept like a slippery eel.

He was bare from the waist up and she noticed a few of the

marks her nails had left on a perfectly molded shoulder. The sight sent a now-familiar shot of heat through her body, but she couldn't linger here lusting after the man and risk being intercepted.

With one last longing look at that decadent male specimen sprawled on the bed, she turned the doorknob. Nothing happened. She tried a second time, pulling with all her strength, but the damned thing didn't budge.

Calma, Leona, calma, she chanted inside her head as she attempted again and again to break free. By the fifth turn, the chanting escalated to internal shrieking and she was perspiring so much her boots were sliding down from under her arm.

"That derriere is even more tempting in the daylight."

Apollo's suspiciously alert voice made her jump nearly a foot in the air, sending the boots and clothes flying.

With her face flaming, she turned around, only to find the Duke of Annan looking—much too spry to have only woken up—like the picture of unabashed debauchery with a key dangling from his fingers.

"Looking for this, Bella Doctora?"

"Give me that," she demanded, extending a hand, but it was hard to take it too seriously when she was doing it all deliciously naked.

It had been a dirty move to let her think he was asleep while she slithered around the bed like an otter. It had taken all his strength not to dissolve into a fit of laughter when he spotted her crawling around the room naked as a babe.

"You'll need this to make your escape, Fiera," he taunted as he slid the key under his pillow.

"I have quite the busy morning, so if you would please hand me the key," she told him, with an air of absolute indignation. From the neck up, she was the very picture of feminine outrage, the lower parts were a different story. The illustrious Doctora Montalban was currently plastered to his bedchamber door with one arm over her luscious breasts and a hand covering that patch of curls he'd hoped to revisit this morning.

"There's nothing you're covering there I haven't had the pleasure of enjoying thoroughly," he pointed out.

"That is beneath you, sir," she huffed with that pert nose up in the air.

"That was exactly where I was hoping I'd find *you* this morning." He did enjoy that little flush of pink on her cheeks. "Alas, we'll have to do this the hard way."

"The hard way?" she asked, then gulped loudly when he threw the covers off his body and set his feet on the floor.

It was a challenge not to laugh.

She was such a damned mess. Gorgeous, a fucking siren. Curves and softness, warm brown sugar he wanted to drown in. But she would fight him at every turn. He sighed, glancing at his raging cockstand, and stood.

"What are you doing?" she asked, eyes fixed on the area between his navel and upper thighs. "I must get back." This was said a bit more distractedly, since her attention was now squarely on what he was doing—or stroking—with his hand. Her nipples had turned into tight peaks before his eyes, and her flush had spread to her neck and chest. He was certain she was wet for him.

She was as lusty as he was. Demonios, but he could devour her.

"First we have to talk about this habit you have of sneaking out of my apartment like a thief in the night."

"I wasn't sneaking." The affront on her face was truly breathtaking.

He couldn't stand it anymore and pressed her right up against that door. "Then why were you crawling on my floor with this rump up in the air?" He squeezed said rump, which made her squeak.

"I didn't want to wake you," she hedged, then melted into him when he slid one thigh between both of hers.

"How considerate of you," he told her without a trace of sincerity. She straddled his leg and he could feel that searing heat burning him. He thrust his pelvis into her, making her gasp.

"This is coercion."

"What is?" he asked innocently, lifting a hand to pinch one of those beautifully taut nipples.

"How can I have a conversation like this?" she protested, even as she offered him her neck. He obliged with a biting kiss.

"I would've preferred to start the day in bed," he said, skating a hand over her flank and down to her heat. "We'd both be in much more reasonable states of mind, don't you think?"

A moan escaped her lips while she gripped his shoulders and began to rock into his fingers. He watched her face with fascination, eyes closed, mouth parted. Ready for more, and he wanted to give her every ounce of pleasure she required, after they talked.

He snatched his hand away.

"What, what?" she protested, absolutely livid at being denied her orgasm.

"Talk first," he said, leaning on the dresser. "Making you come for me, later."

She had the gall to look affronted.

"I don't know what more there is to talk about." She tapped her bare foot on the floor, extremely aggrieved. "We are engaging in some…" She waved a hand in a circular motion.

"Some fornication," he offered. "Very filthy and satisfying intercourse?"

She screamed, then covered her face with her hands. "Yes, that!"

"Our very copacetic copulation is not what I want to talk about, Fiera." He thought she might assault him after that, but she regained control.

"I'd thank you to stop the euphemisms." Even when she was begging, it sounded like an order, and it made his cock throb. "We have an agreement, it's all settled. We can continue without holding a conference about it." She expounded on all this without looking at him.

Nothing was settled as far as he was concerned. After last night, he doubted he could go back to pretending he actually planned to marry one of his aunt's debutantes. He certainly had no plan of allowing Aurora to think she was some kind of entertainment for him.

"I'd be more than happy to continue availing myself of all you'd like to offer, Fiera." She rolled her eyes, hands fisted at her sides, still gloriously naked. He'd keep her like that for days if he could. "But I'd like to talk about your brothers and the clinic—"

"No," she interrupted, the blush replaced by a furious glare. She swept her chemise off the floor and dragged it over her head. "I thank you for being my champion last night, but beyond what we've agreed to, you're not invited to immerse yourself in my life."

"I'm already immersed," he told her, as he reached for his own dressing gown, resigned to the fact that this conversation would not end as he wished. She simply scowled. "I don't like the idea of you unprotected." She looked up from the fight to the death she was currently in with the row of buttons on her chemise.

"I'm not unprotected," she countered, after giving up on the buttons with a huff.

"If you want that building, you need to play by the rules."

Her look of betrayal left him uncowed. He'd be damned if he let her go on like this.

"That is blackmail, Apollo."

He raised an eyebrow in challenge.

"What rules?" she asked, exasperated.

Where did he begin? He hadn't liked the idea of anyone showing up at her rooms and being allowed inside. What if some disgruntled husband came after her? He also didn't know what those brothers of hers were looking for. The thought of her still walking around with those blade gloves, or that little pistol, would likely send him to an early grave.

"The rules I'm implementing right now," he stated, freely using his ducal voice. "Self-defense lessons are not enough. I'd like to send someone with you when you work nights."

"Why?" she asked, with horror on her face. As if she had no earthly idea why anyone would ever think the way she carried on was of concern. It truly made him want to commit violence on those three bastards who shared her blood.

"Because I don't want you getting hurt." The glare she sent him was absolutely homicidal, but she didn't argue. "Starting today, you will have Jean-Louis with you in the evenings, and—" He held a hand up when she began to protest. "One of my conveyances too. I'm not backing down on this, Aurora, or I am not giving you that building."

He could see how much it took her to not fly at him in a rage. But she was too smart not to know he had her.

"I don't like being handled, Apollo," she warned with a tightly clenched jaw. She'd brought those tight fists to her hips, and even through her narrowed eyes, he could see her fury. He could also see the way her sight snagged right at the triangle of skin visible through the dressing gown.

"Jean-Louis won't bother you."

She blew a raspberry then uttered the man's name with disgust, as if its utter Frenchness only added insult to injury.

"I don't like having strange men around when I do my work," she groused, but she still came to him when he tugged on her hand. "You saw how skittish Doña Maria was." He pushed back her hair and planted a kiss on her neck.

"I also heard you say that her husband did not want her getting treatment." She huffed but did not argue that point. "What if some infuriated husband decides to take his frustrations out on you?"

"I can take care of it on my own," she insisted weakly while he made circles with his thumb right at the base of her throat.

"But you don't have to, Fiera." He knew she got scared and all he wanted was for her to do her work without fear. "Your friends would be concerned for you if they knew the risks you're taking." It was a low blow, but it seemed to work. He tipped up her face, but she wouldn't look at him.

"Fine," she finally said, those brown eyes flashing with wounded pride. "But I don't have to like it."

"I did not expect you to," he conceded, and began kissing her again. "Now that that's settled, perhaps we could focus on some of the things you do like," he cajoled. She made one of those lusty little noises, as he began divesting her of the chemise.

"I just put that on," she protested and he let the garment go.

"It can stay on," he told her, leaning in again, but she pushed him back.

"No," she said, pressing a hand to his chest and forcing him to take a step back. "I'm tired of you telling me what to do, Apollo." Her eyes were narrowed and something predatory flashed in them. "I won't let you govern me," she informed him, livid. Then shoved again until he was sitting at the edge of the bed. "I want things too, you know," she said, standing there with her fiercest expression.

"What things?" he asked, undoing the tie of his dressing gown and spreading his thighs apart, noticing her attention was now very much on the nether of his regions. Like every morning, his cock was standing at attention, bobbing for her with enthusiasm. He could read the hunger in her face, but she was still cautious. Still denying herself.

Some imbecile had told this woman to hide her fire. To smother the flames of her passion. Apollo only wanted to stoke them. He wanted to burn in them.

"What do you want, Fiera?" he asked again, and this time it was a challenge. He rested his hands on the mattress, determined to make her come and take what she wanted from him.

She stood there for a moment her eyes eating him up, then went to his knees in front of him.

"This, I want this." She took him in her hands, the scratchy feel of her palm on the head of his cock sent pleasure shooting up his spine.

"I very much want you to have it, sweetheart," he said, with a groan.

"It's like velvet," she admired, as her hand moved over his cock. She cupped his balls, then squeezed them, just enough to make a pearl of liquid form at the tip. With her eyes locked with his, she licked it.

"Aurora," he said through gritted teeth.

"I thought we'd have another anatomy lesson, Your Grace."

"If you keep doing that, it's going to go in your mouth," he warned.

"What, your glans?" she asked, before wrapping her lips around the head and sucking hard enough to make him see stars. She made this little noise of delight, like having his cock in her mouth was pure rapture.

"Open wider," he told her, clasping the nape of her neck, as she lapped delicately at the head.

"Not yet." She shook her head and tickled the frenulum with the hard tip of her tongue. "Oh, that is very sensitive. What about this?" she asked, lazily stroking it from base to tip while he watched. He was so hard it would not take much. He was riveted with the idea of seeing his seed on her lips.

"Stroke it harder," he ordered, pushing into her tight fist.

"Does it feel good?" she asked, and he could only nod.

"Keep doing that, darling," he urged, reaching for her, and his Fiera took that encouragement to heart. Her touch became more certain, rougher, faster, until his harsh breaths echoed in the room. "You're so good at that," he praised her, watching as that pert bottom wiggled in the air. When she reached for his balls and squeezed at the same time, he had to breathe through his nose, to keep from spending.

Then she moved to his sac and he began to see spots. "Oh, the scrotum is quite sensitive, isn't it?" she crooned, as she tickled one, before lapping at it.

"I'm going to disgrace myself," he grunted, while she took one into her mouth and slurped the thing. His hips bucked and he had to count backwards from ten, just to keep from squealing. When she moved back up to his cock, she pressed the tip to her lips. She looked like temptation itself. "Open up, cariño." She parted for him and then he was in that hot, wet heaven. Just the tip, he didn't want to overwhelm her, but his need was strong.

"Can you take more of me, Fiera?" he asked, and in answer she pressed forward, lodging his cock deeper. "Carajo." He shuddered as she dug her nails into his skin, then took even more of him, her head bobbing up and down, as his balls drew up and his heart hammered with the need to come. Then she began humming around his cock and he exploded.

"Aurora," he roared, pulling out as his seed shot out of him onto her hands and chin. It took him a moment to get his breath back and his vision was more than a little blurred.

"That was explosive," she told him, staring at her fingers. He reached for her and brought her onto his lap.

"Me vuelves loco, Fiera." She smiled, her lips plumper from her efforts. But her eyes were already guarded. He slid the back of his hand over her cheek. "Let Jean-Louis come with you, preciosa, please." Her expression was closed and she looked unhappy, but after a moment she nodded.

"Fine," she agreed, turning away when he tried to kiss her. "But I will be keeping that key to the bedchamber."

He pressed his face to her hair and shook his head helplessly.

"All the keys are yours, Fiera," he told her, thinking he was not only referring to the keys for his apartment.

Seventeen

"Where have you been?" Luz Alana demanded as Aurora walked into her friend's parlor an hour later than promised. She didn't blame them for their cross expressions. She looked a mess, and now she was going to be late for the garden party a duke—the *duke* in large part responsible for her lateness—was hosting for the benefit of the clinics.

"Perdon, perdon." She made sure to appear appropriately contrite while she kissed her friends on the cheek, still breathing hard from having run the last two blocks. "I've been behind all day, it's been mad at the clinic."

"Where's the dress?" She looked down at herself with a wince.

At Luz Alana's insistence, Aurora had agreed to wear one of her friend's dresses for the occasion, but it needed alterations and she never took it to the modiste.

"I did not have time to go to Bernadette's," she confessed. Manuela's mouth dropped open like Aurora had just said she'd slapped the seamstress across the face.

She would've worn her sage dress, but Apollo tore at least three of its buttons and there was a stain on the front of the skirt she would never be able to get out. It was ruined. Like her.

"You know how busy she is." Aurora did know that the modiste—formerly in service of Queen Marie-Louise of Haiti—had been doing her a favor by agreeing to do the alterations on such short notice, but the week had gone by in a flash.

"I know," she admitted, even as her face heated. "This week has been one crisis after another, and I never got around to it."

This was not a lie. She had indeed been running an hour behind on everything all day. Partly because she'd had her fistulotomy patient arrive for her procedure without prior notice—something she'd been glad for. And partly because she'd let a certain duke delay her with another one of his morning "therapeutic" sessions. In truth, in the week since she'd stayed over at his den, she'd barely slept at home.

Her days were not much different to her usual hectic juggling of patients, duties around distributing pamphlets and her latest project—and one she enjoyed—self-defense lessons with Gilberto. Though the work was gratifying, and she liked having a lot to do. But now instead of dragging herself back to Claudine's each night, she found herself giving the fiacre drivers the directions to the den of iniquity on a nightly basis.

She'd had more than one painfully awkward encounter with her landlady, who now greeted her with "How is the duke?" every time she walked through the door. Usually with a smirk on her face that made Aurora blush all the way down to her toes. Did any of this detract her from going to the man's lair at every opportunity?

It did not.

She was badly addicted, hopelessly infatuated. She could barely think the moment he was near. His presence covered her like fog. She was utterly fascinated by how her body responded to his touch, to the things he said to her. It was as if Apollo held the keys to the darkest, innermost room inside her, where all her desires lived.

His seemingly endless desire for her was another source of fascination. Always so hungry, and his need seemed to feed her own. She only had to walk into his parlor and he was instantly on her. His hands possessively taking, sliding over her as if confirming it was all where he'd left it. He would whisper all the things he'd thought about doing to her through the day. Would press her against the wall and murmur in her ear as he undressed her.

He'd recite the long list of wicked places he thought of tasting her. Explained in achingly exquisite details where he'd put his mouth, his fingers, his cock. One day, she'd arrived at his rooms and found him waiting for her right beyond the doorway. After wordlessly turning her he'd gone down on his knees, pushed up her skirts while his fingers left an electrifying trail up her thighs, right at the juncture that held her aching need.

He left biting kisses as he described to her how that very afternoon he'd walked out of a meeting with his solicitor to take himself in hand after becoming possessed by the idea of going to his knees for her. On another occasion, she'd walked in so tired she was certain she'd fall asleep standing, only to find him stripped to the waist, holding a box of the bonbons he always kept on hand. He'd carried her to the table, sat her at the end, asked her to eat them, while he feasted between her thighs. Her exhaustion had gone out the window by the second chocolate and she found herself being taken with powerful thrusts as Apollo licked the traces of the confection from her lips.

This morning he'd woken her up by flipping her onto her stomach on his soft linen sheets and proceeding to kiss his way down her back. His big hands squeezing and pressing until he reached her nalgas. There he took his time kneading and massaging them while he regaled her with all manner of deliciously obscene poetry about the shape of her bum.

How much he loved to squeeze it, the way it wiggled when he took her from behind, how lush it felt in his hands...and then ever so gently, he'd parted them while she sobbed with need, until she felt the ghost of his tongue grazing...

"Aurora!" Luz Alana's atypical scream finally snapped her out of her extremely uncouth daydream. "You're an hour late and now you are ignoring us," her friend rebuked. If *Luz Alana* was complaining about her, she truly must be in a sorry state. "We have to start for Apollo's house, they were expecting us thirty minutes ago. We can walk there, it's only five minutes."

Was she truly doing this? She'd not been in public with Apollo since they'd begun their...arrangement and she was not certain what her reaction to him would be.

"We'll just have to arrive with you in this state," Manuela lamented, then reached for the Gladstone. When Aurora tried to protest, her friend held up a hand. "You're not walking into a duke's house carrying this tattered medical bag." She could only imagine her friends' faces if she were to tell them that she had in fact been doing that very thing all week. Instead, she bit her tongue and docilely handed it over.

"It's that man she won't tell us about," Manuela said to no one in particular, making panic balloon in Aurora's chest.

"What?" Playing dumb was the only viable option. There was absolutely no possibility of her confessing to anything. "No," she denied, hurrying out of the room, so they could not see her face. "I had a procedure this morning and you both know we've been struggling to find apothecaries."

She looked over her shoulder and quickly turned away, fearing she'd buckle under Manuela's disbelieving stare. But thankfully the comment about the apothecaries sparked Luz Alana's interest. Nothing brought her enterprising friend more happiness than deciphering a business conundrum.

"Have you not found a new one yet?" she asked with that focused intensity that made her such a sharp businesswoman.

"Not really." She grimaced, feeling like a heel when her friend reached to take her hand. But it was true that the loss of their trusted apothecary was a worrying development. It was only the part about finding the solution she'd lied about.

She'd spoken with Mihn after Apollo told her about his mother Phuong's farm and discussed with him the possibility of purchasing in bulk from her. That was a promising avenue, but they needed a temporary solution while they figured out the details. She bit back a curse when she realized that telling this to Luz Alana would likely lead to questions of how she'd met Mihn, which would steer right back to the Duke of Annan.

"And there's also the fact that your brothers are here." She winced at that and earned sympathetic looks from her friends. Aurora had given the Leonas a redacted version of her brothers' visit when she'd gone to Luz Alana's for that dress. "Have they been to Claudine's again?" Not all of them, but Ramón had sent her a pointed letter informing her of his disapproval of her choices. She'd torn it up and thrown it in the fire.

"Octavio stopped by the clinic the other day." She hadn't bothered to ask how he knew to look for her there, but she had been cautiously glad to see him.

"Did he know anything about Philip?" Her friends had been very alarmed on her behalf when she confirmed that Philip was in Paris. But she'd somehow managed to put the man completely out of her mind in the past few days and was almost surprised at the mention of his name. After all, what could Philip do to her? There was nothing he could take that she hadn't already given up herself.

"No, apparently they tried but have not been able to get more details about what Philip is doing in Paris."

"Was it all right?" Manuela asked, cautiously. "With Octavio?" He'd given her information for where to find him and promised to let her know if they heard anything about Philip. Then he'd asked her to consider making amends with their parents.

This was not something that interested her.

"It was fine," she said with a smile, and felt comforted in the fact that even if she chose not to make amends, she would not be alone in the world. She had her friends and she could always count on them.

"Now that we have covered the basics, tell us about the rest of it," Manuela said, circling a gloved finger in the air, as they walked onto a street lined with opulent homes.

"What rest of it?" Aurora inquired innocently.

"Your brothers, the apothecary," her friend listed aloud. "That's not all that's going on with you." She did not like the look of Manuela just then.

"Of course it is," she contested with a huff, picking up her pace. "Well, that and this cursed garden party!" She did not have to feign exasperation at the mention of the event, which was becoming more and more unavoidable as they reached their destination. Her friends were much too smart to not notice the way she flushed whenever she saw Apollo. She only hoped her reaction to seeing him stopped at that.

"If that's not all of it, then why do you have a love bite on your neck?" Manuela demanded right as they reached the wrought iron gate of the Duke of Annan's residence.

"I do not have..." An innocent person would probably not slap a hand to their neck, but in her defense, she was not accustomed to this much lying.

"I knew it!" Manuela cackled with glee while Luz frowned.

"I'm not ready to share anything," she told her friends as they climbed the steps to the door of Apollo's home.

"Is it—" Manuela began, but Aurora shook her head, denying whatever was going through her friend's mind. "Is it serious?"

"No, there are no feelings involved," she told them, and her stomach clenched at the words. "I simply need to keep this secret awhile longer." This was only biology, nerves, her aversion to deceiving her friends. It had nothing to do with her falling for Apollo or the denial of said nonexistent feelings.

"Let's focus on this, please," she said as she reached for the knocker, which was the same one as that of his rooms, and the mere sight of the thing had her practically breaking out in sweats. "I'm already regretting this, and this conversation is not helping." Manuela clamped her lips together and sighed.

Luz Alana, the sensible one, simply sent her a stern look and said, "Well, you're going to smile all the way through it. You need this and so does your clinic." That did the trick, and by the time the door opened, she'd gotten herself in order.

"Welcome, mesdames." A gentleman in livery opened the door, took their coats and guided them toward a magnificent foyer, where a lovely woman and an equally beautiful, younger version of the hostess seemed to be greeting guests. Apollo was nowhere to be seen. Which frankly was a relief. She could at least make her way through the house without her body rebelling against her like it did at the mere sight of the man.

"That is Doña Jimena, and her youngest, Juliana, the other daughters stayed in Cartagena," Luz Alana explained with a smile. The aunt. There was a nervous flutter in her stomach at the prospect of meeting the most important person in Apollo's life. His savior and protector. The one who fought so he could take his place in the world, the only mother he'd ever known and the one she suspected—in part—was the reason he'd claimed his title. The one whose wish was for her nephew to marry a woman who could be his perfect duchess.

As she walked forward, she was flooded with a feeling of

inadequacy. With each step, she became more and more consumed by the feeling that she did not belong there. That if Apollo's aunt knew who she truly was, she'd toss her out. By the time they reached the two women, Aurora was so tense her neck was in pain. "Luz Alana, estas preciosa querida." The older woman beamed, taking in Luz's aubergine gown, then gestured to the girl next to her. "You remember my Juliana."

"Of course I do." Luz Alana nodded with enthusiasm as she leaned in to kiss the younger woman, who barely inclined her head in acknowledgment. "I adore your gown."

Luz proceeded to compliment Juliana on her dress, jewelry and coiffure with an effusiveness that seemed to escape Juliana. The girl's eyes were frantically roaming around the room while she twisted the fan in her hands.

"Niña, don't be rude." The older woman rebuked her daughter, then sent an apologetic look at Luz Alana. "She has her head in the clouds lately," she said with a familiar glint in her eye that Aurora had seen many times from mothers poised to make a successful match for their daughters. "There's a fair share of suitable young men in Paris."

However, Juliana did not look too pleased with her mother's comment.

"Oh, has a young man started calling?" Luz Alana asked, to which Juliana reacted with a nasty scoff.

"I have no interest in boys." The girl could not have been more than fifteen. She was lanky, in that way of girls who still had growing to do, but she had a lovely face and piercing brown eyes.

"Juliana!" Doña Jimena exclaimed, embarrassed.

"It is so good to see you, Doña Jimena, that color suits you," Manuela exclaimed, with enough oohing and aahing to suffuse the tension after Juliana's outburst. Her mother sent the girl another chiding look, before turning to Manuela.

"Thank you, Miss Caceres, how nice to see you here this evening." The older woman's greeting for Manu did not have the same warmth as the one directed at Luz Alana. Not that you would know from Manuela's enthusiasm.

"It is wonderful to see you and thank you so much for hosting this in order to help my dear friend's clinics." The words were emitted with such sweetness, Doña Jimena could not help but smile. When she focused her attention on Aurora, however, the joy in the woman's eyes dimmed significantly. Aurora could tell Apollo's aunt was forcing herself not to stare at her shabby rust-colored suit. A very inappropriate memory of Apollo peeling off the very jacket she was wearing while informing her he'd begun to become aroused at the mere sight of bolts of wool came to mind and she had to swallow down a giggle. This certainly did very little to contribute to Doña Jimena's overall good impression of her.

"It is nice to meet you, Doctora Montalban. My nephew has spoken very highly of your work."

The things that occurred in her body at the mere mention of Apollo's name could not be good for her system. Everything seemed to come alive all at once. She couldn't believe he'd talked to his aunt about her. About the clinic yes, even the cause, but her personally. She didn't know how to feel about that.

"That's very kind of him, and thank you for hosting this for us, ma'am." She resisted the urge to curtsy and settled on a reverent—she hoped—bow of the head. "This is quite a house." She'd been raised in wealth. There was not much that impressed her, but she had never felt like she belonged in grand houses like this. She wondered now if she would've dared come to Apollo here, if he didn't have his den of iniquity.

"My nephew brought all the furnishings from Cartagena, crafted by our best artisans," Doña Jimena told Aurora, waving a hand at the exquisitely crafted pieces perfectly distributed around the room. Marble and finely carved wood filled every space. From the ceiling hung an exquisite chandelier Doña Jimena said was made especially for their family by an Italian glassmaker in Buenos Aires.

This was a world away from the cozy, warm apartment she'd grown so fond of. While his rooms near the Parc Monceau were a sanctuary, this place was a showroom. The mere size of it was astonishing, and every piece of furniture, every fixture was clearly there to mesmerize.

He'd need a perfect wife in this place. One who could stand next to his beautiful aunt and cousin and not stick out like a sore thumb. Not her, the rebellious doctor, who was dangerously close to becoming a rabble-rouser.

"All the art is from the Americas too," Manuela, their artist, whispered, with a little awe in her voice, bringing Aurora out of her morose thoughts. "He has an astonishing collection." Doña Jimena thawed significantly at that.

Aurora turned her head to look at the paintings and indeed the typical European pastoral scenes were not what lined the Duke of Annan's walls in his rooms. The few portraits in the room were of finely garbed men and women of deeply brown skin in regal poses. This man might want to be in the aristocracy, but he was not willing to hide a thing about himself.

Aurora canvassed the room again, telling herself she was admiring the art and not attempting to find a head of mahogany curls above the crowd. She was half-listening to Manuela and Doña Jimena's discussion about a seascape by an artist named José Ferraz de Almeida when she noticed Juliana's sudden alertness as she spotted a figure on the other side of the room. Aurora could not see much of the man, other than his blond head and lean figure as he briskly crossed the room and disappeared through doors leading to the garden. Something about him sent a shiver of unease through Aurora, but Juliana's face broke into a smile that explained her lack of interest in "boys."

"Mama." Juliana's voice was very high and surprisingly animated given her ennui from only minutes ago.

"You're being much too loud, Juliana," Doña Jimena rebuked her daughter, who was practically vibrating. "What is it?"

"May I be excused?" she begged, and Aurora sensed the girl was trying very hard to not look in the direction where the man had gone. "Please, I just saw Mademoiselle Boucher." That name smoothed the frown lines from Doña Jimena's brows, and with a sigh, she made a shooing gesture toward her daughter.

"Ten minutes." Juliana was off like a shot.

"That child," the woman exhaled, with a shake of the head. "No interest at all in finding a husband. All she does is mope and primp her hair." Manuela and Luz Alana both smiled and made noises of understanding while Aurora kept her eye on Juliana. She hoped whoever the girl had gone to meet was not a blackguard like the one she'd been ensnared by at the same age. "Ladies, if you'll excuse me, I have a few arrivals to greet," Doña Jimena announced. "Doctora, we will ask you to speak to our guests when everyone's arrived." The reminder of her upcoming speech did very little to calm her nerves, but she nodded and smiled, before the woman went to greet her other guests. She wondered what Doña Jimena would make of the women's dressing gown hanging next to her nephew's in his secret apartment.

"Aurora, are you even listening?"

"What? What is it?"

Luz Alana rolled her eyes at her in a manner she usually reserved for Manuela's antics, causing Aurora's face to heat with such intensity she almost pressed her palms to her cheeks.

"I was attempting to brief you on the key players here tonight." Now Aurora was the one rolling her eyes. Luz Alana approached everything as if she were entering a high-stakes negotiation.

"You mean besides the snobs and gossips?" she asked under her breath when she spotted a few of the notorious matrons in the local Caribbean social circles.

"Gossips with fat pockets," Luz Alana countered. Aurora sighed and reminded herself this was all a necessary part of running the clinic. They wanted to help more people, and for that, they needed funds.

"I know *I* will be the source of much gawking and pointing, but I enjoy that," Manuela said primly, with her usual defiance.

"I should've insisted Virginia be the one who does the speech," Aurora lamented, but neither of her friends seemed very sympathetic.

"Darling Virginia is a known anarchist," Manuela reminded her sweetly, looping one arm around the crook of Aurora's elbow. "She might still be a wanted woman in Buenos Aires and the ambassador from Argentina is *here*." She cupped her mouth for the next part and Aurora braced herself. "Cora and his sister were...friendly in the past." She pointed at a tall white-haired man speaking to a lovely older woman.

"Where is your duchess, by the way?" Aurora asked. Manuela and Cora had been inseparable in the months since they'd reconciled.

"She had to attend to some business in Champagne," Manuela said dreamily. "According to the note I received this morning, tonight I will come home to a lusty duchess and chilled champagne," she tittered. "Life is but a dream."

"That sounds much more pleasurable than this," Aurora grumbled again, which earned her a very censorious look from Luz Alana.

"This will be a wonderful evening," her business-minded

friend insisted. "You will develop skills in procuring funding for your endeavors and be forced to socialize." That last part was clearly meant to chastise, but Aurora was too preoccupied searching for the elusive host of the evening to react with one of her usual barbs.

"We could just ask Cora for the money," Manuela started, and Luz Alana shook her head.

"Absolutely not," Luz Alana interrupted. "It's not good practice to rely on only one source of funds. You must also learn to talk about the good work you do, Leona." Aurora nodded dutifully, without much enthusiasm, which elicited a sigh from Luz. "Now, please focus," she demanded, grabbing Aurora by the shoulders to point her in the direction of the refreshments table.

"That man standing there holding court is Don Simón Patiño." Even Aurora knew who that was. The Bolivian magnate who owned most of the tin in his country and had one of the biggest fortunes in the world. "The rumor is that his wife has their three marrying-age daughters here looking for eligible aristocrats. I heard they're on the hunt for a husband for the middle one, Graziella." That probably meant Mama Patiño had Apollo in her sights. She swallowed down the bile that thought incited and looked away.

"You're too quiet, I get nervous when you become too pensive," Luz Alana griped, making Aurora laugh, despite her dark mood.

"The obsession with an aristocracy that was built on the backs of our ancestors will never stop shocking me," she remarked, as if that was the reason for her scowl.

"I should've kept my brief to myself," Luz Alana lamented, finally at the end of her rope.

"Well, it is utterly ridiculous." Aurora threw her hands up dramatically at a very unimpressed Luz Alana. "These people built their fortunes from the exploitation of our countries, our people, and now we're just giving it all back to them for some silly titles."

"At least now they have a brown-skinned duke to obsess over," Manuela remarked.

"Apollo will eat these girls for lunch," she said, before she could stop herself.

"Apollo, is it? Such familiarity," Manu noted, with a coy grin on her lips. "When did you stop referring to him as 'duque de mierda'?" It was one of Manuela's least attractive attributes, her insistence on pointing out truths no one wanted to hear.

"Speak of the devil," Luz Alana said, sending Aurora's heart into a gallop. "And bless him, he's just stopped to speak with Patiño."

That was when she saw him, larger than life and more beautiful than the gods. Even with her negative opinion of the aristocracy, she could not deny the man looked like a duke. He was in a gray suit, cut to show off those impressive wide shoulders. Shoulders that should have a mark or two left there by her hands, and teeth. The thought was a comfort as she watched the young woman next to Patiño, sending besotted looks at Apollo.

"That's Graziella Patiño," Luz murmured. The heiress whose mother was actively trying to marry her to a titled man. She was as lovely as he was handsome, in her pale rose gown, which was almost certainly from Worth's. They looked like a matched pair, his power and height a perfect complement to her regal elegance. She fit perfectly in this stately home, built to be filled with expensive, fine things.

"We should go and introduce you," Manuela suggested, pulling her arm, but Aurora didn't budge. She could not look away from the gorgeous creature who was hanging on every word Apollo said to her. She should look away, go and speak with some of the people here who could do so much for her clinic, but instead she was torturing herself.

"Apollo is clever," Manuela muttered as they looked on at Apollo and Miss Patiño. "She might not be English, but she has connections at the highest echelons of society."

"And her father is actually richer than Croesus," Luz Alana teased, while jealousy pelted Aurora like a hailstorm. The sight of Graziella's hand on his forearm made her sick to her stomach.

Which only went to show how far gone she was. What did she think Apollo did when he wasn't with her? Going after his own plans, securing the future of his dukedom. Doing what he must to ensure he could do things on his own terms. Marrying into one of the richest families in the world certainly would do it.

"I need some fresh air," she told her friends, who were still enthralled by the tableau across the room.

"Don't you want to greet him?" Luz Alana asked, suggesting more than asking.

"I will later." She'd rather flay herself than walk up to him right then. "I want to clear my head before my speech." The looks of concern on her friends' faces told her they didn't quite believe her, but she escaped into Apollo's gardens before she was tempted to confess the whole sordid affair.

By the time she reached the bottom of the steps and took in the absurdly manicured Eden, she was angry with herself for her reaction to seeing Apollo with that girl. She had no right to be jealous or possessive of the man. Apollo wanted a wife and she didn't want to be anyone's duchess. But seeing him with the perfect Señorita Patiño made her inadequacy that much more evident. She hated feeling unworthy, especially of things she had no desire for.

And it was not like any of it mattered. She didn't want this kind of life. There was no having Apollo without losing her hard-fought freedom. This house, this world did not suit her, but still, for a second in there, she'd wondered what it would be like to be the one he chose. And none of this woolgathering was conducive to being in the state of mind necessary to stand up and speak about her work. She had to focus on what mattered, not on the things she could never have.

"Montalban." The sound of a familiar and unpleasant nasal voice announced the presence of someone else in the corner she'd commandeered by the wall of pasionaria. "I heard you were here to make the case for your quacks." She whipped around only to come face-to-face with the two people she wanted to see even less than Apollo's heiress.

She considered the pair of men in their crow-like clothes, their oily, thin mustaches and sour faces and smiled to herself. The surge of anger made her fingers tingle and suddenly she had air in her lungs. A verbal assassination of these two imbeciles was exactly what she needed to ventilate the irritation of the last few minutes and get back to what she'd come here to do.

"Well, well," she said, in a tone as cordial as a punch in the mouth. "If it isn't the Hymen Brothers. Who let you out of your coffins?"

Eighteen

Apollo had been in the process of scheming an escape from a mind-numbingly boring conversation with the very lovely, but astonishingly bland, Señorita Patiño when he spotted a flash of rumpled rust-colored fabric, concealing the pert bottom he'd become intimately familiar with in the last week, dashing toward his gardens.

Barely an hour into the blasted charity event and he'd descended to a virtually vegetative state from the endless string of dull conversations his aunt had pulled him into, but the moment he caught a glimpse of dark coils flashing through the crowd, everything inside him roared to life. The effect Aurora Montalban had on him was something to be studied. He'd been practically dozing off, and suddenly he was alert, primed for battle. It was as if he could feel the blood rushing to his head, his limbs...his cock.

"What are your opinions on ladies riding astride, Your Grace?" Graziella Patiño inquired, her big gray eyes fringed with lovely eyelashes focused on him just so. "It's become astonishingly popular," she tittered coquettishly while he contemplated which corner of his garden would best serve the intentions he had for Aurora Montalban's tasty morsel of a body.

He was still staring at the door she'd disappeared through when Don Simón cleared his throat impatiently. "I can't say I have given ladies' riding habits much thought, Señorita," Apollo said, and watched her smile fade a bit. She did seem like the type to subscribe as closely as possible to the rules. Then again, so had Aurora, and he'd been very pleasantly disabused from that misconception. "In any case, I'd leave it up to the lady to decide how she wants to use her saddle."

"Of course you're correct, Your Grace," the heiress capitulated, doe-eyed and malleable, without even an attempt to contradict him.

He imagined what Doctora Montalban would have to say about men telling women how they could ride a horse or anything else, and from there his mind descended straight into the gutter. Heat suffused him and his head was virtually inundated with images of how the doctor had ridden him, quite energetically, a few nights earlier.

Demonios, he had to go find her. The little diabla hadn't even stopped to say hello. He should've expected that. She was probably making herself mad imagining all sorts of things. He knew she'd be nervous about the speech, and he'd tried to be attentive to her arrival, but his aunt had been on a mission tonight. In fact, she was walking toward him just then with that fop Forsyth. There was something that didn't quite sit right with him about the man.

"Ah, sobrino," his aunt exclaimed, with a happy smile on her lips. This was a common occurrence when Forsyth was present, which made it harder to openly dislike the man. "Look who has arrived all the way from London." While they did their round of introductions with the Patiños, Apollo examined her aunt's beau with barely concealed distaste.

"Forsyth," he said tightly as the man offered him a hand. He was younger than his aunt, by a dozen years or so. A for-

mer Royal Navy officer and a handsome enough sort. With
a recently acquired barony that came with land and a modest annuity, Forsyth was certainly a catch. When Apollo had
pointed this out, the man had confessed that after spending
over a decade on assignments throughout the Americas, he
simply did not see himself with a young British bride. Apollo
could not begrudge the man for his predilections when he'd
spent the last month chasing after a short-assed Dominican-
Mexican whirlwind in lieu of procuring his own English rose.

It was not that he didn't think the Englishman could fancy
his aunt. After all, Jimena Robles Vda. de Salazar was not only
a beautiful woman, but a wealthy one. He wanted his aunt to
be happy, heavens knew she deserved it after the time she'd
had at the end of his uncle's life. Apollo just wasn't certain this
Lord Forsyth was the right man for her.

"Your Grace." Forsyth grinned as he gripped Apollo's hand
a little too forcefully.

"I should've known you'd be with the prettiest girl here,"
his aunt exclaimed in a teasing tone, sending a knowing look
toward Graziella, who blushed prettily before hiding those
guileless gray eyes. The gesture only served to remind him
of the fiery chocolate regard of the woman who'd never give
up her freedom for the cage of propriety and society rules he
came with. Apollo endeavored to give his aunt a smile, but
it was becoming harder to pretend he had any interest in this
plan of hers to find him a duchess.

He didn't need a duchess who was only there as an amenable
trophy. He wanted a partner, a coconspirator. He thought of
Evan and Luz Alana. The way his brother went to his wife to
consult her on every weighty decision. The trust he placed in
her judgment, how he valued her advice. Perhaps Apollo had
gone about this all wrong. After his father died, it seemed vital
to make a strong alliance through marriage. To find a duchess

whose family connections and fortune would cement his status in the world where he now existed. But lately, he wondered if what he needed was a woman strong enough to stand with him in the treacherous paths he would be treading. The face of a ferocious, rebellious physician came to mind, and suddenly, all he wanted was to see her.

"Thank you for a lovely talk, Don Simón," he told the older man, who was occupied discussing maritime commercial routes with Forsyth. The old man smiled amiably as Apollo turned to his daughter. "Señorita Graziella, encantado." She blushed again when he kissed her satin glove.

"Where are you going?" his aunt asked, barely concealing her disapproval.

"I must go see about our guest of honor," he said, smiling at Don Simón. The business magnate didn't seem very interested, but Graziella's eyes lit up.

"I'm quite eager to hear from the doctora," she said with open admiration. "What a fascinating thing, a woman doctor."

"I will make sure to introduce you," Apollo offered, noticing Forsyth's sneer at the young woman's comment. One more reason to dislike the man.

Apollo made his escape only after agreeing to tea and something to do with a pianoforte and Graziella in the near future. By the time he went outside, his skin was buzzing with eagerness to find his quarry.

The air of the garden was slightly chilled for September. There were guests milling about in the better-lit areas surrounding the house. It took some doing to find her. A few turns in the dark, but he finally discovered her by the vines of pasionaria, coldly deploying exquisitely crafted taunts at two very soberly dressed, mustachioed gentlemen who did not seem up to the challenge of that very sharp tongue. She had her hands on her hips, and in profile, he could make out the lines of her. That generous bosom was angled quite menacingly as she leaned forward to deliver insults.

Apollo was not a fanciful man, and the last years had involved more scheming and lying than any honest one ought to be embroiled in. It had all left him quite devoid of romantic notions. But the sight of that wisp of a woman in a rumpled walking suit, which was surely an insult to fashion everywhere, unleashed something in him he should've heeded as the harbinger it was.

"Has it occurred to one of you that my poor attitude has more to do with your idiocy than my lack of humor?" She was furious, her gaze hot enough to burn.

"If we are so idiotic, why were we the ones invited by the academy to present our findings here?" one of the mustachioed fellows shot back. Apollo took a step forward, ready to take up her defense, but Aurora was quick to return the barb.

"Oh, I don't know, Rosales." Every word out her mouth dripped with condescension. "Perhaps because half the academy is filled with maidenhead-obsessed imbeciles like the two of you." The laugh escaped him before he could control it, but the mighty Doctora Montalban was much too focused on her opponents to notice. The other two were busy spluttering nonsense about her insolence and the "place of women," which he was certain they'd come to regret in short order.

His Fiera did not disappoint.

"Why would they care to hear me speak on how they've dismantled a perfectly sound system of women's health for profit when they have you two clowns on a stage parroting nonsense about hymenology and virginity math equations?" That time she almost lost her cool demeanor. He saw her struggling to keep from lunging forward. He was so enthralled witnessing this tableau he almost missed what one of the Hymen Brothers said, until he noticed her reaction to it.

"Why must you always be so angry, Montalban?" She flinched at the insult, her chin trembling with anger. It was the same shattered expression she'd had that night with her brothers. And he'd had enough.

"Because I'm constantly forced to deal with the likes of you, Castañeda," she shot back, as Apollo moved toward the trio, but she'd lost her bluster. Castañeda seemed aware of the fact, because he took a menacing step in her direction.

"If you two gentlemen are attached to your teeth and skulls, I'd advise against coming even an inch closer to Doctora Montalban," he called out as he stepped into the light. It took quite a lot of restraint not to brain the two fops against the flagstone.

The pair, who at closer range seemed to be bafflingly matching in their suits, shot him disgruntled looks but quickly blanched when they realized who they were glaring at.

Good, let the Hymen Brothers quake a bit in their boots.

The Valkyrie he told himself he was protecting stepped out from behind the vine, looking thoroughly unimpressed and muttering things under her breath about dukes and comemierdas no lady ever would.

"Your Grace," she told him with all the sweetness of a Brazilian piranha.

"Doctora, are you in need of my assistance?" He infused the question with a drop or two of suggestiveness. Then his attention drifted to the bottom lip he knew she'd been biting. By the time his gaze arrived at the spot at the base of her throat he liked to dip his tongue into, he could hear the Hymen Brothers scurrying away. "Seems like I've scared them off," he told her, taking the last step he needed to press their bodies together.

"I had that in hand, Annan," she informed him, with a growl.

"You certainly did, you glorious thing," he whispered, as he wrapped her in his arms. It took him a moment to notice she wasn't exactly melting into his touch. He frowned when he noticed her arms hanging stiffly by her sides. Had those two bastards actually done something to her? "What's wrong?" he asked, sweeping a hand over her arms, only to have it swatted away by a very cantankerous Aurora.

"Why are you always trampling into places unannounced?" she demanded, very far from the amorous mood he'd hoped to find her in.

"I like to make my presence known," he retorted in the tone he used when they engaged in their wordplay. This usually somewhat thawed her to his flirtation.

So far, there were no puddles he could see. In fact, she looked positively indignant.

"Being the size of a building doesn't do it?" she shot back with her arms crossed over her chest.

"Now you're just jealous because you get mistaken for a child all the time." He was certain that would induce at least an uptick of her mouth, but she was not budging.

"Did you invite those two buffoons to torture me?" she asked him, then took a step back when he reached for her. Now he understood the trouble. He should've been more attentive to the people his aunt had sent invitations to, but he'd been much too caught up with the tropical storm currently seething at him.

"We invited most doctors from the Americas in Paris for the exposition," he reminded her, but that only made her eyes narrow further. How could she see at all through those slits?

"I suppose you were more focused on the female guests, or was the señorita Patiño also your aunt's guest?" Was that jealousy?

Something a lot like satisfaction panged hard in his chest. But he knew this was very delicate ground. If he inquired why she'd mentioned Miss Patiño in a less than friendly fashion, she would either deny it or become even more cross. Hell, he wouldn't be surprised if she took off and ran.

"Her father was one of my guests," he finally said, hoping this would be enough to be allowed within a foot of her person. "And I was much too distracted watching you trample through my house to pay attention to much of what she said."

"Liar," she groused, with her mouth pursed tight.

"This reminds me of the first time we met," he told her, recalling the soiree at the Mexican Pavilion of the Exposition Universelle, when he'd found her standing outside another party.

"You were also a cad then," she pointed out, but allowed him to wrap his arms around her waist.

"I was also the one on the wrong end of an Aurora Montalban tongue-lashing." He leaned down and traced the tip of his own tongue over the delicate shell of her ear. "And to think how fond I've become of them."

"You were insufferable," she huffed, looking up at him with slighted chocolate eyes.

"I was trying to be friendly," he cajoled, as his hands lowered to that lush rump and squeezed, coaxing a sweet moan from her.

"You made fun of my clothes," she said, pressing her own lips to his neck, turning his hardening cock to stone.

"Watch yourself, Doctora," he grunted when she added teeth. "And *you* insulted *my* suit." He dug the pads of his fingers into her derriere and she made a lusty little sound with her throat. "I recall the words *demented dandy* and *public menace* being tossed in my direction." That impish grin finally made an appearance and Apollo began to wonder why he hadn't just written a check and bedded her in lieu of all this.

"What I recall saying was that you were too pretty," she informed him as he remembered the way she'd stood up to him. That heart-shaped face pugnacious and fierce as she told him he was "ridiculously pretty." She'd flicked her hand and shaken her head at him as if attractive people were the latest in a long line of quandaries she'd been forced to deal with, and he'd barely known what to do with himself.

"Mmm." Something possessive erupted inside at the memory, and he gathered her closer. "I think I remember you lavishing compliments on my sensual mouth and fine jaw, Fiera. You might have even suggested a tryst."

"I did not!" She swatted at him, but he caught her wrist and bit her finger, which made her go soft in his arms. God, but she was damned beddable. "I *said*—" she made her eyes big, and that swirling heat took up in his belly again "—that *you* were probably out there trysting with some poor girl." She did say that, but what she didn't know was that, just like tonight, he'd been out there because of her.

He'd seen her at the soiree with her bellicose way of glaring at every person who crossed her path. Defiantly indifferent to the fact that she was horrifyingly underdressed as she stuffed her mouth with cocadas. After months of uninspiring conversation with beautiful girls with very little dreams beyond the house they'd keep for him, Aurora Montalban was the singular most intriguing thing he'd seen in Paris.

She still was, and that was becoming an increasingly unavoidable fact for Apollo.

The sounds of two people hurrying through the darkness jolted Apollo out of his reverie and reminded them both they were a bit exposed to the elements.

"I was out here rehearsing my speech, and you've distracted me," Aurora groused as she set herself to rights, with a scowl on her face.

"A rebel like you, nervous?" he asked, earning the cut of her eye.

"No woman wants to be a rebel, Apollo," she told him with a tired sweep of her hand. "It's not that I don't enjoy my work," she told him. "I like how good I am at it and mostly I do it because it helps women in need. But I *am* a Black woman born in Hispaniola and raised in Mexico who managed to become a licensed physician." There was as much pride as there was exhaustion in her voice. "I have amassed my share of battle scars."

The truth came upon him like a blow to the head. He could not keep her. He could not drag this woman into a world that would constantly make her feel as though she did not belong.

"You wear them well, Doctora," he told her, when everything else he wished to say breached every rule the two of them had agreed on.

"That, Your Grace, was the perfect thing to say." She smiled at him, and it was a sweet one, and took his hand. "Come on, now I must truly practice this blasted speech."

Nineteen

"*I should've worn something nicer,*" *she told Apollo* under her breath as he guided her along a gravel path. He glanced down at her jacket and waggled his eyebrows in apparent appreciation.

"Are you fishing for compliments again?" he asked, in that teasing voice she'd grown to adore. "You know I'd tear all that tweed off of you at the first opportunity," he told her when they were hidden behind an enormous hedge. She truly wished she didn't find his lechery as flattering as she did.

"Stop pretending you like my clothes," she said, slapping his hand away when he reached for something suspiciously close to her breast.

"I'm not pretending." He had the gall to appear offended. She rolled her eyes at him but offered up her neck for some kisses. When he didn't and insisted on staring at her, the silence began to nettle.

"What?" Her voice was a bit too high.

Perhaps he truly thought she was vying for compliments. But she wasn't. It was that he'd never pretended with her. It was what made things between them so good. Apollo wanted her, even when he didn't like her, and it was the same for her.

False compliments were things friends did, and she didn't think she'd be able to extract herself from this if she began to think of him as a friend, despite what he'd said to her brothers.

"I thought you were aware how far I've come around when it comes to your apparel," he whispered. Their bodies were pressed together and his breath feathered over her ear, making things happen in regions she did not want to be aware of in this particular setting. She should redirect the conversation to less explosive topics, but this was the problem with her and this man. She could never get enough, even of the things she knew would get her in trouble.

Especially of those things.

"Based on the multiple items of clothing you've torn, ripped or generally ruined, I assumed you were sending me a message about my choice of clothes."

A delicious feeling erupted in her belly at the predatory sound he made.

"The message, Doctora, is that I'm very fond of everything you so cruelly keep concealed under this." He ran a finger over the cuff of her jacket, and even that light touch had her gasping for air.

"Fine, you like my clothes." She would not grin at him like a loon. She was a physician, a woman of the world, for God's sake, not a blushing virgin. "No, stop it," she reproached as he reached for a button.

"Is this the thanks I get for opening my home to your cause, Doctora?" he asked with that slithery rasp in his voice that made her insides slip and slide.

"Thank you for inviting the Hymen Brothers?" she bleated, as he undid two of them before planting a kiss right above her breast.

He interrupted his ministrations to the curve of her neck, then looked up at her and winked. "I thought you handled yourself quite well with them," he admitted, to which she responded by pinching his stomach.

"Do you like seeing me suffer?" she asked, peevishly. "You know those two hate me."

"Their invitation was my aunt's doing," he told her, then flashed her a wicked grin. "Though I must say witnessing that verbal evisceration was quite a treat." Which was all well and good for Apollo's entertainment, but those two would do their best tonight to talk her clinic down.

"If you must know, that encounter has only made me more nervous about this blasted speech you're requiring I give."

"Am I to understand that you—" he pointed a finger in front of her face "—Doctora Aurora Montalban Wright, are intimidated by the Maiden Marauders?"

She sucked in a breath to keep from laughing. How was he making her laugh when she was quite close to a panic?

"*Don't* call them that, and stop pointing that thing at me, or I'll bite it off." She reached for it, but he planted the finger with the rest of his hand on the column she was leaning against.

"Don't tempt me," he countered. Hiding in corners with this man was a habit she absolutely needed to break. Especially when he was in formal wear. God, she wanted to climb him. "Are you truly afraid of a few snobs and a pair of sanctimonious pricks in bad suits?" he asked, with genuine surprise.

"No, I'm not afraid of them," she pouted. "My nerves just get the best of me at times." She sighed and looked up at him, and found that steadfast regard that, somehow, she'd begun to trust more than any other.

"Am I hearing right?" The pendejo actually cupped his ear. "That you, the woman who lectures me constantly on how the medical establishment doesn't know what it's doing, are considering missing an opportunity to educate all those aristos?"

"Do you keep a record of everything I say?" she snapped back. He only grinned.

"I might." Why did he say things like this when this could never be more than what it was now? Tonight only made that fact that much clearer.

"Virginia deserved this more than I do." His gaze took that haunted look she'd seen before in his eyes. Like her words clawed at him sometimes.

"But I didn't do this for Virginia, I did it for you." Her chest pounded, and howling, needy things that could never see the light of day almost tore out.

"You're giving me an unfair advantage, then," she tossed out, in a desperate attempt to rein in her emotions.

"That's right, Bella Doctora." He lifted a shoulder, his coffee-bean eyes shining with defiance and something much more volatile. She felt like he was looking right into her soul. "I'm the Duke of Annan, and I'm using my power, my position *and* my money to give you what you deserve. What about it?"

What a terrible thing it would be to have to give up this man.

"Won't this hurt your efforts to make alliances?" She'd been concerned about this for days now. It seemed particularly obtuse, even for Apollo, to advertise a connection to a clinic he knew did things that were not exactly legal and certainly not considered moral by the very people he was attempting to ingratiate himself with.

"Fiera, you underestimate me, as always," he told her with a wolfish grin, and her legs nearly buckled from the effect. "My house is currently packed to the gills with the *progressive* ilk of the aristocracy. They're simply delighted to support my entry into the ton," he informed her, affecting a ridiculous posh accent. "You see, I will be such an excellent representation of my people."

Aurora frowned at that and slowly asked, "What people?"

Apollo's grin was sharp as a blade. "I have not managed to extract that answer from a single one of them. What I have been regaled with are plenty of stories about their abolitionist ancestors and how their great-grandmamas handed out blankets to street urchins." His tone was light enough, but there was a cutting edge to it. "They're always so forthcoming about their good deeds, but things do become quite less jovial whenever I ask if their abolitionist grandparents received any of that twenty million the king awarded the great and good of the Empire in compensation for losing their slaves."

She was struck once again at just how good Apollo was at hiding in plain sight. The ton had no idea they had a wolf in their midst.

"I presume *you* know quite well which ones did," she said, and he made a very gratified sound, like a cat who'd just brought back a tribute to his master and received a nice scratch for his trouble.

"I keep a list of the names on my desk, Fiera." Other women might not find Apollo's dogged insistence on schemes and machinations arousing, but she certainly did. "They might have forgotten the finer details of their Slavery Abolition Act, but I never will."

"They won't see you coming, will they?" she asked, momentarily stunned by his wiliness.

"Not even when I reach for their throats, sweetheart." That smile, it made her ache.

She imagined this was what it looked like when people used their power for good. Not exactly pretty, even ruthless at times, but still righteous. "Now, what do you need to go out there and help all those ladies of leisure feel good about themselves while we extract some of those ill-gotten gains of theirs?"

"What I need help with is focus," she informed him in a breezy tone.

"Focus, you say?" the duke asked, in that molasses voice of his, which sank deep into her bones. It made her weak.

"Indeed." She circled her arms around his neck. "But I keep thinking about kissing you and it's much too distracting." His other arm joined the first on that spot on the column above her head as she raised herself on the tips of her toes.

"What kind of host would I be if I didn't help my guest of honor?"

"Kiss me, Your Grace," she demanded.

"For the good of science," he teased, with a graze of his lips that felt like the static in the air before a thunderstorm.

"For science," she agreed, turning her head, and then he was there, inside. With a kiss like roaring flames. His tongue razing through nerves and thoughts of fickle aristocrats and men who ruined lives.

It was one of his deep kisses. The ones where their lips almost melded together. When their lungs seemed to be sharing each breath. His palm like a brand against her throat kept her where he wanted, and he took her mouth like it belonged to him. Like he'd drawn a map of his property and he'd explore it like he damned well pleased.

Licks and bites, whispered words of praise. How sweet her mouth was, how much he loved kissing her. When she was ready to sink to the ground, he pulled back.

"Is your focus much improved?" She wasn't sure how she ever thought asking the man to kiss her could result in anything but absolute chaos in her head.

"Yes," she lied, as she found her footing.

"You seem a bit unsteady, Doctora," he jested, and planted a sweet kiss to her brow that made her heart flutter.

She was a lost cause.

"Don't flatter yourself, Your Grace," she told him, hoping she'd make it out of this hedge on her own two feet. "I'm simply worried that I'll be booed for my objectionable beliefs."

"You were invited here to share your objectionable beliefs," he told her.

"Apollo, I won't pull any punches for this crowd." She was proud of her work, but it was hard to fully let go of the habit of making her views palatable to people. "I will speak about the clinic's work with midwives, our stance that they should be considered an integral part of the medical establishment."

"How do you mean?" She'd already explained all of this to him, but he was looking at her like he'd never heard any of it and she figured she might as well batten down the hatches with this affable—if troublesome—audience of one.

"As I've told you before," she remarked with a growl. "As medicine has become more formalized, and even with the entry of women into the profession, our access to services has decreased." He gave the finger she was pointing at his face a sardonic glance. She would need to watch that habit. She sheepishly put it away and launched into her speech again. "Midwives have been marginalized and pushed out, which has resulted in men controlling the kind of services women are able to receive. And it's all done in the name of our welfare."

"And who were these midwives again?" he asked, with a furrowed brow. As if the entire thing was much too vexing for him.

"I'm getting tired of repeating myself, Apollo." He only stared at her with blank eyes. "Fine," she harrumphed. How could he do this, melt her one second and drive her absolutely mad in the next? "The midwives," she said the words slowly as if to a toddler, "by and large in the Americas were Indigenous or Black women. Here in Europe, they typically belonged to the working class. For centuries, they safely provided contraception, education, counseling and care for women and their children." Just saying these things made her angry all over again, and she would need to mind her tone in the room with all the aristos. "Now the same women who birthed generations have been branded as quacks and systematically pushed out of the profession."

"Do *you* work with them?" Now he was being intentionally obtuse, and she did not have the time for that.

"Of course I do," she groused. "We work with them at our clinics, and I have been training a few in more complicated procedures, like fistulotomies."

"And contraception," he remarked.

"Yes, contraception too, especially now that the Comstock Act in the United States has prompted other countries to enact similar laws to control women's access to them, you know all this, Apollo," she bit out, none too happy, while he looked at her with a strange expression on his face. She would not explain the blasted American legislation that made all distribution of contraception, or even information about it, a criminal offense to him again. She'd already discussed Anthony Comstock's— who was a postal servant, of all things—war on family planning, ad nauseam.

But when she looked up at the Duke of Annan he did not seem very bothered by her refusal to answer his questions. On the contrary, the man seemed utterly pleased with himself.

"There, now you've given your speech to the most important person here this evening and he fully endorses it," he declared, with a satisfied smile.

"If you wanted me to recite the speech, I could've done so," she told him, much too stupefied by his handsome face to even conjure up annoyance.

"I could've, but now we're both certain that you're quite ready to skewer all the men of science out there." He winked and clasped his hand to the nape of her neck. Something she'd developed a concerning proclivity for. "If not, I could invite them to have a word outside and attempt some of my own methods of persuasion."

Some women might be wooed with flowers. Others perhaps appreciated a serenade. But for Aurora, there was nothing more sensual than a man offering to do violence to a group of misogynistic bastards on her behalf.

"I don't know if dukes ought to be starting brawls at charity events for clinics," she teased, and he flashed her that lupine grin that turned the lower part of her body hot and liquid.

"That would be dukes from around these parts, Fiera. Cartagena dukes do things a little differently." His thumb was making circles on her neck. A motion that she'd also become quite fond of.

There went her focus again.

She placed her palms on his chest and pushed firmly. "It is time to go, Your Grace, or we will never leave this corner."

"Fine, but we will continue this later at the den of iniquity." She nodded in agreement, not bothering to deny what they both knew to be true. She let him kiss her on the neck, and she may have bitten his bottom lip, but this time, she managed to get them both off the column and down the gravel path without any more diversions.

As they emerged into the light, with the comforting weight of his arm looped with hers combined with the slight sting on her lips from his kisses and the fall breeze on her face, Aurora wondered if this was what people felt when they said they were happy.

In the heels of that thought, the sound of a woman's voice stopped Apollo in his tracks. "It's my Tia Jimena," he told her, looking up the path to where a lady and gentleman were walking toward them. She stiffened at the mention of Apollo's relative, who had not been very warm when Aurora had arrived earlier that evening.

"I should go," she told him, ready to make up something in order to avoid a potentially awkward confrontation. And it would be awkward. She knew the condition Apollo's kisses left her in.

"Apollo, querido," the woman called, still concealed by the shadowed path. The man she was with was very tall and had his head bent saying something to her. Something about him sent a cold shiver down her spine.

"Who is that?" she asked as unease flooded her. It was the nerves again, she thought. It was one thing to do her speech for Apollo, another to contemplate doing the same for his forbidding aunt.

"Lord Forsyth. My aunt's beau." By the way Apollo's mouth soured, it seemed he was not fond of the man, but his aunt certainly felt differently. She seemed very taken by whatever he was so passionately parlaying.

"Where have you been? I've been looking all over for you," Apollo's aunt exclaimed as she stepped out of the shadows with a man Aurora had hoped never again to see in her life. "Look who I found when I was out here looking for Juliana."

He was still handsome, the blond hair that mesmerized her at fifteen might have more silver at the temples, but it was still lustrous and perfectly coiffed. The blue eyes she'd told herself shone with interest and desire, instead of the malice she'd later encounter, were still that tantalizing cerulean blue. Tall and beautiful, the kind of man a girl—or a woman—could lose her head over. Except she knew the fangs and scales hidden under the surface. She felt herself begin to shake and locked her legs, clenched her muscles. Forced herself to stand tall as she ignored the frantic hammering of her heart.

Philip Carlyle would not get the best of her ever again.

"Doctora Montalban," he said, extending a hand. "How long has it been?"

"A lifetime," she said, looking at his hand without offering hers.

The last time she saw him, he'd threatened to turn her in to the authorities and destroy her life if she didn't agree to marry him. But by then, the life she thought she'd have was already destroyed. Since that day, she'd wondered what it would be like to see him again. She wondered if she'd be fearful or ashamed of how easily she'd fallen into this charlatan's trap. Only months ago, a moment like this would've brought her to her knees, but now all she felt was rage.

"How do you know each other?" Doña Jimena asked Forsyth, who dropped his proffered hand awkwardly when Aurora would not shake it.

"Miss Montalban's family and I were quite close when I was in Mexico a decade or so ago." He looked her up and down, but she refused to let him make her feel inadequate. He should be the one who was ashamed.

"Was she always passionate about medicine?" Doña Jimena asked Philip about Aurora, as if she wasn't standing right there.

"Miss Montalban was passionate at everything," he said. His tone was innocent enough, but the way he smiled at her made her skin crawl. She thought of Apollo's mischievous smiles, his taunts, and realized that while he infuriated her, his teasing had always been an invitation. He was not interested in dishing out barbs she could not return in equal measure. But this man looked to humiliate, to put her in her place, and she wanted very much to humiliate him.

But if she did, Philip would attack, she could see that in the sly way he examined where Apollo's arm was linked around hers. Could almost hear his machinations as he shot her a look that said "if you expose me, you'll expose yourself."

She couldn't look up at Apollo, who she could feel tensing up at the exchange between her and Philip. But this was going to happen eventually. Her past, her mistakes, coming back to haunt her. It was the choice she'd made after all. She'd refused to let her fate be sealed at age fifteen and that had a cost. The cost was that her place in respectable society would always be in peril.

Apollo knew of her parentage, but that was not something she'd been responsible for. She *was* responsible for the choices she'd made about her body and her future, and she stood by them. But she would not allow him to be impacted by them. It was one thing to let him raise funds for the clinic, but it was another to allow Philip to harm Apollo's standing among his peers. Not when she knew how much he had yet to do.

She had to let him go.

"If you'll excuse me," she said, sliding her arm from Apollo's. When he tried to keep her with him, she tugged free. Her eyes downcast, her heart breaking. But Aurora had never been one to shirk from consequences, and she would not today. "I need to go to my friends and prepare for my speech," she told the Duke of Annan, before walking away.

Twenty

She was in the wind again.

A week. He'd not seen her since that garden party. A damned week she'd been hiding from him, and he'd had enough. He'd known something was amiss the moment they'd encountered Forsyth. He'd felt the change in Aurora, and for the rest of the evening, she hadn't been the same. She'd been brilliant during her speech, as he knew she would. She'd dazzled the charity-minded guests and they'd opened their purses. She'd almost been charming, in that scowling way of hers. But the moment she'd finished, she'd made excuses, claiming she'd received a message about a patient going into labor, and left in a flurry.

That night, she hadn't come to him in his rooms, then the next day, she'd sent him back his key with a note letting him know she couldn't see him anymore and warning him that his aunt should be careful about Forsyth. He'd sent the key back with a note saying they'd made a deal and he intended to make her keep her end of it. A one-word reply came back. A lovely written *Cabrón* with an inspired little curl on the accent mark.

At least she'd kept the key.

She'd also allowed Jean-Louis to continue to escort her on the evening visits to patients, as he'd asked. But it seemed she'd sworn the man to some kind of secrecy pact. Clearly, Jean-Louis's loyalties had changed while in service of Aurora Montalban. So far, Apollo was yet to extract a word out of him about what she'd been up to. As far as Philip Carlyle, Lord Forsyth, was concerned, he'd sent one of his men to dig up information on him.

He'd attempted to speak with his aunt regarding his doubts, but she was adamant Forsyth was instrumental in Apollo's entry into the ton. He doubted that highly and was now convinced the man was up to some grift involving her. He'd asked her if she'd given him money, but so far, she'd denied it. But he also knew his aunt was stubborn and didn't like to appear foolish. She would never admit to judging Forsyth incorrectly unless she was forced to. He *could* have the bastard killed, but that would upset his aunt, and he had enough women in his life angry at him.

"Come in," he called, at a knock on the door, while he examined plans for the building he'd just purchased. The building he had yet to show to its new owner, since she refused to see him.

"Don Duc," Jean-Louis announced himself with that greeting that set his teeth on edge. It didn't matter how many times Apollo told him *duke* was not his new last name. At this point, he figured Jean-Louis was simply entertaining himself at his expense.

"I need to see Doctora Montalban today," he said shortly, his eyes still cast down on the plans.

"I will let the lady doctor know, Don Duc," Jean-Louis informed him with a stubborn look.

"I'm not requesting," Apollo snapped, slapping both hands on his desk. Jean-Louis barely blinked. "I'm requiring her to be here."

The big man twisted his mouth in what Apollo supposed

was his attempt at a smirk, and clasped his enormous hands in front of himself.

"The doctor has some very interesting notions when it comes to gents telling her what to do." Was that admiration in the sod's voice? Was that a sparkle in the eyes of a man Apollo had watched almost kill at least a half dozen men with his bare hands?

"Jean-Louis, are you seeing her today?" he asked through clenched teeth.

"I might be." That was delivered with another of those sparkling smiles and a waggle of busy eyebrows.

His patience was badly frayed, and he would love nothing more than to have someone snap it. Perhaps it would do him good to be pounded to a pulp by this brute. He'd barely slept in the last week.

The worst part was that he knew she'd been there. The smell of carbolic had been thick in the air two nights ago when he'd turned up past two in the morning. But there had been no poorly dressed wildcat to be seen. She was sneaking in with patients without leaving a word.

He had things to do, carajo.

There was Ackworth and his ploy to declare him an impostor, the damned MPs who wanted his vote but not so much his presence, and this blasted bride hunt. But did he attend to any of it? No, he was sitting in his apartment, watching the door, waiting for a five-foot-three-inch headache to walk in and continue to disrupt his existence.

"Then you best make sure she's here, in my house, not one minute past noon." Jean-Louis simply raised an eyebrow completely unbothered. "Not one minute later, or you can tell your lady doctor that I will come for her myself." Apollo knew this was his own doing. He'd been careless somewhere and now things were out of his control. He did not like it when his world was in disorder, and that was exactly what her absence felt like.

"She's really got you sweating." Jean-Louis delivered this observation displaying an impressive number of teeth, and Apollo almost launched himself across his desk and throttled the man. "She's something, that lady doctor," the former pugilist chuckled, as if Aurora's intent on driving Apollo out of his mind was the most delightful thing he'd ever heard.

"Bring her *to me*, Jean-Louis." He thought he felt one of his molars pop, but for once, Jean-Louis kept his mouth shut and nodded.

"Sobrino!" His aunt barreled into the room with that frantic air she carried around recently.

"Tia, I don't have—"

"No, you're not getting out of this, Apollo," she exclaimed, as Jean-Louis scurried out of the room.

"It is barely nine in the morning," he groaned, but his aunt was giving him no quarter. She stood across his desk with a stubborn scowl that spelled trouble.

"I just heard from Claude that you won't see your guests for morning tea."

His aunt's new strategy was matchmaking by covert strikes. She'd taken to bringing gaggles of girls over at random times, as if she could ambush him into picking one.

"They're not my guests," he said tightly. "They're *your* guests."

"What in the world is happening with you?" his aunt asked, looking genuinely baffled.

"What is happening, Tia, is that I have a dukedom to run," he said with as much calm as he could manage. He loved his aunt, but as of late, it was as if she felt entitled to his life. For so long, he'd seen her as his champion for this lost cause he'd been fighting against his father, recently he felt increasingly confined by her intents on his life. "Evan is coming over today to discuss matters of the duchy. We have meetings with businessmen in the afternoon." And he had what was almost surely going to be a battle of wills in about three hours with Aurora. "Can't Juliana entertain those ladies with you?"

"Juliana's gone to see some paintings at one of the galleries in the exposition with a new friend." Lately every time he asked about his cousin, she was out with some new acquaintance, and he wondered if Juli's whereabouts should be his aunt's focus, not Apollo's marital future.

"Then you entertain them, Tia," he said with such force, his aunt flinched. He immediately felt guilty, but then his aunt spoke and made him angry all over again.

"Lord Forsyth has advised that you present yourself as a man of leisure. It is unseemly for a duke to work."

"I don't care what Forsyth says." He was being a brute and that would not help matters. "Perdoname, Tia," he apologized, rubbing his hands over his face. This was not how he wanted for a conversation about Forsyth to go. Losing his temper whenever the man came up would only make things harder. "I will come and say hello to the guests for a few minutes, but I truly cannot spend the morning having tea with debutantes." This mollified her, somewhat, but she was still frowning at him.

"Something's different about you, sobrino," his aunt said, her gaze vexed by whatever she saw in him.

"I *am* different, aunt, I have a world of responsibilities, dozens of families who depend on me, and taking tea with heiresses is not a priority." Again she sent him one of those perturbed looks, her eyes searching, as if there was something she was missing.

"But hosting charity salons for women with murky reputations is? You do know the rumors of the conditions of her birth." This he would not tolerate. Somehow, he knew this was Forsyth's doing.

"Aurora is not up for discussion," he told his aunt, in a hard tone. "And she has nothing to do with this."

"Don't forget who you're here for." For his mother. To honor her name. To ensure her death was not in vain. But he wondered if performing for these aristocrats was the way to do that.

"I cannot be like my father and shirk my duties."

"No, you cannot," she told him after a long pause. With a sigh, she came around and kissed him on the cheek. "Violeta would be so proud of you," his aunt told him, before quietly exiting the room.

The mention of his mother felt like a punch in the gut. All this time, he thought this was what she'd wanted. To see him triumph, to see him reclaim what was robbed from him. But lately he could not stop thinking that his mother, like that patient of Aurora's, had been barely sixteen when she married.

He could only imagine the fear she'd felt when she found herself on her own, with a man who, in many ways, was a stranger and who ultimately never cared for her. He wondered what would make *that* girl proud. He was starting to believe it might have nothing to do with titles.

"Don't tell me you're hiding in here." Apollo didn't appreciate Evan's grin or his confident guess of his current circumstances as he made his way into the room.

"How bad is it?" he asked, and Evan grinned, before taking his usual seat.

"They look quite bloodthirsty."

"Wasn't your wife to be here for this?" Apollo asked, annoyed. The three of them had been working on a plan to erect a bottling plant for Luz Alana's new cordials on a piece of land owned by the duchy near Glasgow. "Her presence is a requirement if I am to tolerate yours." Evan only laughed, but Apollo did not miss the contentment in his brother at the mention of his new wife. He truly would not have believed a mere few months—and the love of a woman—could transform a man so dramatically. But the same Evan, who a year ago told Apollo that once they exacted revenge on their father, he would leave society forever, was now making plans to establish the first association for business and tradespeople that welcomed women.

Apollo did not begrudge him any of it. Not really, but at moments like this, when the weight of his title and the life that came with it seemed beyond his capabilities. Perhaps Evan had been so eager to help him claim it because he didn't want it either.

"You're truly cross," Evan said, with a frown. Apollo grunted in answer as he pretended to double-check his tie. "I would've thought a room full of women poised to throw themselves at you would be a boon."

"There isn't a single woman in that room who sees me as anything other than a novelty or a taste of something exotic." Evan, as he always did when the cravenness of the people of his world came to light, looked contrite. Apollo had no patience for his brother's guilt today. "If there's one thing you are not responsible for, *Lord Evan*—" his brother winced at the title, but Apollo carried on "—it's for overeager debutantes and their mothers. If we were in Cartagena, it would be the same, they'd just look different."

"At least this batch is a bit more varied than the one from London." Apollo rolled his eyes at the reminder of the mothers who had descended on him like locusts after he'd arrived in the city, once his father's death was announced.

"I truly don't have the energy for any of this," Apollo said with finality, then bit back a groan when the image of a certain half-feral physician appeared in his mind.

"You don't seem to have energy for much at the moment," Evan concurred, which only incensed Apollo more.

"I still thrashed you this morning." Evan shrugged, unbothered. These days, the hunted, high-strung man Apollo had first met was a far cry from this smiling, easygoing man.

"Are you certain there's nothing amiss? You seem tired. Are you sleeping?" Apollo only shook his head. He could tell Evan the reasons why he hadn't slept in days. But his brother would most likely laugh in Apollo's face. It was what he'd done to him when he was at his wit's end over Luz Alana. "Is it Ackworth?" Evan asked, now a hint of real concern in his voice.

He shook his head and sighed. "No, but I'm sure he'll be making himself a nuisance soon enough."

"I wish we could get something on him," Evan mused. Apollo did too, but so far they had not been able to find out much that could help them discredit the bastard. "If it's not Ackworth, something else is amiss," his brother pushed. "You've been even more unbearable than usual."

"Do I need more reasons to be cross than the bevy of women in that other room waiting to sink their claws into me?" he asked, with honest exasperation.

Evan chuckled, mollified for the moment. "I can't say I envy you," he conceded, pushing off from his repose on Apollo's desk. "I will go get my wife, and we shall be back to save you from their satin-clad clutches."

"I'll go deal with the debutantes," he announced, peevishly and stood up.

Perhaps Aurora was doing him a favor by keeping her distance. The last thing he wanted was to drag a woman who already took on all of the world's problems into his mess. A mess that was all of his own making.

When he reached the door connecting his study, Apollo sighed, turned the knob and stepped inside.

"Ladies, did I keep you waiting?"

Twenty-One

"We will be going to see the duque after this," Jean-Louis informed Aurora as he helped her out of the carriage. She knew it was useless to argue with the man and that this impending audience with Apollo was inevitable.

Instead of answering, Aurora focused on her patient's well-appointed street as she tried to anticipate what she'd be walking into. At least she had protection, even if it came in a quite aggravating package.

Just the previous evening, she'd received an unexpected request from her fistulotomy patient asking Aurora to her home for the postsurgical visit. Given the young woman's distress regarding her husband in those initial encounters, she'd had been reluctant to come alone, which was how she'd ended up with Apollo's henchman as a chaperone that morning. Which meant there was no escaping the duke's summoning. She had no doubt that if she refused to go see Apollo, she'd find herself over Jean-Louis's shoulder.

"I said I would go after this visit, Jean-Louis," she retorted with a sneer, but the man was utterly unflustered by her annoyance. And it wasn't like she hadn't expected Apollo to do this. In truth, she'd expected him to barrel into Claudine's the very next day after the charity event. But to her surprise, the Duke of Annan had stayed away.

She'd be lying to herself if she didn't admit to missing the man. Despite her efforts to maintain emotional distance from him, she'd felt his absence intensely. She yearned for the den of iniquity and how simple everything was there. So, she'd kept her distance, because she'd rather have him mad at her than make him vulnerable to Philip's monstrosity.

Whatever game the man was playing was a dangerous one and her presence would only make it worse. Philip had been silent, no threats, no warnings about revealing their past connection, and that scared her more than if he had. She knew sending Apollo that note instead of telling him face-to-face had been cowardly, but he would've asked questions she didn't feel ready to answer. She could've contacted her brothers to alert them of Philip's whereabouts, but the last thing she needed was three more overbearing males underfoot.

No, she had matters in hand. Today she would tell Apollo what was happening between them had to end and she'd go back to her life. She'd only been in the man's bed for a week, how hard could it be to give it up?

She decided she was not in the state of mind to answer that question honestly and diverted her attention to the task at hand. For now, she'd leave the worrying about Apollo, Philip and her brothers for after the visit. This was not the time to have her head in the clouds. She had no sense what would await her this morning. The patient had been so skittish before, she could only assume she was a glorified prisoner in her own home.

"You can accompany me to the gate, but you cannot loiter by the door as you do at the clinics," she warned Jean-Louis as they neared the house, which earned her a sound that was not exactly a no but very far from anything that sounded like an agreement. The man took his task of guarding her a bit too seriously and had attempted more than once this past week to dissuade her from leaving the carriage at certain locations. He could also be quite stubborn. "This should not be a very long visit," she reassured him when they reached the door.

She looked up at the ostentatious molding above the doorway and considered what might await her. A potential confrontation with an irate husband who at the very least terrified his own wife.

This was probably too much of a risk. She knew that, but she couldn't leave a patient to her own devices after a procedure. And Doña Maria had made the request herself. This was part of the work, after all, risk-taking. She wasn't asking anyone to incur it for her—other than using Apollo's apartment and then demanding he keep her secrets—and it was her prerogative to help those who needed it. That was the vow she'd made after all that happened with Philip. She would never leave a woman to her fate if she could help it.

She just wished she hadn't started things with Apollo, because for the first time since she'd begun her medical studies, her own needs seemed to be at the forefront of her mind. She missed Apollo, missed the way he took care of her, and wasn't that idiotic? A man who she could never have.

Perhaps it was time to leave Paris. Apollo would get that building for the clinic, she was certain of that. And now with stronger financial support, everything would be all right. She'd managed to ensure that the clinic could provide services for a long time to come.

By the time she grabbed the door knocker, Aurora was in a mood, which became evident by her aggressive pounding on the door. It wasn't very long before a forbidding gentleman opened the door.

"Yes?" he asked haughtily as he gave her a thorough examination. It was quite a feat, considering he didn't lower his head even a fraction of a centimeter. He was quite tall and dressed in dark livery. Not bulky like Jean-Louis, but he seemed perfectly capable of keeping her out if he felt like it. His cold blue eyes and his sneer certainly didn't appear welcoming.

"I'm here to see your mistress, she's expecting me."

He seemed genuinely confused at her words, as if the idea of the lady of the house receiving any callers was unfathomable.

"I'm a physician," she explained. This statement, as expected, only made the man look that much more suspicious.

"It's all right, Collins." Doña Maria appeared at the top of the stairs in her usual sober attire. But instead of that sullen demeanor from before, her lovely brown face was more animated and there was color on her cheeks. "I can take if from here." She rushed forward, pushing the man aside, who emitted a little yelp at his mistress's arrival.

"But, madame, we were told to not allow any company that's not in his lordship's list while he is away."

His lordship.

Aurora had suspected her patient was married to someone of a certain standing. This was risky indeed. The servant had an English accent, which told her it was probably some British aristocrat living in Paris as an expatriate. It was not his words that chilled her to her core, but the reproving, patronizing tone he used. Like Doña Maria was not his mistress, but merely a wayward child. But if being spoken to by her servants in such a derogatory way bothered her patient, she did not show it. On the contrary, the young woman was uncowed by the man's rudeness, as she sent him another defiant look.

"Please come in, Doctora Montal—" Doña Maria stopped short, likely out of caution of not identifying Aurora to the traitorous Collins. "You may go, Collins. I will call for you if I need anything." Aurora watched in amazement as the cowering woman she'd first met was now standing up for herself. "As far

as I know, this is my home and I shall receive whoever I like."
With a cutting glare, Doña Maria walked past her odious servant and took Aurora's hand. That horrid odor from the fistula
was gone, replaced by a lovely fragrance of orange blossoms.

"My apologies, Collins can overstep." Her voice sounded
stronger, and she stood taller. Her raven black hair was in a
thick braided crown around her head. There was a strength
back in her voice, in the way she held herself, that had not
been there before.

It was the kind of change Aurora had seen countless times.
This woman's ailment had taken her dignity, her humanity,
and now she'd begun to recover it. Witnessing this, knowing
that in some small way she'd helped her reclaim something
that had been stolen from her was why Aurora would never
let anything keep her from her work. If she were the emotional type, Aurora thought she might shed a tear or two for
this newly emboldened version of Doña Maria.

"This way," the young woman indicated, pointing down
a long hallway.

"How are you feeling, Doña Maria?" Aurora asked, as they
made their way past a number of large portraits displaying what
looked like generations of prominent ancestry.

"Please call me Sandra," she said with a smile that went all
the way up to her eyes.

"All right." Aurora nodded, then did as asked. "How are
you feeling, Sandra?" She rarely found out her patients' real
names or learned much of their lives. It was part of their strict
rules around anonymity, but she was glad to experience this
rare moment. To see this kind of transformation made the sac-
rifices worth it.

"I haven't felt this well in years," Sandra told her, but it
seemed something else was on her mind.

"Are there any other issues?" Her patient shook her head as she led Aurora into a drawing room.

"Is this where you'd like us to do the examination?" she asked, looking around for a place where Sandra could lie down to have the stitches taken out. She understood the woman's reluctance to have Aurora come to her bedchamber, with her staff being as intrusive as it was, but this room seemed particularly unsuitable. "We will need a place where you can lie down," she said, looking at the two chaises, which could work, if necessary, but they were not exactly the best option. "For me to remove the sutures."

"Yes, of course." Sandra sounded a bit distracted, and when Aurora came closer, she could hear her teeth chattering.

For a second, Aurora panicked and wondered if her patient had set a trap for her. Perhaps informed the police of her visit. The procedure she'd performed was perfectly legal, but she certainly didn't want them looking too closely.

"Has something happened to your children?" she asked, hoping for an answer that didn't involve potential legal troubles for herself. It would break her heart to be betrayed by this woman.

"No, my girls are fine," Sandra assured her, though she was clearly distressed.

"There's another room where we can do the examination, after," Sandra finally said. When Aurora looked down, she noticed the patient was wringing her hands. "I wanted to ask you something first." Something about the way she said it told Aurora the request had nothing to do with doctoring. Her voice was very low, like she was afraid someone had their ear pressed to the door.

"What do you need?" she asked, knowing that no matter how dangerous the request, she would try to help.

"I've decided to leave my husband," the young woman said,

the tremor in her voice replaced by a steel that made Aurora swell with pride for whatever little part she'd had in it. "I don't have a lot of funds for the journey, only the pin money I've saved, but it's enough to get to my sister in Geneva. She's begged me for years to come to her. I'm finally ready." This would not be an easy thing. Even if she was willing to help, there was much to think about.

The law these days was more lenient toward women when it came to divorce, but there would be a scandal. In a court of law, her husband could probably take her children without much difficulty. There was so much to consider, so many pitfalls she could encounter, and Aurora knew she should bring those up before she agreed to anything. She also knew there was no possible way she would not do what she could to help her.

There was nothing to be done for the fifteen-year-old Aurora who had fallen into a terrible man's clutches and paid a hefty price. But this older Aurora had a responsibility to be worthy of that bravery. Just like there was nothing to do for the years Sandra had lost, or for the pain she'd endured at her husband's hands. But the future could be different for her, for her children.

"I know I ask too much," Sandra apologized, as Aurora considered matters.

"How long will your husband be gone?" This was not the first time the clinic had aided a woman in escaping a terrible husband, but never one of this station. There could be repercussions for all of them if the man found out who helped her. But Aurora could not walk away and leave her here trapped.

"He returns late this evening." That was not ideal. Aurora would not have time to get her more funds to escape with. She didn't even know if there was a train she could leave on today. But if Sandra could pack herself and her children up quickly, she could well be on her way to Switzerland by the time he came back.

"Sandra," she said, taking the woman's hand. It was damp and cold, and she could feel the nervous tremors going through her.

"Yes, Doctora?" The hope in her voice almost broke Aurora, but this was not a moment for emotions. This was a time for action. With Sandra's pin money and some of Aurora's own emergency reserves, they could get her and the children away.

"Are you certain your sister will help you? He could come after you because of the children." There was no point in sugarcoating the situation. This would only work if she knew what she was in for.

"She was always opposed to the marriage. She told my father Lord Ackworth was much too old for me." A shadow crossed Sandra's face and Aurora's fury rose at the thought of what horrors she was likely recalling. "She said she'd help me with the divorce. I sent her a telegram after the surgery and she asked me to come."

Sandra had the loving support of a sister and that was worth everything.

"You will have to leave now. With whatever you can carry." Sandra sent her another of those tenacious looks and nodded.

"I'm ready and I'm not afraid anymore." No, she wasn't, Aurora could see it. "I might not get another chance."

"We need to find out the train schedule," she began, but Sandra pulled out a paper and gave it to her.

"There's one train to Geneva, leaving in three hours. I have my bags packed." She pointed at two valises sitting by the door, with two small cloaks draped over them. Once again, her chest swelled with admiration for this woman's resilience. "I just need a conveyance that can take me and the children to the station." They had three hours, which would give them enough time to take out her stitches, have Jean-Louis stage some kind of escape plan and get her away.

"I have a carriage outside," she told Sandra, who looked like she'd collapse with relief at the news. Reluctantly, Aurora sent a thanks to Apollo's overbearingness. "Let me examine you first," she said, pointing to one of the chaises. "Then we'll get you on that train."

It took exactly two hours to examine her, enlist Jean-Louis and create a diversion with the servants that involved a small fire and a nearly disastrous encounter with an alley cat, but they managed to get Sandra and her children out. A feat she knew would not have been possible without the Duke of Annan's carriage or his henchman.

Twenty-Two

Three hours into his aunt's blasted tea service, Apollo was questioning every decision in his life that led him to this room overrun with debutantes competing for his attention with the zeal of gladiators in the Colosseum.

As it was, he should have nothing to complain about. When he'd announced he was in Paris to search for a bride, this was what he'd been after. Wasn't it? Beautiful, well-bred, gracious girls…who left him cold. Guileless, smiling blank canvases for him to fill with his own tastes and preferences until they could anticipate his every whim. Well-cultured girls with enough sensibility to be stirred with just enough sentiment when taking in a particularly moving opera, but with not enough imagination to lose sleep over Apollo's dalliances. Docile and malleable, the complete opposite of the woman who dominated his every waking thought.

How could he be content with any of these kittens, when he'd had a lioness in his bed?

"Your Grace, if I may." With great effort, Apollo forced himself to muster up some kind of enthusiasm for the young woman calling his name. Lady Gertrude, if he remembered. The child of a destitute earl who had gambled away a fortune built on the backs of the people Gertrude's ancestors kept in bondage.

"Lady Gertrude." He nodded and took the gloved hand she proffered. It occurred to him that he'd likely encounter skin as supple and smooth as a baby's under the satin. The thought made him sick with want for a pair of scratchy, battered hands. He would have Aurora in his bed tonight. He'd had about enough of this cat-and-mouse game. He was a damned duke, for God's sake.

"I'd like to sing you a song on the piano," Lady Gertrude offered with a girlish flutter of her eyelashes and an eager smile. He almost laughed at the round of eye rolls and pouts around the room at her coquettish efforts. He did appreciate the girl's initiative, but he didn't think he could tolerate this much longer.

Where was Evan with the damned cavalry?

"I'm afraid I must excuse myself, ladies," he said in an attempt to suppress whatever plans Lady Gertrude had involving a wreath of what looked like silk tropical flowers her mother had pulled out of a bag.

"Per favore, Duca," the girl's mother pleaded in Italian. It would probably do no good to explain to her that he spoke Spanish. They'd only stare at him blank-faced and switch to French.

One of the most tedious aspects of his newfound popularity among the ton was their insistence on relaying their comfort with his "ethnic characteristics." He could not swear to it, but he was certain that a couple of the women had applied some kind of darkening substance to their skin.

"Your Grace, we have also heard of a party you are hosting in Nice." This came from the Portuguese matron whose lovely daughter had earlier impressed upon him her talent in speaking dead languages and reciting a plethora of poems by deader white men.

"Unfortunately, Señora Carmela, the guests to my house party are only residents of countries *outside* of Europe." He took advantage of the stupefied look on all the faces in the room and stood up with every intention of ending this audience, even if he was branded as rude, when a knock on the door caught his attention and, for a glorious moment, shifted the focus of a dozen pairs of eyes away from his person.

He decided to use this distraction as an opportunity to escape when the thing flew open. Standing on the threshold was an extremely cross Aurora Montalban in her usual disheveled glory, and had it not been for the dozen or so ladies of leisure currently occupying every surface of the room, he would have grabbed her by the waist and kissed her senseless.

"What do you want, Annan?" she exclaimed with extreme outrage, after sending his butler a threatening look, while the man hovered behind her like a mother hen.

"Your Grace," the butler pleaded, as he backed away from Aurora. Claude had a few inches on Apollo, which meant he was a good foot taller than his Fiera.

He would put his money on her, without hesitation.

"I can handle things from here, Claude, thank you."

She whirled on him, her eyes flashing with menace. Not even the murmuring which suddenly erupted around the room could make him take his eyes off her. She was in one of her dark suits. For once, her hair seemed to be behaving and his hands itched to tug a curl loose. It was the first time in days he'd felt like there was blood, not ice, running through his veins.

None of these pretty girls with their breeding and lovely manners could hold his attention like this hellion could.

"You called for me," she insisted, barreling into the room,

then stopped short when she realized they had an audience. It took her a moment to register what she'd walked into, but he saw the realization descend on her face. Her expression went from annoyed to confused to…thunderous, in a matter of seconds. Then a very dangerous glint, much like the one he'd seen in her eyes right before she'd pulled her pistol, Juana Inés, on him.

"Ah, have I interrupted your tea, Your Grace?" she asked with concerning sweetness as she took in the women in the room and what had to be miles of tulle and taffeta. When she was done, she bared her teeth at the women. "Ladies, if you would excuse us." She lifted her battered Gladstone and slapped it on top of the sideboard, making the small cakes and sandwiches on tiered trays shake ominously.

Apollo was mesmerized.

"I was about to sing for His Grace," Lady Gertrude explained. His Fiera bared her teeth further. One of the ladies actually whimpered in fear.

"How quaint, but I'm afraid I will have to ask that His Grace cut things short." Aurora Montalban could tell herself as much as she wanted that this thing between them was of no consequence, but the way she was looking at him right then was nothing if not proprietary. He sent her a look he hoped communicated that he'd love to see her stake her claim. "You see—" she turned to the women, with a contrite expression "—we're in the midst of a quite rigorous treatment to rid the duke of a fairly nasty case of foot fungus. But don't worry, he should be right as rain for the nuptials."

A chorus of wails and horrified gasps swept around the room while Aurora positively beamed at him. After that announcement it did not take long to vacate the parlor, and within a few minutes, they were alone in the room.

His aunt would probably have an apoplexy when she returned from her errand to find the house empty of maidens and their eager mamas.

Aurora, on the other hand, looked quite pleased with herself.

"You're very well-versed in deception, Fiera. I'm impressed."

"You were the one demanding I come to see you, only to be entertaining half of the unmarried women in Paris when I arrived." She sounded more than a little peevish and he could not say he minded.

"I should make sure to have you around when I need to rid myself of unwanted guests," he suggested, which earned him quite a bellicose stare.

"You didn't seem to be in much distress when I arrived."

"Have my female admirers put you in a cantankerous mood?" She threw her head back and laughed, as if the mere suggestion was ridiculous. Except she kept looking at a spot on his lapel as if she wanted to walk up to him and tear it off.

The same spot, he noted, Lady Gertrude had daringly brushed with her finger as she'd said her goodbyes. Doctora Montalban might have kept herself away, but indifference was not the reason.

"Why have you been hiding from me, Aurora?" Her head snapped up at his use of her name. There was a vulnerability in her eyes, a caged glint to them that made him want to reach for her, but from the hard set of her shoulders, he knew that would likely lead to another encounter with Juana Inés.

Apollo had a habit of asking questions as if he already knew the answers. It vexed her when he looked at her as if he could discern her actions, before she had herself.

And she could just tell him.

Confess the baggage she trailed with her everywhere. Her fear of what Philip might do to her reputation, to Apollo's. But she could not bear his disdain, or much worse, his pity. Not after what felt like such a victory this morning.

"I haven't been hiding, Your Grace," she refuted, infusing as much tedium into her words as she could manage. "I have been working."

Working and pining for him, wishing on those nights she could barely drag herself up the flight of stairs to her small room at Claudine's that she was walking into the den of iniquity instead. Where he'd have a platter of something delicious waiting for her. But that man, those cozy rooms, none of it was real. *This* was what was real, the opulent residence of the Duke of Annan. Where the most well-bred ladies of Europe and beyond came in the hopes of being selected as his bride.

What was real, and never would cease to be so, was that *she* was the ruined bastard of a man who never loved her and a woman who didn't love her enough. What she had was her work and her skill and herself. Nothing else.

"Jean-Louis said you had something to show me," she said, for once opting for a noncombative approach with this man. She could not afford to lose more battles to her desires.

"Jean-Louis said—" Apollo spat his henchman's name with an aggression she didn't quite like "—that you've been running around in dangerous places again."

That surprised her, she didn't think Jean-Louis would divulge that information. Then again, the man was under Apollo's employment. She'd known him learning about her affairs was a risk.

Now here they were entangled, impossibly knotted in each other, and the ripping apart would leave her bereft.

"What if I am?" She did not hold back, her voice as loud as she could make it. "Any trouble I might find, I will take care of," she told him arrogantly, even when merely hours earlier, his protection aided her in helping someone to safety. It was fickle and wrong, but she was grasping at straws.

"I—" He echoed her exasperated tone, which only made her temper rise further. "Why do you insist on pretending there's no one in the world that cares for you? Is it pride?" She'd never seen him angry, she realized. What she'd witnessed, those displays of temper, had been mere displeasure, because Apollo César Sinclair Robles in a fit of fury was something else altogether. He loomed so large, his face like a thundercloud. Not even a trace of that ever-present humor remained. "Is this some kind of punishment you inflict on yourself?" She flinched at the question, not liking how close it felt to the truth.

It *vexed* her that even when she was furious at him, she could not help but notice how the bow of his top lip dipped perfectly. That the memory of how his lips felt on her breasts haunted her like a wraith. It was devastating to know his kisses and his touch would be someone else's soon.

"As much as I enjoy all this—" she waved a hand between them, to which he barely reacted "—can you please tell me what you asked me here for."

He didn't answer, his eyes roaming over her like he was taking inventory. Then he took a step closer. She could flee, the door was right there. But her feet would not move.

"One week, Aurora," he said, when he was finally in front of her. The back of a settee dug into her rump. If she leaned back even an inch, she'd topple over the thing.

"What do you mean?" she asked, pretending not to know seven days had passed since she'd been in his bed. His finger traced the curve of her neck, up to her jaw, and she clenched it to keep it from trembling. "You're toying with me, Apollo." Her admonition was a little breathless, and she could not focus when he was looking at her like that.

"Do I look like I'm playing, Fiera?" he asked, and again her body reacted in ways that should've scared her.

"You're certainly wasting my time," she protested, clutching the finger he was using to make sensual circles around her nipple. "Stop it." Her demand was feeble, barely a thread. When he leaned in and brushed a kiss to her neck, her hand fell away.

"Stop wanting you?" he asked huskily, then slid his tongue over her bottom lip. "Stop taking myself in hand whenever I think of the honey between your thighs?"

"Apollo." It was a useless plea, because whatever he wanted from her, she'd give him.

"You've deprived me, Fiera," he told her, before he brushed his lips on hers. And her throat clenched almost painfully. "Did you miss my hands on you?" She whimpered as her own hands scrambled for purchase behind herself. "Did you think about how deep I was inside you the last time?" Her sex clenched at the memory of how it had felt. He bit her lip and she moaned. "You remember how I took you?"

Her hands itched to undo buttons, to lift her own skirts, to open the placket of his trousers so she could see him, take him in her hand, her body.

"We said this would only be temporary, that it would have to finish eventually," she countered, feebly.

"I'm not finished yet," he growled, before he lifted her off the ground.

"Put me down, Apollo." She deployed her most forbidding tone, but he was not listening and soon she found herself seated on a desk. "You'll make me late for m…" Whatever else she was going to say flew out of her mind when he did something utterly wicked to her earlobe.

"This should not take very long," he said amiably, sliding a hand under her skirts.

"You're attempting to distract me," she complained weakly, feeling the ghost of his smile against her lips.

"Is it working?" It was more than working, she was seconds from tearing off his clothes. This was why she had to stay away.

"Not at all," she lied, pushing him away with very little conviction while he slid two fingers inside her. He was just on this side of rough as he thumbed her folds apart. "I'm utterly unaffected," she told him, even as she canted her hips to feel more of his touch. The pad of his finger made wet, lazy circles around her clitoris, which promptly turned her limbs liquid.

"You like that," he told her, his voice hot and low against her ear. "You're so wet for me." She was. Swollen and ready for everything he'd give her. "I think about this all the time." He was tapping on that bundle of nerves now, each touch sending a current of the sweetest pleasure through her. "You might be cross with me, but your sweet, tight concha, she's ripe and eager for me." She opened her mouth to protest, but he was inside her again, those thick fingers preparing her for his entry.

"This is unseemly," she gasped as he stroked her walls and suckled her nipple through the cotton of her shirt.

"What's unseemly is you keeping yourself away when you need this as badly as I do." He sounded furious and she didn't bother denying it.

"Would any of your innocent little maidens let you have them like this?" she asked, unable to help herself, using her teeth on him, even as she parted her thighs farther, desperate for more of his touch.

"I'm a man from the tropics, Aurora," he told her between biting kisses. "What use do I have for a gentle breeze of a girl when my blood requires a storm?" She was a storm in his arms, untamed, dangerous.

"I didn't like their hands on you." She fisted the lapels of his jacket. Right where that debutante slid her finger. A frisson of satisfaction ran through her as he grunted in approval at her possessiveness.

"Unbutton your blouse," he ordered. When she sank her teeth into his shoulder instead, he pushed another finger inside her. "Now, Fiera." With trembling hands, she undid three, enough for him to pluck one breast out and take the nipple in his mouth.

She arched her back at the searing delight of his lips and teeth teasing her. The way his tongue grazed the tip made it tingle all the way down to her belly. She circled one arm around his neck and held on as he brought her so swiftly to climax with his fingers.

"You're clenching around me," he groaned, lifting his head. He was so beautiful, those brown eyes that melted her and that mouth that made her want too much. "I have the plans for your building," he informed her, right before he lifted her skirts up around her waist. His eyes fixed at the juncture of her thighs.

"I'd like to see them, please," she replied in an equally nonchalant manner.

"Only once I've availed myself of what you've been depriving me of first," he told her, licking his lips. She canted her hips for him and a feral sound rumbled in his chest as he caught a glimpse of her mound of curls. He tugged at them as her own hand gripped his hard length.

"So ready for me." She was more than ready and quickly verging into desperation. All anger replaced by blind lust. "Where's my Fiera?" he growled in her ear.

Here, she wanted to say. *Wild and hungry for this thing we do. For the freedom this mad, frenzied lovemaking gives me.*

"Now, Apollo," she demanded while her hand stroked him. He cupped her bottom and lifted her to him.

"Take me inside you," he ordered. She had him in hand and she guided him over her folds, her clitoris. The contact sent hot, feverish tremors through her. "Vamos cariño," he urged, and she could hear an echo of her own need in his voice. She pressed her forehead to his and took him inside, pressing into his thickness until he was fully seated. She shuddered happily, just as he rocked into her.

"There's nothing sweeter than this," he whispered. She palmed the sides of his face and brought his mouth to hers, taking greedy pulls of his tongue, nipping at his bottom lip. The thought of leaving sore spots and bite marks as reminders of what they'd done spurring her on.

"Esto es mio, Fiera," he growled as he pushed himself so deep that she felt him pulsing inside her.

"Go to hell, Duke," she shot back, as their bodies collided recklessly. Her hips met his with such force that the sounds of their crashing bodies drowned out everything.

"We're going to have to find some better use for that smart mouth of yours, Doctora."

"Try it," she challenged, as she rocked her hips into his thrusts. She impaled herself on him wantonly. Fast, intense thrusts mingled with his slow, languid ones that made her sigh. She gasped when he slid his hand out from under her rump to the underside of her knee. He pushed her leg back and sank even deeper.

"Ah, demonios," he gasped when she contracted her walls around him. He bent her over and pushed inside her in earnest. Her core pulsed as sparks exploded in her limbs, crawling up to the very core of her. Her climax washed over her like a summer storm. Powerful and swift. He let out a long, deep groan while his hips twitched against her.

"Fiera." It sounded like a prayer, or maybe a lament. As he eased himself from her body, she closed her eyes and wondered what was happening to her. She'd just let the man have her in his parlor. She could make a scene and start another fight, but what would she gain by that? She was growing bored with her own resistance to this.

"We can't do this in parlors," she said without heat as she attempted to put herself back in order.

"We could be doing it in my den of iniquity as much as you like," he rebuked, as he buttoned his trousers. She tried not to think of the flutter in her chest at the thought that he'd missed her. Then she shook her head at the absurdity of what they were doing.

She was still struggling with her shirt and jacket when he pulled a handkerchief from his trouser pocket.

"Let me," he whispered, pushing the cloth between her legs. He didn't seem the slightest bit embarrassed to be doing this for her. Somehow, this tending to, this gesture that took mere seconds, felt much more intimate than what they'd just done. When he was finished, instead of handing it to her, he pressed it to his nose, then slid it back into his pocket.

"I will dispose of it," she said pointedly, with her hand extended.

"It's mine," he retorted, almost petulantly. Then that wicked grin tipped up his face. "I'll keep it under my pillow for those nights when you disappear on me."

"Why?" she asked, nonplussed.

He pressed the grin to her neck, then nipped at it. "Because your cunt smells so sweet, I'd bury my nose in it a hundred times a day if I could."

"Apollo," her voice came out needy at the blatant, uninhibited way he approached sex.

"A piece of cloth with your scent is a very distant second, but it'll do." A gently bred lady would be appalled, horrified at the crudeness of what he'd done. But she was fascinated, newly aroused by his unapologetic displays of ownership. He finally stepped away from her, looking refreshed and so handsome a greedy urge to claim him rocked her.

"You've made me a mess," she complained as he settled her back on firm ground. When he didn't reply with his usual innuendo, she looked up from straightening her skirts and what she saw in his eyes petrified her.

"What is that man to you, Fiera?" he asked, and she didn't need to ask who. There was something so raw in the way he looked at her that her hands began to shake.

"I don't care about your past," he told her, making her heart hammer painfully in her chest. "But if he's hurt you—"

"No one's hurting me, Apollo." *But you will soon*, she didn't say, *when you marry a girl with no Philips in her past.* She swallowed that sorrow and reached for him, needing to kiss him.

"You keep too many secrets, Fiera." If he only knew. He slid his strong arms around her waist and lifted her off her feet. His kiss was slow and sweet this time. Exploratory and thorough. A man like Apollo could make even her begin to dream of fairy tales.

She met him stroke for stroke, gliding her tongue with his. Her hands clasped behind his neck. She thought that maybe she could tell him. They would still part when he left to choose his bride. She knew who he was now. He would not judge her, or at least she didn't think he would. If she was honest, if she spoke the truth now, she might save him and his aunt some heartache. She was considering doing that very thing when the doors to the room burst open and the worst possible thing that could've happened, happened.

"Aurora Montalban Wright, you little minx." Manuela's unmistakable voice rang through the room in an ominous mixture of delight and devilry as Aurora tried to pry herself from Apollo's grip, and frantically tried to muster up some reason for finding herself in the circumstances she did.

"Well, Your Grace," she said, breathlessly, her legs dangling in the air. "I hope my advice helps with that ailment." She was much too disheveled for her attempt at saving face to work. Her cheeks were so hot she thought she could see smoke rising from them, but she bravely turned to look at her two best friends, Evan and Cora standing in the doorway. "I was just helping the duke with an issue." She could only imagine the state her hair was in and hoped she was not flushing too badly.

"Was the ailment inside his mouth, and were you fixing it with yours?" Luz Alana asked, with a wide grin.

She ignored that and pinched Apollo on the arm hard enough that he finally released her. "Oh, Luz, you know how I feel about divulging patient information, and I should get going."

"Oh no, you're not," Manuela exclaimed, extending both arms to block the entrance to the parlor. Luz stood next to her for good measure and for a second, Aurora considered launching herself out the window. Then decided that moving to Siberia was likely the only way she'd escape her friend's interrogation.

"Fine," she exclaimed in defeat.

"Pardon us, Your Grace," Manuela announced, tugging on Aurora. "We will be back as soon as we hear the details on this new miraculous medical treatment that involves climbing men like trees and the use of tongues."

Apollo's lip twitched, even as he nodded solemnly. "Please take your time," he exhorted. "I'll be right here waiting to offer my testimony to the doctor's skills." The pendejo winked at her. He actually winked at her, right before she was flanked by her two friends and escorted out of the room like a condemned woman headed to the gallows.

Twenty-Three

"Aurora, you sneaky little devil," Manuela said with relish, as she shoved Aurora into an empty room. "This is why you've been hiding from us!"

"It's not what you think." That was met with matching expressions that screamed "you're going to have to do much better than that."

"Leona, I hope you know we're not leaving this room until you give us every sordid detail," Manuela shot back. "The man was squeezing your nalgas so thoroughly I'm surprised he could pry his hands off."

Aurora could've used some kind of Act of God in that moment.

"That's who gave you your love bite." Luz Alana pointed at her neck with triumph, making Aurora regret not climbing out that window earlier.

"You little sucia," Manuela gasped, with an expression of such delighted awe, Aurora almost laughed.

"I'm not a sucia," Aurora volleyed back, with feigned outrage.

"Oh yes, you are," Manu crowed, rubbing her hands like she did when things took a particularly bawdy turn. "This is utterly delicious."

"There is *nothing* happening," she insisted, which was received with a warranted amount of dubiousness.

"All right," she admitted, refusing to look her friends in the eyes. "On a few occasions—"

"A few," exclaimed Manuela, with a toothy grin.

"The duke and I," Aurora continued, "have…" The words became stuck in her throat.

She was not embarrassed of the fact she'd taken on a lover. It was just that Apollo was so, so, so *everything* she'd never thought she'd be drawn to, and here she was, so lost in the man she'd been caught in the act.

"You have…" Luz Alana urged, whirling a hand in the air with an alarming degree of urgency. This was what she got for being such a damned grouch during their entanglements. Oh, what was the point in resisting, they'd get it out of her eventually.

"We've had sexual intercourse!" she blurted out, then covered her mouth with both hands while Manuela launched herself from her chair and began a celebratory dance involving pelvic thrusts and truly obscene hand gestures.

"Finally, Leona," she cheered, making pistols with her hands and bizarrely firing them in the air. "We're so overjoyed, we won't punish you too harshly for keeping secrets from us."

"Whatever you think this is, it is not," Aurora warned Manuela, which clearly didn't register, since she added noises to her festivities.

"Well, I'm just happy you've found someone you want to spend time with." Luz Alana was too dignified to introduce a double entendre, but the glimmer in her eyes relayed quite effectively the kind of time she was referring to.

Manuela finally stopped fluttering around the room and sat down. "Yes, very happy," she panted, short of breath from all that gyrating. "I want details, the filthier, the better."

"Well, you're not getting them." She ignored Manuela's pouting and turned to Luz Alana, who was at least pretending not to want a thorough accounting of Aurora's dalliances. "This is temporary, a distraction."

"Are you certain of that, Leona?" Manuela asked in a worryingly sober tone.

"Of course I am." She tried to mask the semi-panicked tone in her voice with a little laugh. "I was reviving that part of me, that's all." Immediately Luz Alana's expression turned contrite, and Manuela softened her stance at Aurora's allusion to her past. "Despite him being the absolute opposite of what I find remotely fetching in a man."

Manuela scoffed at that, and Aurora could not take offense to it. The man was unnaturally beautiful. "Leona, even I find the man appealing and I have no interest whatsoever in his entire gender."

"Fine, he's handsome." He was addictive and deadly without his clothes on. But if she allowed her mind to go down that path, she would give too much away. "But he's also arrogant and manipulative." She wasn't certain who it was she was attempting to convince, not her friends, from the dubious looks on both their faces. "And he's much too boisterous for me." This claim elicited a bored yawn from Manuela. "We could not be more different." And yet he'd come to her aid every time she needed him. Was her defender against her brothers. Insisted on keeping her safe, when she wouldn't even do it for herself. "It's complicated between us, but there's nothing there other than what you saw."

"*I* saw fireworks," Manuela offered, and Luz Alana didn't seem to disagree.

"Maybe you need spectacles," Aurora suggested, making her friends laugh. "I'm being honest, we have an understanding and we agreed to keep it from you because we suspected, correctly, you'd make it into something it's not."

"This is why he was asking after you this past week," Manuela mused, with a sparkle in her eye, which made a warmth spread in Aurora's chest. One more of her body parts actively working to undo her.

"I'm sure he's only mining you for information he can later use to torture me." This only seemed to intrigue Luz Alana further.

"I think he's trying to determine a way to penetrate your very fortified walls."

Manuela waggled her eyebrows at that. If her friends only knew how little there was left of her defenses when it came to Apollo Sinclair. "That choice of words is what I call fortuitous." She should've known her Manuela would grab any opportunity to say something obscene.

"Don't be crass, Manuela." She pointed an accusing finger at her friend.

"Why not?" she asked, innocently. "I'd say the duke seemed like he wanted to give you a few more rides on his—"

"Saddle?" Luz Alana offered, which sent Manuela into peals of laughter.

"On his *very* large saddle." To her great shame, Aurora's mouth twitched with humor. They were ridiculous, her included.

"And all this time, I believed your claims to detest that big, dark, handsome duke, Leona." This was from Luz Alana, who had been squarely in the Apollo César camp for months now.

"I never said I detested him," she retorted, nervously touching her hair as irritating thoughts about his taste for pulling it rose in her mind like a tidal wave. "I merely dislike his... Apolloness." She was blustering again. It was her perennial state of being when he was even remotely part of the conversation.

"Well, that explains it," Manuela joked, but Aurora could see her friend was disappointed in her refusal to admit to any feelings toward the duke. She also knew that feeling came from nothing other than their desire to see her happy. But she didn't want marriage. She wanted independence, and she certainly did not want marriage to someone whom she'd be a complication or, worse, a terrible burden.

"He's looking for a duchess," she reminded her friends. "And you know as well as I do, it could never be me." That dampened their effervescence, but not for long.

"Why can't you be his duchess?" Luz refuted gently, inciting a series of flutters and sparks inside her that she would never entertain.

"Are you truly asking that question?" Aurora was honestly nonplussed. It was one thing for Apollo to believe the rules did not apply to him, but until very recently, Luz Alana had been a rational person.

"You would make a magnificent duchess," her friend said with conviction Aurora didn't doubt she absolutely believed.

"I'd bring him down like an anchor." With her parentage, with the threat of Philip looming over her, with the work she would never give up.

"Apollo would not care," Manuela began. Aurora held a hand up. True love might have impacted her friends' grasp on reality, but she would not entertain the delusion that she somehow was an appropriate woman to marry the first Black man to enter the British aristocracy.

"He might not, but everyone else will care very much if he marries a bastard with a checkered past." As expected, they both opened their mouths to protest. But there was no use in pretending she was not telling the truth. "It is what I am."

"I wish you weren't so severe in your views of yourself," Manuela protested. Aurora knew her friends meant what they said, but they didn't know what it was like to be living, breathing proof of your parents' greatest shame. The reason for whispers and emotional wounds that never quite healed.

"I'm not severe, I'm realistic," she corrected, endeavoring to not sound resentful or cross. "I know you've both recently found your soulmates, but the fairy tale I want doesn't include a prince," she told them, even as her mind conjured up a memory of Apollo carrying her to bed. "Luz, you and Evan are a perfect match," she told her friend, who seemed to be biting her tongue to keep from protesting. When she turned to Manu, she found a similar expression. "And, Manu, Cora was in a position to turn her back on society. But Apollo cannot, he intends to make amends, to do right by his mother, by the people who depend on his duchy, by his siblings. I won't jeopardize that. Now," she continued as jovially as she could manage with a knot in her throat and a gaping hole in her stomach, "tell me, what have I missed?" The question was a desperate attempt to change the subject, but thankfully she was saved by a knock on the door.

"Pardon the interruption, my love." Luz, despite her distress, lit up the moment her husband entered the room. "I was sent to let you know lunch has been served." Aurora's relief at the interruption was short-lived as Apollo came to join his brother in the doorway.

"Doctora, I thought you'd join us." Luz, Manuela and Evan all swiveled their heads in her direction as though they suspected hot spurts of lava to start shooting out of her head.

It was not too far from the effect the man had on her. As if she were churning inside, and more times than not, he used that to his advantage.

Refusing to let her hide her need from him. Forcing her to lay herself bare for him. Using her own need against her. But right then he wasn't looking at her like a foe. Besides, she was tired of being angry, and all these damned confessions had made her hungry.

"I guess I have a bit of an appetite," she admitted, standing up. She didn't think she imagined the gleeful smiles on her friends at her concession to a meal with Apollo. Neither did she imagine the familiar weight of the man's hand on the small of her back as he guided her toward the dining room. And when he whispered a husky, "I can smell you on my hands, Fiera," as she took her seat, she absolutely did not almost swoon.

The meal, to her surprise, was uneventful. At least outwardly. Apollo was unusually well-behaved, conversing quietly with everyone at the table. His countenance the very image of contentment, when merely half an hour earlier he'd practically devoured her in his parlor. One could not tell by his cool demeanor.

The problem, it turned out, was her. At least her awareness of him. Even when she wasn't looking his way, her body seemed attuned to his every move. The worst part was that she kept noticing the evidence of what they'd been doing when they'd been caught.

His hair was a riot of curls, sprouting in all directions. Knowing her hands were the cause of it made her unhinged. Then, there were his clothes. The knot of his tie was loose, the lapels of his jacket noticeably rumpled, and there was one cuff link missing from his shirt. He looked like a pirate attempting to pass for a gentleman and failing miserably.

The fact that everyone sitting at that table knew she was likely the reason for his appearance did absolutely nothing to tamper her desire to crawl over the table, straddle his lap and work on ridding him of his remaining cuff link. The images her brain conjured had her close to fanning herself with her napkin.

"Perhaps you'll all help me in convincing the doctor to join us in Nice," the Duke of Annan announced from his repose at the head of the table. She shot him daggers with her eyes.

"Oh, that's a marvelous idea!" Manuela exclaimed, then sent her a look that screamed "see, he loves you."

In fact, it was a terrible idea. The last thing she wanted was to be there to witness every floozy in the continent throwing herself at the man. She was much too volatile in his presence to even try.

"I wish I could go, but I'm much too busy at the moment."

"We're not leaving for another week," Luz pushed.

"I don't think so," she said, feeling Apollo's gaze searing into the side of her face. "The clinics are quite demanding at the moment," she hedged and stood up with her medical bag in hand—which she'd recovered from the parlor—intending to swiftly take her leave. If all of them ganged up on her, she knew, come next week, she'd be on a train to the French Riviera.

"Don't go, Aurora—" She was about to battle Manuela's cajoling when a piercing cry from somewhere outside the room interrupted her. Before any of them had time to react, Apollo's aunt burst into the room.

"¿Que paso, Tia?" Apollo demanded, reaching her in two strides. The woman who Aurora had last seen smiling radiantly at Philip now looked on the cusp of collapsing.

The screams must've been hers because when she tried to answer, her voice almost gave out. "It's Juliana." Aurora could barely hear the name as it left her lips.

"Is she hurt?" she asked, in the forceful tone she'd learned in her years working in hospitals.

Doña Jimena whipped her head around at Aurora's question, her eyes stark as she took in the room full of people, and belatedly tried to gather herself.

"Yes," she said, as she ran a shaking hand over the front of her skirt. "She collapsed at the gallery, her friend just brought her in the carriage." She began to cry then, deep, racking sobs, as Apollo tried to hold her up.

"Your Grace," Claude, the butler, entered the room, his demeanor visibly less collected than when Aurora had arrived. "We need a doctor for Señorita Juliana."

"I can see her," Aurora told the man, who looked gratefully at the bag in her hand, then glanced at Apollo in question. Before answering, the Duke of Annan bent his head to his aunt's ear and spoke quietly. She nodded once, eyes closed, as she held on to her nephew.

"Yes." Apollo nodded with authority, but he looked dazed, like he'd woken up in a strange room and was yet to get his bearings. "Show Doctora Montalban to Juli's room, Claude," he ordered, leading his aunt out. As they ascended to the upper floor of the mansion, Aurora noticed that the older woman seemed almost scared of what she'd find.

People reacted differently in moments of crisis, some desired to be as close as possible to the patient, others nervously paced in the periphery.

One thing Aurora could not abide were people who could not self-command during emergencies. If you were not injured or in distress, as far as she was concerned, you should stay out of the way. The exception to that rule were mothers, who normally could not be pried from their ailing child, no matter how old their offspring, but Doña Jimena followed Aurora and Claude up the stairs, not the other way around.

Once in the bedchamber, Aurora's focus was solely on the small figure hunched in on herself in a lovely, canopied bed. It was the bed of a girl, she thought, with its frilly pink lace and satin. But right now, the princess of this palace seemed to be in a nightmare.

Aurora's own stomach twisted as she came closer and smelled

the sour scent of vomit and sweat. Her face was barely visible with her head curved into her stomach. She kept moaning, in that droning, constant hum people made when the pain was unbearable.

"Juliana," she said softly, kneeling down to get a closer look at her pupils, which were dilated. With great care, Aurora lifted the girl's face and the eyes that looked up at her had a blankness to them she'd seen many times.

"What's wrong with her?" Doña Jimena asked from the door. The sound of her mother's voice made Juliana start shaking.

"Give me a moment, please," Aurora said to the woman, then turned her attention back to Juliana. Her pallor was a concerning gray and her hair was matted with perspiration. "Juliana," she cupped the girl's cheek, which was concerningly clammy. "I'm Doctor Montalban, do you remember me?" Aurora forced herself to relax her face, smooth the frown she was certain kept wrinkling her brow. With her mask of placid competence in place, she tried asking again. On the second try, she received a small nod.

On instinct, she leaned in closer, so close that she could feel the girl's quick, hot breaths on her face. "I'm here to help you. Where does it hurt?"

"Here." Juliana clutched her abdomen, her pretty face streaked with tears, as Aurora began pulling out supplies from her bag, already fairly certain what was wrong. When Aurora tried to touch her abdomen the girl wailed, which in turn sent Doña Jimena into a fresh wave of sobs.

"I don't want my mother to know," the girl whispered shakily in Aurora's ear before closing her eyes and hiding her face in her pillow.

Once she'd given Juliana something for the pain, Aurora turned to the doorway where her mother waited, she could hear Apollo's heavy footsteps pacing in the hallway. "Can I please have a pitcher of boiling water and a clean basin?"

"I can get them," a young maid said from the corner of the room, her worried gaze pinned to Juliana's form.

"I'd appreciate a few minutes to speak with Juliana in private," Aurora said, turning to Doña Jimena, who was crying openly, her hands clutched tightly to her midsection as if she was physically experiencing her child's pain. And yet, she kept her distance.

"What if she needs me?" the woman asked, with the voice of a lost child.

"Ten minutes, please," Aurora asked, then Juliana complained again, and her focus was back on her patient. She heard retreating steps, but she did not look back to see if the older woman had gone or not.

She ran her palm over Juliana's clammy forehead, forcing her voice to remain steady. "This is just between us for now," she said, hoping she could keep her word. "But I must know what happened."

There was a small moan of pain and a series of shuddering breaths before Juliana spoke.

"He said he'd find someone who could make my menses return," Juliana admitted softly, her pretty mouth in a tight grimace. "He said it would be fast, that no one needed to know." A cold fear spread through Aurora as she listened to the story.

She knew there was more she should ask, but she was afraid of the answers. Once the maid returned with the water, Aurora washed and focused on the examination. As suspected, she found some bleeding and a cut that was already an angry red. There were bruises on the girl's pelvis and thighs, as if she'd been held down. Aurora gritted her teeth as she cleaned up the careless work.

"Where did you go?" she asked a drowsy Juliana. The tendrils of the morphine already taking hold. The girl moaned weakly when Aurora pressed on her belly, feeling for inflammation.

"He took me to a doctor." She gulped down a sob. "He was very rough, and the place was dirty. I wanted to leave, but he promised I would be fine." He *had* been rough with her, but thankfully it didn't seem like the infection was quite as bad as she'd thought. She continued to examine Juliana and was relieved to find her injuries were all treatable. At least the physical ones.

Aurora asked a few more questions that Juliana answered quietly, avoiding the one she knew she must ask. Once she'd taken care of everything she could, she forced herself to do it.

"Was it Philip?" Juliana's eyes flashed open, even half asleep there was surprise and fear in her face. Aurora's own body went cold as she waited for the answer.

"Yes." Tears rolled down Juliana's face. She looked so small and wretched. Like all hope had bled out of her.

"I'm sorry, Juliana." She reached for the girl's hand and squeezed it, which brought on more tears.

"I don't know where he is, he just left me." If she had to guess, the desgraciado was already on his way out of Paris, and quite possibly France.

Aurora breathed through the hot, pulsing fury stiffening her limbs, then relaxed her jaw and settled on fixing the things she could in that moment.

"No matter what you did, you didn't deserve being taken to someone who'd hurt you," she whispered to Juliana, her voice catching a few times. Aurora comforted her patient while she grappled with the fact that over a decade later Philip was still destroying lives.

Aurora wanted to think that Apollo would not cast out his cousin. That Doña Jimena would hopefully see where the true blame lay in this situation. That she could care for her child even if she was disappointed in her. Aurora would try to help the girl, as much as she could. Though she couldn't make the Philips of the world disappear, she could make sure the Julianas received the care they deserved.

Juliana had fallen into a fitful dozing when there was a soft knock on the door. After a second, Doña Jimena walked in carrying what looked like bedclothes, with Apollo on her heels.

"How is she?" he asked, quietly, his handsome face stark with worry. Aurora didn't look at him, or at his aunt, as shame and rage churned inside her.

"She has a minor infection, but I've cleaned up the worst of it and the bleeding has stopped." She stood from the chair next to the bed, which Doña Jimena promptly occupied. "She needs rest and some remedies I'll send for at my clinic." The older woman nodded, her frown deep as she looked at her daughter. "I will stay here tonight in case her fever worsens."

"I should've known," Doña Jimena said, as she lifted the girl's limp hand and kissed it.

"No, Tia," Apollo gently rebuked his aunt, then kissed the top of her head as she started to cry. "No es tu culpa."

Aurora was out of reassuring words in that moment. She was much too sick with guilt to muster up anything other than useless platitudes, but it was a relief to see that perhaps Juliana's mother could stand by her.

"Do you need anything, Fiera?" he asked, seemingly unaware he'd called her by her nickname. Even in her misery, the blunder comforted her.

"Not right now," she said, wanting to lean into him, but knowing now more than ever that she needed to keep her distance. Because he would despise her when he knew what she'd kept from him.

He nodded, then sent his cousin a worried glance before

turning back to her with a smile. But there was a hardness there too. She wondered if he suspected what had happened to Juliana.

"I'll look in on you soon," he told her. For a second, he hesitated and her heart stammered in her chest. She wanted to go to him, feel those strong arms around her. Instead, she put some space between them, by taking a seat on the other side of Juliana's bed. She'd known the end would come eventually. She just didn't feel ready. Had she known she wouldn't have wasted the past week. But this was the right thing to do, even if the thought made her chest ache.

"Thank you, Your Grace," she told him without looking his way, her gaze focused on the rain lashing against the windowpane.

Twenty-Four

The next morning when Aurora walked out of the bedroom after leaving an exhausted and morose Doña Jimena sitting with a drowsy but recovering Juliana, Apollo was waiting by the door.

"There's no fever," Aurora reassured him, holding herself stiffly, avoiding his gaze.

"Because of you," he told her, and reached for a curl that had come loose and tucked it behind her ear. The look of pride and awe on his face made her wish the ground would swallow her. He had no idea it was her cowardice which put his cousin in harm's way. She had to tell him the truth, and once she did, he would never want to see her again. Then she could put Apollo and all of this behind her and go back to her work.

At least now she knew who was responsible for all the women they'd had turning up at the clinic with terrible infections. Juliana remembered every detail of the place Philip had taken her to. That so-called doctor would not be in business much longer, but there was the matter of the man who had caused so much destruction. Philip had ensnared Juliana. Like he'd done with Aurora, he'd made the girl promises he'd never intended to fulfill. Seduced her, and then when the consequences arrived at his door, he took the easy way out.

"I'm taking you home," Apollo told her, wrapping an arm around her shoulders, right there in front of the maid and his butler.

"I'm not going home," she informed him haughtily, to which he simply raised an eyebrow. As though she were a petulant child he was attempting to appease. She was not in the mood for Apollo's highhandedness. "I'm perfectly capable of seeing myself to Claudine's."

She stood there, tightening her muscles to the tremors coursing through her and looking right into those flashing dark eyes. He was furious. Anyone facing the righteous anger of the Duke of Annan would run for cover, but she was not afraid. Never of him.

"I'm not taking you to Claudine's."

"Apollo, you should stay here, with your family." She tried to reason with him. "You should get some rest."

"*You* need rest," he retorted, swiping a thumb under her eyes, which she was certain were bruised from lack of sleep.

"I'm used to it." She shrugged, which only seemed to make him angrier. "Your aunt and your cousin need you. I'll be all right on my own."

"They're taken care of." Something about the set of his jaw sent an uneasy shiver down her spine. There was no reasoning with Apollo when he got like this, overprotective, determined to save her from herself. "Now I'm going to take care of you." He pointed at the carriage, leading her down the steps to the street. "Don't fight me on this, Fiera."

"I—" She began to make more excuses, but the anger on his face made the words die in her throat.

"I think it's time you told me about Philip Carlyle." She only nodded, then climbed into the carriage.

The silence in the conveyance was oppressive, but she didn't know what to say. Apollo looked dangerous, his eyes stony as he looked out the window.

She'd known the moment she'd seen Philip that he was likely up to his old tricks. Juliana would be all right, the infection had not spread. But Aurora knew from experience, the emotional scars would take much longer to heal.

"She should be back to normal in a few days," she said into the silence. Apollo only nodded, his gaze still on the passing street.

"I have arranged for a solicitor to change the deed of the building for the clinic into your name." He'd been quiet for so long, she jumped at the sound of his voice. "I'm sorry I never got to show you the plans." She almost didn't know how to react to this cooler version of him. It was what she'd said she wanted, but after merely minutes of this distant man, she was already crumbling. Because despite everything she knew, she'd allowed herself to rely on him.

"It should not be in my name." He turned to her then, his face harder than she'd ever seen it.

"The building is for you." He was harsh with her, his words cutting, and she deserved it. He'd done what he promised and she'd repaid him by keeping secrets that could've cost his cousin her life.

"It was Philip," she told him, and he stiffened, as though he'd expected those words but was still surprised to hear them. She could hear his questions in the silence that followed. "It's true what he said at the salon, we knew each other when he was stationed in Mexico." The words landed like an explosion in the small space between them. A taut silence stretched for what felt like hours until he finally spoke.

"Did he do the same thing to you?" She knew the question would come and it was still a punch in the gut. The impact of it so swift she almost doubled over. When she didn't answer, his face turned dark with rage.

"That hijo de puta," Apollo seethed, looking around the carriage as if considering simply leaping out of the conveyance to go hunt down the man. "I will kill him."

"It's my fault," she blurted, relieved in a way to finally voice the truth that had been eating at her for the past week.

"What are you talking about?" Apollo asked, his voice laden with frustration when she would not let him hold her.

"I could've stopped him, instead of letting my family hide my secret," she said, her voice barely a rasp. "I should've accepted my fate, faced the consequences of my mistakes and married him." If possible, her words seemed to make him even angrier. She could hear his molars grind as he turned to face her.

"The only one responsible for what happened to Juliana is that bastard," he said, moving closer to her. "If you think I'm going to be sorry for the fact you aren't married to that fucking monster, then you really don't know me." He grabbed her hand and pulled her to him, his eyes boring into hers. "And one thing I can promise you, Juliana will be the last person he ever does this to."

"I'm sorry." She didn't know for what. For not speaking out, for giving him more things to worry about.

"You have nothing to be sorry for."

Unlike her brothers and her father, Apollo didn't think that she deserved to lose everything for falling in love with the wrong man. His fury was mighty, but it was not directed at her. Until that moment, she didn't realize how terribly she'd needed this.

"Your cousin would not be in the situation she's in if I hadn't..." she began, but he took her chin between his fingers and leaned down, so their faces were close enough to touch.

"Stop this, Aurora." His eyes locked with hers as he took her hands in his. "I will not tolerate this self-pitying mierda from you." Even when he berated her, he was a comfort. "We're not playing this game. You're sorry that you didn't throw your life away? You are no one's tribute. And I'm glad you didn't fall in that bastard's trap." She'd always seen it that way. Even when it meant being an outcast, she'd never regretted her choices. She knew doing what she did saved her from a life that would've felt like death. But for many, what she'd done was a travesty. No one other than the Leonas ever gave her that validation, or even saw the value in the life she'd been able to build for herself. "Now, stop being so damned contrite. You saved my cousin's life yesterday. I should be the one thanking you."

"No, you shouldn't," she insisted, feeling lighter despite the tension of the last few hours. "Do you know where he is?" she asked, hoping Apollo hadn't stained his hands with that desgraciado's blood.

"He's gone," Apollo admitted, with his head in his hands. "While you were tending to Juli, I went with Jean-Louis and Evan to find him." She was half-relieved he hadn't. "He's disappeared." She could see the frustration written across his face. "But he couldn't have gone far, and I have one of my men after him. We'll find him and he'll pay, I'll make sure of that."

"Philip is ruthless, Apollo." And now he was likely desperate. "He would not hesitate in trying to spread rumors about you."

Apollo scoffed at that. "I ruined my own father, Fiera," he reminded her with a chilling grin on his face. "Lord Forsyth has no idea what he's just brought down on himself."

"My brothers might know where to find him." She knew Octavio would help her at least. Maybe even Sebastian. In that way, she could do something to fix all this.

"I will go see them," he informed her, with a scowl.

"They won't be happy to see *you*." Ramón would probably try to shoot him on sight. But Apollo's face was like stone.

"You let me worry about that," he said in a tone that brooked no argument. "You're going to the den of iniquity to rest, and you will stay there with me, safe."

"I need to get clothes at Claudine," she told him, and he promptly shouted the instructions to the coach. "I should be helping you find him," she said weakly. But he simply scoffed and sat back with an arm firmly around her.

"Absolutely not, and don't argue with me, Aurora. I'm weary of you fighting me." He sounded tired and worried. He was restless, his fingers pressing into her as if he was afraid to let her go.

"You can't be associated with me anymore." He only shook his head at her, like every word out of her mouth was ridiculous. "I'm serious, Apollo. I'm a liability to you," she pleaded, but he was utterly impassive.

"*You* are *precious* to me," he countered, making her heart break all over again. He gathered her close and though she knew she should fight him, she let him hold her. Desperate for the safety of his arms, if only for the last time. "You let me concern myself with liabilities and assets in my own damned life."

"You're only making this harder." He emitted a harsh laugh and turned to look at her with narrowed eyes.

"I am?" He almost sounded amused. "I'm not the one who keeps running."

"It's not running, it's self-preservation." He softened at that and sighed.

"You're the most difficult woman I've ever met, Fiera."

"I have to be," she said, and he seemed to understand her meaning, because he only leaned over and kissed her cheek, then took her chin in his hand and turned her face toward him.

"From the first moment I saw you, I've wondered what went

into the making of your grit, and now that I know, I want to burn the world down and rebuild it for you." His words made that place inside that had been dry and barren since that night she'd left home stir to life. "Let me take care of you now," he said as they came up to the top of her street.

And what would happen after? Her past would still be there. Her secrets always lurking in the shadows. She should stop this now, but how could she walk away from this man?

"All right, I'll come to your rooms," she relented. "But tell him to stop here. I'll walk the rest of the way."

"I would like to take you to your door and wait for you."

"I'm still attempting some kind of semirespectable life, Apollo." He stared back at her as if she was speaking in another language. "It is one thing to leave with you if you come fetch me for dinner, it is quite another to turn up here at dawn and have you waiting for me in your carriage while I go fetch some clothes."

"You're in a former courtesan's house, five doors down from a tavern of sapphists," he pointed out drolly.

But this was a boundary that she would not allow him to cross.

"If you can't respect this one request, then I can't come back with you." He sighed in defeat and rapped on the door of the carriage.

In truth, she needed some distance from him. It was much too hard to think clearly with Apollo looking at her like he'd slay dragons for her. Entirely too seductive to believe he was all-powerful, that those shoulders could weather anything that came her way. But the truth was that he was just a man. A man who would eventually grow tired of the whispers about her. Who would ultimately realize she was not worth the trouble.

"Wait here," she told him, moving to the door. But as always, he didn't listen and began to help her down.

"I can climb the damned steps, Annan," she protested in vain.
"Your legs are very short."

"You are an oversized cabrón, but you don't hear me pointing that out." He flashed her one of his toothy grins, making her smile despite her somber mood.

It was a few hundred yards down a steep hill to Claudine's. As she briskly made her way to the house, the crisp morning air helped clear some of the cobwebs from her head. She was so deep in her thoughts about the previous night and the consequences that might come, she almost didn't hear the voice calling for her.

"Doctor Montalban." A familiar male voice coming from the alley between the boardinghouse and Claudine's tavern stopped her before she reached her door. It was early, but births happened at all hours, and Claudine told everyone in the neighborhood Aurora was a physician.

"Yes, can I help you?" she asked the figure coming out of the shadows. Something about the man's fast movements, made her take a step back. Had she not been exhausted from the evening before, she might have caught on to the threat sooner.

"I've got a message for you from Lord Ackworth." Ackworth? That was Sandra's husband. When the man lunged for her, she tried to run, but he was already pulling her by the front of her dress.

"Let me go," she cried out, before he backhanded her.

"Where did you hide her?" the man yelled in her face, shaking her hard enough to make her teeth rattle.

When he moved, a sliver of light cut across his face and she recognized him as Collins, Sandra's impertinent footman.

"My lord knows you took the mistress and the bairns," he shouted and hit her again. The back of his hand connected with such force on her cheek her head slammed into the wall.

"Hel—" she began to scream, but he covered her mouth with his hand.

"Shut up, you whore!" The man seethed while she tried to free herself from his clutches. "If you don't tell me where you hid the mistress, I'll make you sorry."

She hoped Apollo heard her and wished she'd just let him walk her to the door like he wanted. As she tried to dislodge the man's hand from her mouth, she remembered she'd learned some things from Apollo and Gilberto. She didn't have her pistol or her gloves, but she *could* defend herself.

She bit down on the man's hand hard enough to hear something crack, he pushed her away, and she slipped on the wet cobblestones. When she tried to break the fall with her hand, she landed on a jagged rock, which made her cry out in pain.

"Now you've really done it," Collins roared, lunging in her direction.

"Help me!" she cried out as she scrambled away from him. But he was fast and grabbed for her again, this time using his feet to try to kick her. Her head throbbed and her hand was bleeding, but she fought with all her might. She managed to make contact with his shin, making him cry out in pain and stumble, then she went for a kick on the man's crotch. The pendejo managed to avoid it and shoved her so hard she crashed to the ground.

"Tell me where she is," he demanded, lifting a boot she knew he intended to aim at her head.

"I won't ever tell you where she is," she told Collins, as she crab-walked on the wet ground.

"My lord will make you pay," he shouted, looming over her.

"Hijo de puta, te voy a matar." The cry came from behind Collins, a bloodcurdling roar that made her attacker whip around. Before the manservant could react, he was being lifted from the ground like a rag doll by the Duke of Annan, who appeared to be in the grips of a murderous rage.

He was already running toward her when she cried for help. He watched as she walked down to the boardinghouse and saw her stop to talk to someone before being dragged into an alley. It took but a second before he was running to her.

Apollo had spent his life bent on revenge, spent half of it orchestrating the downfall of his own father, but he had never thought of himself as a killer. Watching Aurora be snatched in plain sight and hearing her cry out for help was the moment when he truly understood he could kill in cold blood.

By the time he reached her he was in a blind rage. Nothing but snapping bones and drawing blood would do. He lifted the hijo de puta who had dared touch his woman, backhanded him until he bled, then flung him against a row of rubbish bins. The man's head cracked loudly against the wall, but Apollo had to resist the urge to go for him again.

"Get up, Fiera." She winced as she sat up with her hand clutched to her chest.

"I'm all right," she said weakly. "It's just a cut." Her lip was bloody, and she already had a bruise darkening her cheek.

"You're bleeding," he told her. His hands shook from fury and there was something wrong with his breath, which came out harsh and loud.

"I'm fine." She shakily pressed her hand to her face and made an effort to smile at him. "But you're scaring me with that sound you're making." He frowned, unsure what she was referring to, then realized he'd been growling.

He'd scared Aurora's attacker too, because by the time he'd finished helping her up the man had crawled away, and gotten into a waiting carriage.

"Did you know that man?" he asked, as he inspected the

scratches on her face. She hesitated, then sighed, looking in the direction where he'd escaped.

"I think he works for my patient's husband." Apollo had to bite his tongue. He'd known something like this would happen since that first night. She took too many damned risks, running around all of creation like she was invincible with no damned sense of the danger she put herself in.

"What's the husband's name, Aurora?" he asked, as calmly as he could, while passing her a handkerchief. When she didn't answer, he attempted to scoop her up, but she batted him away.

"I'm fine," she insisted, though he could see she was in pain. "I did fight him, you know," she told him defiantly, and if he wasn't seconds from throttling her, he would've kissed her bloody lip right then. But he was not letting her keep anything else from him.

He was done with Aurora's need to protect everyone but herself.

"I need you to give me the man's name."

"You're doing it again," she told him, with a frown. "That noise." He was surprised he was not foaming at the mouth with the state he was in.

"Aurora, so help me, I'm not in the mood to play this game with you." She didn't like his tone, but he was not conceding on this. "My observance of all your rules and all your secrets ended the moment you were almost killed in an alley."

"I was defending myself." She had the gall to look offended. "This is a sensitive situation," she said.

"What happened?" he pushed.

"I still need to get my things," she told him, in place of answering.

"Aurora." His control was hanging on by a very thin thread, and whatever she saw in his face seemed to finally apprise her of that fact.

"It's the patient you helped me with that night." He sighed, sorry for the poor woman, because he would come after her husband with everything he had. "I was at her house yesterday to remove the stitches from her procedure and…" She paused there, clearly struggling with what to say, and he knew whatever it was he would not like it. "She needed help getting away from him, so I did." Apollo closed his eyes and tried to conjure up any remaining reserves of patience before he spoke again.

"If she's gotten away from him and is safe, then all I care about is you." He knew that protecting her clients was important, but if the woman had escaped the brute, then Apollo would make it his business to ensure the man was never tempted to touch another hair on any woman's head.

"I don't want to make things harder for her," she said, as he put his jacket over her shoulders. She was shaking, and even in the muted light of the darkened street, he could see the bruise on her cheek. "Apparently he hid their marriage, he wouldn't even let her leave the house alone, so it might be to her benefit when it comes to escaping him."

He was going to personally dismember that mal nacido, whoever he was.

"I promise to make sure he can't hurt her. Please, Aurora," he begged. Needing to vanquish at least this villain from her life.

"He's a lord," she told him, which only infuriated him more. Of course he bloody was.

"His name, Aurora," he insisted, as he pulled her out of the alley and turned her toward his carriage.

"I need clean clothes," she retorted, attempting to veer back in the direction of her building. That was when he gave up all pretense at civility and scooped her up. "Not this again," she protested, but he did not care.

"I'm not letting you out of my sight until you're safe, in

my house. I can send a note to Luz or Manuela to get you clothes," he informed her even as she attempted to fling herself out of his hold.

"No, Apollo, your aunt has enough to deal with today."

Her words confused him, then he realized what she meant. "I already told you, I'm taking you to *our* rooms," he clarified, tightening his grip on her.

The moment he said the words, she relaxed in his arms. It was the truth. That small set of rooms was one of the few things from his old life that still brought him comfort. Her presence there made it a haven.

"Our rooms?" she asked, and he nodded, brushing a kiss to her brow as they arrived at the carriage.

"I'll never be able to get the smell of carbolic out of it," he told her with a smile. "You might as well claim it." Her eyes went liquid as she looked up at him, and a little tremor passed through her jaw.

"Let me see your hand," he whispered when they were back in the carriage. The white linen of his handkerchief was soaked with blood. His stomach turned at the sight of it. Her blood had been spilled, and someone would pay for that. "He made you bleed." He could not keep the rage from coming out in his voice.

"It's not so bad."

"Tell me who this desgraciado is," he demanded, and hoped she could hear how close he was to losing the reins on his control.

She delayed doing it for as long as she could. She insisted on getting herself settled on the bench. They were almost halfway to their rooms when she finally relented.

"You cannot leave those children as orphans." He knew if he didn't agree, she wouldn't tell him. He could not promise anything other than making the man sorry for his very existence, but he nodded. "His name is Ackworth, Lord Ackworth," she said, utterly unaware of the stick of dynamite she'd just tossed at him.

Ackworth, the man who had made it his business to voice his repulsion at the idea of a person with African blood being part of the aristocracy had kept secret that he was married to one. That he had children with her.

There it was, finally, something about Ackworth that could help Apollo end the man's efforts to discredit him. It would take no more than a few letters and the whispers would start. He could destroy Ackworth with this, but in doing so, he'd expose a woman he would never harm.

A year ago, hell, three months ago, there was nothing that would've stopped him from using something like this to his advantage. He wouldn't have even thought twice about it. But now things were different. He was different. Well, not so much he would not go looking for the man and beat the pulp out of him once he had his Fiera safely tucked away.

"Let's get you home," he said, pulling her to him. "Then I'll deal with Lord Ackworth."

Twenty-Five

"*Your note to the Leonas was much too dramatic,*" they'll think I'm in my deathbed," she told an impassive Apollo as they entered the apartment.

"Saying you were attacked is not dramatic, it's fact," he argued as he guided her to her armchair—or the armchair she now thought of as hers. She wanted to contradict him, but he looked so worried.

"Apollo, you should go home," she told him as he placed her medical case on the small table next to her.

"I am where I need to be." She let that go and watched him open her bag with a hard tug. There was a tension in him she'd never seen before. Like every muscle in his body was close to snapping and then there was that rumble in his chest. He'd looked so fierce in that alley, like he could've dismembered Collins. But when he'd reached for her, he'd been as gentle as ever. "I'll go put on a kettle for tea, then we'll clean your hand."

"I can do it," she insisted, but he was already hastily moving to the small kitchen.

She was still reeling from the night before, from the attack. Not for the first time, she wondered if the path of least resistance would be just to leave Paris. It would be for the best, but the mere thought of never being in these rooms again made her heart ache. Just being there was a comfort. The mingled scent of her carbolic soap and the hints of cedar from his shaving soap loosened the knot she'd had in her stomach for days.

She looked around and noticed the small kit, with tools she'd placed on his bookshelves for when she brought patients. There was that dressing gown of his she loved wearing after they made love. There were traces of her everywhere.

What would people say if they knew that the Duke of Annan had a nest where he played at domesticity with a scandalous woman? Likely that it was exactly what they expected from the likes of him.

When he returned, he kneeled in front of her and took her hand. He'd brought a small basin of hot water and the cake of carbolic soap she now kept in his washroom. She tried not to dwell too much on what all this meant. What it would mean for her when another woman called this place and this man her own.

"Would you fetch the antiseptic from my bag?" He worked briskly, familiar with her things, anticipating her instructions. When she whimpered from the pain as he tried to clean the wound, he leaned and pressed his lips to her fingertips.

"I'm sorry, sweetheart." He sounded like he was going to be sick.

"It's all right," she told him, cupping his cheek with her hand. They looked at each other for a moment, and she recklessly allowed herself to internally voice all the things she could never say. That she wanted him more than anything. That he was dear to her, that he might be worth letting go before everything she never thought she could give up. That no one had protected her like he did. "It's just a scratch." He made a pained sound, then turned his face, so he could kiss the hand she still had there.

She loved him. The certainty of that throbbed inside her like a second heartbeat. What was worse, she would never not love him. Not even when this time together was nothing but a faint memory for him.

"I want you to come to the Riviera with me," he informed her as he finished bandaging her hand, which she pulled away at his words.

"I can't do that, Apollo." Though she tried, she could not hide the hurt in her voice. "I don't think it's fair for you to ask."

"Aurora, you were just attacked in the street."

"I'll stay with Virginia." She knew she was grasping at straws. Given her current state, she was not exactly in a position to reassure anyone she had her affairs in order.

"Virginia can't protect you from Ackworth." No, no, she couldn't, and being under her friend's roof would likely result in trouble for her and the clinic. Leaving Paris for a couple of weeks was a reasonable solution for her situation. But she could not bear the idea of watching him select a bride.

"Your friends won't come without you, you know that." She slumped her shoulders and put her face in her hands. She was so tired and she was scared. Fearful of the retribution Sandra's husband would bring down on her. Heartsick for what she was about to lose.

Strong arms wrapped around her and she felt the tears begin to fall. She'd held on for so long, but she didn't know what to do.

"I'm scared of what Ackworth will do to the clinic," she whispered, and his embrace tightened around her.

"You leave him to me," he told her, kissing the top of her head. "When your Leonas arrive, I'll go and deal with Ackworth and Forsyth." She wanted to argue, but she needed help.

There was no use in denying it. Aurora could be stubborn and she didn't relish this feeling of helplessness, but she was not a fool. She needed Apollo's help, and she'd let herself take it.

Once she knew Virginia and the clinic were safe and that Ackworth could not harm his wife, she'd leave France and start over. She'd done it before.

"How did it go with the Montalban brothers?" Evan asked hours later as Apollo climbed back into his carriage after his visit with Aurora's siblings.

"Unpleasantly." On their second meeting, Aurora's oldest brother, Ramón, had been just as loathsome as the first time. He'd had the gall to ask questions about his intentions for their sister, which Apollo had answered with some unfriendly rejoinders about their less than stellar record at caring for her safety, which had almost led to blows.

The truth was, he'd been asking himself the same questions. The mere thought of having anyone else but her was practically repellent to him, and he'd seen her face when she'd talked to him about Nice. He had to make it clear to Aurora that everything had changed for him. He knew convincing her would not be easy. But that would have to wait until he had her out of Paris and safe.

"They've agreed to help track Forsyth down," Apollo told his brother. "They said their man might have some inkling as to where he's gone." The Montalban brothers had no qualms about breaking a law or two when necessary. If they hadn't put Aurora through so much anguish, he might actually like the two younger ones. Not Ramón, he'd happily knock that cabrón's teeth out.

"Which means…?" Cora asked. Both her and Evan had refused to let him go after Ackworth alone once he'd told them about the attack on Aurora.

"Which means, we're going to pay Ackworth a visit at his club." Simply saying the man's name made him see red.

"Can you explain again how it is that you're after not one but two aristocrats at the moment?" Cora asked, as if inquiring the time for the next train to London. Apollo exhaled, slapping the side of the conveyance after calling out the directions to their next destination. "Or maybe the better question is, whether it's advisable to seek out Ackworth at a club full of English expatriates in your current state?"

The question for some reason made his temper flare. He was bloody exhausted of being asked for restraint, to mind his temper when the Ackworths and the Forsyths behaved like there were no consequences.

"Was it advisable for you to crash your way into Manuela's wedding and rip the scalp off the groom merely months ago?" Apollo retorted, not even attempting to moderate his anger. "Likely not, and yet you did."

He didn't expect the formidable Cora Kempf Bristol to cower under his accusation and she did not disappoint him. She merely lifted a shoulder before smoothing a hand over her skirts.

"But I was not trying to garner clout for my entry into the Lords." She sent him a sardonic look. He scowled back. "On the contrary, I was very much aiming to be completely erased from all polite society. It's why I live in Paris, querido."

And that was the crux of it, to gain favor with these people, he'd need to overlook their villainy. He thought he could do it, if it got him what he wanted. He wasn't sure he could anymore.

Apollo sighed as the carriage weaved them through the congested Parisian streets. "Nothing is stopping me from giving Ackworth the beating he's had coming, and if that means I lose my footing in the Lords, then so be it."

Evan emitted one of those long-suffering exhales he seemed

so fond of whenever Apollo was in the vicinity. "We have to consider that despite the man's despicable character, he will find favor in the aristocracy for losing his wife—"

"He did not lose his wife," Apollo interrupted. "She escaped him." He understood that his brother was giving him sound advice. But the sight of Aurora on the ground with a bloodied lip would likely give him nightmares for the rest of his life. If he had gotten there a minute later, the lunatic Ackworth sent after her would've been stomping on her head.

"We can use this, Apollo, if we play our cards right," Evan insisted. "The man had Aurora attacked on the street."

"And has a secret wife with the same skin color as the people he vocally despises and blames for every problem in Britain. Que comemierda," Cora added, drolly.

Evan's face darkened at that, his attention still on Apollo. "You have more than enough to put a chink in his petty claims regarding your title, but if you attack him at his club, there will be no going back from that."

With every word out of Evan's mouth, Apollo's fury rose. Not at his brother, but at this murky, twisted thing he was now part of. He was tired of the English stiff upper lip and the pretense that their prejudice and bigotry wasn't violence. Was he supposed to allow the man the courtesy to save face after he'd sent his attack dog after Aurora? This monster had kept his wife a virtual prisoner, had cheated, lied and stolen with impunity for years, and only now did they have enough to put a "chink" in his armor. Meanwhile, Forsyth continued to ruin lives and was only rewarded with more power and position, and Apollo had had enough.

"I have a question for you, brother," he seethed, well aware he was lashing out at the wrong person and yet was unable to control himself. "What would you do to a man who sent a thug to backhand your wife in some filthy alley?" The mere suggestion of someone hurting Luz Alana had Evan bristling with malice.

"I would kill him with my bare hands." His brother's eyes shone with intensity. Cora, on the other hand, made a sound of appreciation that had the hairs on Apollo's neck rising.

"But Aurora isn't your wife, Your Grace." Cora delivered this with an infuriating amount of self-satisfaction.

"There's a reason why no one likes you." Apollo's response elicited one of those feline grins from Cora and a startled laugh from Evan.

"I'm liked by those I care to be liked by," she volleyed back, then turned to his brother. "What do you say, Lord Evan?"

"As always, you arrive just at the heart of it, Duchess."

"Jodanse, the both of you," Apollo grumbled.

"You ought to devise what you want, Your Grace, we will be on our way to the Riviera very soon," Cora pointed out unhelpfully.

To Nice, where he was supposed to select his future duchess. Yesterday he didn't think he could do it, today he knew he'd already found her. She was sitting in his apartment with a bloody lip. "I'm not choosing a bride," he declared as they came to a stop. "Not unless it's her."

"Does Aurora know how you feel?" Cora asked, with uncharacteristic sympathy. Apollo scoffed at the thought of his Fiera hearing him declare his undying love.

"She'd be halfway across the Atlantic, if I had." Both Cora and Evan sent him pitiful looks, but he could not dwell on this. He had Ackworth's head to tear off.

"Neither of you need to be involved in what I'm about to do here," Apollo said, as he reached for the door.

His brother sent a baleful look to the green door of the Circle D'Anglais, the gathering place for the English aristocracy in Paris. "I'd be remiss not to tell you again that going after

Ackworth in this way will have its repercussions. He's not the only one who wants you out. He's just the only one willing to be vocal about it."

Apollo considered his brother. Evan had proved himself not only loyal but a man who lived by his convictions too. Apollo trusted his brother, but there were things that Evan, even as much as he loved his wife, a Black woman, could never understand.

"This is a line in the sand," Cora told him. "If you come for one of them, you'll make a lot of enemies."

"There isn't a single thing that will stop me from getting out of this carriage and using my fists on that man." He could feel the rage surging in him. "Not out of some moral principle, but because he dared to touch Aurora. If that makes me a fool, then I will live with the consequences."

"There, was that so hard?" The duchess had that look that was a cross between an anaconda and the Cheshire cat.

"Go to hell," he muttered, before he launched himself out of the carriage.

"May I help you, sir?" a valet asked as he walked through the door of the club. Apollo barreled in without a word.

"Ackworth, where are you?" he bellowed up the stairs as Evan and Cora caught up with him. His blood was boiling as he searched room by room, rousing members from their post-luncheon stupors.

"Sir, I beg your pardon." A small man with the look of a harried cockatoo made his way up to Apollo. "Lord Ackworth is not available at present."

Apollo ignored the man and ran halfway up the stairs. "Come down, you coward," he shouted with his brother and friend closely behind. He knew they were there to make sure he didn't kill the man, but it was good to have reinforcements. "Where is he? I know he's always here at midday," Apollo demanded of the man, who was now huffing at the top of the stairs as if he could hold Apollo back. "If he is here, I will find him and God help who is keeping him from me," he told the man, who paled at the threat. He suspected Ackworth would have champions at the Circle who would attempt to keep Apollo from getting to him, but so far no peers had come to the man's rescue.

"Monsieur, please." The little man raised his hands in supplication, sending a terrified look at the door at the end of the corridor. Apollo reached it in three strides.

"Hiding won't save you, Ackworth," he bellowed, as he turned the knob, only to find it locked. "You have to answer to me for what you did to Aurora Montalban." He thought of Aurora bruised and scared, and with two kicks, the door splintered open.

He saw the scrambling figure hiding behind the curtain, like the sniveling coward he was. "There are witnesses here," Ackworth wailed as he plastered himself to the wall. Apollo grabbed him by his shirt and yanked him out of his hiding place. "You helped her take my wife," the man cried, his eyes red-rimmed and wild. Apollo punched him in the mouth twice, quieting him.

"If you make him bleed, do it off the carpet. You already have to pay for the door," Cora advised from where she stood.

"Now you'll have the same bruise you left on Aurora," Apollo told Ackworth, who was calling out for the authorities. "Your wife is not coming back you shit louse."

"They belong to me and I demand restitution," the man cried, his yellowed teeth stained with blood. "They're mine." He talked about his wife and children as though they were property, like someone had taken his horse and he wanted it back. Apollo wrapped his hand around Ackworth's neck and tightened it just enough to serve as a warning, even as he felt his control begin to fray. He wanted to inflict pain on this man, almost enough to throw everything he'd worked for by the wayside.

"They're not things, they're human beings, you fucking pustule." He had to make himself breathe to keep from choking the man right then. Ackworth was keening now, blubbering like a child, begging for the mercy he'd never shown his wife or children. "You like to send others to do your dirty work for you." Apollo's voice was garbled and raw, which seemed to terrify Ackworth. Good, he should be scared. "Yes, you're quite the big man, scheming behind your little desk, while you terrorize those who can't defend themselves against you, demonizing people with your pen. Not so bold now, are you? You pathetic piece of shit," he bit out, his face barely inches from the trembling aristocrat.

"You don't belong among us, you're an animal, a savage," Ackworth screamed, his eyes bright with a frightening zeal. "And now everyone will know." How did men like this do it? Decide that keeping their wife in virtual captivity did not in any way hinder his ability to moralize. He could call Apollo an abomination because of his race, while he married a woman of similar ancestry. Because to the Ackworths of the world, rules only applied to others.

Apollo lifted him roughly, and slung him into a wall so that his feet were scrabbling for purchase a few inches off the ground. "If you value your life, listen to me carefully, Ackworth." Something in his voice must've finally alerted the man of how precarious his situation was, because he quit fighting. "The only reason I'm not snuffing the life out of you is because the woman you had attacked this morning asked me not to leave your children orphaned." He made his point by slamming the man one more time. "If you think I care enough about being a duke that I won't make it my business to destroy you, I suggest you think again."

"You cannot threaten me. She took my wife…" Ackworth started sobbing then, but Apollo knew it was all about losing control over her rather than actual affection for his family.

"And I will take much more than that from you. I won't expose you and your lies to save that poor woman more misery." The man opened his mouth to protest but quieted when Apollo shook him again. "You will leave her in peace and forget Aurora Montalban's name," he warned. "You can do what you want with me," Apollo said, lifting a shoulder. "Keep telling lies about me, invent whatever you want. But know that each time you do, you will have to look over your shoulder just a little more often." A tremor passed through Ackworth, his body going limp in Apollo's grip. "I will be out there waiting for just the right moment to rid the world of your miserable fucking existence."

"You can't do this," Ackworth wept, looking around and finding no one there to defend him.

"Can I share a secret?" Apollo asked, his voice low and menacing. "You were quite right on one thing, Ackworth, I might look the part in my superfine wool, but the truth is, I can be quite the savage." The man was openly crying, and the sight made Apollo's stomach turn. "I'll be waiting for a statement from you announcing you're retiring to a private life in your country seat, without your wife or children. I could destroy you and I know you care very much of your standing among peers. Make sure you do what I say, or you'll find out what consequences look like."

With that, Apollo let him go. Ackworth crumpled to the ground while two footmen rushed to help him up. Two others escorted Apollo, Cora and Evan from the club, before informing them their membership, if they had one, would be rescinded.

"Well, that was worth leaving my warm bed," Cora commented, climbing back into the carriage, but Apollo was in too dark of a mood to engage in any kind of banter.

"I thought you were going to kill him," Evan said with a bit of awe in his voice.

He was not himself. Since he'd seen her fall to the ground that morning, he'd spent every second worried about her safety. He was almost scared of the things he'd be willing to do to make sure she was. "I don't know if I have the constitution for this."

And there was more to do. He'd have to get Aurora out of Paris. Take care of Juliana and his aunt. Find Forsyth. Even Ackworth would remain a headache until he sent his lawyers after the man.

"The Leonas will turn your life into utter chaos," the duchess said at length, with more sympathy than he'd ever heard from her. "But if there is any life left once they're done with you, it is a very enjoyable one."

"I have no complaints," agreed his brother as he sent Apollo a toothy grin.

"She will probably scratch my eyes out for my trouble."

"Only if you're lucky," Cora quipped, and for the first time that day, Apollo had something to smile about.

Twenty-Six

It took much doing to get Aurora out of Paris. *Once* she'd received news that Sandra arrived in Switzerland, she tried to get out of coming to Nice. A concerted offense involving emotional blackmail from the Leonas and multiple bribes from him was enacted in ordered to get her on the train. They'd finally departed from Paris the previous evening and that morning arrived in Marseille, where he'd planned a stop.

"When you said 'farm,' I imagined something much smaller," she said, her gaze darting left and right as she took in the vineyards flanking the road leading up to the villa. This stop at Mihn and Gilberto's farm was one of the bribes. She was so damned contrary, he'd wondered if it had been a mistake to bring her here, but watching her face open up at the sight of the fields, Apollo knew he'd done the right thing. "The lavender goes as far as the eye can see."

"They're a big supplier of lavender and other herbs, but I'm sure you already know that from your clandestine meetings with Mihn." He winked at her when she sent him a cheeky grin over her shoulder. But inside he was still unsettled by the events of the past week.

Forsyth remained in the wind, and with each passing day,

more came to light of the man's treacherous intentions. In addition to seducing Apollo's fifteen-year-old cousin and then putting her life in danger, he'd also borrowed a large sum of money from his aunt, which he'd taken with him. His aunt was humiliated and heartbroken, but she was standing by Juliana's side. Juli at least was recovering well and had left for Nice with her mother a day before Apollo and Aurora departed Paris.

"I am so looking forward to meeting Phuong." She turned her face toward the sun. The yellowing bruise a stark reminder of how close he'd come to losing her. "It would be such a boon to secure them as our supplier for our products."

"You'd think I'd just brought you some diamond mines." He pretended to be cross at her enthusiasm. But in truth, it was a great relief to see her this animated.

Since she'd been hurt, he'd rarely let her out of his sight, and for once, she'd heeded his wishes to be careful. She'd become so quiet since that day of the attack, since Juliana. Sometimes she barely spoke for hours, as if she was going to a place inside herself. This carriage ride from the station to the farm was the first time he'd seen her truly smile in days.

"I would not be anywhere near as excited about diamond mines," she shot back, eliciting an honest shake of his head. He knew it was true. This jaunt to see medicinal herbs was better than gold for his Fiera.

For as long as he could remember, the greatest satisfaction in his life had come from settling the score with his father. But now he found that making this grave, tightly wound woman smile was an even more powerful addiction.

"Mihn said she's growing herbs from the tropics in a hot-house," he told her and bit back a grin at her hungry expression.

"I didn't know they could grow things from the tropics in Europe."

He lifted a shoulder, pretending to know a lot less than he

did. "It's warmer here near the Mediterranean, and they do a lot in the greenhouses," he explained as she hung most of her torso out of the carriage. "Please don't do that." Instantly, his heart began to race and he pulled her back by the waist, which landed her on his lap. To his surprise, she let him hold her there. Likely because she could see better from the height. Still he liked her there. Lately he could only relax when she was in his sights.

"That is beautiful," she said, her focus on the fields.

It does not hold a candle to you, he thought but kept the maudlin words to himself. He would tell her the truth here, he could not let her arrive in Nice still thinking he intended to take a wife. Well, one who wasn't her in any case.

"From what I hear, Phuong is as interested in meeting you as you are to meet her."

She narrowed her eyes at him. "Have you been meddling in my business again, Your Grace?" There was nothing that Aurora viewed as more of a threat than an infringement on her independence.

And it was true he had schemed a bit with Gilberto and Mihn. He knew she'd spoken with them about supplies for their clinics, but Apollo hoped this visit would plant a seed for a much larger endeavor.

"For someone who spends her days and nights giving help to others, you're certainly resistant to it for yourself." She received his comment with a cantankerous, if slightly contrite expression. "But I agree that it will be good for you to speak with Phuong. She's had to make her way on her own. She might be of great help." She turned around to look out the window again and, in the process, ground that delicious rump right on his cock.

"I hope so," she mused, so distracted with her thoughts, she didn't notice the torture she had him under. The carriage came to a stop then, and he had to bite back a groan when she pushed back into him. When he was forced to adjust himself or risk a public embarrassment, she finally noticed his aroused state, and the imp grinned. "That's what you get for plotting behind my back."

"There are many things I'd like to do behind your back, Fiera," he told her, taking that stubborn chin between two fingers and pulling her close. "Plotting is not nearly at the top of the list."

Her breath caught, and that fire that seemed to always be roaring between them was suddenly ablaze. He leaned in, needing to taste her mouth again.

She bit him.

"Carajo, Fiera," he grunted when she pulled back, her countenance the picture of devilish satisfaction.

"And that's what happens when people try to derail me from my professional endeavors," she said haughtily, reaching for the handle of the carriage. She jumped down from the thing before the coachman even had a chance to place the stepping stool by the door.

"An endeavor I secured for you," he flung back half-heartedly as he followed her off the carriage.

"Try to keep up, Your Grace. Enterprise waits for no one."

"Ah, I should've known the beautiful Doctor Montalban had arrived from the wounded rhino noises coming from my friend," Gilberto announced happily as he greeted her outside a lovely stone farmhouse. Next to him and Mihn was a minuscule woman Aurora assumed was Mihn's mother.

"This is my sogra, Madame Trần Phuong," the handsome Brazilian said, wrapping an arm around the older woman. It was very unusual for a man to claim his lover's mother as his mother-in-law, but that only made Aurora more curious to meet the famous Phuong.

"Madame Trần Phuong." Aurora extended a hand, but the woman grabbed her and kissed her on each cheek. She smelled like lemongrass. She was shorter than Aurora, who was barely three inches over five feet, but she was very trim. She was beautiful, her face bore laugh lines that spoke of a life well lived. Her son had her intelligent brown eyes and her golden complexion.

"It is a pleasure to meet you, Doctor Montalban," the woman said. "My son has told me about you, it seems our Apollo has finally met his match in you." The older woman sent a playful glance in the duke's direction, and to her astonishment, the Duke of Annan, the most shameless man in France, actually blushed.

She'd noticed Apollo seemed a bit more at ease here. From the moment they'd gotten off the train, he seemed, if not relaxed, certainly less tightly wound then he'd been for the past week. Since everything with Philip had come out and the attack from Ackworth, he'd been constantly uneasy. He stayed at the den of iniquity, refusing to leave her alone. Some nights she'd wake up and find him staring at the ceiling, with his arms wrapped tightly around her. It took four days to arrange the departure from Paris and she didn't think Apollo had slept more than a few hours each night.

"Aurora would like to see the fields and the greenhouses," Apollo told Phuong, who raised a hand to pat his cheek. He received the touch humbly, rewarding the woman with a warm smile. It was interesting seeing Apollo here, in a place where he wasn't doing his usual grandstanding.

"I would love to see your farm," she said, eagerly.

"Of course, we would be delighted to show you." Phuong took her by the hand and began a brisk walk down a stone path leading away from the house. "Let's go to my personal garden first." She pointed to an expanse of perfectly aligned garden beds covering an area that had to be as large as the main building. "The men can catch up with us." Aurora, for all her own walking through Paris, could hardly keep up with the energetic Phuong.

"Do you grow all this yourself?" Aurora asked, as they made their way through the patchwork of greenery.

"No," Phuong said with a smile. "I have botanists and horti-culturists who help with the seasonal planting," she explained. The small plot in front of them contained what Aurora could recognize as rue and aster flowers. Both important ingredi-ents in some of the contraceptives they provided at the clinic. "These are of interest to you, no?" the older woman asked, with a knowing smile. Aurora tried to listen for a suspicious note to her question, but there was nothing but warmth. She'd shared very vague details with Mihn, mindful that he could assess the things she needed and reach his own conclusions.

"I'm not sure what Mihn has told you about my work," she began, careful not to offend the woman, but wary to divulge. The work she did was not something she could share with just anyone. If it were only her, she might be more forthcoming, but there was Virginia and Abelardo and the others to think about.

"He did not say much," Phuong reassured her, lifting a shoulder in a very Gallic gesture, and winked. "But he said you're a doctor, and that you work to help women from the islands, former colonies." Aurora thought Mihn might not have needed to say anything to his mother, because Phuong figured it all out on her own. The thought, to her surprise, did not alarm her. Apollo was right. She needed more allies if she truly wanted this endeavor to grow as much as she hoped. Maybe she could start having a little faith that there were others beyond their small band of doctors willing to do this with them in order reach even more women in need.

"We help any woman who comes to us," she explained, while she pulled off a bit of rue from a bush and pressed it to her nose. "But there are many women from former colonies in Paris who are not able to find care from those who understand their needs and we make sure to provide that."

Phuong turned to her then, her lovely brown eyes surveying Aurora's face. "I see you, Doctor Montalban," the woman whispered, as she reached up to touch the spot on her cheek where her bruise was beginning to turn a sickly yellow. "You do what must be done, even when it costs you."

Aurora's throat tightened at the approval and respect she saw in the woman's eyes, and wondered what price Phuong had paid for the life she'd made for herself. A life where her son and his lover were welcome.

She didn't like being seen so clearly. She much preferred hiding behind her prickly walls, but this gentle touch from a woman who already felt like a kindred spirit eased something inside her.

"Isn't this a marvel?" Gilberto asked jovially, as he walked up with Mihn and Apollo trailing behind.

"Yes," she said, a little breathless. "What do you do with all of it?" If this was the house garden, she could only imagine the farm produced an enormous amount of product.

Phuong took her hand again and led her forward. Apollo, for once, didn't seem interested in his usual place at the head of the pack. He was content to talk with Gilberto and Mihn while she and Phuong charged ahead.

"How many people work on the farm?" she asked, when they reached the enormous greenhouse sitting in the middle of what seemed like endless fields. All around them things were growing. The lavender was straight ahead, but from where they stood, she could see fruit tree orchards. She also noticed a few small cottages dotting the land, plus a few scattered buildings.

"That is a complex question." Phuong sent Apollo a questioning look, as if wanting permission to speak further. He nodded reluctantly, which peaked Aurora's curiosity.

"We own half of the land, and the other half my mother's sold to other women," Mihn explained. Aurora looked between the two of them. Mihn's tall, slim form, his jet-black hair, so similar to his mother's. They were both so elegant and proud. But they were not what the typical landowner looked like in this part of the world.

"This land belonged to my father's family. He left it to me and my mother when he died." That cleared up a few things.

"I'm sorry to pry." He laughed at whatever he saw on her face and waved her off.

"We get the question quite often."

"When Mihn and Phuong finally took possession of the land, it was a wasteland," Apollo chimed in. He was leaning against the glass structure. Imposing and magnificent even in repose. "She now produces about fifteen percent of all the lavender in Provence."

"We had help," Phuong said soberly. Apollo's words finally dawned on her. He'd said "finally took possession." It was not hard to imagine that there were people in Mihn's father's circle who were likely none too pleased with having a Vietnamese woman owning land, even if it had gone to waste on their watch.

"I'm curious about the women you've sold the land to." She was intrigued. Phuong didn't seem like the type to exploit the vulnerable, but Aurora had seen a lot of people take advantage of widows or women in desperate circumstances.

Instead of answering, Phuong tore a stem from a row of flowers. "Anise hyssop," she told Aurora. "Helps women heal after childbirth." She'd been handed a basket as she entered the greenhouse, and it was already half full of the things Phuong cut with a little knife she'd pulled out of a pocket in her skirts. "We began selling portions of the land a few years ago," Phuong told her, and Aurora noticed the motherly demeanor from earlier had melted away some, and she now had in front of her a woman who was very much about her business.

"I've never heard of women being able to acquire land on their own," she said. Aurora knew widows could do so. She imagined women of means could too, if they chose, but it was hard to imagine a bank giving poor women loans. "It must be hard to deal with the banks."

"You're looking at the women's bank," Phuong announced, pointing at Gilberto and Apollo.

"What?" she asked, genuinely stumped.

"You two are the bank?"

"Sogra, you're confusing our guest," Gilberto claimed, then pounded Apollo on the back. "Are you going to enlighten the doctora, hermano?"

Apollo responded with a lazy lift of a shoulder. "Technically, we're the vault," he told her, with the air of someone utterly aggrieved at the need to explain himself. "Phuong and now my sisters are the ones accepting the applications and approving the loans." Apollo's half sisters, from what she'd heard, had welcomed their brother into the fold with open arms, but it seemed it went beyond that.

"The interests are so low, and favorable for the women, they're more like gifts," Mihn clarified, and Phuong nodded in agreement.

"I didn't even think women could purchase land." She knew she sounded like a dolt, but this was beyond anything she had ever imagined possible. Her head was spinning. Apollo had been funding loans to help women own land all this time?

"Here in France, we have to be creative, but we've found ways to maneuver where we can." This came from Gilberto.

"Some of the women have continued to work with us, growing lavender, fruits or herbs to be sold in the market." Phuong continued as if it was an everyday occurrence to see men funding women's enterprises. "Others have used their lands to grow crops they use to make their own products."

"One of the women joined with another three and they now make a very popular Marseille soap they sell to apothecaries all over the continent." Mihn pointed at one of the larger buildings on the southern part of the farm, which she assumed was the soap factory.

Something occurred to her.

"Would it be possible to work with some of the women on your farm to create the herbal blends we provide in our clinics?" Even as the words came out of her mouth, she wondered if those self-defense classes were just an excuse to introduce her to Mihn.

"I think that would be a wonderful endeavor for us." Phuong sounded enthusiastic and perhaps like she already had been informed of this possibility by an interfering duke. "We would love to work with your clinics."

"What you're doing is revolutionary," Aurora told the small group, who quietly, with little fanfare, was changing this corner of the world. She thought of all the times in her life she'd heard the word *no* when she wanted to strike out on her own. The ways her family held money over her head to get their way. She thought of the friends from finishing school who had dreams of being architects, scientists, but were told girls were meant for one thing only. All they'd needed was choices, someone to believe in their potential.

"My sister," Gilberto said, and his voice cracked just slightly on the last word. "She wanted to be a businesswoman." The hollowness in her voice told her this would not be a happy story. "She was convinced that if women were given the means, they could rule the business world." Aurora turned her attention to Apollo, who somberly watched his friend. "But my parents forced her to marry instead, a few years later she was gone at the hands of the brute."

Apollo looked grim as he clutched his friend's shoulder. "Just like my mother, like Evan's mother." The look he gave her then seemed to penetrate her very soul. *Just like it would've happened to you, Fiera.*

Aurora was not a believer of fate. She knew from her own life that one's destiny was what one made it. But then how did she explain Apollo's presence in her life?

"We wanted to do this for them," Gilberto finally said.

"Helping women fulfill their dreams is a lovely way to honor your sister," she finally said, in a choked voice.

"We hope so."

Aurora stood there for a moment contemplating the Duke of Annan. The man who had once told her he'd have to be a better man to honor his mother's memory.

"Apollo César Sinclair Robles," she said, her voice taut. He gave her one of those sardonic looks she now recognized as his mask of choice. But she knew all about wearing masks and Apollo's no longer worked on her. "One of these days, the world is going to find out there's a hero under all that cynicism and bluster, and then what will you do?"

He shifted, sliding that big body up and off the column he'd been leaning on, and took a few steps toward her. "I'll just have to keep you distracted so you don't reveal my secrets, Doctora." He wasn't touching her. They were a good foot apart and still, her face heated. His gaze on her made her feel translucent, like everything inside her was in full view to everyone there. She needed an escape.

"This has been lovely, but I'm afraid we must go now if we're to catch the afternoon train to Nice," she said to Phuong, who was busy gathering cuttings and putting them in her basket. "I would like to pay you another visit on my return from Nice."

"Nonsense, you will stay for dinner and we will discuss our new business then, and you have not been in the lavender," the older woman decreed, as she piled more herbs into Aurora's basket. *That* would not be advisable. Her defenses were already dangerously low. After an evening traipsing through lavender fields, she would be even more impaired to resist Apollo, and she'd promised herself she'd end all this before he picked his bride.

"But we must get to Nice." She looked to Apollo for support, but none was forthcoming.

"Please consider staying, Aurora," Gilberto cajoled, then attempted to offer her his arm, which Apollo thwarted by pushing him out of the way. The Brazilian laughed, reaching for Mihn. "My apologies for my friend's brutish behavior, but before I was attacked, I was going to say my sogra was planning to make feijoada in your honor tonight."

"Really?" She didn't look in Apollo's direction, but she knew what she'd find. His checkmate grin. This was a low blow, using her weakness for a good meal to bribe her into staying. "That is very tempting."

It was more than tempting, it was a siren call. She adored feijoada. She'd been to Brazil a few years earlier and had been enamored with the dish of black beans and salted pork. She'd thought of it constantly after she left. More importantly, she wanted very much to discuss the possibility of making the clinic's teas and other contraceptives here at Phuong's.

"I really should go, I have no clothes," she pleaded weakly.

"I can find something for you," Phuong promised, with a cajoling smile. "One of the ladies up the road makes beautiful linen dresses." Aurora's defenses were weakening with each second. "Take her, cher," Phuong instructed Apollo, who instantly snatched Aurora's hand. "I will have your rooms readied in the meantime."

And that was how she found herself in the singularly most romantic moment of her life, with a man she had foolishly, irrevocably fallen in love with, and absolutely could not have.

Twenty-Seven

"You don't need to admit I was right. I don't want you to embarrass yourself." She did not give Apollo the pleasure of turning around to look at his self-satisfied countenance.

"I knew I'd regret not bringing my blade gloves with me," she tossed back.

He barked out a laugh as he pulled her by the waist. She went to him, done with resisting the closeness she wanted. The more she learned about this man, the more confused she became about how she'd give him up.

"I love it when you threaten me with bodily harm." He had her plastered to his front, and she leaned into him, struggling again to recall what she was mad with him about. "It's very arousing." His voice was very low now and it seemed to slither through her, weakening her inch by inch. "I liked when you clawed my back, mi gatita." He pressed his lips to her neck, parted them just enough to lap her heated skin.

"I'm not a kitten," she protested, her voice embarrassingly breathless. He'd been careful with her since the attack, treating her like spun glass. Even when she knew it was wrong, she could not deny she'd missed this.

He made a sound of agreement. Scraping the edge of his

teeth on the spot below her ear that coaxed a sound from her very close to a purr. "You're a leona," he whispered, indulgently. "Fierce and wild, and deliciously prickly." He'd called her those things before. But this time she didn't feel mocked. She felt worshipped, appreciated, praised. Then she remembered she was supposed to be annoyed at him.

"It would've helped to know about those loans when we first met, you know," she reproached him, pulling away from his attempt to incapacitate her with kisses.

When she turned to face him, he was looking at her with that curious expression he sometimes affected. Like she was the most fascinating riddle.

"You're claiming that my boasting about all the things I do for women would've made for a more positive impression of me." She'd have thought he was a self-important comemierda who was probably lying to paint himself as a hero.

"It might have," she hedged, making him laugh again.

"You hated me instantly."

"I didn't hate you."

"You *detested* me," he volleyed back, greatly entertained by her fib. Dios, that laugh burrowed right into her bones. It was her favorite one, the one that made his eyes twinkle. How was it fair that a man this handsome, this powerful, had dimples and sparkling eyes?

"I can't reason with you when you're like this," she huffed and took off down the path.

"What am I doing?" He chased after but kept pretending like he couldn't catch her. Extending his arms until he could almost reach her, and then letting her escape his grasp. When had she ever played like this? She could not remember.

"You're being charming again and it is very unsettling!" she yelled over her shoulder, before she picked up her skirts and raced up the field.

"Ven aca, Fiera," he called. "I thought we were friends." When she looked back again, he crossed his eyes and stuck out his tongue, making a laugh burst out of her. This was perhaps the most concerning effect this afternoon had on her. She seemed unable to hold on to the irritation that before Apollo seemed to always be simmering under her skin.

It could be knowing that women owned the land she stood on. That they owned everything she could see. That despite all the work yet to be done and the horrors happening even in that very moment, she could hold on to the knowledge that she was one of many working to right some of the wrongs in the world. It could be that Apollo made her common sense evaporate.

She kept running, her face up to the sun, until a stitch in her side made her stop to catch her breath. Her chest heaving up and down as her heart pumped blood to her limbs.

"Caught you," he said, low and husky in her ear as he wrapped his strong arms around her. She turned so that they were face-to-face.

"You have to give me back," she told him, trying very hard to make light of the storm of feelings roaring inside.

She loved him and she could never, ever tell him.

He pushed back an errant curl as she worked to get her heart to slow down. "What if I want to keep you, Fiera? What then?"

She wanted to latch on to the promise in his eyes, but she knew what this was about. Apollo's need to protect the women in his life. That didn't stop her from yearning for what he offered her. Didn't stop her from foolishly wishing she could accept it.

"You'll have to learn to live with disappointment, Your Grace." She expected one of his acerbic remarks. Hoped for something that would put them back on familiar ground, where she flung insults that he punctured with his sharp tongue. But all he did was bring her closer. His own chest rising and falling as he looked down at her. He opened his mouth, but she stopped him. Pushed up on her tiptoes and circled her arms around his neck.

"I'm not done with this conversation, Doctora," he said against her mouth. "But I will let you win for now." She should fight, remind him that not even the South American families vying to befriend the new duke would tolerate a duchess with such a history as hers. He could not be tied to scandal, and even he could not ignore the ones in her past.

"Kiss me, I'm out of breath," she gasped, and the side of his mouth tipped up. He shook his head, brushing their lips together.

"You need my air in your lungs, Fiera?"

"Yes." He held her too tight, his body a harbor against anything that could harm her.

"Dame tu boca," he demanded roughly as he took her mouth. Any man would've soothed her with soft kisses, but what she needed was exactly this. To know the ferocity of his desire for her. He sucked on her tongue as his hands gripped her tight. Her waist, her rump. He touched her like he could never have enough of her.

She gave as good as she got. Her own teeth scoring his neck, marking, like he belonged to her.

"Deja tu huella, Fiera," he encouraged as she dug her nails into his skin. She wanted to leave traces of her on him. So that when she was gone, he'd remember. He searched for her mouth and took it again, his tongue sparring with hers. She could feel herself sinking, but he held her up. "I'm not going to make love to you on this field," he groused, when her hand slid over his hardness.

"Why not?" she asked, coming up for breath. Who was she? This reckless creature ready to make love in the open air?

"Because these bushes are full of bees," he said, pointedly looking at one buzzing only inches from them. She yipped and burrowed closer into him.

"I don't like bees." He made one of those low-in-his-throat noises that made her think all manner of sinful thoughts and kissed her head.

"And I don't want you plagued with stings when I undress you tonight." Her nipples puckered at the promise in his voice.

"I don't want to be disreputable in Madame Phuong's home," she demurred, knowing it would only make his next remark more incendiary. One of his hands slid up her bodice until his thumb was flicking one of those puckered nipples.

"You love when I do disreputable things to you," he told her, with the air of a man who knew he was standing on solid ground, before biting her earlobe and sucking on it. "First we'll have dinner," he said, pressing soft kisses to her forehead while his fingers took turns pinching her nipples. The contrast between the gentle caress of his lips and the harsh work of his fingers had her caught in this exquisite space between pleasure and pain.

"After dinner, we'll go to sleep, separately," she taunted him.

"After dinner, Fiera," he began, sliding a hand down her front until he was cupping her sex, "I'm going to take every inch of clothes off your delicious form." His touch was too clever, too good. "Then I'm going to lick you from head to toe."

"Apollo," she whined, and began to wonder how painful it would be to acquire a few bee stings.

She knew she was on borrowed time. That every moment she spent with him, she was exposing him to wagging tongues and scandal.

"You're thinking again," he complained, gently tapping her right temple. "You're much more amenable when you don't think so damned hard."

"If what you want is an empty-headed trollop, you should've left me here and gone to Nice." The moment she said the words, she regretted them. She didn't want to think about Nice or what—and who—was waiting for him there. She stared up at him, attempting to pierce him with an unfriendly glare, but she knew she was much too besotted to manage anything of the like.

"Encabronada." With the way he uttered the word, sultry and slow, one would not think he was calling her bad-tempered. But those eyes simmered with heat as he looked down at her. "There is nothing in Nice that I want more than what I have right here," he told her, making her heart thump painfully against her chest. "And you know damned well, I'm obsessed with your mind." This was how she'd lose this war, the praise, the delight he took in her ugly moods and her penchant for overthinking. "I just don't want you to be in here all the time." He rubbed a circle on her temple, then bent down to tear a piece of lavender from one of the bushes and slid it right over the errant curl he'd tucked back earlier. Then kissed her again.

She could try to argue more, remind him that they'd agreed she would be a terrible duchess. Ask what he meant with that comment about Nice. Tell him that he was making things more difficult. That he knew as well as she did there was no future for them. Not if he wanted respect from his peers, or from the elite from the Americas and Africa he was courting.

But she didn't. Instead, she exhaled a long breath and let her head fall on his chest. She let him brush his lips on the top of her head. She let him take her by the hand and lead her down the rows of lavender and pretended this stolen afternoon could be her life.

"I know the way back to the room, Apollo," she told him that evening, as she swayed those hips down the long hallway leading to the bedchambers.

"I'm merely escorting you, to make sure there are no monsters under your bed," he shot back, attempting and failing to lightly pinch that gorgeous backside.

"The only monster I've seen so far is the one in your trousers." A sly grin over a bare shoulder. Dios, but he wanted her. All through dinner, he'd barely been able to keep his hands off her.

When they reached the door, stood at the threshold, her arms splayed to the side, blocking him from the room. "Respectable houseguests don't let rogues ravish them in their rooms."

"And here I was thinking that time I had you in my parlor had disabused you of that penchant for respectability." She made a lusty sound when his palms connected with the door's surface above her head.

"It's not a penchant," she protested, even as she turned her face up to him. He pressed forward, wanting to feel her. "Contrary to what my behavior as of late indicates, Your Grace, I have managed some semblance of restraint for most of my adult life." That pretty pink flush colored her cheeks, and there was a brightness in her eyes that pierced the very heart of him.

She was open to him. Soft and wanton, his, if only for this moment.

"It's because you find me irresistible, Fiera."

He took her mouth, a little roughly, letting her feel his hunger. Their tongues warred as her nails raked over his back. He loved how she unleashed on him. He would never get enough of that fury.

"I want to be inside you," he whispered hotly, as he lowered one hand to touch her. They hadn't done this since before her attack. He'd been cautious, not wanting to pressure her when she seemed so vulnerable. But now with enough distance from

Ackworth and the rest of the fires still to be put out, he needed her. Badly enough to beg if necessary.

He pressed the heel of his hand to her sex, making her moan for him. The other hand pinched the hard bud of one nipple and she fed him all her needy sounds. He felt her scramble for something, heard the sound of her fingernails scraping on wood, and before he knew it, they were tumbling inside her room.

He'd forgotten they were in the damned hallway.

"I'm not letting you tear this," she warned, already busy unfastening the row of buttons down the front of her blouse. It was a gauzy pale blue garment, with a matching skirt that Phuong had procured for her. She looked lovely in it, serene, and he wanted more than anything to ensure she could always be like this.

"Then you better hurry," he warned, taking a step forward. She backed away with a grin, walked to the large open window and flicked the drapes closed. Her bottom pertly lifted as she leaned over a small desk to reach them. The image of her over the surface of it, those strong hands gripping the edge while he surged into her took hold of him like a fever.

He'd told himself the craving would subside. That, like it always had before, the urge would wane. But his need for Aurora Montalban seemed to feed on itself. The more he had her, the more he wanted. Not just her body. He wanted to possess the very essence of her. Hoard those smiles she rarely offered him. Squirrel away every moan, every lusty glance. The world could have Doctora Montalban, but Aurora the Fiera was his.

"I'll help with the skirt," he offered, making quick work of the hook at her waist and pulling it down, before she could deny him. "I'd very much like to fuck you right against this desk." She made an eager little sound as he worked to undress her. There was no bustle, no petticoat, just a bit of linen covering the swell of her backside. Beneath it, skin the color of the most luscious milk chocolate. He slid a hand up her back, gripped her nape possessively, his fingers digging into her flesh as she arched into the touch.

"Apollo." The way she said his name in these moments tore at the very foundation of his control. He was obsessed with the raspy way she called to him. Asking him without more than a sound for everything. His body, his mind, his damn soul.

He'd tried to convince himself he could let go of this. That eventually he would have to come to terms with his title, with the path it set him on. That he had an obligation to show these aristocrats he was better than all of them. But the moment he'd seen her on the ground, bruised and bleeding, everything else ceased to matter. Her safety, her happiness was all he wanted.

He didn't care about higher causes. He would honor his mother's memory and he'd try to do some good, but his purpose was this woman. Making way for her to do the healing and repairing she so desperately wanted to do.

Otherwise, it would be destroying Forsyth and Ackworth and every other man like them. Without her, he'd be lost to the darkness that had always lived in him, because he might be his mother's son, but he was very much his father's spawn.

"Eres mia, Aurora Beatriz," he whispered against her skin. He skated his hands up the dip of her waist, up her spine. "This is mine." He sank his teeth into flesh, making her whimper. "Mia. Mi Fiera." She stiffened at the possessive declaration, then a humming thrummed through her.

"I belong to me, Your Grace," she countered, even as she parted her legs to his touch. He countered her statement by cupping one breast with a hand while he speared her heat with the other.

"I own this," he insisted, struggling to free his hard shaft from his trousers. The sound of tearing fabric elicited a surprised laugh from his lover, who was circling her hips like a demon on his aching length. "Coño," he moaned when he finally wrenched it free. "Let me in, amor," he coaxed as he kissed the tip of his hardness to her entrance, then slid it over her drenched folds.

Always so good. So perfect.

They both cried out at their joining. It was always like this. Consuming, unbearably perfect.

"Move, Duke," she demanded, making him laugh.

"My blushing maiden," he teased, nipping at her skin, then she was the one laughing. The sound of it, so bright, so light, even when he knew there were so many shadows in her heart. But for him, in these moments she sparkled. He lifted her up until she was on her knees on the desk.

She cried out as he sank further. "It's so deep," she moaned when he pushed inside again and again. He ran his hands over her, leaned down to kiss the nape of her neck, her shoulders.

"You're perfect," he moaned, as he reached under her and rubbed that tight nub of nerves. She jolted at the touch, her sex gripping him so tightly his eyes rolled in his head. "So good, mi Fiera." He wanted to say it then. That he loved her. That he could not let her go.

"Ah, Apollo," she cried when he increased his thrusts. He felt her flutter around him. Her slickness warning him of her nearing climax.

"Come for me, amor," he coaxed, leaving open-mouthed kisses on her hot skin as he entered her in rough, short strokes. "Your cunt is the sweetest thing," he growled in her ear, making her buck into him.

"You have a dirty mouth," she rebuked, even as she turned her face for a kiss. She puffed a breathless little moan into his mouth, then cried out.

He found his own orgasm in the next instant, his forehead

pressed to her shoulder and words he knew he was afraid to utter biting his tongue.

"I will have to live in this room now," she grumbled moments later, her voice muffled with her mouth pressed to the desk. "There's not a soul in Marseille that didn't hear us." He laughed tiredly, still catching his breath, while he caressed her heated skin.

"I assure you Gilberto and Mihn are too busy with their own evening endeavors," he told her, carefully sliding out of her. They both groaned at the loss, but he did manage to resist the urge to paint her with his seed like a Neanderthal. "Let's get you to bed." He scooped her up and she let him carry her there. Her face buried in his neck.

He laid her down gently, his heart beating so aggressively in his chest he could hear the pulsing. She was so lovely in the moonlight, her skin glorious against the pale sheets. This woman had carved a hole in his heart and nothing else could fit but her.

"I need to stop letting you debauch me whenever you like," she said with feigned peevishness as she modestly brought the sheets up to her neck.

"But you always look so refreshed after a debauching," he told her from the foot of the bed. She scoffed, but her eyes didn't leave his naked body. She might not ever vocally stake a claim to him, but those brown eyes roamed over him like a queen surveying her territory.

"You might as well sleep here," she said, reaching for him. "You're so damned loud you'll wake up the entire house getting back to your room."

"You can just say you want me in your bed, Fiera." She rolled her eyes and tugged on his hand until he relented and toppled over her. He cradled her face and kissed her, and she kissed him back. He did so with his eyes open, tasting, looking, inhaling her. Wondering how to say it as he watched her lashes flutter from his kiss. He'd asked her this before but pretended to do so in jest. But nothing about keeping her was a joke, not anymore. He didn't think it ever had been.

When he pulled back, her eyes slid open and he thought he could see every minute, every second of the rest of his life in their depths. His future right under him, cradling him, holding him.

"Marry me, Aurora." He let her go, expected her to fight him. She did.

"Apollo," she cried out, as if the words terrified her. "You know I can't. Philip is still out there."

He dearly wished he could erase Forsyth's filthy existence from the face of the earth. How much damage could one man do?

"Forsyth doesn't matter, you and I do." It made him sick to his stomach, it made him homicidal to see her like this. The bravest, best woman he'd known huddled under the weight of other people's judgments. People who were not worthy of kissing her damned feet.

"It's not just Philip and you know it," she finally said, blinking madly as if she was holding back tears. When he reached for her, she pulled away. Right before his eyes, she retreated into herself, that hair shirt she loved so well tightly wound around her. She wouldn't look at him, her gaze fixed upward. "Not even a duke can make a bastard acceptable to the aristocracy."

The word hit him across the face. The violence of it, the way it made her sound so small. Instantly the warm glow of their lovemaking was replaced with a glacial aloofness. He could almost see her shields going up. The defenses he'd so painstakingly tried to demolish back in full force. They were so close he had but to slide his hand an inch and he'd touch her, like she was sitting on her own little island, with an ocean of fury around her.

"That doesn't matter to me, Aurora—"

"You say that now, but you *will* change your mind." There were a thousand things he wanted to say, but he knew this woman by now and she needed to say her piece. "I'm the child of my father's indiscretion with his wife's younger sister." Her lip quivered, and he could see her struggling not to cry. "Do you truly think the aristocracy will abide that?" He wanted to take her in his arms, but he also knew that would not be welcome. She wasn't wrong. If he was someone different, they might tolerate it. But he had to be above all reproach and even then, they'd make him feel like he didn't belong. "You have a chance to show them who you are, who *we* are. And my presence would be a stain on that."

Not for the first time he repudiated the burden of being the first, the only.

"Don't say things like that about yourself, Aurora." It was an effort to keep from shouting. He hated the way she looked right now. He could practically feel the self-loathing rolling off her in waves. "You're already better than all of them, than I am. Just as you are."

She looked brittle, like the lightest wind could knock her over. "What about all the women in Nice right now waiting for you to make your selection?"

"I've already made it." That was the only thing he was certain of. "You're my duchess."

"Don't say that, Apollo." She sounded scared, like every word out of his mouth terrified her.

"It's true, you're who I want and none of this other mierda matters," he began, but she cut him off with a swift shake of her head.

"No, don't tell me it doesn't matter to you."

"It doesn't matter to me," he insisted. There was no gently bred, aristocratic lady who could ever compare to this woman.

"It will matter." She was pure defiance now. It cut him to the bone to see the fear in her eyes, refusing his words. "It will matter when the whispers start, when you can't find a single ally. You'll hate me or you'll hide me." Like her father hid her. Like that whore's son Ackworth hid his wife.

She was up from the bed now, wedged into a corner of the room with that sheet wrapped around her. She looked hunted, her eyes traveling over his face as if looking for a diagnosis. Excavating for some feeling she expected to see but was yet to locate.

"I would never hide my duchess."

She laughed, a broken sound, and turned away from him. He tried to stand, to go to her, but she held her hand up.

"No, stay there." She squeezed her eyes shut, her mouth in a flat, miserable line. "Or I won't say the things I need to say." He wondered if this was the true reason she'd given up her family fortune. If she was imposing some kind of penance on herself. "Remember when you'd tease me about my sanctimoniousness?" God, he could be such a pendejo. "Why do you think I'm like this?" she asked, through tears.

"I don't know, Aurora," he answered helplessly, as he watched her rip herself apart.

"Because I need to make up for my birth. Because no matter how good I am, how well I behave, any mistake, any misstep comes down to that. The bastard who can't rise above her nature."

The words were not easy to hear, and it took everything in him to not go to her. But it all made sense now. The way she held herself. The distrust, the walls she built up around herself. Her certainty that she wasn't enough. In the beginning, he'd thought they were similar in their stubbornness. That, like him, she forced herself into places because she had to show people she was just as good as they were. But now he saw it was about earning her place.

She killed herself with the clinics, with the work, because she didn't think they would allow her to stay. She kept secrets even from her friends because she believed their love, like her father's and even her mother's, would only be there as long as she didn't cause them trouble. His heart shattered for that little girl who was neglected and ignored, never knowing why she wasn't wanted.

He had seldom felt this powerless. Fury churned in him at what the world did to women. The cycle of misery and shame inflicted on them.

"Mi cielo."

She scoffed at the endearment. "I'm no one's idea of heaven." But when he stood and went to wrap his arms around her, she came to him. She pressed her forehead to his chest. "I don't want to ruin things for you, Apollo, and I will. Promise me you won't risk what you've fought so hard for, for me."

He was tired. Weary of having to take on the world, simply to be allowed into a room he had every right to be in. He didn't want to battle anymore, he just wanted to love her.

"But what if all I want is you?" He tried to pull her chin up to look at him, but she wouldn't let him.

"I won't marry you, Apollo. I won't do that to you."

He wanted to fight her, bully her into seeing that she was the only thing he wanted. But he knew that with Aurora, words only went so far. He'd have to show her.

Twenty-Eight

Aurora should've known her tearstained rejection of Apollo's proposal would have the opposite effect she imagined, because the man never reacted to anything like a sensible person.

What other duke in the world would only grow *more* convinced he wanted a woman after he discovered she was a bastard, dabbled in crime and had a terribly checkered past?

The man was impossible. But no matter what he told her, or even what she told herself about his feelings for her, there was no future for them. Apollo had the possibility of making a great difference in the lives of many, of creating a different kind of legacy, and she would not interfere with it.

And now she was in Nice with him. The fact that he would not be selecting a bride like he'd promised did nothing to ease her nerves. She should've gone back to Paris that morning instead of boarding the train to the French Riviera. But he'd woken her up with his lips working themselves up the inside of her thighs. He'd stroked, licked and bitten her to a blinding climax before taking her from behind while he told her that her tight sex was surely better than anything the heavens could ever offer a man.

She'd taken the train to Nice.

"Are you all right?" Apollo asked for the tenth time. She nodded tightly, trying to descend from the train without being noticed by two of her brothers' friends who were already on the platform. Vicente Reyes and Jose Maria Alva were two of the engineers who had designed the Mexican Pavilion for the exhibition. Both had attended university with her brothers Octavio and Sebastian. For all she knew, they'd been sent to keep an eye on her.

She quickly lifted the fan to her face and almost fell as she took the last step off the train. Apollo caught her before she tumbled to the ground. The man was so damned...devoted.

"Why are you covering your face like that?" She winced and then he made a sound of understanding, his thumb caressing the small of her back. "You can hardly see the bruising, Fiera."

For an instant she felt guilty about letting him think she was self-conscious about the remnants of her encounter with Collins.

"I'm only feeling a bit warm." She fanned herself furiously as Apollo diligently moved her along the crowd. There was a sea of brown faces here. Women in lovely gowns and gentlemen in well-appointed suits arriving on the French Riviera at the invitation of the Duke of Annan. If she weren't in such a rush to avoid being recognized by her brothers' potential spies, she'd stop to take it all in.

It was not like she hadn't been in environments like this. The well-to-do families of the North Coast of the Dominican Republic and the upper crust of the Yucatán Peninsula her parents socialized with had many people who looked like her. But she hadn't been anywhere in Europe where a gathering like this had occurred.

"This is quite an event you are hosting," she told him, genuinely impressed with what he'd managed. It would be quite a message to the copious members of the British aristocracy who frequented the South of France at this time of year. "You've done well, Your Grace," she told him, unable to help the bit of pride in her voice.

"*We* have, Fiera," he corrected, and she let him win this time.

"Leona!" The scream was unmistakably Manuela, and soon she was being pulled into an embrace and kissed by her two best friends. Instead of stopping in Provence, the two of them, with Evan, Cora, Tia Jimena and a recovering Juliana, had arrived in Nice the day before.

"He's still alive, so I assume things went well," Manu joked, sending an amused glance in Apollo's direction.

"Aurorita." They'd just reached the carriage when a man's voice called out her name. She froze at the use of the diminutive of her name.

"Who is that?" Apollo asked with unvarnished hostility.

She suppressed a sigh and turned. As expected, Reyes and Alva headed toward her.

"They're friends of my brothers," she told Apollo, who narrowed his eyes at the information. Despite their truce in order to find Philip, Apollo harbored no warm feelings toward her siblings. She could not blame him.

"Señor Alva, Señor Reyes," she said, tilting her head in their direction. "These are my friends Lady Luz Alana and Miss Caceres Galvan." The greetings were quick and warm, then it was Apollo's turn. "This is the Duke of Annan." She didn't think she imagined the growl she heard when the two men extended their hands.

"How do you know Doctora Montalban?" the duke asked with audible hostility.

"We grew up with her older brothers," Alva explained amiably. Apollo's eyes were all but slits by then.

"It's a pleasure to see you again, Aurorita." Reyes had always been somewhat of a flirt.

"I've been traveling," she said, at the same time that Apollo practically barked. "She's been saving lives." Then he proceeded to pull her closer with an air of ownership she dearly wished she didn't enjoy as much as she did.

"Of course." Reyes grinned amiably, seemingly unaware he was in the sights of a dormant volcano.

"She likes to be addressed as *Doctora Montalban*." Apollo bared his teeth at the two men, which finally got Reyes to back away, holding both hands up in surrender.

"Pardon me, Your Grace." Both men shared an amused look and Aurora knew without a shadow of a doubt her brothers almost certainly would hear about this.

"Gentlemen, will we see you at the Promenade des Anglais this afternoon?" Luz Alana chimed in, clearly aware of the tension. Aurora groaned internally at the reminder of what was on the agenda for the afternoon.

"We will see you on the paseo, then," Alva said with a nod, as Apollo helped her into the carriage after sending both men more pugnacious glares.

"That was uncalled-for," she said, when he finally settled beside her, not caring that the Leonas could hear.

"You're much too self-possessed to be addressed with diminutives," he countered, as if that was a justification. "What do you think, ladies?" She scoffed at his appeal to her two friends, who were apparently elated over his behavior.

"It's what her brothers used to call her," Manuela explained, amused.

"Were either of those two pendejos her siblings?" he asked pleasantly, even as he directed daggers with his eyes in the direction where they'd left Alva and Reyes.

Manuela and Luz Alana, who were absolutely no help, only

laughed at his insults to the two men. "They're not my siblings, but they've known me for a long time."

"Well, they'll have to learn they can't be so familiar to future duchesses." This, as expected, prompted a series of oohs and aahs from her friends.

"He's not being serious," she told them, nipping that line of conversation in the bud.

"I'm *perfectly* serious," Apollo returned, taking her hand and placing it on his knee.

"Aurora," Manuela exhaled with bright eyes.

"Don't start, Manuela," she groaned, covering her ears. "I'm *not* the future duchess. I'm certain you will have your pick of lovely debutantes from respectable families from the Americas throwing themselves at your feet."

"I don't want debutantes," he told her, with a stubborn set of his jaw. "I want pugnacious physicians who threaten me with scalpels."

Manuela and Luz Alana could barely contain themselves, but they managed to not react to Apollo's claims.

"I'm not duchess material, Apollo," she declared, looking out the window, and for once, Apollo left it alone.

An hour later she found herself in one of the lavish bedrooms overlooking the Mediterranean Sea, draped in an excessive amount of yellow silk.

"This is too much," she balked, staring at her reflection in the mirror.

"No, it's exactly enough," Manuela shot back, bending down to adjust the hem of the gown she'd bullied Aurora into.

In truth, it was not one of the ridiculous designs with those atrocious bustles. The skirt was wide, but not so much that she looked like a wedding cake. The raw silk felt lovely to the touch, and the filigree embroidery in a slightly darker shade of yellow on the collar and sleeves were the exact amount of embellishment she approved of. The delicate pleats under the breast enhanced her shape and brought attention to her bosom. Her face heated at the thought of what Apollo would say. Then it heated further when her brain answered the question with alarming detail.

She still could not make sense of the night before. Of the certainty in his eyes when he asked her to marry him. She knew he believed it when he told her he didn't care about her past. But he couldn't know what it would be like. And though giving him up would be hard, she thought she could survive it. What she knew she couldn't was to see his love for her turn into resentment and regret.

"Why can't I wear that?" she asked, waving at the suit she'd been wearing when she left Paris two nights earlier. Knowing it would at least provoke enough of an argument with her friends to serve as a distraction.

"Aurora, you will be on the arm of the duke at the promenade."

"Oh, stop calling him *The Duke*," she snapped with irritation. "I don't know what's gotten into the two of you."

Luz Alana rolled her eyes and Manuela threw herself on the chaise.

"He cares for you, Leona," Luz Alana said in a gentle tone, as though she feared the words would set Aurora on fire. "It's evident. Evan said he's canceled this bride selection business—"

"No." Aurora could not hear any of it. It would only make things worse. "He knows everything, even about my real mother." That day they'd come to the den of iniquity while Apollo went looking for Ackworth and Philip, she'd told the Leonas that Doña Jimena's beau was the same man who had almost ruined her.

"Leona," Manuela said, her voice brimming with emotion.

"He insists he doesn't care," she rushed to say. "But he will. Eventually he will." Just like her father had. He'd tolerated her presence as a condition to having the woman he loved with him, but in the end, his position and his reputation were more important.

"Apollo doesn't care about any of that," Luz Alana told her, her hands gripping Aurora's shoulder in the reflection. "He repudiates all that snobbery and hypocrisy."

That didn't change the world he was part of now. Their opinions would matter. Even for the families who were here in Nice, eager to make alliances with him, it would matter.

"But it will be of importance to everyone else. You should know that better than anyone, Manuela." Her friend, who had turned her back on society and the world she'd known, to openly live with her beloved, had to understand what Aurora could cost Apollo.

"It's his choice to make, Aurora. You can't decide what you are to him." She knew they would say this. Now that they each had found love, they were convinced everyone should have it. That nothing was high enough of a price. But they weren't her. They hadn't done the things she had.

"Eventually I will become a burden." She said it while looking in the mirror. Already changing for the sake of this fantasy that could never be for her.

What did she think she was doing in Nice? In frilly walking dresses, going on promenades? This was not the life she'd chosen. She preferred her independence above everything. A life where no one cared where she came from as long as she could do the job at hand. This impostor she was looking at would end up with a broken heart or much worse.

"You don't know that," Manuela insisted, frustration clear in her voice.

"Yes, I do!" she volleyed back. "I'm trying to be sensible."

"Sensible like you were running around putting yourself in danger?" Luz Alana scolded her. The accusation stung, but she knew her friends were hurt by all the secrets she'd kept from them.

"Sensible like I don't want my heart shattered." She kept her focus on her sleeves, which she tugged on so roughly she thought she heard a tear on the seam of the cuff.

"He's mad about you, Leona," Manuela pushed. "You must see that."

"He asked me to marry him last night," she confessed. Unable to keep the bewilderment from her voice.

"Do you want to marry him?" Manuela asked carefully, then quickly added, "Please don't attempt to lie to me, I have seen you look at the man. You're worse than Luz Alana is with the Great Scot."

"You practically dissolve into a puddle whenever your duchess walks into the room," Luz Alana protested. Manuela offered a wordless grin around the hairpins between her lips. "And stop calling my husband the Great Scot."

"He likes that nickname, and we're talking about Aurora," Manuela argued. "The duke is going to choke when he sees you in this."

Aurora rolled her eyes and took herself in. She didn't look like herself, sucked into all this silk and fine thread. She didn't look like the woman who worked nights on end. Who was chased by police and helped women escape their violent husbands. She didn't look like a woman with roughened hands and a wary heart.

"This isn't me," she pointed out, turning this way and that.

"I don't think any of us are exactly as we were when we arrived in Paris five months ago." Manuela and her irritating wisdom was beginning to grate.

Her friend had become so self-assured in these past few

months. For Manuela, peculiar soul that she was, love had brought out her more sober, judicious side. While everyone else seemed to lose their heads for love, Manuela had gained the temperament of Solomon.

"Has it only been five months?" Luz Alana asked, looking heavenward.

It was unbelievable.

Their lives had changed so much in such a short amount of time. She'd arrived here still attempting to atone for her mistakes. Striving to be outwardly perfect in the present, so people forgot her past. But that had made her miserable, her life small. Despite everything, she liked this Aurora better. This Aurora had a purpose, had learned to be resourceful, to ask for help. Had a community of colleagues as dedicated as she was to their cause. This Aurora had risked her heart and been rewarded grandly, even if only fleetingly.

"I don't want to change." Both women widened their eyes at her impassioned tone. "I want to be a doctor, I want to be independent."

"Apollo won't take those things from you," Manuela insisted. And perhaps he wouldn't do it on purpose, but his position required a kind of woman she simply could not be.

A knock on the door offered Aurora a much-needed escape from a conversation she knew would not end with any kind of resolution.

"Come in," Luz Alana called, and the Duke of Annan's head appeared in the doorway.

"The men are becoming restless," he told Luz Alana with a grin, then he looked at Aurora. For a second, he seemed almost dumbstruck, but then he focused on her and his gaze ran hot. "Muy bella, Doctora." He did nothing to cull the lust in his voice, he did even less to conceal the possession in his gaze.

The hunger she saw there made the already-tight clothing constricting. "I will be the most envied man at the promenade."

The way he looked at her. Like a dragon with his treasure.

It was so tempting to believe that she could have what her head and heart wanted, but she had never lied to herself. It was a rule that had served her well, but Apollo came into her life to make her want to break it.

"We will be there in a moment, Your Grace," Aurora said, ignoring her friends' little gasps at what they'd seen pass between her and Apollo. With one last incendiary look, he left, leaving her with a thumping heart and a fire under her skin.

"It does seem like she has it all under control, doesn't it?"

Aurora grabbed her parasol and pointed it at her friend like a saber. "Manuela Caceres, you do not want to be the one to snap the last of my nerves."

Twenty-Nine

"I'm still partial to your working clothes, but this shade of yellow makes you glow," Apollo whispered in her ear as they made their way up the Promenade des Anglais.

It was difficult to entertain his attempts at charm in the state she was in. "I can't feel anything above my hip bone and I'm fairly certain I'll never regain sensation in my left breast, but I'm jubilant that you find the color to your liking." He emitted one of those rumbling sounds that made her feel like prey.

"I can't say I recommend you begin listing body parts I have a particular fondness for." Not even his uncouth behavior—which she usually found distressingly arousing—could shake off her dark mood. She thought perhaps arriving in Nice could finally cement the truth of their situation. That Apollo's life required things from him she could not be part of, but instead her friends, the dress, the walk by the Mediterranean Sea, were all conspiring to do away with her better judgment.

"There have to be over a hundred people here, Apollo," Luz Alana commented from behind, as they made their way along the promenade, which brought a welcome distraction to the gray cloud looming over Aurora's head.

"It is quite a sight," Evan concurred, and Aurora quietly

agreed. "This promenade was built in the '20s for all the British peers that descended on the place," the Scot said as they came up to where the walkway curved into the sea. Aurora took a look around the wide boardwalk lined with those tall palm trees. She didn't think she'd ever see a coastline that compared to that of her mother's homeland in Puerto Plata, but this place was stunning in its own right.

"That's why it's called Promenade des Anglais." As always, there was a contrite tinge to Evan's voice when he spoke about the aristocracy. "We do enjoy our walks by the sea." Luz Alana made a sympathetic sound and pushed up to kiss her husband.

"I can imagine my decision to overrun the place with some of the elite families of the Americas, Asia and Africa will only increase my popularity in the House of Lords." Apollo beamed at the prospect, but Aurora shook her head. Why did he have to be so defiant?

"I'm delighted with our current invasion of the Riviera, but are we truly going to walk the seven miles?" This came from Manuela, who was strolling alongside them, shoulder to shoulder with Cora. The duchess wore shaded spectacles and her usual scowl.

"I'm not fond of perspiring in public." She sent a cursory look over the splendidly azure waters of the Mediterranean Sea and tightened her hold on her lover.

"It was not an obligatory invitation," Apollo volleyed back at the duchess, who sent him a mutinous glare from under her glasses. Aurora and Manuela sent each other amused looks at their bickering. It was not surprising that Cora and Apollo had become close, despite their efforts to make it seem otherwise.

"Who is that?" Luz Alana asked quietly, looking at an older gentleman being pushed in a wheelchair by a much younger and very scantily dressed woman.

Apollo's grin widened when he saw the pair. "*That's* the

famed Peanut King," he told her, then sent Evan an amused look. His brother sighed.

"The Peanut King?" Luz Alana asked, eyes bright with curiosity. The older man had a weathered brown face, and even in the chair, it was obvious he'd once had a formidable form. He could've been an older uncle of Apollo's.

"That's Charles Heddle," Evan explained. "His mother was from the Wolof people in Sierra Leone, but his father was a Scot, from the Orkneys. That's his new wife with him."

"His fifty-years-younger wife," Apollo added. At that, all the women in the group whipped their heads to stare at the old man, then shuddered in unison.

"That's disgusting," Cora declared, with an expression that matched the sentiment.

"It might be, but the man is a genius," Evan informed them. "He almost succeeded in shifting the economy in Sierra Leone from the slave trade to peanut farming."

Luz's eyes lit up at that. "Fascinating."

Apollo nodded approvingly and waved at the old man when he passed them. "He's also incredibly influential among Scottish burghers and some of the more progressive peers." That was delivered with a wink that made Aurora's heart flutter. "He's an admirer of the way my brother and I made our father aware of my existence."

"I might want to meet the man," Cora relented, after sending one last look in the direction of the Peanut King.

After a while they all began to go their separate ways. The first to go were Cora and Manuela with the excuse of needing something from their carriage. From the way Manuela's eyes lit up at Cora's excuse, Aurora decided what the duchess had misplaced was somewhere under her lover's skirts.

"I see Tanaka, brother," Evan announced a moment later, tipping his hat in the direction of two gentlemen descending from a carriage. "He's the Japanese emperor's man," Evan explained when Aurora sent him a confused look.

"Make sure you invite them to the fete tomorrow," Apollo reminded his brother, who was already headed for the man's carriage with Luz Alana in tow. Which left only the two of them. As if people weren't already gaping at Aurora, wondering who the duke's companion was.

"That is a very deep sigh," Apollo muttered, as he tightened his hold on her.

She looked up at him, and her heart constricted just at the sight of his face. The sun was in his eyes and he was squinting at her. He looked young and capable, the kind of man people should want to lead them. The kind of man any woman would be glad to build a life with.

She would've, if her own life were different.

"I'm thinking of this brave new world you're attempting to forge," she told him, instead of casting up the muddle of conflicting feelings roiling inside her. Apollo, who could see too much, gave her a dubious look. "I'm serious. There's such potential here, to do good. You could have such influence on so many, and I…" She didn't want to be a hindrance. She didn't want to do to him what she'd done to her mother and alter the course of his life. She didn't want to be greedy.

"You could do it all with me," he told her, unmoving in his certainty of her. If only she had his faith. "You're hungry," he declared into the taut silence between them.

"You won't change my mind with food," she protested with a laugh, but he was already walking toward a small stand on the side of the street. There was a sign on it that read Socca.

"These are a specialty here," he informed her. "Chickpea-flour pancakes." She had no idea if that sounded good or not, but she knew better than to resist him trying to feed her.

There was much to yearn for when it came to a man like

Apollo César Sinclair Robles, she thought as she watched him stride toward the unassuming stand. His wide shoulders, that lone, unruly curl that always ended on his forehead. Most of all, she would miss the way he looked at her with those dark eyes. Like he craved her and cherished her. Like he saw something in her no one else could see, not even herself.

He was talking with the gentleman making the pancakes when an older man and a tall, slender woman with a parasol approached him. She only recognized them when the lady lowered the sun barrier and beamed up at Apollo.

Graziella Patiño looked perfect by his side. Poised, wealthy, free of any scandal that could mar Apollo's chances. He watched her speak animatedly at him, like she had at the salon, while Apollo smiled politely. Don Simón observed them with the air of a man looking at a critical investment. She ought to go, let him fully claim the life he'd fought so hard for.

"She'd be the perfect duchess for him." The voice came from somewhere behind her.

When Aurora turned, she came face-to-face with Apollo's aunt Jimena. She was as elegantly dressed as ever. The diamonds around the older woman's neck and dangling from her ears shone brightly in the autumn sun, but the light in her eyes was significantly dimmed. Still, no one would suspect she'd had her world turned upside down merely days earlier.

Aurora had always considered that kind of stoicism a virtue, but she was beginning to wonder if it was worth the toll it took. She expected to find venom in the older woman's gaze, or at least recrimination. Pity was much worse.

"Doña Jimena." She hesitated, unsure what to say, then she remembered that despite the circumstances, this was the mother of a patient. "How is Juliana?" She'd wanted to see the girl when they arrived at the villa but was told she was resting.

"She is feeling stronger, she's remorseful, embarrassed and

scared, but she's healthy and that's all that matters." Doña
Jimena's voice broke for a moment, but with two breaths she'd
gathered herself. The raw pain in the woman's eyes eased Aurora's worries about the girl's future. Juliana's mother might
not be happy, but she would stand by her. "I'd like to thank
you for what you did for her."

"You don't need to thank me, I'm glad I was able to help,"
Aurora whispered, quickly feeling uncomfortable when Apollo's
aunt continued to stare at her in silence.

"Philip told me about you, you know?" Aurora didn't respond, certain Doña Jimena had more to say. Apollo was still
smiling at the Patiños, but she could almost sense he was looking in her direction. "He didn't say he'd been involved," she
explained, her mouth twisting into a bitter grimace. "He said
you'd be a liability for my nephew, that you could hurt his as-
cent into the ton."

"I see." It was the only thing she could muster in that moment. Besides, what more was there to say. Philip would know
about ruination.

"It's not that I judge you for what you did," Doña Jimena
claimed, as Aurora's heart hammered in her chest. "In a way,
I admire you." Her face suddenly felt cold, like a sheet of ice
was hardening around her, while Apollo's aunt continued to
talk. "You refused to be forced into a marriage with a scoundrel
like Philip, even if it ruined your name. It was brave, bold."

"I'm not sure what you're saying," Aurora muttered, even
though she was fairly certain she did.

"I am grateful to you, for your discretion, for saving Juliana,
but you made your choice," the older woman said unflinch-
ingly. "You have your independence, your profession." She
lifted a hand in her nephew's direction and Aurora could see
the woman's pride. "He's the first of ours to have this power
and position. You must know that a woman like you would

hurt his chances." Her eyes were hard, almost angry. But Aurora didn't think it was directed at her. Maybe at the world, at men who forced women into such choices. "If he marries you, it will ruin everything."

She flinched at the Doña Jimena's words, which hurt all the more because they were not delivered unkindly.

"I don't want to be duchess." The words sounded like a lie. Because the truth was, she might not want the title, but she wanted the man.

Doña Jimena clucked her tongue and turned to look at Apollo. "Perhaps not, but you want him, and I know he wants you." Despair tore at her, because she could not keep her heart from soaring at hearing the words. She could also not deny the truth. "He needs a duchess like her." She nodded toward Graziella, who had her delicate hand on Apollo's forearm without noticing his regard was fixed somewhere else. "Someone who's not dragging scandal behind. I know I sound like a hypocrite, but I would say the same thing to Juliana if she was in your shoes." The widow shrugged, then sighed wearily. "I understand the desire for autonomy, but that comes at a price."

The words were like lashes against her face.

"I know you were given a rotten hand." This time it was Aurora who looked away, not wanting to face the pity on the woman's face. "But our survival depends on facing our reality. None of us can have it all, Doctora Montalban, and neither you or my nephew can fix the aristocracy."

She considered the older woman and wondered what she'd had to negotiate to be standing here at the Promenade des Anglais watching her nephew, a duke, when her own mother had been born a slave.

Doña Jimena was right. Why was her personal happiness more important than Apollo's future?

She'd sealed her fate at fifteen when she'd risked scandal to free herself from Philip. She could never regret that choice. But now she was trying to break the rules. She knew more than most just how few choices women who went against society's norms ended up with. She'd had the privilege and resources to make a life for herself, and that had to be enough.

"Thank you," she said quietly, swallowing down her tears.

"We all deserve more," Doña Jimena said, not without sympathy, reaching to squeeze her hand. "I hope someday we're able to get it."

"Tia, I didn't know you planned to come." Apollo's booming voice jolted both women, who flinched at the sound. He was holding what looked like an overcooked crepe in a cone paper.

"Hola, querido," his aunt called in an overly bright voice. Her heart broke at the sight of his easy smile, which turned into a frown from whatever he saw on their faces.

"Is Juliana all right?" he asked the moment he reached them.

The older woman's lips trembled and her eyes filled with tears, but her face split into an adoring smile as she looked at her nephew. "She's fine," she said with a nod, then looked at Aurora. "Thanks to the doctor." Apollo's own face split into another one of those smiles that pierced her soul.

"She's quite magnificent," he said huskily while her heart shattered into a million pieces.

She took a deep breath, shivering from the cold air brought in by the mistral and choking on unshed tears. "I'm a bit cold, and I have a headache," she said, unable to control the chattering of her teeth. Goodness, since when had she become so dramatic?

Since you fell in love.

Instantly Apollo came to the rescue. "Come, I'll take you home." He put an arm around her shoulder, then turned to his aunt. "Will you come with us, Tia?"

"I'll return with the Patiños," she told her nephew. Apollo

sent her a questioning look, but she waved him off. "Go, mijo, take care of the doctora."

"Vamos, Fiera." Without caring who saw him, Apollo tucked her to his side all the way to the carriage while Doña Jimena looked on.

Thirty

"She's called a footman to bring down her luggage."

Apollo stood up from the chair on the veranda, where they were all taking breakfast, at Luz Alana's announcement. All except for Aurora, who had arrived from the promenade claiming a headache and had not been seen since.

"Who called a footman?" He asked the question, knowing damned well who the *she* in question was. He'd tried to slip into her bedroom the night before, but the door had been locked.

She hadn't been the same since the night at Phuong's. But he'd thought she only needed time. He was asking a lot from her. It would probably be kinder, more honorable to let her go, but not having her was unthinkable.

She was *his*, dammit.

He was certain something had passed between Aurora and his aunt when he'd insisted on getting the damned pancake.

The moment he'd come back, he'd known. Her eyes had been dull and her shoulders curling in on themselves as he'd handed her the thing. She'd eaten it, all the while with a tight, dead smile on her lips as she chewed and painfully swallowed. It had been agony to watch her pretend to enjoy it. Being in love was not for the weak. Even the simplest things turned into torture.

"Where is she?" he asked Luz Alana, before looking over at his aunt, who was examining the toast on her plate much too closely.

"Still in her room."

He was at the bottom of the staircase when a harried Manuela appeared at the top. "It's locked, she won't open it."

"Give me a minute to talk to her first," he told the women as he mounted the stairs two at a time. He reached her door in seconds and had to exercise an enormous amount of restraint not to kick it open.

"Open the door, Fiera," he demanded, projecting his voice. He lifted his knuckles to rap on the thing or tear it off the hinges if he had to, but after a second, she opened the door.

She looked pale and the bruise had turned a sickly green. She was back in her usual attire. This time a dark gray suit with those slit skirts she loved so much. Her back ramrod straight as she reached for her gloves. Most disturbingly, every piece of clothing on her was unrumpled and pristine.

She'd opened the windows, and the room was blindingly bright. From where he stood, the sunlight cast her in shadow. His heart hammered in his chest as he watched her move. That ruthless efficiency of hers. The detached composure she employed in everything. Except with him. In his bed. There she was wild, impulsive, greedy, happy, his.

"Your Grace." Her voice was like a faint echo. She was right there in front of him and yet she could've been a hundred miles away.

Apollo was not afraid of very many things, but in that moment, he feared that she might already be lost to him. The way she'd been discarded by her parents, her brothers. Her own mother. It all had left a hole inside her that Apollo didn't know if even he could fill.

"Why are you sending your bags downstairs?" There was no controlling the emotion in his voice.

"I'm going back to Paris," she informed him in that overly friendly tone she used when she was at her breaking point. She refused to look at him and kept that eerily vacant stare on something over his shoulder.

"What did my aunt say to you at the promenade?" She flinched at the question, her chin quivered for an instant, but she quickly regained her control.

"Nothing." This was the calmest, the politest he'd ever seen her. "I asked after Juliana." She didn't raise her voice. She didn't look at him.

He'd always been so good at keeping a distance from any unpleasantness. He'd mastered the ability to regard anything he didn't like with detached disdain. He was not a man who let his emotions command him. But in that moment, he was as close as he'd been to coming undone.

"You promised me, Aurora." She blinked, then tipped her lips farther up in a brittle smile, before turning away from him. "You said you'd stay until we knew it was safe for you to go back to Paris."

"I should've never promised that," she told him, while she puttered around the room, until there was nothing left, but to face him. Her matching gray hat, as always, was precariously perched on her head. "I should not be here."

"That is for me to surmise," he told her, remembering all the times she'd said she was not his problem. "You're my guest, my companion, my—"

"No," she almost shouted, putting her hands up, as if she wanted to force whatever he was about to say down his throat. "Please don't say things you will only regret later."

"The only thing I'll regret is letting you leave here now, knowing how I feel about you." Her eyes widened, a hunted, panicked glint in them.

"I have to go," she said, hurrying to the door, but he wrapped his arms around her before she could slip away. "I need to go. My train is in an hour, Your Grace."

"I'm not *Your Grace*, carajo," he told her, taking her chin in hand and forcing her to look at him. Even now, within that shroud of misery, he could feel that current of wanting running through her. "I'm your man, your lover." She shivered in his arms. "I love you, and you are mine," he insisted, and even as she shook her head, she pressed her forehead to his. He could feel her racing pulse, her breaths ragged as she fought that war she always had waging with herself. "Tu lo sabes, Fiera. Tu eres mia," he told her, searching for her mouth. Her sob and his harsh breath mingled in a kiss that tasted of her tears. "Y yo soy tuyo."

He kissed her again, wanting to feed her the storm raging in his heart. The devastating, undeniable truth of his love for her. She fisted the back of his jacket, so hard he thought he heard it rip.

"No, Apollo," she said, wrenching herself away. "You have to let me go."

He took one of her hands and pressed it to his heart. "This is yours, and there's nothing that can change that." That seemed to only make things worse. A flurry of emotions passed through her face. Despair, yearning, anguish, ending in something that looked like cold determination.

"I won't let you ruin everything over your misguided honor." She poked his chest hard with her finger. "Do you think you can just change the rules, Apollo?" she demanded.

"Maybe they need to be changed, Aurora."

"You have a hundred potential allies coming here tonight,

do you think you can just walk in there with me with impunity?" This was what it was all about. She could not believe she deserved him choosing her over his position. That the devil's bargain she'd made when she was just a girl in order to escape the hell Philip Carlyle had in store for her meant she needed to live in penance forever.

"You don't believe you deserve to be happy," he said, finally seeing things clearly.

"What are you talking about?" she balked, breaking free from his hold.

"Your defiance, your need for independence, it's not freedom, it's your prison." How had he not seen this before? "You've bought their lie. You think that you don't deserve to be happy because you broke their rules."

"You just want a woman to save." She was ruthless, looking at him right in his eyes as she said it. Making sure he'd despise her afterward. "I'm not your mother and I am not Juliana. I don't need to be saved."

"But you need to be loved." His words seemed to shatter her. "I love you and I know you love me." Her face crumbled, her chin quivering as she fought back tears.

"I don't love you." She said it like her heart was breaking. "I don't love you, Apollo." Her voice broke on his name.

"I don't believe you," he told her. He knew she was lying. Maybe to herself, to him. He didn't know. "You're scared that I'll stop loving you, but I am not your father." She shook her head, as tears welled in those brown eyes.

"I can't," she pleaded with him.

"Aurora!"

Before they could say anything else to one another, Manuela's panicked voice and frantic knocks made them both start. "Please, open up, there's been an accident and they're looking for doctors."

Apollo took a step back, knowing that the conversation was

over. "Duty calls, Doctora," he bit out, as she went to open the door.

"What happened?" she asked, already reaching for her medical bag.

"There was an accident. A coach turned over near the train station," Manuela informed them, while Luz Alana sent him a nervous look. "They know you're a doctor and were hoping you could come and help."

"If you go, you will take Jean-Louis with you." For a moment he thought she'd fight him on it, but after a moment she nodded.

"All right, I will return to collect my things after," she told him as she left the room with her friends in tow.

She'd done the right thing. Then why did she feel like she had a hole in her chest? Hours after she'd arrived at the accident, she could not achieve the focus she'd always been able to command for her work.

She was distracted. She'd made mistakes, and she was heartsick. She was miserable for what she'd told him. Her stomach roiled every time she remembered the way he'd looked at her. He hadn't believed her, she knew that. But he'd finally seen the depth of her cruelty, and instead of hating her, he'd pitied her for it.

"Can you dip that in the carbolic solution, please?" she asked Jean-Louis, extending him the needles she'd used to suture a patient. Yes, because despite how horrible she'd been to him, he'd still made sure she had Jean-Louis with her. Despite her complaints, she had to admit the duke's henchman had turned out to be quite a competent assistant, and a surly one.

"Drink this first," he told her, offering her a glass of lemonade.

"I don't have time," she said dismissively, already turning to take care of the next person lying on a pallet.

One of the many they'd had to temporarily set up inside the train station after a coach carrying two dozen people intending to board the morning train to Lucerne had overturned only a few dozen meters away.

"The boss will have my head if I don't make sure you take care of yourself," Jean-Louis insisted, his hulking body seeming to take up half the space in the train station.

"I can take over, Docteur," said one of the women from town who'd come to help with the wounded. "You have been on your feet for hours." Aurora sighed and stepped outside with her bodyguard, who watched her drink the lemonade with the air of a sullen headmistress disciplining a wayward student. She finished the thing in three gulps and handed him the glass.

"There, happy?" He sent her a stubborn look as he pulled a parcel from his jacket pocket.

"Eat," he ordered, handing her the bundle.

"I don't have time, Jean-Louis," she complained even as she unwrapped it. She was starving. She hadn't had an appetite since the afternoon before at the promenade. Then again, her stomach had been in knots for days now. She was sick of herself as much as she was of this entire situation. What was worse, she knew that distance would not make any of it better.

Apollo was in her blood now. He was running through her veins, stuck under her skin, and nothing she did would change that. And she'd brought this misery on herself. She took a few bites of the apple and cheese she'd been handed, then turned to Jean-Louis, who was eating his own apple.

"How did you even have time to pack food?" she asked, just to have something to do that wasn't think of the way Apollo had looked at her when she'd told him she didn't love him.

"Le caid told the cook to make us a basket while you were talking to Mademoiselle Manuela and Madame Luz." Even after she'd spoken to him as she had, Apollo made sure she had food and water.

Her gut roiled at the mention of her conversation with her friends. Both Luz and Manuela had pleaded with her to stay in Nice. Begged her to let them come help her to the station, but she'd refused. She'd snapped at them, said ugly things she didn't mean. That she had no interest in handing over her freedom like they had. That she didn't need someone by her side to give her life meaning. She'd been awful and cold, and for the first time in all their years of friendship, they'd looked at her like there was no hope for her.

They'd both embraced her stiffly and turned back to the house without another word.

"Are you all right, Docteur?" Jean-Louis asked, jolting her out of her thoughts. She looked down and realized she'd dropped the slices of apple to the ground. They were caked in the rocky dirt under her feet.

Ruined.

"I'm fine," she lied, offering the man a smile that hurt her face. The big man did not seem very impressed by her effort.

"I've known him since he was twenty years old and making trouble for himself in Paris." She didn't have to ask who the *"him"* was. Jean-Louis spoke softly for such a large man, and despite his penchant for picking her up without permission, he had kind eyes.

"I commend you for your patience," she said with a cynicism she didn't feel.

Jean-Louis smiled sadly as he looked into the distance. "I've never met a more unbothered little prick," he told her, with an air of bafflement. "For all his bluster and peacocking around, the man needs very little. He barely goes to that big mansion he bought for himself." She knew that. He spent more nights in his little apartment in the eighth arrondissement than he

did at his formal residence. She didn't think he'd set foot in
the Parisian town house he'd inherited from his father yet.
"And though he's a fair and generous boss, he never seemed
to need people."

Her throat closed at his words and she didn't know why.

"Apollo's very self-sufficient," she told him, contracting her
muscles to smother a shiver spreading through her.

Jean-Louis made a noise that she took as agreement, then
he turned to look at her. "He's a ruthless bastard. Destroyed
his own father without a second thought." He made that statement with a grin, so she didn't think the man considered that
a flaw of Apollo's. "In the fifteen years I've been with him,
he's only ever asked me for a personal favor once." Something
about the way he said that to her made her start shaking. It was
hot outside, and her usual wool suit was making her sweat, but
she could not stop the tremors.

"What was that?" she asked, unsure if she wanted to hear it.
Her walls were crumbling rapidly, and this quiet man's defense
of Apollo would likely decimate what was left.

"He asked me to take care of you." A humming sound escaped her throat at his words, and she began to swallow com-
pulsively. She'd cried more in the past week than she had in
the last thirteen years. "When he went looking for that cochon
who hurt you, I have never seen him like that. I was certain
he'd kill the man. I'm amazed he didn't." He hadn't killed or
exposed Ackworth, even when it would've helped him, because she'd asked him not to. There was a clicking sound in
her throat she'd never heard before, and her teeth were rattling.

"May I ask you something?"

She nodded, certain he'd ask it regardless of what she said.

"Do you truly believe he doesn't love you?" That was the
trouble. She believed it all too well. She could feel it when he
looked at her. Could taste it when he kissed her. Saw it clear

as day in his eyes when he was so deep inside her she felt like one half of a perfectly locking puzzle.

But love never stayed as love. It morphed into resentment, obligation, disdain, control.

"Love won't be enough when he realizes I can't be who he needs me to be." The large man gave her a pitying look, like she was beyond reasoning with. That made her angry, because when had the entire world begun to behave like scandal and ruined reputations didn't matter?

Was she the only sensible person left?

"Look at me, Jean-Louis," she demanded in a choked voice, gesturing to her soiled skirts streaked with blood, piss and dirt. "Do I look like a duchess to you?" Jean-Louis set his mouth stubbornly as if she was the difficult one. "You know what I do, you know how unfit I am to be sitting in parlors and hosting dinners. I'm no duchess."

The man sent her a long look, clearly unmoved by her tantrum. "A lot of people would say you're not what a doctor looks like and yet here you are," he told her, and she remembered the man was known for knocking out his opponents with a single blow. "You can't actually believe all those snobs are better than you." He waved a hand in the direction of the villa or maybe England, she couldn't know. "Besides, *he's* the *duke*, and *he* thinks you look like a duchess."

"Well, he's wrong," she declared, pressing a fist to her sternum and turning toward the makeshift clinic in the train station. A barrage of shouts and screams coming from the site of the accident caught her attention, then she saw two men running toward her carrying another man between them.

He was bloody and one of his legs looked mangled. He was wailing in agony.

"Take him inside," she ordered as she ran after them with Jean-Louis on her heels.

"He was thrown far, landed in a ditch," one of the men said as he laid the victim down on a pallet. "We only just found him." The injured man's face was darkened with dirt and there were bloody spots all over it where broken glass had nicked him, but his leg was the biggest problem.

"Sir, can you hear me?" she asked in French. The man was conscious, but only barely. Jean-Louis, bless him, handed her a pair of shears, which she used to cut through the trouser leg. To her relief, the wound was not as bad as it seemed.

"Marion," the man moaned as she worked to assess if there were any fractures or internal injuries.

"Marion?" she asked one of the men who'd brought him in, but he only shrugged.

"Marion," the man insisted, becoming distressed. "I need to talk to her."

"We will try to find Marion," she reassured him while she did the examination. But with each passing second, he became more agitated about this Marion. "Sir, what is your name?"

She had to lean down to hear him, but after more desperate calls for his Marion, he finally told her. Damien Allard.

"Damien, do you have family here in Nice?" He nodded and began to say Marion's name again like a prayer. She tried to get some more information, his direction perhaps, but the more questions she asked, the worse his agitation became, so she gave it up.

"Does anyone know who Marion is?" Aurora finally asked loudly enough to get the attention of the other nurses and doctors. "Jean-Louis, look through his pockets," she said as she prepared the wound for suturing.

"Damien!" The woman's cry came from outside as Aurora was bandaging the wound. Her patient, who had finally managed to settle, sat bolt upright the moment he heard her. It took three people to keep him from standing and tearing the stitches.

"Monsieur Damien, you must stay lying down," she ordered to no avail. The man insisted on getting up. Finally, a small, slight woman reached the pallet, her pretty face streaked with tears. She was wearing a country dress with an apron and her entire front was soaking wet. Aurora had to move out of the way when she threw herself at the man.

"Damien," she exclaimed as terrible sobs escaped her. Aurora stood stiffly to the side as she watched her reach for him. "Damien, my love," she cried as she attempted to kiss him and confirm he was still in one piece at the same time. "I'm sorry," she cried on his chest as he wrapped his arms around her. "I shouldn't have let you leave as I did."

"Shh," he soothed her, kissing her hair.

Aurora's skin felt tight on her face, on her entire body, witnessing the intimate moment. When she looked around to see if anyone else was watching, she noticed that everyone else was busy with the chaos in the room. Only Jean-Louis had his attention on the two lovers.

"It's all right, my love," Damien whispered to Marion. "I know why you said it."

"I was afraid," she confessed, as Aurora backed away. She should leave, she was intruding on an obviously private moment, but she was transfixed by this woman's ability to expose herself in a room full of people. "I love you and I would've never forgiven myself if I'd lost you thinking I didn't."

Damien's body convulsed and Aurora took a step forward, thinking he was having a seizure, but then he looked up and she saw he was crying. He hid his face in Marion's hair and wept.

"That is all we need," he told her as he kissed her again. "All we need."

Again Aurora looked around, wondering if everyone else's heart was close to exploding. When she found Jean-Louis's gaze, she was confronted with a look that communicated something along the lines of "ignore *that* at your own peril."

"Oh, go to hell, Jean-Louis," she mouthed with a roll of her eyes. What would be next, a staging of *Romeo and Juliet* by the nurse and train conductor?

But the more she looked at the pair of lovers, the more she felt like a very small boat in a raging storm. Water whipping around her, splashing over her until she didn't know which way was up. Only that she was drifting farther and farther from the only place that had ever felt like safe harbor.

She was here on the stark, flimsy vessel she'd built for herself. On it was her work and her purpose, but no love, not any love that would require any kind of gamble. She'd never been enough for her father, her mother. Philip had used her need for love against her. Opening her heart had left her wounded and scared, and Apollo's was so big, so bright, it terrified her. Because she didn't think she could survive watching it disappear.

The room started to darken, and when she looked out the window, she noticed the sun was setting.

The station was quieter now. Damien had been the last injured passenger they'd brought in in hours. She was done here. There was nothing more to do. She pulled her watch from her pocket and winced when she saw that Apollo's party was starting soon.

"What now, Doctora?" Jean-Louis asked a bit too smugly.

After taking off the apron she'd put on to work, she walked over to the man with her hand up. "I do not want any lectures, just take me back to the villa without comment."

"Of course, you're the boss." She didn't look straight at him, but even in her periphery, she caught a glimpse of Jean-Louis's satisfied grin.

Thirty-One

Hours after Aurora left for the accident, Apollo sat in his study, contemplating what he'd gotten himself into. He'd have more than a hundred people whose alliances could very well set the course of his dukedom in a completely different path than his predecessors. He didn't care about any of it. He wished he'd never come here.

He ignored the knock on his door, then sighed when the door opened anyway.

"I thought I was the worst hostess in the peerage, but you have managed to supersede even my abhorrent hospitality." Cora stopped in front of him and sent him an appraising look.

"Go ahead," he told Evan, who had also arrived to rub salt in his wounds. "Laugh at me like you promised you would."

His brother made a pained sound, then glanced at the gold band on his left hand. "I have no intention of laughing at you," Evan told him with much more sympathy than Apollo deserved. "I'm merely trying to assess how much thought you've already given to deserting your title."

Apollo groaned and covered his face with his hands.

"That you can't do," Cora exclaimed, before shaking Apollo by the shoulder. "You're not robbing me of the satisfaction of knowing that you will be making all those bigots in the House of Lords squirm."

"I was thinking about the plans to build schools, hospitals, and improve the situation of our long-suffering tenants," Evan retorted with a roll of his eyes. "But your personal petty vendettas are just as important, Cora."

"I'm not abandoning anything," Apollo sighed, feeling like the weight of the world was on his shoulders. "Aurora would despise me if I did." Cora made a sound of agreement and Evan let out one of those world-weary exhales. "She told me she doesn't love me," he confessed into the taut silence of the room.

"You didn't believe her, did you?" This was Cora, who was now standing by the drink cart pouring whisky into tumblers.

"I don't know," Apollo admitted.

He knew she cared for him, knew she even needed him sometimes, but he was starting to think that was the problem. That Aurora was petrified of wanting someone too much and then being cast aside. "I don't know how to make her believe she's the only thing I want. That I would give this all up for her." He'd seen the fear in her eyes when he told her he loved her, the despair when he'd said she was punishing herself. "She won't hear of it. She's convinced she'd ruin everything for me." He pulled on the tufts of hair that were probably already standing up on his head.

"She thinks you'll eventually wash your hands of her," Cora said, her voice unusually tender as she spoke. When Apollo turned to stare at her, she had a faraway look in her eyes, like she was recalling something buried deep in her memory. "She'd rather push you away now than let herself trust that it won't happen later."

She'd told him that. Said time and time again that she knew he'd eventually hide her. The problem was that there was nothing he could do to prove to her that he'd never do that.

She would have to take a leap of faith. Maybe he'd just have to keep proving it until she could believe. He was considering this when his aunt and cousin appeared in his doorway.

"Juli, should you be out of bed?" he asked, then regretted it when the girl flinched at the question. She'd always been such a vivacious girl, curious and whip-smart, but the light in her eyes had been dulled by what she'd lived through. He would make the man pay, even if it took him twenty years to find him. He'd done it with his father, after all.

"Mama has something to tell you." He frowned at the unfriendly look his cousin sent her mother. His aunt had a caged glint in her eyes, and for the first time, she looked her age.

"I talked to Aurora," his aunt confessed, confirming his suspicions. "I told her to let you go, that she'd hurt your chances as duke." His aunt's sense of ownership over him was becoming cumbersome. He loved her, but his life was his own and when it came to Aurora, nothing and no one mattered more.

"You had no right to do that, Tia," he told her, his voice hard. "If you cost me the woman I love, I will never forgive you."

"We have fought for this for so long, sobrino," she argued, her voice breaking. "I wanted this for you, for my sister's memory."

He had too, but he was beginning to wonder if this was ever really about what his mother had wanted.

"I want to think my happiness would've mattered to her, that it would matter to you." His aunt's eyes filled with tears. "I love Aurora, Tia. She's worth more to me than any position."

"She won't stop her rebelliousness," his aunt pleaded with him. "She won't ever conform to your world." He almost laughed then, because that was exactly what made her perfect. Aurora would never compromise what was right for a place in society.

"That's right, aunt, Aurora will never lie to me to save my pride, she won't ever turn a blind eye to an injustice because it's inconvenient." His tone was harsh, but his aunt had crossed a line and he would make sure she knew that doing so again would be unforgivable. "She will never choose her comfort over another's well-being. She's better than I could ever aspire to be, and there's no woman who could be a more perfect duchess, for me." That was the heart of the matter. He needed her and everything else they'd figured out together. "If you'll excuse me, I have to go find Aurora." He reached the door in two steps.

"Be ready to beg," Cora called after him, and he had every intention to.

He was down the stairs and out the door in seconds, heading for the stables to procure a horse, but was intercepted by a cariole barreling up the gravel path like it was being driven by the hounds of hell.

"Don Duc," Jean-Louis shouted triumphantly as he raced toward him with—to Apollo's horror—Aurora precariously hanging on to her seat.

Was Jean-Louis trying to kill her? Apollo was going to break his neck for driving so recklessly with his woman in tow.

"What are you doing, Jean-Louis?" he bellowed, ready to tear the man's head off, but the moment the horse came to a stop, Aurora jumped off.

Apollo almost went to his knees from relief as she leaped into his arms.

"I'm sorry I left," she told him as he lifted her off the ground. This was the only thing that mattered, this woman in his arms. If he had her, he could face anything.

"It's all right, mi amor, I was coming to find you," he told her, before kissing her on the mouth without caring what the crowd now gathered outside after Jean-Louis's chaotic arrival thought. "Wherever you go, I'll go. I won't let you run from this."

"I thought it would be easier if I left, Apollo," she told him in a small, defeated voice he never wanted to hear from her again.

"It will never be easier for me without you," he promised, his eyes soaking her in. He pressed a small kiss to the fading bruise and pulled her to his chest. "I've known you're mine for a long time now." He lifted her chin and a knot formed in his throat, when he saw the tears in her eyes. But he thought this time maybe they were happy tears. "If only to save a few men losing their heads at your hands if they attempted to woo you."

She offered him a rueful smile at that, casting her gaze upward. "Heads will not stop rolling just because I'm in love." He was certain everyone in Nice could hear the beating of his heart.

"You love me," he said, lowering his head, needing to taste her lips.

"Did I say that?" she hedged grumpily.

"Docteur, just put the man out of his misery," Jean-Louis shouted from somewhere behind them.

"Don't pressure me, Jean-Louis," she volleyed back, before rising up to meet Apollo's mouth.

"Tell me," he pressed, desperate to hear it.

"You say it first."

"I love you." He did not hesitate, then pressed a kiss to her mouth for good measure. "I adore every inch of you." He continued clutching her tight. "I'm jealous of the damned wind that rustles your skirts, because it gets to touch you." She swayed in his arms and made some kind of protest, but he would tell her everything. Would leave absolutely no doubt in her mind he was hopelessly in love with her. "I love your scratchy hands and your frumpy suits. I love every single little thing about you, and I will worship you for the rest of my life if you let me." She nodded, her eyes shining with something that cracked his chest open.

"I love you too," she whispered in a voice like an ember, bright and hot, and burning. "I will believe that you always will, even when I can't love myself," she sniffled, shaking her head. "I don't know if there's anyone else who can love me like you do. I don't ever want to be without you."

"You never will," he told her, with the blood rushing between his ears.

"Damn you, Apollo," she said wetly. "I don't like to cry."

"Not even happy tears?" She shook her head, an adorable pout on her lips. "Not even I'm-going-to-be-a-duchess tears?" She scoffed, but there was a tiny lift to the corners of her mouth.

"Especially not! Which reminds me, if I am to go to this party on your arm, I should probably wear something with less bloodstains." She looked down at herself with a frown and he had to kiss her. "I look a mess," she said with a wince.

He bent down to kiss her again. "I think you look perfect."

"Are you ready?" Apollo asked, as they made their way to the garden where the party was already in full force. It had taken a concerted effort and some true miracle work from Luz Alana and Manuela, but in less than an hour they'd managed to make her mostly presentable.

She looked down at the lovely gown and to her surprise, she was. She was ready. Scared, nervous, but ready to be loved by this man. Ready to, day by day, embrace that this was the life she deserved.

They set out together down the path to the garden as Aurora thought of the day they'd had. Of what she'd come so close to losing and she stopped.

"What is it, amor?" Her pulse raced at the warmth in his words, and she lifted her face up to him.

"I need a kiss," she told him, and as always, he obliged.

"Just one?" he asked, before pressing his mouth to hers.

"For now, we'll save the rest for when we're in private," she told him, thinking anyone could walk upon them.

"I have many things in mind for our private time this evening," the duke promised, and she could not resist another kiss.

At that precise moment a male voice came from the other side of a row of rhododendrons.

"Annan." For an instant, Aurora thought it was something to do with the train accident, but then she saw a man pointing a pistol at her. Apollo quickly pushed her behind him and stepped up to the threat.

"Ackworth," he said with derision, as the man came out into the light.

"Don't move!" he seethed as he waved the weapon in the air. He looked disheveled, like he hadn't slept in days.

From the corner of her eye, she spotted Evan behind the man, as he took a careful step forward. Meanwhile, Ackworth was waving the weapon in the air while he ranted about being made a laughingstock. "If anyone comes near me, I will shoot."

"This will only make things worse," Apollo said in a surprisingly calm voice, as he confronted the erratic Ackworth.

"Worse than you humiliating me in my club? Worse than my father threatening to disown me?" He was screaming. His face mottled with bruises. He looked unkempt, and there was something unsettling in his eyes. He seemed like a man with nothing to lose. "Worse than her taking my wife and children!"

"Your trouble is with me," Apollo told him, pushing Aurora out of Ackworth's sight.

"She started this trouble." Ackworth's eyes were wild and he was not very steady on his feet. "And now she took my

Sandrita from me." From where she hid behind Apollo, Aurora saw Cora emerge from the bushes to stand next to Evan. She suspected Manuela and Luz Alana were somewhere looking for help. Ackworth might be here to do mischief, but they had their cavalry.

"If anything happens to her, you won't walk away from here," Apollo warned the man.

Ackworth pointed at her with the gun, then fumbled with it when it almost slipped out of his hand. Which was the opportunity Cora used to throw something at the man's head. The impact knocked him to the ground while Apollo jumped into action.

He knocked the pistol from Ackworth's hand and proceeded to beat the man to a pulp. Soon Evan, Cora and the Leonas had half of the footmen and a very cross-looking Jean-Louis drag the bloodied Lord Ackworth away.

"What will happen to him?" Manuela asked Apollo, who shook his head in disgust.

"Not nearly what he deserves," he answered, tucking Aurora under his arm. "Did he hurt you?" She just shook her head as they watched the men carry out the man.

"Are you sure you are all right, Leona?" Luz asked.

"Yes," she said, her heart still pounding. "But I ruined my dress again," she lamented, looking at the grass stain on the hem. "Will I ever enter a ballroom properly dressed?"

"There's never a dull moment with you, is there, Fiera?" Apollo asked, with a grin.

"I told you someone would eventually try to shoot you," Cora told him, making them all laugh.

"I may have a go at him next," Aurora groused, palming his clammy face. "What were you thinking jumping in front of a gun?" she asked, beyond annoyed at his damned antics.

"I was thinking, I won't let anything happen to the woman I love. I was attempting to be heroic."

"Well, I don't need a hero. I need you."

"Does that mean you'll marry me?" he asked, reaching for her hand. She was amazed no one else could hear the battle drums inside her chest. "You might as well do it. Before one of us ends up dead."

"We have a party to attend," she reminded him. Miraculously it seemed no one had noticed the noise coming from the scuffle with Ackworth, since there was still talking and music coming from the garden.

"This is more important," Apollo said, pulling her toward him.

"I will be a terrible duchess," she said, looking between him and their friends.

"How terrible?" he asked in that teasing voice that filled her belly with butterflies.

"Hopeless," she wailed, gesturing to her stained dress. "I will never be dressed properly. I'll likely offend someone important at every function you bring me to. I won't ever stay quiet when I think someone is being prejudiced. And there's no solution when it comes to my hair in the rain."

"You know what I think, Fiera?" She raised an eyebrow in question and shook her head. "I think you are the absolute perfect duchess for this duke."

She let herself feel his love, believed what she saw in his eyes and pushed up on her tiptoes to kiss him.

"I think this time you may be right, Your Grace."

Epilogue

"You know, most men tire of their wives eventually," Aurora told her husband, as he rid her of her nightshirt in two decisive tugs.

"Most men are idiotic sods," the Duke of Annan informed her as he gripped her waist. She was sitting astride his narrow hips, a position she was quite fond of, as it allowed her a perfect view of that impossibly sculpted chest and shoulders.

"Are they now?" she teased, cocking an eyebrow, while she ran her hands possessively over his pectorals, letting her nails press into the skin.

"They are indeed." He bucked into her at the touch, and she pressed her heat into his skin, making him suck in a breath. "And I'll be happy to offer further evidence of this later." His hands descended to her rump, another part of her body he had not grown tired of celebrating yet, she hoped he never did. "But for now, be a good girl and sit this luscious culo on my face and allow me to properly worship you, wife."

"This culo?" she asked, circling her hips invitingly. He groaned at the friction, then swatted one cheek.

"The very one," he answered and licked his lips. "Ven amor," he coaxed her. Those brown eyes hot with desire. "Dejame probarte."

It was hard to resist that request, and she loved mornings like this.

They were in a new bed, canopied under a mosquito net, which made this early morning lovemaking feel almost dream-like. As she moved up his body, she lifted her eyes to the still dark predawn waters of the Caribbean Sea. But even *it* did not take her breath away like the sight of her husband, when he looked at her like he was now. As if every one of his prayers had been answered in her.

"Mi amor," he crooned, as she settled over him. Her thighs on either side of his head as he pressed his nose to her heat.

"Apollo," she sighed his name as his fingers parted her folds.

"I love your smell, Fiera," he growled, inhaling her. Her body responded to that sound with a familiar intensity. She held on to the bedpost as he worked, his tongue lapping at her slowly, cat licks, little nips which sent delicious shivers down her spine. But this morning she craved that bone-shattering intensity only he could give her.

"I thought you said you were hungry, Your Grace," she teased, and then his mouth was on her. His lips latching to her clitoris, making her see stars. By now, he knew her body better than his own. She was not an easy woman to love, she was prone to dark moods, and some days it seemed like the shroud of the past would suffocate her, but he never stopped loving her.

With his words, his actions, his body, he showed her that there was nothing in her he could not love.

"Muevete, mi cielo," he urged, as he mouthed her folds.

"Come me gustas," he growled as he sucked on her labia and entered her with two fingers. "Is this good, mi Fiera?"

"So good," she answered, gripping the bedpost as his mouth took her to heaven. He let his teeth graze her engorged flesh and the contact sent sparks of pleasure through her limbs. Her duke, her man, her husband. "Te amo, Apollo," she gasped as her climax began its frantic swirl inside her. He tongued her heat and spread her for his hand until she was shouting out in pleasure, her body arching in exquisite agony.

"I need you inside," she whispered, frantically scrambling down his body.

"You need this, wife?" he asked, taking himself in hand. With frantic nods she lifted herself and plunged onto that impossible, unrelenting hardness that filled her so perfectly. She planted her hands on his chest and bent down to kiss him as they worked together until he was fully seated inside. "Muevete, Fiera."

"Like this?" she asked, grinding her hips into him, until she saw his eyes roll in his head.

"Just like that," he grunted, thrusting hard into her. "Ride me, amor." She did, moved like the tide, with this man in her body, in her heart, her blood. He bit his lip as she rocked with him, his eyes half-lidded and that caramel skin glowing with perspiration.

God, he was beautiful and all hers.

"Vamos, mi vida," he said, with a swat, making her laugh. She tightened her muscles, making him cry out. He pumped his hips into her with a force that made her teeth chatter. A few more thrusts and he was spilling inside her. He wrapped his arms around her, pulling her down for a kiss.

"I love you," she whispered, lifting her head to see the sun rise over the horizon to reveal impossibly turquoise waters.

"Te amo, Fiera." That was the only thing she needed.

There was much to do that day, but for now, she had nowhere else to be, but in her husband's arms.

"Are you ready for today?" Apollo asked, some time later as he joined her on the veranda of the new midwife training center she'd built on the site of her mother's old home.

"Better, now that you've roused from your slumber to join me," she said, reaching a hand up to cup his cheek. After they made love, he'd dozed off, but she'd been much too excited to fall back asleep.

He turned her around and kissed her. "My wife wore me out, using me for her pleasure," he teased, nipping at her lip.

"What good is having a husband with the body of a god if one doesn't use it?" she asked, then demanded another kiss.

It was almost three years since they'd married, and still, the thrill of calling him husband had not waned. He was still too brash, a little vain about his beauty, but there was no more perfect man for her than Apollo César Sinclair Robles.

"The rest of our numerous family members will be here any minute," he informed her with a kiss to the cheek. She smiled at that too. It was the third time in the past year, they'd done this particular ceremony. Evan and Apollo with the help of the women in their lives had put to use the resources of the duchy to create a different kind of legacy. They'd started with the inauguration of a women's sanatorium named after Evan's mother, which would provide humane and holistic care for women suffering from psychological ailments. Just six months ago, they'd all made their way to Venezuela for the opening of the art school for women that Manuela and her lover, Cora, had installed in Puerto Cabello, honoring the dream Manu's grandmother had not been able to accomplish in life.

And now it was her turn, a midwifery school where women from the Caribbean would be trained by other women and prepare to go on to medical school if they desired. It was a dream that she had only been able to envision once Apollo encouraged her to think bigger.

And she had done so. The clinics with Virginia were now being reproduced at a larger scale in France, and expanding to the Americas. Virginia had launched two in Uruguay and Aurora's former patient Sandra—who was now divorced and in Rio de Janeiro with her children and training herself to be a midwife—was using her family's resources to open a clinic in her city. Their remedies were now being mass produced with the help of Mihn, which meant that those who needed it could access them at a reasonable cost. That was just the beginning of what she had in mind.

"Are you happy, Fiera?" he asked her quietly as they walked around the room that would be used for dining and rest. The large bay windows overlooked the turquoise waters of the Caribbean Sea.

"I am," she told him, inspecting the art on the walls and the comfortable furnishings they'd selected as she looked inward and found that her heart, too, was fuller than she could ever imagine on her own. "And I'm proud of us," she told him, putting her bare hands on his cheeks. Hands that were softer now, because her husband massaged them every night with Phuong's salve. "Proud of the legacy that you're building, my love."

"That we're building," he corrected, and brought her closer to him. "You were the one who taught me purpose, mi vida." She sighed at the casual manner in which he called her "his life" and kissed him.

Since that night in Nice three years ago, Apollo forged his own path as duke. Choosing her cost him his aspirations of rubbing his existence in the aristocracy's face, but what he'd been able to do despite this still amazed her.

She *was* proud of him, she was proud of herself too. They had no desire for children and had no plans to leave a bloodline to perpetuate the riches of the duchy. They would build institutions that would give women means to foster a different future. The names of the mothers and grandmothers in their family would live on longer and further than any of the men who underestimated them ever would.

Their sons and daughters would make sure of that.

"My taste truly is immaculate." Manuela's booming voice broke their intimate moment, and in the next instant, her two best friends, their spouses and the rest of their brood were standing in the room with them. Her brothers—Sebastian and Octavio, as Ramón remained an utter comemierda—would arrive that evening, and in the morning, they'd open the doors to the Gloria y Violeta Midwifery Institute.

"I see that the Caribbean air has not affected your humility, Manu," Aurora teased, as she reached for her friend while Cora looked on adoringly.

"No, it has not," Manu exclaimed, waving a hand around the room. "If it were up to you, this room would be like a hospital." Aurora rolled her eyes in jest, but her friend had been the one to help with the selection of furniture. Luz Alana had also contributed by finding local women to make all the curtains and bedding.

"You will have to help me soon, when my business laboratory is further along," Luz Alana quipped as she kissed Apollo on the cheek before doing the same to Aurora.

"Mo Chride, we only broke ground last week," Evan lovingly told his wife from where he sat with Luz Alana's younger sister, Clarita, who at thirteen was as tall as Aurora.

"Your lady likes to be prepared, brother," Apollo said as he took Aurora's hands. "That is why they are such mighty lionesses."

She felt like a lioness, one who formed her own pride with women she admired and loved. With a man she adored. A Leona who made a life that was in many ways like something her fifteen-year-old self would've been bold enough to aspire to, if she'd only known it was possible.

"I love you," she told Apollo as she slid her arms around his waist and laid her cheek against his chest.

"And I love you, mi Fiera," he whispered, kissing the top of her head. "What wild dream will we conquer next?"

She had a few in mind, and she knew with him at her side and the people in this room around them, the future truly would be what she made it.

★ ★ ★ ★ ★

Author's Note

At the same time I was writing Aurora's story, nineteen different attorney generals were requesting access to federal records to monitor women crossing state lines to receive abortions. Women died unnecessarily because of the draconic laws enacted across the country keeping them from receiving life-saving care.

The world in which Aurora would've lived was one where women's agency was being viciously contested.

From the Comstock Act that I mention in the book to the rise of forensic medicine as a means to penalize women, the late nineteenth century was a time when women had to be resourceful and bold to maintain some level of bodily autonomy. As Aurora mentions in the book, the arrival of the medical profession eroded much of the established networks of midwives that provided women with essential care.

The Hymen Brothers unfortunately are based on a real historical figure, Francisco de Asís Flores y Troncoso, a Mexican physician who quite literally wrote the book on the hymen in Mexico, his contribution to the field of hymenology (yes, this was a thing that existed).

Nora E. Jaffary in her book *Reproduction and Its Discontents in Mexico: Childbirth and Contraception from 1750 to 1905*, wrote:

Flores's text on the Mexican hymen, along with a host of materials dealing with public sanitation, policing and incarceration, and health was included in the works Mexico chose to represent its national scientific achievements at the 1889 Exposition Universelle in Paris.

Though at the time women physicians in Mexico were merely few, they were courageous and I can only imagine what they thought of Dr. Asís y Flores Troncoso.

Men in the medical profession spent a lot of the second half of the nineteenth century developing scientific methods to control women's bodies. The biggest advances in forensic medicine were largely credited to Ambroise Tardieu, a French pathologist, whose obsession with detecting traces of abortion in women became a full-fledged field of study. Men and their shenanigans when it comes to legislating women's bodies are nothing new and neither is our resistance against it.

Virginia's character was actually inspired by a few Argentinian women who were indeed anarchists. There was a strong movement in Buenos Aires that fought mightily to organize unions for suffrage and reproductive freedom. There was also a robust "free love" movement that I must write about in another book. Sarah Loguen Fraser, Aurora's mentor, was in fact the first woman licensed to practice medicine in the Dominican Republic and one of the first Black women to graduate from the medical school of Syracuse University.

There were also quite a few nascent feminist publications in Latin America, including *Fémina* in the Dominican Republic, which espoused for a place for women outside the home.

Lastly, the medical field was experiencing many milestones during this time, and many of the procedures, tools and protocols used by Aurora are based on real ones. Like Dr. Benguay's anesthetic canister, which was offered on sale for the first time at the 1889 Exposition Universelle. Those blade gloves also existed!

Aurora's clinic, though not real, was certainly not unlikely.

The networks of women supplying each other with information, aid and support have always existed. But I'd be remiss to not mention that the actual inspiration for the clinic was the legendary Chicago underground abortion service run by a group of courageous women during the late 1960s.

Though Nice and the French Riviera are only a small portion of the book, I was compelled to include them for a few reasons. The first is that I really wanted Aurora and Apollo to make out in a lavender field. An important second was to shine a bit of light on the connection between Britian and the French Riviera. In the late nineteenth century, Nice became a favorite destination for the British aristocracy. There was even a British consulate, given how many Brits spent their winters in the south of France. It seemed like the perfect place for Apollo to gather all the people he actually wanted to build alliances with, right under the noses of the British aristocracy.

There are so many other stories I would've loved to dive more deeply into, like the outlawing of the practice of capoeira in Brazil at the end of the nineteenth century, but I could not fit them into the book. I hope this inspires you to read much further.

Thank you for coming on this journey to Paris with me and my Léonas. It's been the ride of a lifetime. I hope you join me on the next adventure.

For those who love a reference list, below are the texts and essays I used for my research.

"Abortion in France: Women and the Regulation of Family Size 1800–1914" by Angus McLaren

"Designs of Deception: Concepts of Consciousness, Spirituality and Survival in Capoeira Angola in Salvador, Brazil" by Margaret Willson

French Riviera and Its Artists: Art, Literature, Love, and Life on the Côte d'Azur by John Baxter

Madame Restell: The Life, Death, and Resurrection of Old New York's Most Fabulous, Fearless, and Infamous Abortionist by Jennifer Wright

"Midwives of Guadalajara (Mexico) in the 19th Century: The Ousting of their Art" by Laura Catalina Díaz Robles (in Spanish)

"No God, No Boss, No Husband: Anarchist Feminism in Nineteenth-Century Argentina" by Maxine Molyneux

"Obstetrics and the Emergence of Women in Mexico's Medical Establishment" by Lee M. Penyak

The Once Upon a Time World: The Dark and Sparkling Story of the French Riviera by Jonathan Miles

Reproducing the British Caribbean: Sex, Gender, and Population Politics after Slavery by Juanita de Barros

Reproduction and Its Discontents in Mexico: Childbirth and Contraception from 1750 to 1905 by Nora E. Jaffary

Sex and Herbs and Birth Control: Women and Fertility Regulation Through the Ages by Ann Hibner Koblitz

The Story of Jane: The Legendary Underground Feminist Abortion Service by Laura Kaplan

Acknowledgments

The very last adventure with the Leonas is done, and this was certainly one I could not have made it through without the many Leonas in my life. I always knew Aurora's book would be a tough one, but I didn't know I'd be doing it without my cocaptain for eleven books, my former editor and friend, Kerri Buckley. I missed her steady hand very much on this book, but I am grateful for my community of friends in romance who lent a hand during my many moments of doubt.

As always, thanks to my agent, Taylor Haggerty, steadfast and wise as ever.

My virtual office mates: Alexis Daria, Zoraida Córdova, Mia Sosa and Tracey Livesay. When I say this book could not have been written without them, I mean that literally.

Thanks to my friend Jen Prokop, who read this manuscript for me and talked it through with me ad nauseam. You have the best eye in romance.

Thanks of course to my "call a friend" friend, Sarah Maclean, who probably knows the Leonas better than I do at this point.

With every one of these books I have tried to do as much research as possible and in that process have found incredibly generous people. I must thank Nora E. Jaffary, author of *Reproduction and Its Discontents in Mexico*. Thank you for taking the time to speak with me and give me such amazing insight into the work women in Latin America were doing in reproductive rights at the turn of the nineteenth century.

Thank you to Jhensen Ortiz at the Dominican Studies Institute at the City College of New York, who has been the MVP in my research for this entire series.

Thank you to all the booksellers who have championed this series. I will never not be grateful to see you selecting my ladies for your book clubs. I appreciate you beyond measure.

Thank you to the team at Canary Street Press, my editor Errin Toma, my publicist and the rest of the crew for their support in getting this series out into the world.

As ever, thank you to my husband, Andrew, not only for listening to me plot, replot, deplot, unplot and everything in between, but for offering support and kindness when I am deep in the weeds. Thanks to my kid for being everything and more.

Finally, the biggest thanks to my readers, those who have been with me since the Dreamers and those who found me through the Leonas. I write because I want more stories out there about Caribbean women being intrepid and mighty but also loved and seen. I hope that in some measure these books make you feel seen and loved too.